The Chosen Man

The Chosen Man

J.G. Harlond

www.penmorepress.com

The Chosen Man by J.G. Harlond

ISBN-13: 978-1-942756-04-0(Paperback)
ISBN —978-1-942756-05-7 (e-book)

BISAC Subject Headings:
FIC002000 FICTION / Action & Adventure
FIC014000 FICTION / Historical
FIC027050 FICTION / Romance / Historical / General

Cover Illustration by Christine Horner

Address all correspondence to:
Michael James
Penmore Press LLC
920 N Javelina Pl
Tucson AZ 85748

*for
Tony*

Acknowledgements

With special thanks to Sarah Harrison, Shirley Mitchell, Manuel Arredondo Braña, Diane Brewer, Joan Fallon and Rachel Hunt.

When the first alarm subsided, the tulip-holders in the several towns held public meetings to devise what measures were to be taken to restore public credit. It was generally agreed, that deputies should be sent from all parts to Amsterdam, to consult with the government upon some remedy for the evil.

—from *Extraordinary Popular Delusions and the Madness of Crowds* by Charles Mackay (1841)

Prologue
Cornwall, England, Early March 1635

Using her clever knife and humming the necessary chant, she scored a circle into the turf beneath the ancient cross.

The beginning at the end at the beginning...

Into the circle she placed an acorn for him and marked a tree growing from its shell. Beside the tree she placed the flowers for her, blue periwinkle and an early primrose, then a twig of wine-red hawthorn buds for the future. Gradually, she began the next sequence:

Blow the wind blow, rain the rain down...

She had timed it exactly, the first drops of spring rain pattered on the weathered stone of the Celtic cross.

Blow the wind blow and rain the rain down,
Bring us a summer to grow more than grain.
Growing and growing, circle give life...

Aggie hummed meaning into the words, the shape, the petals and buds, then scraped soft green turf back over them. The rain would do the rest.

For a moment she rested on her haunches and looked about her. Had she been seen? She put her knife in its special pocket and struggled to her feet. A storm was brewing over the sea to the south, the wind in her face.

"Well, how can that be?" she asked the small dog waiting at her side. "How can she come from all the way over there?"

Aggie peered through the blustering rain at the line where the old river met the sea. "That's not right," she said. "Not from foreign lands."

1

Chapter One
The Vatican, Italy, Early March 1635

"Another particularly tenuous idea from Spain. Grasping at straws."

"Stems."

"What?"

"You mean grasping at stems."

"Is that supposed to be amusing?"

"Well, the whole thing is ridiculous."

"Perhaps, but it could do significant damage," replied the younger man, who had been made a cardinal at twenty-three. He sat down behind his desk and picked up the Spanish envoy's gift to examine its jewels.

The pope's other, less effective nephew watched his cousin raise an exquisite crucifix to the light: silver on mahogany, emeralds and purple-blue lapis lazuli from the New World; a gift from Spain—or a reminder of their territory.

"A set back in finances won't damage established Dutch tradesmen very much. I certainly can't see it having any effect on their war with Spain," he said.

"It will if they're using this new banking system. If the hard-working middle-classes, artisans and the like, are selling tulip flowers at high prices then putting their profit in banks, and the Dutch government is using that money to finance resistance to Spain—when the market suddenly collapses there'll be a run on those banks. And if the money isn't there.... Can't you see? That's what the Spanish are after; trying to undermine Protestant confidence, shake and weaken new foundations."

And this is why I am a cardinal and you are my secretary, he added silently to himself.

"So, if an ordinary Dutchman buys one of these plants then sells it and makes a profit, and he puts that money into a bank, but the bank uses it to finance the war—then if everyone wants their money back at the same time and it's not there—"

"The Dutch economy *could* falter and Spain's Flanders army *could* march straight back into the Dutch United Provinces. Except," the young cardinal placed the crucifix back on his desk, "that is not exactly what our Holy Father wants. He's not convinced Spain should regain The Netherlands. Of course he can't say that, and nor must you."

"But if we act against the plan or ignore it, we alienate the King of Spain and the Emperor in Vienna."

"Yes. Rather more than 'ridiculous', isn't it?" The young cardinal looked at his older cousin. "*I* shall have to handle it carefully, and use the right people."

"Who are...?"

"To start with, we need someone who won't be missed to deliver messages. Then we need someone that doesn't miss anything as our overseer, preferably someone with undercover experience. Father Rogelio would suit. He's been involved in the Black Order for years, runs agents in most European cities and no one has any idea who or what he is. Naturally *we* cannot be involved."

"And who will bring about the desired outcome? Or are you going to let the Spanish arrange that?"

"Oh, no, our desired outcome is not quite the same as theirs, remember."

"Ah, well, in that case you need someone who travels between Italy and the Low Countries, who already deals in tulips so he knows what's what, and someone completely unethical. He'll demand a high price for his silence afterwards, I should think."

"Rogelio will arrange his silence. First, we need to choose the right man."

"Our family in Florence uses a Genoese silk merchant. He has something of a reputation, and not just for dealing in exotic goods."

"Genoese? Convenient. The Genoese virtually run Spain; they certainly fight her wars."

"I say Genoese, he's actually from Portovenere, which means—"

"He's as good as a pirate. Mm—that also means his loyalty goes where the booty lies. He could be in anybody's pay."

"Or nobody's. I thought pirates only looked out for themselves."

"Precisely the point I'm making."

The older cousin tried to avoid looking confused and said, "Pirates are not known for loyalty or scruples. I doubt anyone will come looking for him later."

"Is he dashing?"

"Dashing?"

"Good-looking, well-favoured."

"Ah, that. Yes. My sisters met him once, don't know how. They tittered about him for days—weeks afterwards. If that's what you mean?"

"That's what I mean." The Pope's younger nephew weighed the priceless Spanish gift in his hands. Without looking up, he said, "Find him."

Chapter Two
Off the coast of Spain, April 1635

The big man wearing black, the chosen man, was standing arms akimbo leaning into the wind. The feather of the wide-brimmed, black leather hat he grasped tightly in his right hand fluttered limply like a dead cockerel.

The young Jesuit priest from England, John Hawthorne, took a deep breath and spoke, but his words were whooshed up into the air and he was left silent. He waited, his heart pounding like the high surf, until the man turned and nodded a greeting. He tried again, but in his rush to communicate spoke in English, "You are bound for Sanlucar, sir? Or do you sail further?"

He was answered in English, which surprised him.

"Both," said the man in black, turning back to face the sea beyond the prow of the small vessel.

"Both?"

"Look at those waves!"

The man gestured with a wide, open hand as if commanding the sea to rebel. His hair and beard glistened with spray as he braced himself against the screaming wind.

John Hawthorne, caught up in the drama, stared not at the oncoming wall of waves but at the man they called Ludovico da Portovenere and shuddered. Black hair, black cape, a look of mad rapture as the sea churned about them; the very image of a pirate—or the devil himself.

The Genoese merchant rode the next wave with his arms folded across his broad chest and laughed out loud. John tried to speak, but once again the air grabbed his words and tossed

5

them high into the indigo sky. It was no good; he would have to find another opportunity. Clinging to the side of the small ship he began to shuffle away.

"You are what the English call a land-lubber, I see," shouted the large man, but not unkindly. He moved and placed his hand under the Englishman's elbow, bracing him firmly as a sheet of water, sharp as ice, showered down upon them.

"It is always rough here. We are too near to the coast. I'd move her out, but it's not my ship. It's Venetian. You can't trust Venetian captains outside lagoons."

"I was raised among hills and trees, sir, I know nothing of ships, nor am I a good sailor." John Hawthorne slipped and the big foreigner righted him. "I shall never travel by sea again. I shall never travel again, anywhere, ever."

As they edged their way towards the tiny starboard cabins, Ludovico da Portovenere kept his hold on the smaller man and chatted on as if they were taking a morning stroll.

"It is a question of upbringing. I was born at sea; my mother likes to tell how a mortal storm threw her into her travail and how I emerged flailing like a swimmer determined to survive and kicked the ship's surgeon in the eye."

"It makes a good story."

"A good *true* story."

John Hawthorne was too exhausted to continue talking. When they reached his cabin the man in black helped him open the door, then ducked down to follow unbidden into the small, wood-panelled space. He placed his hat on the small table, then removed his vast cape, folded it wet side inward and sidled into the bench seat. It was a tight squeeze.

John stared at the hat. Its feather was long and multi-coloured, and belonged to some exotic bird he could not name.

The Italian merchant followed his gaze. "Tail feather of an Indian cock pheasant," he said. "Was that what you wanted to ask me?"

"Ask you?" John was flustered, out of breath from the tearing wind and fearful excitement of the storm. "No. I— um...." Endeavouring to regain his breath and conceal his discomfort, John removed his wet coat then reached into a cupboard for two cups. Willing his hands not to tremble, he poured sweet wine from a lidded jug then, keeping his head down to avoid eye-contact, he said, "As the captain mentioned at dinner, my name is John Hawthorne, sailing to Plymouth."

"And I am Ludovico, travelling on this stage of my voyage to Sanlucar de Barrameda in Spain. But you know that."

Not wanting to admit the claim, John said nothing and drank from his cup.

The Italian drank from his then said, "You must call me Ludo, the world calls me Ludo."

"The world?"

"Well, everyone I know from the Levant to Amsterdam. I haven't crossed the ocean to the New World yet, but I will. Then there will be Americans calling me Ludo."

"It seems a very familiar appellation—Ludo."

The Italian looked the English priest in the eye and said, "That comment, sir, tells me all I need to know about you."

John Hawthorne's cheeks flamed scarlet, "Oh, I.... Shall you be sailing north to Flanders or England after Sanlucar?"

Ludo cocked his head to one side and gave a half-smile. "Holland, not Flanders. I might disembark at Sanlucar, sail up to Seville and sell my wares there. It depends."

"Your wares? You have a cargo aboard?"

"A few barrels of this and that, some spices. These days I mostly broker sales for others; silk for Florence—that has been left in Livorno; uncut gemstones for various jewellers; some aromatics from India and Cathay. However," he paused for dramatic effect, "on this voyage—as I think you know—I travel with a very special, very, *very* special commodity."

"Diamonds?"

Ludovico da Portovenere shook his head.

"Rubies?"

"No, Mr Hawthorne, more precious than diamonds or rubies. Tulips."

Ludovico da Portovenere, who spent his life at sea and acknowledged no place as home, except a small house on the rocky pirate stronghold of Portovenere in northern Italy, smiled a wide, cheeky smile. "I bring tulip flower bulbs all the way from Turkey. Isn't that what you want to discuss?"

John Hawthorne tried to ignore the question: it interfered with his prepared speech. "Turkey! Goodness gracious. You have been in the land of the—" he paused on the verge of uttering the word 'infidel', noting the swarthy skin between the raised cup and the dark hair of the foreigner, "—in the land of tulips? How interesting. It was a commission?"

"A commission for personal profit, yes." Ludo drained his cup and leaned conspiratorially across the table. "I often commission myself, you know." A long, black-lashed lid closed slowly over a sea-green eye.

John Hawthorne was confused. Fearing he was being made fun of he said hastily, "No, forgive my impertinence. I understood the... um... er... the tulip was losing its attraction. Now there are so many of them."

"Not so many of them. I keep a careful watch on distribution. Apart from those growing in Dutch yards, which obviously I can't calculate, there are just enough in circulation to make them.... But why am I telling you my business strategies? Why is an English priest interested in bulbs coming from the land of the infidel and going to the land of the heretic? Do you plan to start your own enterprise?"

"Heavens above, no! I have no interest in trade."

"So?" Ludo pushed his empty cup across the small table.

"I am just interested in...." The young priest made a show of checking the contents of the jug. "I was told by someone that the high prices meant they would, um... sooner or later lose their value."

"You were told—interesting. But not yet, and even if they do drop in value it may only be temporary. It depends on the speculators. The tulip grower, the real connoisseur, always wants to see variations, new colours and new frills on petals; he is still very much interested in buying bulbs, whatever the price."

"A foolish occupation for a man." John spoke without thinking.

"Men are mostly foolish. When we are not being foolish we are either asleep or dead."

"I fear you are right."

"There are wise men, of course; some of them I'm told live in monasteries. And there are other wise men who—"

"Stay at home and till their lands."

"And raise broods of children, flocks of sheep, gaggles of geese, and die of hard work having never lived a moment."

"Hmm," John pursed his lips and tried to hide his opinion in his cup.

"Forgive me; I did not intend to offend. One doesn't often meet a priest who is also a Puritan."

"I don't dress as a priest. Do I look like one?"

Ludo braced his hands on the table and leaned back, grinning a one-dimpled, cheeky grin. "Mr Hawthorne, you are not a merchant and you are travelling from Ostia; what else would an Englishman be doing in Rome this time of year, unless you are an antiquarian—you have the look of an antiquarian. However, I believe your desire to speak with me is somehow connected with Rome. I currently trade in tulips in Holland and I'm a merchant from the state of Genoa, which is as Spanish as Madrid these days. So this must be to do with the Flanders war or England's return to the 'one true faith'; I'm fascinated."

John Hawthorne gulped wine to cover his embarrassment. He was also cross: he had been wrong-footed. His opening statement would have to be adjusted, and he'd spent hours choosing the right words, the appropriate phrasing, correcting the syntax. Slowly, deliberately, he put down his cup, ready to deliver the cardinal's message, but just as he opened his mouth to speak the cup slid off the polished surface and tipped over the table's protective rim. The ship gave a stomach-churning lurch and there was an almighty crack.

Ludo da Portovenere grasped the edge of the table.

"Hold tight, Mr Hawthorne; I fear we are about to run aground."

Chapter Three
Sanlucar de Barrameda, Spain, April 1635

John Hawthorne felt the ship lurch then dip again, and was launched across his cabin table to collide with the window.

Ludo tried to get to his feet, gave up the struggle and crawled to the door. It took him several attempts to get it open. John gasped as water surged in, confirming his worst fear. The ship was sinking.

"Come, Mr Hawthorne," bellowed Ludo. "Follow me."

Ludo made a grab for his cape and stuffed his hat inside his jerkin. Then he pulled himself nearly upright, grasped John around the waist and dragged him out of the cabin.

The ship was balanced on her starboard side against huge boulders. The surf rushed up underneath them and, just as Ludo was setting John to his feet, shoved the galleon further up the rocky shelf. They fell with a crash onto the slippery deck, drenched in sea water.

John Hawthorne lay where he was, too terrified to move. "I can't swim," he gasped.

"No need. If we're careful we can scramble over the side and onto the rocks."

"I shall slip!"

"Here, grab this." Ludo threw his cape over the gunwale. "Hold onto that as long as you can. Then let go and jump."

"Jump!"

Ludo got back to his feet, threw his cape over the railing and, holding it with one hand, picked up the small English priest again with his other arm. He held him over the wooden railing. "Go on," he said. "Jump—now!"

A sea-wolf of water hurled itself, snarling and slathering at the priest. For a moment John clung to the cape, then—as another wave threatened him—he did as he was told and jumped.

God was with him. He landed with his face flat on a wet, but not too slippery, surface. Embracing the rock as his salvation, he let the world surge around him, then slowly, very carefully, he edged a foot forward. And then hands were grabbing at him, pulling him upwards to safety. A miraculous minute later, he was sitting amongst long wet grass, giving thanks for his deliverance....

John Hawthorne was wide awake now. Sitting bolt upright, grasping rough sheets to his chest, he muttered a prayer of gratitude. After which, taking deep breaths to calm himself, he set his thin legs over the side of the narrow bed and gazed, unseeing, at his knees.

The wind and waves had tossed the laden galleon out of the Guadalquivir estuary like a cork. He couldn't rid his mind of the image; a wall of water crashing about him and Ludo—as he must call him—holding him like a child, telling him what to do.

He put his hands on the hard mattress and levered himself up. His legs were still wobbly. Despite growing up on the banks of the River Tamar he had always been terrified of water. If it hadn't been for Ludo, he would most surely have drowned.

The Genovese merchant's selfless act confused him greatly; it was so at odds with his first impressions of the man as the very image of the Anti-Christ.

Slowly, John began to get dressed. He had dry clothes, thanks to Ludo.

Once the group of Rota fishermen had got the passengers off the ship and onto dry land, various other locals had appeared to save their belongings—or steal them. Ignoring the boatswain and first mate, who were trying to take charge of the rescue because the captain had stayed aboard, Ludo had offered a king's ransom to whoever saved the cargo. Struggling against the screeching wind and lashing surf, he'd organized the men into a chain and made secure the barrels and bales in the cargo hold.

John stopped—one leg poised over his breeches—suddenly seeing the Italian's efforts in a new light. The cargo taken off the ship was all brought to Sanlucar with them. Every item, except his own small trunk, belonged to Ludovico da Portovenere. Perhaps not such a hero, then.

Setting thoughts of the Italian aside, John finished dressing more quickly; he had a report to write. He had at least done something right in accordance with his instructions; he'd insisted on being brought to Sanlucar, where their ship had been due to put in. Something had been pre-arranged in Sanlucar... what?

John took a wooden box containing his writing implements and journal from his trunk and put them on a tiny desk, biting his lip. He had to write a report, but there was still nothing relevant to say. Nothing regarding what they wanted to know in Rome about the Italian merchant. There was, of course, much he could say about the shipwreck.

For a moment he stared into his own blank mind—what was the arrangement for Sanlucar? His head was too full of crashing waves, wind and rocks to think straight. He had nearly drowned. Would nearly drowning be of any concern to the Cardinal?

He tried to run through his instructions again. First he was to deliver the message, then he was to accompany Ludovico da Portovenere when he disembarked in Sanlucar and report on what transpired with a certain Don Emilio de Gaspar, who would come to the hostel in Sanlucar, where they *must* lodge. After which, he was to send a coded report to the Cardinal on the Italian's attitude and how he had reacted to Don Emilio and... another man—who?

Events had gone awry. He was still at sixes and sevens. How on earth was he going to instigate a 'casual conversation' and bring it round to personal religious conviction and 'specific loyalties', as instructed, after what they had just experienced?

Well, there had to be a way, because he now remembered the Cardinal's words—all too clearly:

"You will have to use your own judgment in this. Choose your moment. I am told you are a cautious man: exert great caution. If you believe the man has specific loyalties to a particular entity or state, or of a heretical nature, say nothing. A merchant, who travels as far and wide as he, could be providing intelligence for any number of interested parties. If he is involved with anything in France I want to know immediately. You will be provided with a code...."

The Cardinal had paused, tapped his manicured fingers on his vast desk, and stared at him as if he were a naughty schoolboy. "You will be watched, you know." Then he had laughed, as if it were a matter of little importance. "'We shan't be pleased if you bungle this. You will be punished. Bear that in mind. All the time."

The priest returned to the present and put the stopper back on his ink pot; there was nothing to write. He stretched his thin neck and wriggled his shoulders to relieve the tension that had accumulated since he had been taken from the scriptorium in the English College and marched to his terrifying interview in the Vatican Palace. For the hundredth time he told himself that all he had to do was deliver a message and report on a meeting. After that he was free to return to England—until summoned again.

But he had to be very tactful—diplomatic—cautious. Oh, it was all so—he searched for an appropriate word—clandestine. Clandestine: a charming word for such a dubious undertaking.

John got up and went to the high window of his attic room. Standing on tiptoe he stared out. White sheets flapped like flags of surrender on a neighbouring rooftop. There was nothing to see, nothing to write, except his journal. He had written nothing of the shipwreck yet. He returned to his desk, opened his private journal and began to set down the date. By his

14

calculations it was Resurrection Sunday. They had been in this house for three days and... *and on the third day...* He must find a church, immediately. Bells had been ringing all morning; how could he have overlooked such an important day? He must wash, shave, and go to Mass.

With a new sense of purpose, John scraped his razor over the sparse stubble under his chin. He was just starting on his left cheek when his hand froze as if seized by an unseen presence. *You will be watched. You will be punished. Bear that in mind. All the time.* He put the razor down with a shaking hand and wiped his face with a cloth.

Very well, today, this very morning, he would stop at the room where the merchant was lodged, ask what had to be asked, and then get to the nearest church as fast as he could.

Motivated by the simplicity of the new enterprise, John finished his ablutions, then rushed down the stairs to the well-appointed room and knocked on the door in such a positive manner he surprised himself. It was opened by a girl holding a slop bucket. This anti-climax drained the colour from his cheeks. The girl said something incomprehensible. He had a reasonable command of Castilian Spanish from his seminary years in Valladolid, so he asked her if she knew where the *señor* was to be found. The maid giggled and edged past him with the foul-smelling waste.

As he descended the last flight of stairs, he heard a familiar laugh and stopped outside the ill-lit dining parlour. Seated at the long table facing each other were two men: Ludovico da Portovenere and a colourful figure with a ridiculous frilled cape pushed up over his left shoulder.

Could this be the meeting pre-arranged in Rome? Should he stay and listen, or join them? They were in such earnest discussion an interruption would be impertinent. The matter was decided by the arrival of the landlady's good-looking son bearing a tray with a jug and two cups. John was forced into action. Raising a hand he said, "Good day, sirs."

The Italian looked up, then got to his feet and came to the door of the parlour saying, "Mr Hawthorne, good morning. I thought you'd be at church."

"Yes, yes, good morning, I am indeed on my way, but first I was going to—"

"Tell me something?"

John tried to gauge the Italian's tone of voice: was he angry or amused? It was hard to tell; the way he spoke English had such a curious intonation it always sounded as if he were amused.

"Yes, but you are busy—that is, I have no wish to interrupt."

"Busy, yes, but you are welcome to join us." Ludo waved a hand towards the parlour table. "I believe you know Don Emilio de Gaspar."

The man in the frilled cape inclined his head as a greeting. John knew he should stay, but he simply couldn't do it, not today of all days; he should be in church. He said, "Er, well, no, we have never met. That is, um, I am on my way to Mass. Forgive me. We may speak later—if you are here."

"I'll be here," replied Ludo, "and anxious to know your special news."

"Good. Yes, well, thank you. Excuse me, gentlemen." John tried to lift the cap he'd forgotten to put on, then made a small bow.

Before he could leave, however, Ludo placed a hand on his shoulder and said, "When you return, come to my room. I would like to speak with you about an excursion we are to make tomorrow."

It was not a request, it was an order. John quailed; he was going to be involved in the Cardinal's scheming after all. He didn't know what was going on or why Don Emilio de Gaspar was there, but something was afoot and he wanted none of it. Ashamed of his cowardice, he turned, barely missing the landlady's fair son Marcos, who was still waiting to enter the parlour with the tray of wine.

"Sorry," John gasped, and rushed into the street.

In so doing he bumped into the vast belly of another large man: a man dressed in the sober vestments of a bishop.

The Spanish clergyman looked down at the scrawny foreigner with a scowl and stood his ground. John stepped aside. Trying once more to doff his missing cap, he bowed his apology and scuttled on. The bishop turned his head to watch him go then entered the hostel.

You will be watched. John fled down the street for the sanctuary of ritual.

The stone wall was warm to the touch; Marcos Alonso Almendro, just eighteen, blond and bright as a new doubloon, stood in what had once been the doorway of a shepherd's hut, impatiently studying the road below. The two men staying in his mother's hostel would have to pass this way, but so far only two farm carts and an elderly peasant leading donkeys with laden panniers had passed by; no foreigners in carriages— nothing, for what seemed hours. Time had passed; he now needed to shade his eyes from the sun. The view from the low hilltop was good; it would be impossible for anyone to get by without him knowing.

A sudden sharp breeze, peppery with dry grass and herbs, scuttered in a whirlwind around his rope-soled shoes, making him sneeze and blowing down the precious heraldic standard he had left leaning against the wall. Marcos swore under his breath and picked it up, carefully dusting the white soil and burrs from the painted fabric. He was inordinately proud of this family pennant; it was quartered with a castle that included a maiden in a tower, a dragon, the insignia for Cadiz, and the almond tree of his mother's name. It was a very attractive standard and entirely of his own invention.

The pennant named him *un hidalgo*, the son of 'a somebody', which was perfectly true, he was somebody's son; but in his imagination that 'somebody' was very important, and very rich. He rolled the silk around the stave and tucked it under his arm, then went to check his horse tethered to an ancient olive tree. The horse lifted its freckled grey head and pricked its ears, attention focused on something in the distance. The boy ran back to his lookout post.

It wasn't the carriage he'd been expecting; it was two men on horseback. At this distance it was hard to tell, but it did look like the Italian merchant and the weedy Englishman. Marcos Alonso was in his saddle and cantering down the stony hillside before it occurred to him that the men might be travelling modestly for a reason. However, as he drew his poor nag to a walk, he thought the whole thing seemed a little odd.

After the fancy visitor Don Emilio de Gaspar—he remembered the name because he recalled the frilly cape, and the reason he wore it thrown over one shoulder—had left, Marcos had gone into the parlour to collect the wine cups. The Italian had asked him for directions to the *Cortijo el Gallo*, which was interesting, because the *cortijo* was part of a huge area of land belonging to the Conde-Duque de Olivares; and, after the king, the Conde-Duque was the most important nobleman in Spain.

That was why he was on this hillside, pennant at the ready. One day someone was going to see him for what he was: a highly intelligent, handsome youth with a glorious future ahead of him. And where better to start that future than in the Conde-Duque de Olivares' household?

But—there were a number of buts—was the Italian's visitor, Don Emilio, part of the household at the *cortijo*? If so, why hadn't *he* given the Italian the directions? Marcos felt his skin crawl; there was more to this than tax-free trade. And now that it was too late to get away without being seen it dawned on him that not one of those men was exactly what he seemed. Certainly not the merchant, for all he'd fussed until his cargo was safely under lock and key. And if he was more than a merchant, he would also be more than wary of likely lads on empty high roads.

"Look!" John said.

"I seen him."

"An outlaw! A highway robber! A *bandolero* for sure. They said this could happen. Do you carry arms?"

"Not an outlaw, he's got a pennant. Could be a trick, of course." Ludo watched the young rider rein in his nag and settle the shiny pennant on his stirrup. "Not a *bandolero*, my friend, but not a coincidence either. Do you recognize him?"

John looked at Ludo, then ahead at the young man on a bony horse.

"No, of course not! I've never been here in my life. He'll probably lead us into a trap, a snare, an ambuscade. We shall be circled by his fellows and stripped of all we possess, all our belongings, chattels.... We'll be obliged to...."

"Possible. But unlikely."

The fair youth nudged his horse with his heels and trotted ahead for a few minutes, then halted and dismounted. As he saw the travellers approaching he dropped his pennant onto the dusty road and ran a hand down his mount's near foreleg, making a fuss around the hoof as if extracting a stone.

"*Buenos dias*," hailed Ludo in Castilian Spanish. "Do you have a problem?"

"I hope not, as I have a long way to ride. I'm on my way to Jerez. Good day, sirs," Marcos replied, doffing his cap, then picking up his pennant and smoothing its silk back around the pole.

John twisted in his saddle; no one was in sight, but that didn't mean anything. It was certainly a ruse, a trick, a stratagem.

"If your horse is not lame and you are travelling inland, why not join us for a while? There's safety in numbers on these dangerous roads," Ludo said, winking at his companion.

"Thank you, sir. Let me walk my horse a few paces, see how he goes."

The horse obligingly nosed a sharp flint then reached out his skinny neck and followed the boy a few paces.

"Looks fine to me," said Ludo, who had been studying the nag's saddlebags, not its legs. The boy was travelling very light for one who had 'a long way to ride'. They paused while he got back onto a cracked leather saddle, then set off again in silence.

Realizing the flaws in his plan, Marcos was running through his options: leave them as soon as possible, take them to an inn and abandon them there, ingratiate himself as planned and go with them, or feign runny guts and squat behind the nearest tree for an hour or three.

"There's an inn not far up the road," he heard himself say. "We could take some refreshment. I'll ask the ostler to take a look at the hoof."

"Precisely," muttered the English priest. "A plot, plan, ploy, and we are literally walking into it."

"Mr Hawthorne, Mr Hawthorne, come back to us!" Ludo leaned across and shook him gently by the arm. The priest blenched as the large hand circled his arm.

"Yes? Has something happened?"

"This young man invites us to take refreshment with him at a nearby hostel."

Marcos gaped at the phrasing. He didn't have a single coin on him. "No, not exactly, sir, I just thought...."

"Hm? So you're not inviting us to a cup of your delicious local wine? Pity."

"No! Well...."

"Never mind, if—and only if—we like the look of the place, we may stop. But I regret we have little need of a guide, groom or general servant. *Dio mio*, I sound like Mr Hawthorne here, he thinks in trinities."

"That is blasphemy!" hissed the small priest with horror.

Ludo ignored him and smiled his one-dimpled smile at the boy. "Not that your appearance suggests you fit any of these modest categories; your pennant tells all. Well, not quite all. You tell us. It is a bonny family emblem. Are you meeting someone important in Jerez?"

Marcos' jaw dropped again—it had seemed such an easy project. Not knowing what to say, he said nothing.

Ludo smiled again and inclined his head knowingly. "Perhaps we should stop, Mr Hawthorne," he said. "This dusty road is making me thirsty. We'll have to ride back to Sanlucar this afternoon and it is a hot sun for the time of year." He raised an eyebrow in the boy's direction, looking for a reaction, but Marcos kept his eyes focused on the horizon.

The roadside tavern was a one-storey, wood-framed structure built haphazardly around an open patio. Apart from two piglets rooting under a long trestle table and a few scabby hens pecking at the dirt floor, there was no sign of life. Marcos waited outside in the open doorway, holding his horse's reins in case he needed to make a quick getaway. Ludo dropped his dusty leather hat onto a table in the centre of the patio and selected the safest looking chair. John Hawthorne pulled out the chair next to him and sat down; keeping his cap in his hands for fear someone might dash by and grab it. Marcos stayed outside and made a show of calling for a groom. No one answered his calls, so he tied his hack alongside the others at the rail provided and entered the shady interior.

"Here he comes, you see," laughed Ludo, raising his arms in the air. "My mean-spirited companion has just accused you of stealing our horses."

John Hawthorne jumped to his feet. "That is not true!"

"Well, you were thinking it. Don't you fellows believe wicked thoughts are tantamount to enjoying the sin itself? Or is that just reserved for women's titties and little boys' willies?"

"How dare you, sir! How dare you!"

"Oh, sit down. Today is going to be difficult enough without you having a tantrum."

"Sir, what right have you to address me in such a manner? I have never been so insulted in my life! I have a good mind to leave you right here."

"Very well, off you go. You don't have to be here as far as I know, or is there something else you haven't told me?"

John Hawthorne marched towards the entrance.

"Come back, come back! I apologize. Where are you going anyway, back to Rome or back to England?"

"Neither. I need the privy."

Ludo roared with laughter. "Use the back wall, it'll be cleaner." He watched the Englishman exit, then turned his bright eyes to Marcos standing behind him. "Now, you, sit down and tell me what's going on."

Marcos straightened his shoulders and pulled out a rickety chair with as much dignity as he could muster.

"Out with it. What are you up to? Why have you got us here and what do you plan to do with us now we're here?"

Marcos settled his cap on a knee and ran his fingers around its rim. "I thought you might like to pause in your journey...."

"In our journey to... to... Where is it we're going? Come on, I remember you hovering about with a tray listening to what was none of your business." Ludo waggled a stumpy forefinger at him with mock severity. "Did you honestly expect me not to recognize you? Come along now; think it through a bit more clearly. I was the person that asked you the whereabouts of the *cortijo,* remember, after my visitor had left?"

Marcos lowered his eyes.

"You were too quick with your directions, my lad. From which I infer you know *exactly* where we are going."

Marcos nodded and muttered, "*El Cortijo el Gallo,* sir."

"Correct. Now tell me more."

"About the *cortijo*? It belongs to the Conde-Duque de Olivares, or so they say. It was all shut up, but I think someone lives there again now. Some say it's haunted." Marcos lifted his head and looked the merchant in the eye. "I'm sorry, sir, about the... You won't tell my mother? She'll flay me alive."

"I don't tell tales. But I need the full story and be quick about it. That skinny priest's got a bladder like a pea; he'll be back here to listen if you don't get on with it."

"Full story, sir? About the *cortijo*? I don't know anything else."

Ludo leaned back, causing his chair to creak alarmingly, and blew out his cheeks. "About you and that pretty flag. You don't want to lose that, can't have been easy getting the girl to part with her petticoat."

"She won't notice it's gone till the morning...." Marcos stopped and bit his lip.

Ludo raised an eyebrow. "Enterprising. Being able to sew is a useful little skill."

"We learned with the monks, sewing their cassocks and things for the church."

"You've got some education then, good. Do you still attend?"

"More or less."

"But less rather than more."

"You won't—"

"Tell your mother? No, but all this secrecy is going to cost you."

"Oh, yes, sir, that's all right." Marcos' face lightened. Perhaps his plan was going to work after all.

He was telling Ludo how he'd acquired the paint and created the devices for his pennant when John Hawthorne returned to the patio, cross now because no one had appeared to offer them refreshment.

Ludo got to his feet. "Not much to be had here by the look of it," he said. "Let's go." He turned to Marcos, "Put your flag somewhere out of sight for a while; you won't need it again—today at least."

Marcos grinned and ran to hide his pennant among some dusty oleanders.

Chapter Four

They reached the Cortijo el Gallo well after midday. Marcos jumped from his horse and pulled at a black ring beside the closed gates, setting a discordant bell echoing off cracked walls and startling their horses. Eventually a sour-faced retainer peered out of a spy hole.

"We're expected," Marcos said.

"Oh, yes? Who by?" the retainer replied.

Marcos Alonso looked toward the merchant for a name.

"Tell him the Count."

"The Count."

The retainer sighed and began to pull at the gate as if the effort would kill him. They rode into a wide courtyard set around a pretty fountain. Two immaculate, snow-white horses were tethered to rings in a wall. Each horse had a mane that fell below its shoulder; their hooves had been blacked and they looked as if they had stepped out of a fairy tale.

John Hawthorne gazed at them. "What beautiful creatures," he sighed.

"Mmm," replied Ludo. "And why are they here, I wonder."

The retainer pointed at vacant rings in the opposite wall but made no attempt to hold the reins while they dismounted.

"This way," he grunted and shuffled towards the main door.

Ludo looked meaningfully at the boy. "Marcos, loosen the girths, water our horses at the trough over there, then go to the kitchen and make yourself known."

The visitors followed the ill-tempered servant into a silent house. Glass-eyed black bulls and wild boar glared at their intrusion from high, white-washed walls.

John Hawthorne shuddered, removed his cap and moved toward the empty fireplace at the far end of the great hall. As he did so a figure emerged from a high wing-backed chair by the grate, making him jump. It was an elderly man, as grumpy-looking and ancient as the retainer. He pointed with an ebony stick at the vast table in the centre of the room; it was laid elaborately with fine crystal and bright silver for five.

"Take a seat," he said.

Ludo made a show of removing his hat and bowing, but the elderly man ignored him and went to sit at the table, making no attempt to introduce himself.

In the kitchen a wide-rumped maid with a face like a pumpkin was stirring a pot hanging over a cooking-fire. Marcos stayed as quiet as possible in the doorway as he sought other bodies in the relative gloom, then knocked politely on the open door. A small white dog with a brown patch over one eye suddenly dashed from nowhere and began yapping round his feet. He bent down and let it smell his hand, then scratched it behind an ear and, staying hunkered down, said, "May I come in?"

"Who are you?" demanded the girl, turning to face him.

"My master's servant."

The girl shrugged. "There's water in the jug on the table. Help yourself to bread. There's no spare oil or dripping."

"No oil or dripping?"

"There's not much cooking done here. You do know where dripping comes from, I suppose. What's your name?"

"Alejandro del Aguila." Marcos had a fancy to try out a new persona for his new role in life. He struck a pose, hands on hips.

"I'm known to some as '*El Aguila*'. But you may call me Alex."

The girl stared at him blankly. "I'm Maria de los Dolores. You can call me Lola."

Marcos picked up a cracked cup, poured himself some water then cut a slice of doughy bread and went to look in the pot.

"Not much cooking done here you say, but this smells good. What is it?"

"Kid. Special occasion."

"Why don't they let you do much cooking?"

"The old man only likes these new potato things, mostly he just eats bread. Leastways he don't spend money on anything else."

"What a waste. You're here on your own then, just the old boy at the gate and you?"

"He's my grandpa."

"Must be lonely, no one your own age to talk to."

"Fuff," Lola huffed. "You can't guess. It's like I'm all on my own all the time—only that dog for company. Then suddenly he expects me to cook up a meal for five and nothing in the larder. Well, there wasn't till last week. I've had to make marzipan and get out the last of the bottled cherries. Must be something special going on, I says to my grandpa, he never wants fancy things as a rule. We sometimes get visitors from his country; they get potatoes and chicken. He's Dutch, from Holland."

"Is he, now?" With his father fighting in the Flanders war for as long as he could remember, Marcos knew that a Dutchman choosing to live in enemy Spain was not normal.

"Well at least my master was expected and you had time to prepare. Four people, you say?"

The girl put a tureen on her work table and took a ladle from a rack. "Where you from? Grandpa said we was expecting more foreigners, but you're not foreign."

"No."

"Is your master from Flanders then?"

"Mmmm, this bread's good, may I have some more?"

Lola wiped a bead of sweat from her forehead and smiled. "If you look in the larder you might find something to go with it; there's not much there, though. I'll save you some of the stew."

Marcos stepped into the cool larder. The only illumination came from the open door behind him. It was as she had

26

warned, virtually empty. An ossified leg of ham rested on a frame under some muslin; a sharp goat smell indicated a piece of cheese lurking on an earthenware plate. There was the musty whiff of soggy potatoes and turnips, some wrinkled apples in a dish, and a series of funny looking onions lined up along a shelf. He went over to sniff them. They weren't onions. They looked and smelled exactly like the strange roots the Italian kept in his room. Except the Italian's were in delicate little crystal vases and tucked carefully into straw nests in a leather casket that looked like a miniature sea chest. He'd had to pick two complicated locks to even get a look at them.

"These are funny onions," he said, coming back into the kitchen with a bulb balanced on the palm of a hand.

"Oh, mercy me, don't touch them! Put them back, he'll go mad if he finds you've touched them!"

Marcos did as he was bid. "If they're not onions what are they?"

"They're called *tulipanes*, and my grandpa says they're worth a fortune."

"What are *tulipanes*?"

"Flowers."

"Flowers!" Marcos slapped his knee. "Who keeps flowers in a kitchen larder!"

The girl looked over her shoulder and lowered her voice, "You can laugh, Mr Don't-Know-Anything. That's why your master's here, that's why the old man don't want people coming to the house—and that's why," she chucked him under the chin with the end of her wooden spoon, "you're going back outside and saying nothing, or there'll be no dish of kid in rosemary and thyme for you, nor anything else while they're doing *their* bit of business later on."

Marcos looked at the girl, confused. Then, twigging her meaning, he pecked her on the cheek and skipped outside, hastily followed by the little dog.

The farm buildings had been left to go to ruin, except—and he gazed around him—there wasn't a weed in sight. Limewashed walls were cracked and crumbling, an old hand-plough had rusted into the white soil, even the weather vane on the stable block had come to a halt, but otherwise everything was spotless. He moved round to the door of the first outbuilding and peeked into the granary. The dog wandered around the empty space, wagging its tail as it picked up a trace of mouse, but there was little to attract rodents here; it was completely empty: not a mote of dust, nothing except two sacks of grain tied tightly with string.

The stables were also empty and far too clean. It was hard to believe the white horses were kept here. Further on, a solitary cockerel and a few dowdy hens were shut in a tiny, high fenced compound. The place seemed lifeless until he walked round the back of the outbuildings and noticed a fenced square of land alive with the brightest colours nature could boast. Tall green plants topped with blooms like brilliant turbans stood in military rows. He was walking towards these flowering splendours when the action of the dog caught his attention. First it sat down, then it ran back a few paces, then it turned round in a series of agitated spins and sat down again. It had obviously learned the hard way it was not allowed beyond this point.

How very odd, thought Marcos. *How very, very odd.* There was however, no time to investigate this forbidden territory because the entrance bell clanged again and he was back in the kitchen in an instant. The girl was pouring stew into the tureen.

"Lola, which is the door to the dining hall?"

"That one," she said indicating behind her with an elbow.

Opening the door quietly, Marcos stared into the dimly lit room. His new master glanced up and nodded imperceptibly. He slipped in quickly, went round to the merchant and whispered, "The new tenant, he's Dutch," then took up a position beside the door, his hands behind his back.

Ludo put down the fine crystal goblet he had been examining and smiled. He'd got very little out of the priest about what was going to transpire at this meeting, but knowing their ill-mannered host was Dutch led straight to his barrel of tulip bulbs and the special casket he'd left safely locked and hidden in his bedroom at the hostel.

Two minutes later, with a bluster of hat slapping and boot stamping, a well-dressed stranger was ushered into the house by Don Emilio, the Spaniard Ludo had previously met at the hostel. The frilly cape was once again pushed over his left shoulder to hide what remained of the arm he'd lost while fighting in Flanders. Don Emilio wore no riding glove, but the other man was removing his, finger by finger.

Ludo turned and caught Marcos' eye, gesturing with his head toward the travellers. Marcos nodded and briskly crossed the room to receive the visitors' capes, gloves and wide, be-feathered hats as if he had spent his life as a nobleman's page. With the apparel across his arm, he exited through a door at the end of the room opposite the great fireplace and did not return for some time.

Ludo and John Hawthorne rose to greet the visitors. The Dutchman remained seated.

Don Emilio addressed Ludo as he crossed the large room.

"Don Ludovico, a pleasure to meet you again. I am so pleased you decided to come. You will not regret it, I am sure. Please, let me introduce...." he paused a moment to look at his companion.

"Count Azor," said the man.

"Count Azor," repeated Don Emilio, evidently surprised at his companion's somewhat juvenile choice of appellation: 'the hawk'. Nevertheless, with habitual good manners he extended his good arm in Ludo's direction and continued, "Count Azor, I present Don Ludovico da Portovenere, from Genoa."

Count Azor gave a barely perceptible bow, ignoring, as had Don Emilio, John Hawthorne, which suggested to Ludo the priest was indeed only a messenger with no part to play in the current proceedings, and both men already knew about him.

Before anyone could speak further, Count Azor seated himself at the long table. On cue, Lola emerged from the kitchen with a steaming tureen. She placed it in the centre of the table but did not stay to serve. The Dutchman, who had said not a word thus far, silently grabbed the ladle and helped himself. John Hawthorne looked appalled at the man's rudeness, but neither the count nor Don Emilio appeared surprised or put out.

Ludo noticed John mutter something in Latin, assumed it was a prayer for what they were about to receive, and wondered why he didn't do it aloud: they were in a Catholic country. Then he wondered if it were a prayer to get through the next couple of hours. Or perhaps it wasn't a prayer and he wasn't a priest after all. The two Spaniards might be ignoring him as part of a preconceived strategy. If so, all the assurances he had received *ad nauseam* the previous evening in his room were meaningless. Mentally cursing the priest as a nuisance, he passed the ladle to the count before helping himself to the stew.

The food tasted as good as it smelled, and after exchanging a few words about the unseasonal heat and the lack of spring rain, the men ate in silence, interrupted only by the regular clatter of the Dutchman's spoon.

After a while, Ludo decided to provoke conversation. Looking directly at Count Azor, he said, "You have travelled far today?"

The count looked at him. "A good distance."

Don Emilio said, "Count Azor is with the royal court, which I believe is still in Madrid." He turned to his compatriot. "You will be moving to El Escorial soon, for the summer months, no doubt?"

Count Azor nodded, refusing to be drawn into small talk.

Ludo watched Don Emilio, trying to gauge his attitude towards the count; but Don Emilio maintained a passive expression, so he turned to Count Azor again and said, "It must take many days to travel here from Madrid?"

This question went unanswered as well, for Lola came in, collected their plates, exited with a banging of doors and clatter of trays, and then returned with five silver dishes of bottled cherries.

Ludo watched the men around him with amused distraction. Two messengers, a third who was perhaps an envoy from Olivares in the royal court or even the king himself, and no one was saying a word.

John Hawthorne had gone pink in the face. Out of the corner of his eye Ludo watched him shift a cherry stone around his mouth with his tongue, not daring to swallow and too well-mannered to remove it with his fingers. The count from Madrid sitting opposite made a fancy fist and delivered each stone neatly onto his plate; the Dutchman spat his into an empty goblet. Ludo didn't touch the fruit at all.

Lola came back to remove the dessert dishes. Once she'd gone, the count from Madrid leaned forward, picked up the second carafe of wine and poured himself a healthy measure, saying, "Well, de Kuyper, if you're not going to get this started, I had better do it myself."

John Hawthorne immediately rose to his feet, excused himself politely and sidled through the front door.

"Is that the priest from Rome?" Count Azor addressed Don Emilio. "Not what I'd been expecting."

"He's English," said Ludo.

"English! I hope they are not involved as well."

"No. He was sent by—from Rome," Don Emilio bit off his words.

Count Azor made a moue with his mouth and wiped his moustache on a stiff napkin. "Nevertheless, an unwelcome and unnecessary addition, I hope there's nothing else to surprise me." He looked meaningfully at the Dutchman. "Well," he continued, "I'm glad he's out of the way; we don't want the Vatican knowing every little detail."

He got up and crossed the room to open the outside door as if expecting to find the priest with his ear to the keyhole, then swaggered around, making a show of examining the stuffed trophies. Eventually he returned to his seat saying, "Oh for God's sake, de Kuyper, do your bit."

"It's not *my* business," grunted the Dutchman in bad Spanish.

Ludo leaned back in his chair and raised an eyebrow. "Can I help you, gentlemen? Is there a valuable piece of merchandise to be traded? Is it a delicate assignment and are we, including the priest, representatives of the parties involved?"

"Close," the count said, touching at his whiskers with a napkin. "Continue."

Ludo looked at each man in turn then said, "The Roman Catholic Church, an exiled Dutchman and one, possibly two, representatives of the Spanish monarch—or his government?" He turned to the count. "Who do you speak for, Count Azor, monarch or ministers? The two do not always act in accord these days. Although I understand this house belongs to the Conde-Duque de Olivares, which perhaps answers my question."

Don Emilio placed his hand on the table and turned to Count Azor, expecting him to answer. The count dropped his napkin on the table and stared at Ludo, saying, "You have a reputation for being astute, sir. You are also—by reputation—an unscrupulous merchant. Being Genoese means your allegiance is to Spain and the Pope, or do you have no particular sense of duty?"

Ludo inclined his head but remained silent.

Count Azor, however, required an answer. "Are you what they call 'your own man', or can we rely on your discretion out of loyalty to Church and State?"

"You can rely on my discretion; my motives are my own business," Ludo said, politely but firmly.

"As you wish; the success or failure of the war in the Low Countries makes little difference to me, personally," replied the count.

Don Emilio's head shot round. "I lost an arm fighting in Flanders, and this country had been engaged in war for years. You have no right to dismiss the issue so lightly." He was genuinely angry but modified his tone and added, "Although, naturally—"

"All I need at this stage is your word that you are willing to cooperate with us." Count Azor addressed Ludo, ignoring Don Emilio's outburst. "When I say 'us', I mean I report to the Conde-Duque, who in this matter works entirely in accordance with His Majesty's wishes."

"And the matter is....?" Ludo asked innocently.

The count now scowled at Don Emilio.

Dio mio, thought Ludo, another ineffectual messenger. Don Emilio had omitted something important in their jovial chat at the hostel. Whatever it was, it was making the count from Madrid nervous, which was good. If, underneath it all, the count was afraid of returning to Madrid empty-handed, he could demand better terms—for whatever it was. A nervous buyer always paid over the odds.

The count took a long drink then said, "I am informed you trade in rare flower bulbs from Turkey?"

"I do."

"Interesting. It's not easy to obtain these roots in the Levant; the Turks don't care for Christians on their soil, yet you are said to have an unlimited supply."

"Not unlimited. A healthy supply, yes."

"That is what we want to stop."

"To stop? You want me to cease trading in tulips! The Dutch are obsessed with them and now the French are speculating in them as well. With respect, I sincerely doubt you can compensate the loss of such a livelihood." Ludo paused, intending to close the interview with a polite refusal, but curiosity got the better of him. "What exactly do you have in mind?"

"We suggest that de Kuyper here takes all the plants you have at present and keeps them at this *cortijo*. He knows how to split them, multiply them. That is why he is here today. He might explain how to propagate them if you care to learn."

Horrified, de Kuyper shook his head in an emphatic negative.

"Well, that's a minor detail. You continue with your trip to Amsterdam, taking some special rarities from here: de Kuyper will provide you with two of the famous Semper Augustus and some others—what are they called?"

The Dutchman mumbled some names, but the count wasn't listening. "We also are very interested in high prices. In fact, we are especially interested in seeing just how high prices will go. To that end, we will provide you with a significant amount of cash to stimulate purchasing. You are to offer this to anyone wanting to play the tulip market."

Ludo considered this, then said, "If prices are allowed to go too high the market will collapse."

"Precisely."

"I see."

"Do you?"

"Count, I think you—and your advisors—overestimate the outcome of... what do you want to call it, this plot?"

The Spanish nobleman sniffed and dabbed again at his moustache. "I find the word 'plot' rather crude."

Ludo leaned back and folded his arms over his chest. "Nevertheless, this is a conspiracy—plan, if you prefer—to destabilize the new Dutch United Provinces' economy."

The count made the slightest movement with his head to confirm the suggestion.

"I see," said Ludo. "And you think you can seduce wily Dutch burghers from their habitual common-sense with...." he paused for effect, "flowers? If you said you had a scheme to prevent your own countrymen sending silver and gold to bank vaults in Amsterdam I might take you seriously, but tulip bulbs...."

Ludo was doing his practiced best to remain aloof, but the idea amused him, and he could make an awful lot of money in the process. He cocked his head on one side as if considering the proposition, "Mmm."

Count Azor wiped the palms of his hands nervously on his napkin. Ludo gave no indication he had noticed the act and remained silent.

Eventually the count said, "People in the very highest position in this country *and in Rome* would be most grateful. They will show you their gratitude."

Ludo nodded slowly, then leaned forward and in a quiet voice said, "I, we, should not voice our doubts, of course, it is not our place; but do these people *in the very highest position* seriously believe they can chase Protestant black sheep back into the Catholic fold with a bunch of flowers?"

The arrogant aristocrat from Madrid avoided making eye-contact and reached for more wine. Ludo leaned back in his chair and waited. It was almost laughable, except no one laughed at this Florentine Pope. Maffeo Berberini, now Pope Urban VIII, had a special retinue of secret agents resident in each European capital: intelligence gatherers, spies. Among these agents was an elite group of highly efficient assassins known as the Black Order. They worked at night; no one ever saw them, although they often left a calling card, a square of black silk. So the wise were cautious and kept their thoughts to themselves. Here in Spain, everywhere in Spain, there was the Inquisition, who could fabricate what little evidence they ever required to torture a man into false confession. The thought was sobering; he would be a fool to get involved.

On the other hand, it could be amusing, and it would turn a healthy profit. Naturally, he would have to stay ahead of the game; he would have to stay *well* ahead of the game. And know when to get out. Then he'd have to make a run for the North African coast or the Balearic Islands where he'd be safe. For that, though, he needed his own vessel.

Ludo looked at the Conde-Duque de Olivares' personal envoy, the man who called himself Count Azor, waiting for him to make the next move. Don Emilio was doing the same.

The Spanish count said, "So you are not willing to...." then became lost for words.

Ludo smiled a crooked smile and tapped the table with the fingers of his right hand. "You *could* engineer an *upset*, but if you go supplying funds for private loans it will be the ordinary people that suffer, not the wealthy or politicians. Banks won't lend money for tulip trading anymore. So you aren't going to hurt them unless the middle-classes suddenly withdraw all their savings to make purchases—or pay their debts."

"Perhaps you can explain the business to me, then I can inform the Conde-Duque accordingly."

Ludo refolded his arms and began.

"At present there are two types of bulb trading. There are the connoisseurs; some are fairly wealthy—many are academics or professional men who treat the flowers as works of art. I find bulbs for them and they propagate them to get fancy petals and unusual colour combinations. Then there are 'new men' coming up from the labouring and artisan classes. They buy and sell bulbs like any other commodity for profit. Some of these men call themselves *florists*. These florists have established links with horticulturalists and grow plants for sale. This type of trading goes on in taverns, not the Amsterdam Stock Exchange. The Stock Exchange keeps itself very professional; I doubt you'll ever manage to create even a ripple there."

Ludo paused for some reaction to what he'd said, but there was none.

"Continue," said the count again, without emotion.

"Florists sell to carpenters, butchers, bakers, anyone who wants to risk their savings on what's proving a pretty safe bet. If the market collapses too fast, it'll be these working men, artisans and the like, that suffer. Tulip connoisseurs and city burghers are cushioned by their wealth. You might make a dent in their savings but you won't ruin them—unless you can turn the tulip market into something like a gambling mania so they spend everything they've got. As to the wealthy bankers, they're as safe as the houses they live in. No, it'll be the humble that suffer. If working men start to borrow money so they can gamble on the price of bulbs rising... Can't you see? It'll be these ordinary men and their families who'll take the knock. They won't be able to honour their debts, and they'll lose everything they have trying to pay what they owe."

"So what are you saying? Manipulating the market will have no effect on Dutch finances?"

Ludo could see the count was wondering how he could convey this to King Philip and—or—the Conde-Duque. Could they really believe this was a foolproof, cunning means to undermine the protestant Dutch economy and bring the war to an end? He waited before responding, giving the envoy from Madrid time to panic a little longer, then began to speak again, pacing his words in his accented Spanish so there was no misunderstanding.

"Well, obviously it would affect spending power to an extent. The professional bulb traders, the *florists*, are already working taverns throughout the United Provinces; they're encouraging speculation and now everyone wants tulips. If you've ever been to Flanders you'll know that a bright flower in that climate is a joy in itself. It blooms after a very long, very grey winter. You could, I agree, bring a few of the wealthy to ruin if they are putting *all* their resources into the tulip market, but their Protestant faith makes them careful by definition. Knowing you'll take your sins to the grave tends to make a man think twice."

Ludo shook his head and sighed. "Count, I'm a merchant, I work in what the Dutch call the 'rich trades', spices, silks, tea; I'm not interested in becoming a florist or dealing with clerks and butchers. My business is with wealthy connoisseurs who commission me to bring rare plants from Turkey. I do not rustle up business in alehouses."

"But you know people who do."

"Possibly."

"So?"

"So I am trying to help you see that bringing down a government by undermining its source of finance, thereby reducing the amount of money the Dutch spend on fighting your Spanish soldiers... well, this is probably not the best way to go about it. Although, I do think, if you are absolutely determined, you could turn this tulip business into a full-blown mania."

Count Azor inclined his head. "I was not told you had a conscience, nor that you were a Protestant."

Ludovico da Portovenere lifted his fine crystal goblet and sighed. "If you are merely trying to rock their confidence, and this is just a small but irritating element in a plan to reclaim your lost provinces, it will be easy enough to set up what they call a futures market. But if all this is a means of reclaiming your lost territories and bringing Holland back to the Catholic Church it's a damned strange way of going about it. I can't see many ruined heretics running to the nearest priest for forgiveness. However, that's your problem. I have no interest in anyone's soul—not having one myself."

"Does that mean yes, or no?" snapped the count.

Ludo gave the count a long look and then focused on the vacant glass eyes of a black bull suspended over the fireplace. After a moment or two he shrugged his shoulders and gave a one-dimpled grin. "I'm always interested in making money. Tell me what you have in mind for me. Organizing this means I will have to stay in that miserable climate longer than I like. You also need to take into consideration the risk factor: sooner or later someone will be after my skin. There's also plague in just about every town. I'll want danger money. And you can forget those pretty palfreys you've got out there."

The count looked across the table at the merchant, then opened the palm of his right hand, indicating the gilt-edged tableware and silver cutlery that lay before them. Then he opened the palm of his left hand and wafted it around the room.

"I am instructed to offer you this house and all the land pertaining."

Ludo burst out laughing. "And will you give me the fancy title of Conde-Duque to go with it?" He shook his head, "Thank you, but no. Houses are of no use to me."

The two Spaniards exchanged glances, perhaps wondering what kind of fool rejected a *cortijo* belonging to the Olivares estate.

Count Azor sighed and eased his shoulders. Ludo gazed at nothing but noted every move. The count was tired and cross, in no mood to appease or cajole.

"I wonder," Ludo said quietly, leaning forward, "if it were up to you, sir... would you take my refusal and be done with it? The whole idea is ridiculous, this you know. My response has not been what you expected, and herein lies a serious problem: the Conde-Duque will be displeased and report this failure to the king. Shall you be excluded from court? Am I right in thinking," his voice barely a whisper now, "that you fear the great Conde-Duque might alert the Inquisition to your failure?"

Count Azor swallowed hard.

Ludo watched him shift uneasily in his seat. Timing his final parley, he drank from his goblet. There was silence. The Dutchman belched.

Ludo leaned back in his chair and, addressing Count Azor quietly but very clearly, said, "A ship. That would tempt me. A well-equipped barque with a smart and willing crew: that might persuade me into your nasty little conspiracy. Arrange it, and in the meantime I'll make my way to Amsterdam as planned. I'm sure you'll be able to get word to me there; you have a whole retinue of messengers at your disposal."

Count Azor gulped despite himself, but just as he opened his mouth to speak a very rosy-cheeked Lola came into the room with a tray of marzipan sweetmeats and what remained of a decanter of brandy.

Chapter Five

Ludo, John Hawthorne and Marcos rode away from the *cortijo* in silence. The Italian merchant was angry, the English priest was anxious, and the boy couldn't stop smiling. After about half an hour Ludo turned to Marcos and said, "Ride on ahead and tell your mother we'll need hot baths when we arrive. And don't forget your pennant on the way; you might need it again."

Once Marcos was out of earshot, he said, "Mr Hawthorne, the time has come for you to tell all. Thanks to you I have just been involved in an unnecessarily surprising interview. I asked you for information last night regarding this meeting and you failed to inform me. Forewarned is forearmed, an old adage but true for all that."

John Hawthorne bit his lip, then said, "What do you want to know?"

"Just tell me how you come to be here in Spain, and start from the beginning. I want details in chronological order."

"I can't tell you more than you already know. As I said last night—"

"Last night you fed me porridge!"

John Hawthorne sighed, then, staring between his horse's ears, he took a deep breath and said, "Two weeks ago, I was summoned to speak to Cardinal—to a cardinal. He told me I was to join your ship and approach you. He seemed to know when and where you were travelling. I was charged to find out if you were inclined to the Protestant faith or were a loyal Catholic...."

"And which is it? I'd like to know for my own benefit. Oh, never mind, carry on."

40

"They said that if you showed no specific... allegiance... I was to communicate a message."

"That is what I want to know. Have you communicated this message and did I blink and miss it? Were you supposed to tell me the topic of today's small-talk or what?"

"No, well, the ship nearly sank with us on board! I was distracted. Once we were in the hostel I tried to find an appropriate moment. I tried to speak to you but you were always talking to someone and...."

"So were you being cautious, or were you afraid I might laugh at you and go about my business?"

"Well, both, I er—I knew about Don Emilio."

"Who you hoped would do your job for you?"

"Yes. No!"

"So all you had to do was tell me I was to meet a tall dark stranger and that I'd learn something to my advantage?"

"Yes."

"And what made that so difficult?"

John Hawthorne muttered something to himself.

"What?" insisted Ludo.

"The Cardinal—and his older cousin, his private secretary—everyone in the Vatican knows the power of these men. How could I even begin to refuse? I did want to. I wanted to say no—or something. But it isn't only the message that scares me."

"What scares you? *Dio mio*, explain yourself. You're turning me into the damned Inquisition with all this mumbling."

"It's the fact that I was chosen to deliver it—the message—that worries me most. Why me? I mean, I suspect I know, but...." The small, thin priest opened and closed his mouth, searching for the right words, "I assumed you would know what it was all about."

"How was I to know that? Divine intervention? You didn't even give me an address."

"I got us to the hostel—in the storm!" John Hawthorne was indignant. "That wasn't easy."

"Ah, so the hostel was the key venue?"

"I didn't know about the *cortijo*, or what's been going on today. I just got us to the hostel, as I was told to; then when I saw Don Emilio and then the bishop I knew it had all been arranged—without me."

"What bishop? I didn't see a bishop. He must have come to check up on you, you fool."

John Hawthorne gasped in dismay.

"Mr Hawthorne," Ludo's voice was barely a whisper, "who and what exactly are you? You are more than just a messenger."

"No!"

"Then you had better tell me who it is that knows where I am going to be and when. Who is this omnipotent master of yours? I had planned to come ashore in Sanlucar, but I'd like to think the way we fetched up isn't within his powers."

"It was an act of God."

"Quite."

Ludo shifted in his saddle and sighed. He hated travelling overland: he disliked dust and the smell of horse sweat; above all, he hated not having the upper hand, and in this instance there was a whole network of people who were at least one big step ahead of him.

For a while he considered the advantages and disadvantages of taking the next ship back to Genoa. It would be easy enough to sell his tulip bulbs to merchants sailing north once he was there. He could stay on for a while, spend time with Maria Grazia or Teresa and check on his sons' schooling. Then he could return to the Levant and lie low until the whole stupid conspiracy had been forgotten. He looked across at the English priest and started to ask him if he were planning to return to Rome immediately, but the priest was so lost in thought he didn't hear him.

John Hawthorne was examining not altogether dissimilar alternatives. He could find a ship sailing for Plymouth and go straight home to his mother, or take the dangerous road to Madrid before travelling on to his old seminary in Valladolid.

He could take a less direct route across country towards the north east, beg admission to a remote monastery in the Pyrenees and remove himself from the material world forever. The appeal was strong. He had been sent to the Vatican not because he was a priest in whom the Spirit shone but because he was a scholar. How ironic that his quiet personality had led them to choose him as a messenger.

At this thought, he sat bolt upright and unintentionally pulled his horse to a standstill. That was why he had been chosen! If he did not disappear of his own accord they would arrange for him to vanish anyway. The fact that he was a mere scribe, working on rare manuscripts away from the daily life of the Vatican, meant no one would ever remark on his absence. They would assume he had returned to England and leave it at that. He shuddered, and knew that was what he should do—go home.

As they finally neared the town of Sanlucar de Barrameda, Ludo broke the silence. "Before we return these nags and are surrounded by nosy people again, I'm going to give you one more opportunity to tell me the truth, Mr Hawthorne. Where do *you* stand in this tulip business?"

"Tulip business?"

Ludo looked at the priest. "So all you had to do was tell me about today's meeting?"

"Yes and no."

"Yes *or* no?"

"It does seem odd, I confess."

"You confess! Are you trying to tell me you're strong-willed enough to defy the laws of your country to travel to Spain, an enemy nation, to become a priest and *confess* that you can live with knowing that if you return to England you're likely to be burnt at the stake—I presume they still enjoy cooking Catholics in London—but you haven't got the guts to tell me why a man wants to speak to me on a farm? Mr Hawthorne, I do not believe you are just a messenger."

"A very unwilling messenger."

"And once more: apart from the address, what, for God's sake, is this message?"

"That Don Emilio was to come to the hostel to speak to you... and when the time comes you will be contacted in Amsterdam."

"Amsterdam! So you knew I was going to Amsterdam, and you know about the tulips."

John Hawthorne hung his head in shame. "I don't know anything about tulips. You mean the flower? I have heard of tulips, but I don't think I've ever seen one."

An hour later, Ludo lowered himself into an overfull bath tub cascading of water across the wooden floor. Lying back, he began to soap his black-haired arms and legs, washing away the day's dust and discomforts. For a few minutes he lay in the tub with his eyes closed, then sat up with a start. "That's it!" he shouted, splashing the water with a fist. "Play them at their own game!"

All he had to do was keep to his own rules, never let them get ahead of him again, and make sure he was on the Arab side of the Mediterranean when the market crashed.

In the tiny room above, John Hawthorne was running a square of grey soap up and down his skinny arms. As they had returned to the hostel, the vast, black-skirted bishop had emerged from the front door. Their paths had crossed. The image was imprinted on his consciousness. He was now reviewing his decision to run home, thinking perhaps it would be wiser to stick with the arrogant Italian as commanded. His watchers would see him at the merchant's side—at least until they got to Holland—exactly as he'd been instructed. Once in Amsterdam, he could find a way to get lost then, on his own, find a lugger or some other merchant craft sailing for Plymouth. Once he was home he'd be safe. Relatively safe. Until the Cardinal's men found him. And they *would* find him. The Cardinal's secret agents could find anyone, anywhere. Still, at least he would be at home for a while. After that, it was the will of God.

Decision made, John raised his small lump of soap into the air and dropped it into the bath water, making a sad little splash.

Two days later, John Hawthorne climbed into a tender carrying passengers and cargo out to a galleon. A short distance up the beach, Ludovico da Portovenere was standing arms akimbo, supervising the loading of his salvaged barrels. Once he had seen them safely aboard he returned to the hostel across the way to collect his precious hand luggage. As he was ascending the stairs to his room he heard a squeal of laughter and a deep-throated chuckle from the kitchen. On his way back down he saw an imposing clerical figure leave the house.

The landlady, Marcos' mother, appeared in the kitchen doorway pink-cheeked and smiling; when she noticed the Italian merchant she lowered her gaze.

Ludo said, "I need to settle my account with you, dear lady, or has it already been done?"

"And who might do that, sir?"

"A priest, a bishop...."

The woman looked at him blankly, "No sir, you owe me for four nights in a double room and the single room for your companion."

"Am I to pay for him, too?"

Marcos peered round the door. "Do you need me, sir?"

"And what might I need you for? I'm leaving."

The boy looked sheepish.

The woman spoke, "He wants to travel, sir, wants to see the world. Wants to go to Flanders and get killed like his father." She cuffed the boy affectionately under the chin. "He's fed up with being tied to his old mother's apron strings."

Marcos went scarlet.

"Ah," said Ludovico to the boy, "so that's what it's all about. You didn't mention this when we spoke the other day."

Marcos stared at the floor as the woman spoke again. "Take him, sir," she begged. "It'll break my heart, but it's going to be broken sooner or later. I can't keep him here like a girl, can I?"

"Mmm," replied Ludo equivocally. "Here, Marcos, take this to the tender bound for the *Esmeralda* and wait for me there."

He handed Marcos the leather-bound casket in the form of a miniature sea chest that he had kept hidden in his room. "Don't get on the boat, and don't let that casket out of your grip!"

Marcos took the small chest, walked across the street and down onto the beach. As he went, his mother said, "His father's in Flanders, leastways he was when we got his last letter. I don't want Marcos in any war, though. Can you not use him as a servant? Let him work off his wanderlust that way."

Ludo shook his head, "I don't need a servant, I'm sorry. You should find someone more reliable than me for this."

The woman smoothed her apron. "Ah, well, never mind. He'll have to sort himself out. It's just that he'll have to go soon or the Berbers will get him. They're raiding this coast almost every month and taking boys like him. So far we've managed to hide, but they'll get us one day." She sighed, then said, "Will you pay me now, sir?"

Ludo settled the bill, including the costs for the Englishman, and walked over to retrieve his chest. He gave the boy a handsome tip and slapped him on the back, saying, "You stay with your mother, boy. She's lonely without your father, and if Berber slavers are raiding along this coast you should be here to protect her. A woman needs a man, and you're all she's got."

"Like hell I am! What d'you think that black-garbed bastard is doing in our house every day?" The boy strode off without saying goodbye.

Ludo suddenly saw himself aged fourteen, desperate to grow up and get away. "Marcos!" he shouted.

The boy turned.

"Pack your things."

Chapter Six
Santander, Spain, April 1635

Alina picked up the plates for their evening meal and began to set them out around the table. Fernando, her youngest brother, galloped into the room on the remains of a hobby horse, slapping his side and charging purposefully into her.

"You're too old for that thing now, put it away," she said, rubbing her hip.

"And you're too old to be my sister." Fernando whipped his charger around the long table.

"What's that supposed to mean?"

Head down, the boy ignored her question, stomping the floor with ill-shod feet; then, lurching forward, he was off again around the table.

"Fernando! Stop that and help me with this."

The charger reared up on its hind legs. "That's servants' work," hissed the knight, and he galloped off in pursuit of danger, nearly knocking his king over in the process.

"He's getting too old for that," said the king his father.

"He should be having proper riding lessons, like his brothers," Alina replied, not looking at her father, and not without malice.

"Hmm. What's for dinner?"

"Knuckle soup, ham-fist cutlets, and finger and thumb pudding." Alina went to the drawer and began counting out what remained of the good spoons.

"Is that what you tell your brothers?"

"Sounds better than 'same as yesterday' or 'lentils and rice—again'."

"Hmm." Her father sat in his chair and began to tug at his right boot.

Alina put down the spoons, hitched up her skirt and straddled the boot, much as Fernando straddled his wooden charger. With a practised twist of the wrist, the boot slipped off, revealing three bony toes poking through a much-darned stocking.

"Stitching's gone again," muttered the impoverished grandee, and lifted the foot onto his left knee to examine it.

Alina plonked the last spoon in place and turned toward the kitchen, but her father called her back. "Don't go, the cavalry are busy elsewhere for the moment, stay and chat with me."

"Juana needs help in the kitchen."

"She can manage on her own. I have something to tell you."

Alina took a chair and sat near her father, fearing the worst. He was usually downhearted for a few days after a return from Madrid or Salamanca, or wherever the king's whim or the queen's demand had established the royal court, but this time he was particularly low, and he had returned before the Holy Week pageant, which suggested the worst. Now she would be forced to listen to his woes; she could hardly escape without being very rude.

Her father had started to tell her something on his arrival, but after months of making do and managing the boys on her own she couldn't bear to hear him whining; she had feigned a headache and retired early. It was foolish perhaps, but she preferred the loud, over-dramatic, flamboyant man who told a dozen lies a sentence and believed every one to the humble creature now speaking.

"First and foremost, I have to say how sorry I am and ask your forgiveness."

"For losing my mother's inheritance that was to be my dowry, or for not winning whatever it was you gambled for?"

"It was a fine house in.... How do you know?"

"It was all we had left after last year."

Alina hoped her father could feel the icy chill in the air: she was no longer a child to be gentled into deceptions.

He looked at her and said, "Ah, my Angelina, you have your mother's lovely soft hair."

"But not her soft nature."

"No. You are angry—I understand. But I have a plan! At the very next baptism, wedding or funeral—indeed, on this very Sunday—I shall seek out and woo a certain wealthy widow." The count slapped his knee with gusto, as if he'd created a fool-proof solution to their genteel poverty, then sighed at his impending sacrifice. "She is no beauty, but—"

"She'll take us on—five unruly boys, a leaking roof, one overworked maid-of-all-work and one ageing horse without a carriage?"

Her father had the grace to look shamefaced rather than offended. "I have to find a way to send Alvaro to Madrid, it is his due."

"Then Juan, Jose Luis, Miguel and Fernando, each to make a start in a profession suitable to your *noble rank*."

As if hearing her unspoken plea, her father added quietly, "I shall do something for you, never fear. I don't want to see my one darling daughter an old maid."

Alina lifted her chin and straightened her back. "Would you call the boys, please, Father? Supper is ready."

That night in her room, Alina sat down to continue the story she was writing in her journal about a young woman called Alicia who, dressed as a boy, sails across the ocean to Florida seeking love and fortune. She turned to a clean page, dipped her favourite quill in the ink, then wrote in large letters *I SHALL NOT DIE AN OLD MAID* before hurling the leather-bound journal across her chamber. The ink followed in a perfect arc, leaving a large and satisfactory splash against the wall. She was not dismayed: the stain would serve as a daily reminder.

Chapter Seven
Santander, Spain, April 1635

John Hawthorne was nearly asleep by the time the ship's tender reached the harbour wall. The dip and whoosh of the oars in the thick morning mist was gentle, relaxing, comforting after the tip and tilt of the ship, the slap and frightening crack of the vast sails. For the first three days he had stayed in the cabin he shared with Marcos, only daring to come out for main meals. Marcos said he'd never been onto the open sea before, but he seemed to enjoy the Atlantic swell, the way the ship rode up a wall of water and plunged down the other side. He strode the deck like a life-long mariner, like that devil in the black leather hat whom everyone called Ludo, except Marcos, who called him *patrón*.

As a mariner tied their boat to a mooring ring, he shook himself awake and followed the Italian up the rope ladder to *terra firma*. Once ashore he felt his knees buckle beneath him and would have fainted like a maid if Marcos hadn't steadied him. The miasma of stinking fish and tar nearly knocked him back down. He cast about to see whether the Italian had witnessed this latest debility, but the merchant was already striding purposefully towards some unnamed transaction. Seeing him go, Marcos ran after him.

"I don't need you, boy. Go and get some food and clothes," he said, handing out some coins. "And stay away from the women. They've all got the clap."

Marcos returned to where John Hawthorne was still trying out his land-legs. "What will you do, sir?" Marcos asked.

"I shall find a church. You should come with me."

"Oh no, I'm done with churches. I'll get some fresh cheese and milk."

They parted company and Marcos wandered off down the quay, evidently fascinated by how different it was from his home port.

A young woman, wearing a dress the colour of red wine and holding a fine woollen shawl around her shoulders, was wandering among the small upturned boats and fishing gear along the quayside. She paused to watch a big man in a black hat hand money to a fair-haired boy. The man then stood, arms akimbo, gazing about him as if he were lord of all he surveyed. He was dark like many Spaniards, but his features were unfamiliar to her. Was he, she wondered, a Lusitano or what they called a Moor? A Berber? A Turk?

Her thoughts were interrupted by a raucous squawk. It was a bird in a high domed cage. The cage was filthy, but the creature's gaudy feathers shone like firelight.

Somewhere behind her, a group of lads repairing nets began to laugh. One of them got to his feet and mimicked the way she was bending down to look at the bird. She ignored them and poked a finger between the bamboo bars of the cage. There were hoots of laughter as the bird took a mighty peck and drew blood. She stood up straight, raised her chin, pretending the boys didn't exist. She was good at ignoring ignorant boys; she had plenty of practice.

Just then a small boy ran out of nowhere and stopped when he saw the cage. Hunkering down, he too poked a finger between the bars, but he was younger and quicker and escaped unharmed.

"Corr, Alina! Where did you get him? Is it for us?" asked the boy hopefully.

"Don't be stupid, I've got enough to look after without that as well."

The boy looked disappointed. "I'll look after it."

"No, you won't. Forget the bird. Have you found them?"

The boy shook his head and pushed at the cage, tipping it until the bird screamed *hijodeputahijodeputa*.

Alina slapped his head. "Leave it alone."

"What are we going to do?"

"We? *You* are going to go round again until you find them. I'll stay here, that way we shan't lose each other—again."

"That's not fair; I've got to do all the running."

"You're a boy."

"Oh, and you're a fine lady who's too elegant to get her dress dirty!"

"Yes, actually. Now clear off."

The boy began to saunter away.

"Fernando!" Alina called after him. "Remember, I'll stay here until you've found them. Bring them here. All of them. Understand?"

Fernando looked up at his tall sister, stuck out his tongue and ran back in the direction of the town and the taverns.

Alina looked about for somewhere to wait. There was a pile of new rope coiled like a barrel close by. Examining it carefully for traces of tar, she sat down and arranged the taffeta folds of her skirt around her like a duchess.

It was a beautiful dress. Her mother's wedding dress, which was why she had decided to wear it for her father's betrothal. Unfortunately there were no lace gloves to accompany it; she had spent all her time during the petty ceremony trying to hide her hands in the voluminous skirt and had been embarrassed throughout the interminable meal that followed. Now the bodice felt very tight, and even sitting here on the coiled hemp she was obliged to stay ramrod straight. It was, however, a wonderful dress, and it had made her feel exactly what she was: a real lady.

Marcos straightened his shoulders, lifted his head to appear taller and began to stroll towards the beautiful young woman. He had taken three steps when the harbour exploded with noise and panic. Ships bells jangled, harbour bells clanged, whistles blew, a hundred men shouted at once. The boys loading the fishing boat and mending nets careered past him. One shouted, "The Turks!"

Marcos froze. Should he run for the tender, jump into the water, or climb into the nearest vessel and lie flat? He'd never been here before, where could he hide? They'd have him this time and he'd be rowing them back to Algiers or Salé if he didn't make shift. He scanned around for a bolt hole and caught sight of the girl: she hadn't moved. Didn't she know what was happening?

He moved towards her again, but it was too late. A dozen dark-skinned bodies in brightly coloured pantaloons were swarming over the quayside. Shots were fired. He dashed towards the girl, fighting against the current of local seamen running for the relative safety of their streets and homes. Grabbing the girl round the waist he pulled her down behind the coiled rope onto the ground. She righted herself immediately and gave him a sharp slap across the head.

"Get off me!" she shouted, scrambling to her feet. As she did so, she was swung into the air by a woolly-headed giant who bundled her under his arm in a practised clinch. He turned back toward the edge of the quay ready to toss her into a boat. She squirmed frantically under his arm in a froth of white petticoats.

Then suddenly she was sprawled on the ground again. The African giant was flat on his face and Ludo was standing over them.

He swore at the corsair in galley slang and pulled the girl to her feet. The huge galley rat stayed cowed on the ground, but a couple of other corsairs abandoned their own catches and turned on him, weapons drawn. He spoke again and they halted.

Marcos nipped between them and stood as close to Ludo as physically possible.

The girl smoothed down her skirts, straightened her shoulders and started to walk away. Seeing her move, Ludo reached out and caught the back of her dress, but she deftly turned out of his grip and kicked him. The men laughed. Ludo grabbed her arm and pulled her to him once more. She bit his hand and he let her go with a yelp, "*Regazza disgraziata!*"

The slavers screeched with laughter. He spoke to them and they slapped their thighs. The girl lifted her nose as if there were a disgusting smell and stared out to sea.

Marcos straightened his back, lifted his chin and folded his arms. Standing in what he hoped was a position demonstrating strength, he watched his *patrón* deal with the licensed pirates.

"She's mine, but I'm tempted to let you have her," Ludo was saying. "She's nothing but trouble."

The men guffawed. "You'd get a good price for her."

"That's what I tell her. If she doesn't mend her ways, I say, it's a one way trip to North Africa for you."

"The wild ones are more fun," said a low-bellied pirate, swinging out with a club to stop a runaway in his tracks.

"Nah, let him go, he's got a limp," said another.

"Since when did that matter?" demanded Ludo.

"Only young, healthy ones this time, captain's orders, and we're nearly full."

The pirates looked pointedly at Marcos. Ludo shook his head. But the pirates were torn: here was a pretty youth and a yellow-haired maid to please the most fastidious sultan.

Seeing their doubt, Ludo said, "And the ship out there?" He nodded at the vessel in the bay. "She's carrying silver from the New World."

"Not for us to decide," said the low-bellied pirate. "Come on, let's move. We've got work to do."

The men broke into a run towards the fishermen's hovels.

The girl watched them go, eyes as round as saucers. Marcos started to shake.

Ludo let out a protracted sigh and said, "Don't faint, we're not safe yet. Get into that boat over there."

Marcos moved mechanically towards a small rowing boat now bobbing on the high tide at the level of the stone quayside. The girl stayed stock still.

"Follow him and get into the boat," Ludo ordered.

"I live inland, why should I get in the boat?"

"Because I have just saved your life and they think you're mine! If they see you again you'll be in that galley and in a pasha's harem by the end of the week. That's if they can keep their hands off you for that long. It's your only chance. Get into the boat!"

Ludo pushed her so hard she would have fallen head first off the quay if Marcos hadn't caught her. The little skiff rocked wildly, shipping water. Ludo stepped in regardless and shoved off. Marcos took up the second oar and they pulled out into the Bay of Biscay.

Their ship had been left untouched, but all on board, passengers and crew alike, were in a state of prolonged panic. They had heard the harbour bells and ships' bells clanging, heard the sound of gunfire, and the shouts had carried across the still water of the bay. The crew knew exactly what was happening, although none of them had seen the pirate galley approach in the thick mist. The captain was still ashore and his First Officer was in a dither.

Ludo took control. "Give the order to set sail. We must get out into open sea as fast as possible."

The officer looked at him blankly. "Not without the captain."

"Look, they left you alone going in because it wasn't part of their strategy, or because they didn't see you; but if they don't get what they want in the harbour they'll be over us like a plague of rats. You and your crew would be a useful prize, and if you're not worried about saving your own skin you'd better think about your passengers. And what about all the silver you're carrying? It's your soldiers' pay and they deserve to get it. No one and nothing is safe from a Barbary corsair, except me. They won't touch me. Now, give the order to set sail. If you don't, I'll do it myself."

"You can't do that!"

"I can do that. I have done it in the past. Now move before I organize a mutiny."

"We'll have to come back on the evening tide for the captain."

"If we do that we can put the girl ashore," piped in Marcos, keeping himself attached to Ludo by some invisible caul. He looked behind him. The girl wasn't there. "Where is she?"

Ludo shrugged, "I said she was trouble."

"*Patrón*, what about the priest?"

"Oh, we'll get him tonight as well. He'll be all right: he's not worth the taking. Go and find the girl and put her in our cabin, and keep her there out of sight."

Alina ran her hand along the polished rail and stared into the mist. It gave everything a fairy tale quality. Tall masts disappeared into the white sky above; carved wooden monkeys swung among immobile branches, and painted flowers bloomed on the decorated poop. She climbed some steps to an upper deck and looked over the gunwale; it was as if the vessel were suspended over the ocean. This was the first time she had ever been on a ship, and it was magical.

Marcos didn't find the girl for some time. When he did he was short of temper. "You are to come with me."

"Why?"

"My master wants you in a cabin out of sight."

"Why?"

Marcos looked at her as if she were stupid. "What's your name?"

"Maria de los Angeles Catalina Fernanda Santoña Gomez de los dos Castillas. My brothers call me Alina. You may call me Maria de los Angeles."

"Well, Maria de los Angeles-Alina, this is a galleon full of soldiers and sailors, and there are a hundred licensed pirates out there ready to come and get you. Do you want to be taken to Morocco? Do you want to spend your life in a harem? Do you *want* to see us worked to death in a slave pen, *señorita*? Do you? Do you?" He grabbed her wrist in a fury of indignation, but she pulled away.

"I'll come—you don't need to drag me like a child."

Marcos' anger subsided, but he stayed alert, the girl was taller than he was and well built; a Cantabrian country lass in her best dress, putting on airs and graces with her invented name. She was probably used to swinging a scythe and baling hay. He didn't want look foolish again—or get bitten.

"We are taking you ashore on the evening tide. Your family will be worried."

"I don't think *we* need to worry about that. The likelihood of my father even being aware of the incident on the quay is very small. My brothers, though, if they have escaped, which they surely have because they weren't on the quay, *they* will be looking for me."

Marcos watched her carefully: either she was putting a brave face on it or she had plans of her own. She was nowhere near as scared as she ought to be. Perhaps she was just ignorant. He shrugged. "You'd better come with me, anyway."

He led her to a low doorway and she stepped inside. One look at the narrow bunks, one whiff of the stale, sour odour of enclosed space was enough. "I'm not sharing this cupboard with a boy!" In a single movement she whirled round, gave him a tremendous push, and slammed the door shut.

Marcos fell back ignominiously against the gunwale. Winded, he slithered onto the damp deck and lay slumped like a rag doll. The girl packed a punch like a trooper—and spoke Castilian Spanish like a lady. Who was she? He thought back to how he first saw her, trying to find a category in which to place her. Recollecting how she'd examined the coiled rope, then settled herself elegantly upon it, brought the chaotic events on the quay into focus. They had both been very, very close to being captured for the white slave trade. Everyone on that quay had been in danger. Except the Italian; *they won't touch me*, he'd said. And he'd spoken to them in their own language. Who exactly was his new *patrón*, Ludovico da Portovenere?

Marcos' thoughts were interrupted by shouts. They were here! His skin prickled, his stomach churned; he looked up and saw sailors swarming up ropes and masts. Staggering upright and climbing the nearest mast himself, Marcos saw the captain and the English priest John Hawthorne among a small group of bashed and bruised crew members come aboard. There'd be no need to return on the later tide now; they could get away safely. With a huge sigh of relief he slid clumsily back down to the deck, then twisted an ankle trying to jump the last couple of feet the way the mariners did. He began hobbling towards the cabin, ready to warn the priest about Maria de los Angeles, then realized someone was going to have to take her ashore. An instinct for self-preservation that was not quite cowardice made him turn back towards the mast.

He thought he was well out of reach when he heard Ludo bellow, "Marcos! Get the girl."

Reluctantly, Marcos limped across the deck to the cabin. The door was open. John Hawthorne was lying prostrate on his narrow bunk, a large wooden crucifix clutched above his heart.

"Where's the girl?" asked Marcos.

"What girl?" asked the priest.

Chapter Eight
Cherbourg, France, late April 1635

Alina watched the three men standing around her get angrier and redder in the face. Within minutes of their arrival in Cherbourg, the English priest had secured a crossing to England with some fellow countrymen. He said he wasn't going any further than England on any ship ever again. This suited her very well because he was such an irritating little man. But Ludo—she thought of the Italian merchant as Ludo—was furious with the priest for some reason and didn't want to let him go off on his own.

Marcos pointed at the English cargo vessel and remarked, "Looks as if they've nearly finished loading; they'll be sailing soon."

Alina looked in the direction Marcos was pointing, but her attention wandered as a hideously ugly mariner staggered by with a hand deep down the bodice of a low-life tart. She had seen that on the streets of Santander; so it happened here in France, too. Then she spun round sharply. They were talking about her.

"I don't see why we can't just leave her here," said the priest petulantly. "She insisted on coming, let her fend for herself." Then he looked at her and lowered his head. "I confess I am ashamed of what I am saying, but recent experiences at sea have been worse than a nightmare. I only want to get home, and.... Frankly, I do not see why we can't simply put her on a ship going south and send her back that way."

"*The girl! Her!*" Alina stamped a foot with indignation. "I do have a name: Maria de los Angeles Catalina Fernanda Santoña

Gomez de los dos Castillas y... various other surnames if you want to know. I told you, my father is a grandee. You may call me Angelina or Alina if you must, but show a little more respect."

Ludo raised his eyebrows and looked meaningfully at the English priest, who shook his head in resignation. Alina was delighted to see that the fact they had a daughter of *un hidalgo* with them meant they must change their attitude. For a moment or two, however, there was silence.

Then Marcos suddenly said, "I'll take her—Alina—back to Santander."

"That's a solution," said Ludo. "Do you plan to marry her here, or on the way back?"

Alina was appalled, "Marry? That boy! I'm not marrying an under-age nobody like him!"

"*Señorita*," Ludo said, placing heavy emphasis on the word, "if you are who you say you are, then returning to your father's house unmarried means you will remain in that condition for the rest of your days."

Alina tilted her chin and stared at the roof of a building behind the Italian's head. The smoke from the chimney trailed up into the sky in a single plume; it was the first day without mist, wind or rain since their ship left the Spanish coast. She tried to focus only on the smoke and the sky, tried to ignore the fundamental truth of Ludo's words, but she knew he was right. And in typical male fashion he was determined to prove his point. At least he had the decency to lower his voice.

"By pulling that foolish trick on the galleon, by hiding until we all lost patience trying to find you, you committed yourself to a life wholly unsuited to a *lady*. What did you think you were doing, playing with the lives of a shipload of men? The captain needed to get out of that harbour as soon as possible and you put everyone at risk."

Alina lifted her chin a little higher and refused to answer.

"It's over a week now. Word will have gone round that you were abducted. Your family will assume you are already a fallen woman on your way to a harem. And if anyone saw you going out to the ship with me... not your fault, of course, but your name is, shall we say, 'sullied'. What'll happen if you arrive back now *on your own*? I can't see any man of your class, any namby-pamby *señorito* risking his precious family name marrying a girl with that sort of experience. If you have any sense, any one single remaining grain of common sense, you'll accept Marcos' offer. Why he wants to burden himself with a wife, especially a shrew like you, defeats me, but you could do worse. In fact if you don't accept his offer, you will do a lot worse. Am I making myself clear?"

Alina stared at him, clenching and unclenching her hands in the folds of her skirt, a look of contempt on her face. She was however, suddenly and very desperately aware of the consequences of her foolish behaviour.

"Now, I haven't got time to stand around arguing if we're crossing to England," Ludo said. "Hawthorne, arrange passages *for all of us* on that ship to Plymouth. I will arrange for my cargo to be transferred."

Ludo strode off and Alina watched him go, giving in to another realization: she did not want to go back to Santander. What was there for her there? The house was no longer her home: another woman had the running of it. In re-marrying, her father had displaced both her and her mother's memory.

There was also something else. She wanted to stay with the Italian merchant. He was overbearing, always telling her what to do, but if she had to marry anyone it would be him.

Ludo knew she was there the minute he opened the cabin door. She had a strangely fresh yet musky scent. Even when he had found her hiding on a pile of greasy sheepskins that first night at sea she'd smelled clean. Warm, clean, smooth, and soft, and under other circumstances he wouldn't have hesitated. But his instinct told him this was a sharp miss, too much time with her and she'd turn into a scold. Her bearing, manner and name all suggested breeding, but a woman was a woman in his opinion, and a woman with a mind of her own was best avoided. And now she was here, putting temptation in his way.

Standing in the low doorway of his tiny cabin, Ludo waited for his eyes to become accustomed to the gloom. Gradually, he could see her profile against the light from the porthole.

She had loosened her hair; its thick gold mass was on her shoulders; her shoulders were smooth and her breasts were round and—she was unlacing her bodice.

"No."

"What?"

"No."

That was all he said before turning round and making his way back onto the upper deck of the Plymouth-bound cargo vessel.

He spent an hour or so chatting to the mate, then stood watching young Marcos hunkered down in the chill drizzle with some English sailors. They were showing him how to tie knots. The boy was trying to speak to them in their own tongue.

"Useful lad," he said, ruffling the boy's hair as he walked past him some time later.

This time Ludo opened his cabin door more slowly and left it wide open behind him. She had gone. For a moment he looked at the vacated bunk, and the fingers of one hand ran over the bite mark on the other.

Chapter Nine
Plymouth, May Day 1635

Ignoring his travelling companions following in his wake, Ludo pushed his way through the crowds, the carts and laden mules, taking care not to jolt the precious miniature sea chest clasped protectively to his breast. His silk, tea and spices were already safely stowed in a Plymouth wharf warehouse, and he was now ready for a decent meal. He was aiming for the Ship and Crown, a higgledy-piggledy affair of beams and mismatched windows, where there was a good kitchen and relatively clean beds with feather pillows.

When they finally reached the lee of the building, however, John Hawthorne spoke up, saying, "We cannot go in there with a lady."

John refused to see why Ludo couldn't simply abandon Alina to her own fate. She put their lives at risk. Growing up on a tidal estuary, he knew all about the slave pens of the infidel. He had grown up with tales of abductions. Turks, as they were called in the West Country, were always raiding coastal villages. They had raided his home village of Tamstock not so long ago.

There was another reason he wanted to be rid of her, and it shamed him. Her hair fell in such a way as to make his eyes travel to her breast. As the days had passed at sea, the seed pearls sewn into the bodice of her low cut gown had come unstitched. Each day he noticed another one or two were missing. The fine lace covering her shoulders had become grubby and torn, it needed washing, repairing. He had a quite desperate need to take her in his arms and care for her. Every aspect of her appearance conspired against his vows. He simply couldn't allow her to be subjected to the carnal gaze of sailors and the common man in a public drinking house.

"You cannot take Alina into a tavern!" he insisted.

"Why not?" replied Ludo. "She's with us."

"But—"

"Mr Hawthorne, let me tell you something you may not know, then you can decide whether you want to stay with us long enough to eat a meal, or rush straight off home to your mama." Ludo placed an arm slightly to the left of the priest, pinning him to the wall of the inn. "I was talking to the captain as we crossed your English Channel. I learned that England is more relaxed in its treatment of your co-religionists these days. In fact, they tell me the common people suspect King Charles will convert any day, if he hasn't already done so. His French queen has taken the upper hand, it appears, and she is a devout Catholic. Which means you can go straight to wherever it is you come from without fear. Your behaviour in the last few days has convinced me that you are what you told me in Sanlucar—a cleric of little importance. Frankly, I am weary of our enforced companionship. So please do not feel obliged to stay with me a moment longer. Feel very free to make your farewell. I'm sure your mother is anxious to have you home."

"*Obliged* to stay with you? Sir, it is *you* who insisted on coming to England with me!"

But Ludo was not listening, he was opening a heavy oak door and saying, "Now, it's time for a meal and a comfortable bed. Before you go, Hawthorne, be a good chap and arrange rooms for us. My English is adequate but I find the way people speak on this part of the coast incomprehensible. For tonight, Marcos can have a truckle bed in my room. Get a single room for the girl—I don't want her sharing with anyone."

John gave him a sideways look.

"Oh no, she's quite safe from me: too young, too vicious and too volatile. There's a tripling for your collection. You need have no fears on that score."

Lost for words, John went to find the landlord and arrange accommodation for the impossible Italian.

Ludo ushered Alina and Marcos into a space by the crowded bar. "Keep your voices down," he said, "the Spanish are not well-loved in Plymouth."

The interior of the Ship and Crown was dark: there were low beams and oak panelled walls, steps up to uneven landings, corridors that led round corners. What had once been a public house for seafarers had grown into a tavern, and then a better class of inn as the port of Plymouth expanded. Ships now sailing to the New World brought in a new type of customer, the New World coloniser—yeomen farmers off to acquire their own land where, they were told, grass grew waist high, tobacco shot up on its own, sugarcane grew thick as forests, and there was no lord and master to take his fee or limit the crop. Merchant adventurers crowded aboard any ship they could find, eager to create new trade routes for new trade goods. Copper miners were sailing off to find silver and gold; religious exiles followed in the wake of the little *Mayflower*. Those who were leaving with nothing but the shirts on their backs lodged in the labyrinth of hovels that skirted the harbour. The more respectable voyager lodged for a night or two at the Ship and Crown.

As this trade grew, so did the tavern. The spit and sawdust mariners' bar was replaced by a more genteel dining-room with a saloon above where merchants might do business. Captains came here to arrange victualing and discuss fees with enquiring passengers. It was a place Ludovico da Portovenere appeared to know well.

Marcos stared around him. Alina stood straight, her spine a perfect vertical, her chin lifted in the arrogant manner that Ludo now identified as her defence strategy. When Alina was in doubt she became the lady.

A dough-faced youth in a long apron offered them a jug of small ale and another of sack. Catching Alina's expression he made a bow. "Would the lady and gentleman like some meat? We've got a fresh ham, and there's a mutton roast on the spit."

Ludo was delighted. "Excellent! Find us a table, then bring some of each—and proper, clean plates for four."

Amongst the press of bodies he saw John Hawthorne return through a side door and look around. Locating them, he began to cross the busy dining room, stopping on his way to speak to an old man accompanied by a younger man very like the priest himself. There was a moment of greeting, then a round of back-slapping and earnest chat. The old man said something and John turned, pointing across the room; he then spoke with the men a few moments more before beckoning them to follow him.

When they arrived, John turned to the old man and, raising his voice above the hubbub said, "Sir Geoffrey, let me introduce you to the Genoese merchant Ludovico da Portovenere, and our lady companion, Doña Maria de los Angeles Gomez Santoña— and other names I forget."

Ludo smiled as he watched Alina, who clearly did not understand what the English priest was saying, but just as clearly was so affronted by his obsequious manner she wanted to slap him.

The older man extended a thick-veined hand. Alina inclined her head. The younger man offered her a limp paw. After an embarrassing moment it slithered back against his side, untouched. Ludo raised an eyebrow. Alina shifted her gaze to a smoky beam above his head.

"Forgive me," said Ludo in his most formal English, "with the noise, I did not hear your full name or where you are from."

John Hawthorne had not completed the introductions even the crude limits of British courtesy required. He might be fluent in classical Latin and a clerical scholar, as he insisted, but his behaviour with these men, Ludo decided, suggested humble origins.

Sir Geoffrey reintroduced himself and his son, adding, "We are not from Plymouth; we live a good way inland on the Tamar

River. We have been in town for livestock, and I've purchased some new, rather exotic furniture, which is exciting."

"Ah," said Ludo, "you must have a fine estate. You are unaccompanied today, or are your wives entertaining themselves in the shops?"

"Good Lord, no. My wife isn't one for fripperies, and Thomas hasn't got one at all."

Yet, thought Ludo, but said, "Forgive my impertinence." As he spoke he intercepted a conspiratorial look between John Hawthorne and Sir Geoffrey's son. *Aha,* he thought, *caught you!* And instantly began fabricating a plan.

Alina leaned towards him and whispered in his ear. She wanted to wash her hands and tidy up before sitting down to eat.

"Excuse us, for a moment." Ludo interrupted the small talk. "Marcos, accompany your mistress."

"Mistress!" Marcos looked at Ludo with surprise and horror. His expression met with a silent command: play the game. Marcos, mimicking Hawthorne, struck an over-deferential pose, and with barely concealed mockery ushered his new mistress before him towards the inner door. The four men watched Alina cross the room.

"I commend you on your wife, sir," said the older man.

The younger man licked his lower lip and said nothing.

With a rueful grin Ludo cocked his head to one side, "I regret she is not my wife. I am a merchant of an uncertain status and thus unworthy of milady. I wish it were otherwise."

Sighing with palpable regret he said, "Let me explain how we come to be here before she returns." He lifted his mug, gauging his audience over its rim with twinkling eyes. "I am charged with accompanying milady to Flanders. She is determined to arrange for the repatriation of her dead father. He is—was—a Spanish *hidalgo* of importance; a grandee no less. It is a dangerous enterprise, but she insists on carrying it out in person. Her father's death makes her an orphan of considerable means and therefore, one has to accept, mistress of her own fate—to a degree. She had a lady companion of course, but the poor dame fell ill as soon as we set sail. Milady sent her home to her relatives. It would not have been fair to submit an infirm woman to such a demanding voyage. Milady has a strong mind, but she has a gentle way with her, too. So here I am, playing the gallant knight to this rather special damsel in distress."

Sir Geoffrey drank from his cup then said, "You say she is a lady of means."

"She must be, sir. I command no specific fee, but she must pay all expenses. And it is no light undertaking to sail for the Low Countries in time of war."

"Ah, I thought the war in Flanders was finally petering out. Last I heard, Spain's coffers were empty."

"Empty? That is hardly likely with all the plate, gold and jewels that arrive daily from the New World. Have you ever been in Seville, sir? The city is a glittering vault. Gold bars cross streets on carts like giant carrots." He laughed and waited for a response.

Sir Geoffrey passed a palm over the white hair of his goatee beard; the son passed his tongue over his lower lip. John Hawthorne half-turned his back and examined his mug of watered ale.

"So the war continues," Sir Geoffrey said at last. "I have to say we are somewhat out of touch with world affairs up at Crimphele—my estate. The name itself proclaims it. *Hele* is the old word for something hidden. The Crimp part, of course, comes from old Cornish *crympau*, meaning a ridge of rock, or something of the like. I expect John here can tell you more, he's our scholar. Our house is tucked away behind trees on a ridge above the Tamar—that's how we get Crimp-hele. Nicely remote from hustle-bustle, and I am most glad of it. But I digress; where was I?"

John leaned towards the florid Cornishman and said in a respectful whisper, "World affairs, Sir Geoffrey."

"World affairs? We don't get many of them where we are. It wasn't always like that, of course. In fact my ancestor was knighted by King Henry VII after the War of the Roses. Now I come to think about it, he travelled to Spain with the retinue to collect Prince Arthur's wife. Yes, yes he helped bring poor Katherine of Aragon to England. A blessed woman destroyed by a tyrant, may her soul rest in peace. So our family has been in Spain too, albeit some generations back."

Ludo interpreted the message: Sir Geoffrey was a Catholic nobleman of respectable lineage. Better and better.

"The landlord is arranging a table for us," he said. "Would you join us, Sir Geoffrey, for a meal?"

"Why not? wWe were hungry when we came in, weren't we, Thomas?"

It was the first time anyone had addressed the fair-haired son, standing like a lesser mortal behind his father.

"Good, here comes milady. Let us be seated." Ludo lifted out a chair for Alina and she settled herself at the tavern table like a Spanish queen.

During the meal, Thomas couldn't keep his eyes off Alina. Marcos, in his role of servant, was obliged to stand and watch. He shifted from one foot to another infuriated by the little lord's feeble mannerisms and soppy gaze. Catching his mood, Ludo handed him some coins and sent him off to eat on his own. Alina watched him go, her face expressionless.

"I was telling Sir Geoffrey about your sad loss," Ludo said to her in English. She gave a slight nod, acknowledging the fact that she had been spoken to. It was evident to him, however, she didn't understand a word. Satisfied, Ludo launched into the second stage of his extemporized plan. John Hawthorne made no attempt to interrupt him at any time.

After Ludo had finished speaking, Sir Geoffrey looked at him, then, wiping mutton gravy from his sparse beard, said, "Perhaps we could take a brandy in the salon above while these young people enjoy a sugar dessert."

"I have some American cigars," replied Ludo, getting to his feet and carefully lifting his leather sea chest from beneath the table. John Hawthorne scrambled hastily off his seat as they pushed back their chairs. Thomas half-lifted his rump. Alina didn't even look up.

"As you see, my son is of a retiring disposition," said Sir Geoffrey sadly, after he and Ludo had seated themselves in the quiet saloon above the bar. "This is very unfortunate for us because his only remaining brother died last year—childless. We had three fine sons before Thomas was born and we have lost them all—except Thomas. His quiet ways have kept him out of trouble. He's a bookish sort of lad, you know. In fact I was concerned at one time that Thomas might choose to follow young Hawthorne and," he lowered his voice to a whisper, "join a seminary. A brave act, but it would not be good for our family." He stopped and looked about him. No one appeared to be listening. "I've funded John Hawthorne for years, and I was thoroughly delighted when he chose a future in the Church. He's one of the family... well, not family, exactly, no. I shouldn't be telling you all this, but you see...."

Ludo cocked his head on one side, offering encouragement for the old man to continue, not wanting to break the sense of being in his confidence.

Sir Geoffrey raised his hands, and then dropped them squarely onto his knees again, as if making a decision.

"When I die, Crimphele naturally goes to Thomas. But if Thomas dies without issue, the house, land, the whole estate will fall to my wife's nephew Percy—unless my daughter can produce a son beforehand, which is unlikely. Kate's a dear in every way; she's a widow, soon to remarry, but she's getting on in years now, so regrettably I can't count on her either. This boy Percy likes killing small birds. There is a cruel streak in my wife's family. I do not care for him, and I cannot believe he will have any interest in the estate. He'll sell it off in portions or ignore it. Lord knows, it is hard enough for me to maintain

Crimphele as it is, but when I am gone it will go to ruin, then what will become of my tenants? Some families have been on Fulford land since well before the Normans."

Sir Geoffrey had run out of breath. He shook his head sadly and rested his head against the hard wood of the high-backed settle.

"And your son is reluctant to fulfil his duty as heir?" inquired Ludo.

"Reluctant and disobedient. Not in a shouting way, you understand, not like his brothers. They were full of character, and they liked the girls. They were roistering lads and then proper men, if you catch my drift? Thomas just keeps to himself and reads books. He collects butterflies."

"Perhaps he has his reasons for avoiding matrimony."

"What reasons can a young man with a large estate and a future title have for not marrying?" Sir Geoffrey was genuinely angry, "It is his obligation!"

"Well then, sooner or later...."

"Sooner! I have made up my mind. The lady appears to be healthy, she is good-looking and not without means; she is also of our religion and has no family to hold her in her own country. I would say, from what I have seen, that makes her ideal in every way."

And the small fortune you think she has will patch up your estate nicely, thought Ludo. He sighed at man's cupidity. It was rarely difficult to mislead an acquisitive man, and always easy when that man believed himself in straitened circumstances.

"Mmm," he said, "it is an interesting proposition. But we shall have to handle it carefully." His voice was low, his countenance grave. "I must add I shall be disappointed to lose milady's—sponsorship."

Sir Geoffrey passed his hand over his thin beard. "Naturally, I would be happy to defray your expenses, your loss of income, that is. Can you give me an estimate?"

"Well, I will have to travel to Flanders to repatriate the defunct father. This cannot be accomplished overnight. There will be lodging and transport expenses."

"Quite so, quite so," said Sir Geoffrey.

Ludo touched a fresh taper to their cigars. "We still have to consider milady. If she is willing to forgo her filial duty...."

"One hundred English pounds," Sir Geoffrey said, and smacked his knee with his right hand as if to close the deal.

"Of course," continued Ludo, "she may prefer to proceed with her plan, in which case I may have to stay here a few days more to persuade her. I will leave you to make a bid."

Sir Geoffrey's jaw dropped. "A bid? Over one hundred pounds!"

Ludo looked at his cigar. "Milady is strong-willed. Perhaps you yourself can offer something extra that might encourage her. A title, a settlement, should she be widowed?"

The Englishman was lost for words, so Ludo quietly added, "We have passages booked on a ship sailing tomorrow."

Sir Geoffrey absorbed the deadline and swigged down his brandy. Placing the empty glass on the counter he said, "Persuade the lady and name your price."

Ludo smiled his one-dimpled smile, but said nothing, waiting. Eventually, Sir Geoffrey spluttered, "I have never been a businessman, I leave that to my steward. He handles all things financial, and my wife checks the steward's books every Saturday so we know what's what. But I do, sir, keep an eye on my estate. I visit the farms and the farmers' wives—to keep an eye on butter production and the like. I keep a personal watch on the woods and arrange practical matters with my steward on a day-to-day basis. I may not be astute in business matters, sir, but neither am I a complete fool."

He turned, looked about them to see if anyone was listening, then looked Ludo straight in the eye. In a measured tone he said, "Tell the lady you will arrange the repatriation. It is, as you said, a risky enterprise and hardly appropriate for a young woman of breeding. Furthermore, it is unnecessary; the poor man's dead, how could it benefit him? You will receive adequate monies to cover all your *personal* costs. Do I make myself clear?"

"You do, sir."

"Good. Are you are lodging here tonight?"

"Yes, we have requested rooms."

"Then we shall stay here as well. Do you think you can expedite this matter overnight?"

"I believe so."

"One question before we return to the young people: if I pay you in coin tomorrow, do you think it wise to travel with so much money about your person? Why not accept a promissory note from me now and collect it on your return? I assume you will be passing through Plymouth on your return voyage."

"I can keep any sum safe in here, Sir Geoffrey." Ludo tapped his small leather sea chest. "I never let it out of my sight. I sleep with it in bed. Once I have arranged the repatriation of milady's father I shall go on to Amsterdam. I can always place it in a bank there for safety."

"I don't follow. You'll give my money to a Dutchman? Then how will you pay your expenses?"

"The money goes into the bank's vaults and they give me a paper bill for transactions. The Dutch pay interest on money stored in their vaults. If I use that paper to purchase something, then the vendor can take it to the bank and retrieve hard currency for the sum I have spent. In the meantime they pay me interest to lodge my gold with them."

"They pay *you* to look after your gold! And all you have is a piece of paper to prove they've got it!" Sir Geoffrey began to laugh, the laugh turning into a choking noise and his face becoming an alarming shade of purple. Ludo slapped the man's back with the palm of his hand, but he was waved away. "Water," spluttered the patriarch.

Ludo got up to fetch the water himself. It gave him a few moments to gather his thoughts and consider how he was going to handle Alina.

Sir Geoffrey's face gradually returned to its normal florid hue. After some moments of companionable silence, the Cornishman looked at Ludo and said, "A strongbox and a house like a fortress; I thought that was the best protection in difficult times. It seems I am getting very old. Using paper for money, who'd have thought it?"

"You have a castle, Sir Geoffrey?" said Ludo. "Milady will be delighted."

"Never a complete castle with a moat and whatnot as I believe they have in Spain, but a sizeable fortress, yes. We Fulfords like to keep ourselves safe from invaders—and impostors."

Chapter Ten
Crimphele, May 1635

Alina was expecting a coach with a coat of arms on each door, soft leather upholstery, a liveried driver. But it was a cart, an ordinary horse-drawn farm cart. In the back, two large crates and a barrel had been secured firmly to one side. Tethered to the boards on the other side were two confused ewes and a malodorous Spanish merino ram.

John Hawthorne checked his luggage, which had been stowed perilously close to the sheep, and climbed up next to the driver.

Ludo tucked his precious little sea chest containing a number of very lucrative tulip bulbs and a bride price in English coin under his left arm, then offered to help Alina onto the front seat with the other. John Hawthorne shuffled closer to the driver to make room for her.

"Where are you going to sit?" Alina asked Ludo in Spanish.

"Oh, I'm not coming. You don't need me now."

"But I thought you were coming too." A moment of cold panic stabbed Alina's chest. "You said you wouldn't let him," she gestured towards Hawthorne, "out of your sight until he was back with his mother."

"I did, but it's not necessary now. All doubts clarified by Sir Geoffrey. Our Mr Hawthorne is precisely what he appears."

John Hawthorne bridled at the manner in which they were discussing him but said nothing.

"So where are you going?" demanded Alina, trying not to cry. "This isn't what you said last night. I thought..."

Her words were cut short by the arrival of Sir Geoffrey Fulford and his feeble heir Thomas on horseback.

The Cornish nobleman waved a greeting. "So sorry about the conveyance, we came down to collect some sheep, never dreamt we'd be collecting a prize..." He broke off with an embarrassed laugh. "All set?" Sir Geoffrey smiled at Alina, "Robert will take care of you until we get to Crimphele, and you've got young Hawthorne to keep you company. Body and spirit safe and sound for the journey. Let's hope it doesn't rain too hard."

Alina looked at Ludo for translation, but Sir Geoffrey was leaning from his horse, handing Ludo a document tied with red ribbon. His son Thomas watched them for a few moments, then turned to stare at Alina. Aware of his gaze, she straightened her shoulders and stared in turn at the carthorse's ears. Thomas ran his tongue over his thin lips and urged his mount a few steps closer to the cart to speak to her, then noted her discouraging glare and slumped back in his saddle.

Marcos stood back and watched the scene. Sir Geoffrey had struck some sort of deal with his master. It suddenly dawned on him they were planning to marry Alina to the spineless son. Marcos felt his stomach sink. The bastard had arranged for her to be married! Had she agreed? She must have agreed: Alina only did what suited her. Fury and disappointment made him go hot and cold all at once. He breathed deeply and tried to relax. Simulating a lack of interest, he stood legs apart, arms folded across his chest in the manner of his *patrón,* and considered the Englishmen before him. The father was elderly and very red in the cheeks, but he was straight of back and carried a sense of authority. Given the apparent age difference between father and son, Thomas was probably the youngest and the runt of the litter. He had wispy greenish-blond hair and his skin had the same pasty tinge as Hawthorne's. In fact, now he looked closely, Thomas Fulford and John Hawthorne were very similar in appearance and mannerisms. They both had what he thought of as sissyness, an effeminate manner.

How could the Italian shackle the lovely Alina to such a puny creature? He was furious. What had she been offered? What sort of bribe would persuade a young woman like Alina to wed a creature like Thomas? Had the Italian allowed her to have a say in her disposal? Perhaps she didn't know. Perhaps she thought this was just another stage of the journey. But it wasn't. It was very, very clear—to him at least—there had been a transaction. Could the cold-blooded Genoese merchant have passed her on to the old man? Various unpleasant images crossed his mind. Without a further rational thought he strode up to the cart and grabbed Alina's sleeve.

"What?" she said.

"Do you know what's going on?"

"I might."

"And you might not."

"What business is it of yours, *niño*?"

"Alina, stop being stupid and listen! Are they taking you some place to be married to that creature over there?"

"When the father dies I shall be the lady of the manor, the wife of a baronet. That 'creature' is the last surviving son—he'll get the whole estate."

"And you'll be a titled lady at last," Marcos retorted sarcastically.

"I *am* a lady."

Marcos lifted her right hand and turned it over. "You'd better wear gloves until your hands go soft or people might get the wrong idea. And stay out of the sun, that brown neck tells everyone you're...."

Alina snatched back her hand and turned to face the other way.

Marcos grabbed her arm again and squeezed hard. "Listen! Listen to me—it's not too late. I'll take you back to Santander. I'll get us passages back to Spain. I said I would. You can't trust that black-haired devil: he's up to something, look at him."

"He says if I'm not happy he will come and fetch me. He says..."

"It's a lie. Everything he says is a lie and you know it." Marcos sighed angrily, "Look, even if you think it's true, you can't be sure. He says a lot of things, or haven't you realized?"

At that moment Ludo moved away from the Cornishman's hack and raised a hand in salute.

"We'll be off, then," said Sir Geoffrey to the assembled company. "Come, Thomas, we'll ride on ahead. We'll see you at Crimphele, fair lady." He waved a gloved hand at Alina and spurred his horse into a trot down the early morning street. Thomas followed him without a word or gesture.

"Well," whispered Marcos, "are you coming with me or risking a life of misery with them?"

Alina tilted her chin and ignored the question. Ludo strode over to the cart, waving the document in the air.

"What is that?" asked Alina.

"Your marriage portion, milady, and a handsome portion it is, too. Be grateful to your humble protector for that." He bowed low, his eyes sparkling with mischief. "You'll have two hundred English pounds a year when your husband dies, and control of an excellent property while he survives."

Alina stared at Ludo; Marcos could see conflicting emotions fighting for supremacy.

"A grand house with servants; a nurse to look after nuisance children," Ludo went on, as if to close the subject.

"A home with strangers who don't speak your language," Marcos put in hastily. "Is that what you want?

But Alina was elsewhere in her thoughts. "But my father—my dowry—what did you tell them? My father said I couldn't marry according to my station because he no longer had the funds, and," she faltered at a moment of truth, "I know he can't..."

"I told Sir Geoffrey your dowry is land, and a fine flock of these curly sheep." Ludo pointed at the ram, which lowered its head and glowered as if guessing the falsehoods in the air. "Upon your marriage, the Fulfords get five hundred acres of best Cantabrian pastureland."

"You can't tell them that!"

"I already did, last night. They took it hook, line and sinker, as the English say."

Alina gaped. "But...."

"But what? Anyway, they think your father is dead."

"Dead! They'll throw me out when they find you've tricked them!"

"Ah, no, no, no, who's tricking who here? Sir Geoffrey needs a brood mare—there's not one grandchild so far. And young Thomas is dead keen! He'll be in your bed tonight if you let him. Just make sure you say. 'Thomas Fulford, I will be your obedient wife' in a loud voice before he jumps in. In this country that's as good as a wedding. They don't fuss about marriage ceremonies unless they want to spend money and show off."

"You seem to know a lot about weddings."

"I should know, I spend my life avoiding them."

Alina looked at Ludo sharply, biting her lower lip.

He responded with an exaggerated wink. "Now then, none of that. I told you, you're far too young for me. There was never a chance, if that's what you're thinking. Anyway, I'm a blackguard and a blighter and full of vice, not right for you at all." He smiled a gentle smile and tweaked her chin. "Milady, keep your own counsel, keep your thoughts to yourself. If you can do that you'll keep those around you on their toes. Now then, give me a smile, you're as good as married and I'm your humble servant, who," he tapped his leather sea chest with the marriage contract, "has important business for some very important people, who," he leaned across the girl to speak directly at the English priest, "have asked me, personally, to expedite a very particular task—for which I will be rewarded handsomely. And if I'm not, they will find Ludovico da Portovenere also has some very effective contacts in the Old World."

Then Ludo stepped back and, addressing the driver in English, said, "Now you, Robert, Egbert, Cuthbert, whatever

your name is, get going before milady decides to jump ship."
Laughing, he turned away from the Fulford's cart and set off
towards the harbour, "*Adios*! Farewell, Goodbye!"

"Ludo!"

He turned back and stopped laughing. "What is it you
want?" he asked, reverting to Spanish in a serious, low voice.

"I want to stay with you," Alina whispered.

Ludo shook his head. "Not now, Alina. Not yet. Perhaps
when you are older."

"But—"

"I'll come to find you in your manor when you're married.
I'll come back to this rainy place, and in the mud I'll go on my
knees, and you'll be too haughty to even slap my face."

"You *will* come to find me?"

"I promise. Don't worry, milady, I know exactly where you
are going; it's all written down in this document."

Laughing again, the charming rogue once more, Ludo raised
the meaningless marriage contract aloft and set off towards the
wharf.

For a moment or two, Marcos watched his *patrón* march off
towards the quayside, then he rushed up to Alina in the cart.
"I'm coming with you, to protect you," he said, putting a foot on
the running board to climb in.

"Oh, no, you're not!" Alina replied, giving him such a shove
he landed on his backside in the street.

"Hawthorne, tell the driver to move on," she said
imperiously, then, looking down at Marcos still sitting winded
in the middle of the road, she hissed, "Run back to your master,
boy."

The cart lurched forward. A foot-crushing wheel brushed
the tip of Marcos' rope-soled shoes. He jumped to his feet and
lifted a hand in sad farewell. Alina didn't look back.

Noticing that Marcos was not beside him, Ludo turned just
as the boy was attempting to climb into the cart. Was he going
with John Hawthorne? A host of doubts crept back into his

mind. Hawthorne had admitted that he'd been told to get him to the hostel in Sanlucar. Had the black-garbed bishop in Sanlucar been courting the boy's mother for a reason? Was the boy in his pay? Had the whole thing been a set up from the start? If so, the Vatican secret service really was involved.

Had he, sharp-witted Ludo, with more tricks up his sleeve than all the magicians in all the markets of Christendom and beyond, been duped after all? A moment of anger emerged in a bellowing command, "Marcos, *ven!*"

The journey from Plymouth in Devon to the manor of Crimphele in Cornwall was fifteen miles. It included crossing the wide Tamar River on a horse-ferry and took all day. They stopped to eat and rest the horse at various stages, and at each place Alina felt more despondent: she had not escaped. The hills around her were round and green just like Cantabria; the river they followed was wider, but just as sluggish and grey as the river that flowed by her father's family home; the trees were the same. The people at the stage-houses used a different language, but otherwise they were the same peasant-folk of Cantabria: low and round, black-haired or fair-haired, they had the same weather-worn faces.

Each time they stopped for refreshment they were offered bacon on thick bread trenchers and mugs of cider. Men gossiped in corners of the smoke-darkened hostelries, women swept and carried food. She might as well have stayed in Santander, except in Santander her father had run out of credit and she had no future.

On the road, John Hawthorne and the driver conversed in their West Country English and ignored her, so she dozed despite the uncomfortable seat and the pot-holed highway. Eventually the main horse-road from the coast became a lane, with other lanes leading off into narrower tracks. Wheels splashed through stagnant puddles; high hedges of hornbeam, hawthorn and bramble scratched the side of the cart and snagged Alina's once beautiful wine red dress. She was cold too, and inwardly she blamed Ludo, who could have bought her some clothes in Plymouth, a new shawl to replace the one she'd lost in Santander at the very least. She pulled at the tight bodice of the dress and felt tears welling up in her eyes. She was chilled, tired, hungry, and felt very dirty. This Sir Geoffrey was obviously desperate to find his son a wife if he was willing to take her looking like this.

Hearing her muffled sobs, John Hawthorne patted Alina's skirt. With icy fingers she removed his hand.

As evening approached they began a slow descent into a tree-filled valley. At times Alina could see the river wending its way to the sea; then, in the late afternoon light, the river disappeared behind vast old beech trees, elms and oaks. There was an utter stillness, disturbed only by the soft clop of hooves and the shush of wheels on uneven tracks. Alina felt her eyes close; weary, she leaned against the English priest and fell asleep.

She awoke as the cart halted. A herd of russet red cows was coming towards them in the twilight. A woman with her skirt looped up round her waist and wooden patens strapped over boots staggered up the steep lane behind a couple of stragglers, their heavy udders swinging low over churned mud and green slop. The woman looked up and smiled. The smile relieved the tiredness that belied her age. She pushed a swathe of wavy blonde hair away from her face and looked at Alina as if they had been childhood friends.

Alina returned the smile because she knew the woman, although they had never met. She knew the sort of house she lived in, the quilt-covered bedstead she slept in, the blue and white cups she drank from on Sundays. She knew how she fell asleep with exhaustion at the first screech of the owl, and what time she rose on dark mornings. She sighed; to have come so far and found no escape.

The woman closed the farm gate after the last cow, and the cart bumped on down the narrow track, stopping again at a small cottage. The driver called out, and an older woman in a drab, mud-stained skirt opened the cottage door. Catching sight of John Hawthorne, she raised her arms and ran up to the cart, shouting something incomprehensible. Hawthorne reached across the driver, holding the woman's hand for a moment or so as she gabbled away fifteen to the dozen. Then the driver clicked his tongue, and the old horse leaned into the traces and off they went again.

Lower down the valley, a wide gate bordered by trimmed hedges was opened by a scrap of a lad with a cap over an eye and a catapult behind his back. The driver shouted at him jovially, then turned to Hawthorne to say something. Hawthorne called out to the boy, but he was closing the gate behind them and pretended not to hear.

When at last they came to her new home, Alina saw at once it wasn't the grand house Ludo had promised, but she wasn't surprised. At first sight it looked like a small, square fort of beige and grey stonework, surrounded by trees. They stopped briefly at a substantial but not imposing arch, then clattered into an enclosed cobbled courtyard just as night fell. A hunchback moon leaned out of a cloud to light the scene: the arrival of Maria de los Angeles Santoña Gomez at Crimphele.

The driver and the priest immediately jumped down. Alina stayed in her seat. Two large bloodhounds followed by various sharp-nosed mongrels lurched out of a doorway, angry that they had been caught unawares. Their barking and yapping echoed in the courtyard, filling the night with pandemonium and yanking Alina's already taut nerves to catapult tension. A scream welled up inside her. She gripped the rough boards that had served as her chaise, closed her eyes and willed the beast within her to stillness: she must not lose her temper. As suddenly as it started, the barking stopped. Opening her eyes she saw Sir Geoffrey in a rough woollen jacket coming from a doorway into the courtyard. When he reached the cart, he held both arms up to Alina as if she were his small daughter and he her adoring father.

Alina felt tears prickle at her eyelids and stood up, but her legs were wobbly and she sat down again with an unladylike plump, and they both burst out laughing. She tried again; it was as if she were still at sea. Sir Geoffrey stepped onto the running board and took her in his arms. As her feet touched the cobbles she was lifted again, and held for just an extra moment. And then she was standing on her own and a dark, square figure was beside her. Alina turned and looked into the face of Sir Geoffrey's wife and nearly burst out laughing again. The woman had hooded brown eyes and jowls exactly like the bloodhounds.

The sharp-nosed mongrels were now jumping up behind the cart, yapping and wagging their stumpy tails and snapping at the poor Spanish sheep.

"Silence!" boomed Sir Geoffrey's wife.

The smaller mongrels disappeared under the cart; the larger hounds slunk into the shadows.

"Well, well, here we are," gushed Sir Geoffrey. "Bit of a journey, eh? Never mind, should be a hot supper waiting." He turned to his wife for confirmation, but she was more interested in the contents of the cart.

"What are those?" she demanded, pointing at shapes in the dark.

"That's the Chinese chest, my dear, and a lacquer chair. The barrel is sweet sherry sack, and of course we've got this woolly fellow and—"

"Only two ewes?"

"Ah, yes, er—this chap proved rather more expensive than I anticipated. We'll get more ewes another time. He can keep himself busy with the natives for now."

The woman gave a humourless *humph*. "Where's her luggage?"

Sir Geoffrey looked at John Hawthorne and raised his eyebrows.

"We were attacked, ma'am," responded John hastily, "by corsairs, in the Bay of Biscay."

"You escaped capture."

84

"Yes, but what a fright. A clever man came to our rescue...." John Hawthorne gave Alina a look that said, *I'm sorry, I'm doing my best*, then added aloud, "but they took all her luggage, her jewels, her clothes, her... fans... everything. But she is safe. As you see. And untouched."

"She'll have to send to her family for replacements, I can see the state of her dress from here."

"Yes, well...." Sir Geoffrey and John Hawthorne spoke in unison. The situation was saved by the arrival of a pretty girl in a white lace-trimmed cap. Sir Geoffrey held out an arm to her.

"Here, Kate, come and meet your new... um...." He twisted between his daughter and Alina. "Kate, this is Maria de ... well, we'll call her Alina. That's all right, isn't it?" he said, smiling at his future daughter-in-law, who smiled back. Delighted, Sir Geoffrey continued effusively, "Excellent, excellent. Now then, Kate, help our guest; she'll need a meal and a warm bed."

"And a bath," added Sir Geoffrey's lugubrious wife.

Alina stood by the cart, picking at the few remaining seed pearls on the bodice of her dead mother's wedding dress.

The ugly woman pointed a stubby finger at the ram. "Good wool."

"Precisely, my dear, and new blood, we need new blood."

"If you say so, husband." She started walking toward an arched doorway.

"I do say so, wife," Sir Geoffrey whispered behind her back. Then he looked at Alina and winked.

Lady Marjorie Fulford waited for her husband in the recently completed family parlour off the old great hall. She stood with her back to the fire, her arms folded like a barricade across her ample bosom. The moment he entered the room she said, "Shut the door."

Sir Geoffrey reluctantly did as he was told, regretting his decision to provide private spaces in what had been little more than a vast granite hall adorned with the relics of a more bellicose past. His wife could now shut doors and bully him at will. Hitherto, she had at least maintained a veneer of the humble, if not obedient, wife.

"Where did you get her?" she demanded.

"Get her? I told you my dear, she, um... she..."

"She's a Plymouth tart pretending to be what she's not."

"Good Lord, no! Absolutely not. What young Hawthorne said is true. They were on a ship which was attacked by corsairs. She was on her way to Flanders to collect—"

"That's what you said earlier."

"But that's what I was told."

"And that's what you believed!"

"What reason is there to doubt it? John Hawthorne was with her; what reason might he have to lie?"

"Well, it's strange. I don't like it. What will our neighbours think? What will my sister think? She's *Spanish*, you say?" Sir Geoffrey nodded. "A Catholic; well, that's something. We can make something of that if we have to. But it isn't what we discussed. She isn't what we need here."

"How can you know that, my dear? She's lovely and—"

"And you are *very* taken," Lady Marjorie sighed and shook her head. "I suppose Thomas knows what's going on."

"Obviously." Sir Geoffrey looked at his squat wife standing in front of the fire and said, "That poor girl: bad enough that she's an orphan and in a foreign country, now she has unwittingly unleashed your.... No, no, you are quite wrong. Really, I do believe we have to do what we can to protect her." He sat down in his chair at the head of the family dining table and placed his hands on its polished surface. "Marjorie, my dear," he said, "take a seat, please. I need to outline the plans for the wedding."

Marjorie Trerice sat down beside her husband. He knew she disliked it when he took the upper hand. It made her angry. But he also knew she despaired of the soft Fulford streak: a man should be a man. Marjorie should have been a man.

It seemed to Alina that she was locked in a dumb show of freaks and monsters. The spring day had turned itself inside out as darkness fell and was now sending smoke back down the chimney to choke people in a fit of winter spite. The great hall, where Alina was sitting opposite John Hawthorne, trying to eat a late supper, was a cloud of vaporous yellow that neither the substantial candles on the table nor the dull light from oil burning wicks could dispel. As she and the priest sat in the gloom, a series of strange creatures appeared, disappeared and reappeared around them. Some entered the main door, staring at them without comment and exiting without stopping; others came in and placed themselves at the ends of the table to gawp. A beetle-like creature with a hunchback who had brought their food lingered by the fire, gazing at them with disapproval for what seemed an age.

"That's the cook. Crook-back Aggie they call her," John mumbled in Spanish between mouthfuls.

Alina looked up: the creature had gone.

Dogs of various breeds and crossbreeds and no recognizable breed whatsoever snuffled under the table, registered their presence with detailed attention, sniffing at their clothes, at their feet and legs, and as high as their snouts could reach. Alina was accustomed to dogs, but in Spain they did not enter the house.

She was struggling with her final crust of bread when an elongated, angular shape loomed out of the shadows created by the asphyxiating fire. Emerging from nowhere, it seemed to hover above her like an avenging angel. She all but choked with alarm.

John reached across the table and patted her hand. "It's only McNab," he said.

Not knowing who or what a McNab was, she searched the faces of the others to gauge their reaction, trying to make sense of the weird presence. As she turned round to directly see its corporeal form, it shifted from sight. Alina gave an involuntary shudder.

Her hand was patted again. "It's only McNab. He does that. Just when you think you're alone, he'll pop out of a corner. You'll get used to it."

No, thought Alina, *I won't get used to it, because I am leaving this madhouse at first light tomorrow.* And then there was someone else behind her, but this time it was Sir Geoffrey's daughter in the white cap.

Kate smiled at Alina, then spoke to the priest. "Is she all right? It must seem rather strange, all these people coming and going. Mother has been trying to limit who comes in and out at night. They can't get used to the idea that they've got their own sleeping quarters now. It's worse on chilly nights like this; they just wander in like their parents used to and lie down to sleep by the fire. Mother's tried fining them, but they don't understand why. Father says, if we've got fires upstairs we should let the fire down here die out. Perhaps they'll keep to their rooms then."

"Have they finished all the new building?" John asked.

"Ages ago. You have been away a long time. There's a complete new storey over the stables. Father's given McNab his own suite."

Kate gave an involuntary shudder and John said, "So it's still the same with him, is it?"

"The same, except he gets creepier by the day. You should warn—what's her name? Eileen? Arleen?"

"Her first name is Maria de los Angeles, which in Spanish is sometimes changed to Angelina. But she says she's called Alina."

Hearing her name mentioned, Alina looked up.

"You look worn out, poor thing," said Kate, patting her shoulder. "John, tell her I'll take her back up to her room. Father goes too far sometimes. Fancy making her travel in the farm cart. My husband would never...." Her voice trailed away.

"You still miss him, Kate?"

"How could I not?"

"Of course...."

"Did you know I am to be married again?"

"No, tell me."

"Tomorrow, I'll tell you everything tomorrow, and you can tell me all about your travels and about Rome," she looked warmly at Alina, "and about this lovely lady here. But now it's time for bed." Kate placed a hand under Alina's arm and helped her to her feet.

John explained to Alina in Spanish that Kate was going to take her up to her room and added, "I'll stay here tonight, but I'm leaving early tomorrow to go to my family. You'll be all right, though. This is a good family, Alina, and I'll be back soon. In a strange way I think you have been lucky. Just watch out for...." He was about to say *McNab the steward, and Crookback Aggie the cook*, but he didn't. Instead he said, "Be polite, and I'm sure they will all come to love you."

Alina stared at him for a moment, then offered him her hand. He bowed his head over her sunburnt fingers and smiled with his eyes, a look she had not seen before.

McNab watched the two young women ascend the short staircase to the first landing, then insinuated his angular frame between the shadows and smoke until he was on the outside of the house. A greyhound fell in at his heels. A cold, bony hand gently stroked its head. The dog trotted on ahead; it knew the nightly path. Dog and man turned to the left beyond the arch. Stepping silently alongside the great barn, they proceeded down the path that led along the new front of the house and turned left once more past the kitchen and kitchen courtyard. Looking up, McNab registered the feeble glow of a low-burning candle through a thick-paned window. He removed a soft pouch from his jacket and primed his American pipe. Inhaling deeply, he leaned back into the thick ivy under the narrow window-ledge of Kate's bedroom.

The dog whimpered once as the steward wandered off to investigate the scents and sounds of the Cornish night. A gust of wind licked at the ivy and ruffled the Scotsman's fine grey hair, warning him it was no night to linger in damp, river-laden air, but he tucked a hand into a pocket and lifted his chin to the elements. Neither wind nor rain nor river mist would deter him tonight; they never had before.

Chapter Eleven

The chapel at Crimphele was an integral part of the house. It had been licensed in the early days of the previous century, when notions of religion went unquestioned, when a pope was the highest authority on Earth and every man knew his place. Lady Marjorie and Kate followed Thomas through a door leading off what was now the family parlour into the cool, vaulted space. John Hawthorne, officiating at a wedding for the first time, had entered earlier through the courtyard entrance.

Sir Geoffrey stood beside Alina in the parlour.

"Ready, my dear?"

Alina had spent a week watching what went on about her, not understanding actual words but getting the gist of what people might be saying from their body language and facial expressions. She had been sharing Kate's room, sleeping on a made-up bed by the window. Each morning she had risen, pulled back the curtains, opened the narrow casement and stared at the scene below. The house was built on a promontory or low ridge beside a creek. From this window she could barely see the River Tamar beyond the tree tops, but in her mind's eye she could visualize exactly where the old river met the sea.

Crimphele had its own landing stage for barges, skiffs and luggers, where goods brought up from Plymouth or across from the village of Tamstock were unloaded. She stared at the view and knew she could, if she really wanted to, escape.

All she had to do was tell John Hawthorne, who, after he conducted Mass for Lady Marjorie, was giving her English lessons, that she had changed her mind. She only had to say she wanted to go home. Each morning she made the decision to leave; but then, when she came down to this family parlour and sat by a welcoming fire, and breakfast was offered by a servant with a smile on her face, her resolve weakened. Each morning the grate had been cleaned and logs re-laid for the fire; she hadn't had to help bake the bread or wake up five brothers and chase after them to make sure they were washed and ready for their tutor; she didn't have her day already portioned into inescapable chores. In that moment, on each of the days she had been at Crimphele, she touched the solid pewter plate before her, picked up the good silverware, looked at the fine glassware on the sideboard, and knew this was how her life should be. Then Thomas would arrive.

He was not ugly, nor did he appear to be unkind or have unpleasant habits; indeed, he was clearly trying to be nice to her. On the first morning he accompanied Kate as she showed Alina around the big house and the various courtyards. Each afternoon he took her down to the landing stage and then back up to the house via another route, or they would go up round the old knot garden and come back to the house via the water mill. He pointed at trees, at distant fields, at the river and other aspects of the estate, and using simple English he tried to communicate with her. She nodded and smiled and tried to keep her excitement at bay. All this would be hers.

There was of course a price to pay: a husband she did not love. But what girl in her class got to choose a husband she could love? The only real difference was the fact that Thomas was English and she would have to live in England. Not that this part of England was so different from Santander; it rained often, everything was green, paths and roads were always muddy. But now she didn't have to go out in the rain if she did not want to.

So here she was, in a borrowed dress, standing beside her future father-in-law, who seemed to be a truly good person. She smiled at him and nodded.

"Ready," she said.

"Well done!" replied Sir Geoffrey, tucking her arm under his and patting her hand.

Sir Geoffrey walked Alina up the short aisle of the tiny chapel to the altar and left her facing the priest. Alina looked up. Sunlight streamed through the stained glass window behind him, lighting up Saint Catherine being led to her wheel. In another pane the Virgin shone with pious hope before the Archangel Gabriel.

Thomas shuffled at Alina's side; she turned to look at him. His face was expressionless, ashen; was he afraid? What could he be afraid of? She smiled at him as she had smiled at his father, and he went crimson.

John Hawthorne read the marriage service in Latin. Alina understood the words perfectly, but they washed over her as she gazed up at Saint Catherine.

Sir Geoffrey stood beside his short, fat wife, his rosy cheeks aglow with satisfaction. Alina was a fine lass: a long-legged filly with good wide hips, she would foal easily and the colts would be tall and strong. He was going to see his estate and the Fulford name safe for the future after all. And if, just if, his wife was half-right, if that black-bearded smooth-talker—whom Marjorie didn't know about unless Thomas had blabbed or Hawthorne had said too much—if that foreign devil *had* set up this marriage to get rid of his paramour, well, they only had to count nine months from today. He did a fair bit of trade with Spain on the quiet; it wouldn't be difficult to ship her back where she came from. If push came to shove he could tell Hawthorne to take her back to her family and leave her there.

He switched his gaze to a spot where there had once been a very fine crucifix. It had been removed in his father's time because Queen Bess had threatened to visit. They had been a family of substance in those days—and they would be again.

Across the aisle from her parents, Kate watched her brother and Alina rise to their feet after the blessing and wondered what they knew of marriage. If Alina had been English, she would have taken advantage of the dark nights in her room to explain, in the gentlest way possible, what to expect: that she should relax in the marriage bed, that the act with a man you cared for could be pleasurable and loving. She thought of her late husband George and gave thanks for his kindness. God had granted them no children, but He had granted them each other. She had been lucky; her father had chosen well for her. This time, however, it was Henry Rundell himself who had asked for her. Had her father accepted his offer wisely? She looked at her father and wondered. There were times when she feared he wasn't well: he didn't always hear what they said, and seemed distant, detached from them in some way.

What sort of husband would Henry Rundell be? What sort of husband would Thomas be? Thomas had never shown any interest in women. She had never heard them gossiping in the kitchen about him, never seen a maid colour up and giggle in his presence. They should have let him go with John to become a priest; it was what he had wanted. They were such good friends, John and Thomas, so similar they could even be brothers.

Alina seemed larger than them in some way, and yet now she and Thomas were standing side by side they were the same height. Thomas only appeared smaller because he had a slight build, narrow shoulders and small feet for a man. Not that Alina was a big woman in an ugly way; she had a lovely face and a wonderful mass of shining, wavy hair. She just seemed *more.*

There was a slight draught. The door behind her had been opened. The sudden chill told her it was McNab. Kate focused on her hands and said a silent prayer for the future of two married couples. Her marriage to Henry Rundell, whatever he proved, was an escape from McNab.

Thomas made a conscious effort to breathe slowly. His hands were clammy with nerves and he fumbled with the ring his father had given to him for the occasion. It had been his grandmother's. Surprisingly, it slid onto Alina's finger as if made for her. He held her hand in his for a moment more: it seemed so different to his: wider, the fingers longer, less smooth. An element of doubt crept into his mind concerning that hand, a doubt that the long-winded forename and various surnames John had just read aloud did nothing to dispel. For a moment, as his friend the priest droned on in classical Latin, he chastised himself: he should have tried to speak to Alina in Latin. It wasn't as easy for him as John, but they could have managed a semblance of conversation, if, that was, she'd had a basic education. And there was the doubt again. A girl with workaday hands would almost certainly have no Latin; she could be completely illiterate. His heart sank.

Still, the girl's ignorance might be an advantage. There would be no chance of her countermanding him or giving orders the way his mother did. And once his mother had gone, God bless her and forgive him for such dreadful thoughts, but once she had gone, and his father, of course, then against all odds he would finally be lord of the substantial manor of Crimphele. Thank God for McNab. At least with McNab as steward he would be free to create his library, a library to rival any fine house in the West. He would become the very model of the 'new man' and indulge his passion for poetry and natural philosophy.

John Hawthorne raised the chalice and offered it to Alina. She sipped, took the bread, and stood back. Thomas stepped up and put his hands around the chalice as the priest offered it to his lips. For a moment their eyes met. Slowly, John Hawthorne nodded and Thomas relaxed. He let the sweet wine that was Christ's blood touch his lips and accepted the host. John had once told him the Eucharist word 'host' came from the Latin *hostia*, meaning sacrifice. Did 'hostage' come from the same root? He looked around while his parents and Kate took the bread and wine. McNab was just inside the chapel by the parlour door. He beckoned to him with a 'your turn' movement of his head, but McNab shook his head and left as silently as he had entered.

After the private ceremony, they sat down at the parlour table and ate quail and jugged hare and generous helpings of honey pudding. There was sweet sherry sack and home-brewed ale, but no one sang and no one told jokes. After the long dinner, Kate and Alina went out into the spring evening to get some air. Thomas played backgammon with John Hawthorne until Sir Geoffrey nudged the priest and told him to get home before it was dark.

McNab opened the door and levered the bridegroom into his chamber. The curtains of the high bed had been carefully doubled back and candlelight illuminated the girl leaning against her over-stuffed pillows. The wench had tits like a barmaid; he noted the way they strained across her chemise. The chemise was borrowed from Kate, because she'd arrived with nothing, like a common stray with no pedigree. But the master had chosen well: she'd whelp twins or triplets without a whine in the night—with the right dog to fill her.

He waited by the door and watched the pathetic form of Thomas Fulford climb up onto the bed like a child, then drunkenly arrange himself in a sitting position. He waited for another minute or two while the bridegroom tried to pull himself together. No doubt the bed seemed to be gyrating—as it should be; he'd helped the boy drink a second and a third bottle. The Spanish bitch didn't move. My God, but he'd make the bed gyrate if.... He felt himself harden and placed a hand over his cock. He rubbed once, twice.... He'd plow her until.... The bitch was watching him. The dirty bitch could see him. He pulled out his full dick—but her look....

McNab staggered out of the room like the drunk he'd helped enter and closed the door. Across the stone passage was another door, Kate's door. He opened it, then closed it silently behind him. The room was very dark.

Slowly, he manoeuvred himself between the closed door and the writing desk. The bed hangings were closed tight; she might hear him but she wouldn't see him approach. He took a step, then another, and pulled back the heavy bed curtain. Now, with one hand laid on the shape of a leg, he began again on his hard, fuck-her-till-she-yells dick. It was so good, so good. He pulled the blanket down, he pulled the sheet down. Kate slept on. He unlaced his breeches and pushed up her nightdress. That was what woke her. Placing one large hand over her mouth, he forced the other between her legs.

Disgusted by the steward, Alina now faced her wedding night with a drunken sot of a husband. Wobbling on the high bed, Thomas removed each item of clothing except his wine-soaked shirt, and let them drop on the floor. Carefully, he lay down sideways facing her, then moved and flung his top pillow across the room and pushed the second away too. Now, resting his head on one hand, he placed the other over her breast, then clumsily fumbled with the string of her chemise and pulled down the thin cotton to reveal a nipple. He placed his mouth on it and sucked. Then fell asleep.

Alina gently shifted away from the slack mouth and tucked the sheet up over her husband. She lay back and stared at the light coming through the open window. The room backed onto the hill. A dog fox barked, an owl hooted. In her mind she heard the sound of night-time animals scurrying about their business, heard the badger move from his sett and saw the creatures around him freeze until he was out of scent. She heard a dog whining. It was scratching at the door. Her door. Thomas's door. Scratch, scratch. The whining didn't stop. It was an anxious whine. An unnatural whine. Why did the English allow animals in the house? She slid down onto the cold floor and opened the door. There was nothing there. Yes, there was, outside Kate's door: McNab's greyhound.

Alina flung the door open. There was no light but there were sounds, and Alina knew what they meant.

She ran to the room, to the bed, and beat her fists down on McNab's spine. She slapped the back of his head, hitting him, pulling him, pummelling him. Eventually he turned, rolled off the bed and slapped her hard across the face. Alina put her right hand to her painful cheek, then she drew it back and threw the hardest punch of her life. McNab staggered back and fell. His head hit the corner of Kate's writing desk and he slithered into a heap.

For a moment neither woman moved, both staring at the shape on the floor as if it were a snake. Alina picked up a heavy brass candlestick from beside the bed and held it aloft, ready to strike again.

Kate pulled her nightdress over her legs and got into a kneeling position. "Is he dead?"

Candlestick at the ready, Alina moved closer to the inert form. She didn't bend over him; she'd learned that much from fighting her brothers in the barn. Bend over and your opponent can pull you down, then he's on top of you and you lose. Staying beyond arm's reach, she stepped around him so he couldn't see her, in case he was pretending. She jabbed his back with a bare foot and poked at his shoulder with the candlestick. He didn't move.

"Oh dear God, he's dead," whimpered Kate.

Alina put the candlestick on the writing desk and bent down to grab the man's shirt. She pulled. Gradually, with back-breaking slowness, she dragged him towards the door. The hound was beside her now, its claws pitter-pattering on the stone flagged floor as it danced about in distress.

Eventually the man's body was stretched out on the landing. Alina stood up and listened. Silence. She bent down again and pulled the body bump-bump down the first few stairs of the tower, then a little further until its head was lolling down. The dog licked the man's face. Alina turned, ran up the steps, entered Kate's room and closed the door. There was no key in the lock, so she pushed a chair up against it. If he tried to get back in, it would topple and make a racket.

Kate was still kneeling on the bed, but now she was holding her stomach and rocking to and fro.

"*Calma,*" whispered Alina. "*Calma, querida, calma.*"

She climbed up onto the high bed and held her sister-in-law in her arms, wiping away the tears with the soft muslin frill of her sleeve, then she pulled the blankets up over them and lay holding Kate's shaking body.

"I need to wash," said Kate suddenly.

Alina sat up and started to get out off the bed to leave.

"No! No, please, stay here, don't go, don't leave me here alone," Kate begged.

Not understanding the words but sensing the tone, Alina lay back and Kate went to her wash stand. With a cold flannel she tried to rub away McNab's presence.

After a few minutes she said, "My feet are freezing," and climbed back up into the bed.

Alina put her arms round her and pulled her close for warmth. They stayed awake for what seemed hours, but when a pink May morning crept behind the curtains they were fast asleep.

Alina woke first. What should she do? Stay and comfort Kate, or go and pretend nothing had happened? If she stayed and he really was lying dead on the tower stairs, it would raise all sorts of questions. Why was she in Kate's room, they would ask. Why hadn't she called for help? She felt quite sure Kate would not want a fuss. John had told her Thomas' widowed sister was to be married before the end of the month. If the bridegroom heard about the rape he would cancel the wedding. Then Kate would have to live in the same house as McNab forever. For one thing was quite certain, if McNab was alive he would survive any scandal. She had watched him strutting around the house as if he owned it. A steward who had his own quarters but came and went in the main house like a member of the family, this was a steward with special privileges. Her father would never tolerate a servant getting above his station in such a manner. As soon as she was Lady Fulford, McNab would be out of the door and off the property for ever. But she wasn't Lady Fulford yet, and the current holder of that title was clearly besotted with him. So McNab's story, whatever it might be, would be believed. If he was alive to tell it.

Gently, she eased her arm from under Kate's shoulder. For a moment she sat on the edge of the bed clenching and unclenching her fists; then she got down and stepped lightly over the freezing floor. Moving the chair from under the door handle she silently lifted the catch and peered out.

Sunlight glared down from a tall window onto an empty stair well. She felt her stomach lurch with fear: McNab would be a terrible enemy. Turning her back to the door, she sat down and lifted her cold feet up onto the chair and under her nightgown. Hugging her legs, Alina considered what was best for her new sister-in-law and what would be best for her. McNab would be a silent enemy, so the rules for engagement would be devious, underhand. She grinned; if there was one thing she had learned from living in a household of males, it was that attack was always the best means of defence. Well, she had attacked, and actually she had no need to defend herself; what the man had done was totally unacceptable, he was a criminal. So that is how she would treat him. McNab was her inferior: as soon as she could, she'd blacken his name and get rid of him. For now, though, she had to protect Kate, and to do that she needed to consolidate her role as Thomas' wife and future lady of the manor.

Alina quietly slipped back into Thomas' bedroom. If he asked where she had been she would say she had got up early to see the dawn, or whatever else she could make him believe without words.

But Alina need not have worried. Thomas was sound asleep, face down on the bed in a dampness of his own drool.

Chapter Twelve
Holland, May 1635

"Where are we, *patrón*?"

"Off the coast of Holland."

"I know that. I mean when the ship goes into harbour, where will we be?"

"Flushing."

"Are we getting off there?"

"Disembarking, Marcos, learn the lingo."

"Are we *disembarking* there, *sir*?"

"No. I am going on to Amsterdam. You can 'get off' here or anywhere else you choose."

"Shall you be staying in Amsterdam?"

"Yes. For a while."

"What's Flushing like?"

"Where, what, when! How old are you, Marcos? You're asking questions like my five-year-old son."

"Have you got a son, *patrón*? You never said."

Ludo cuffed the back of Marcos' head amicably and wandered down the deck.

Marcos stayed by the gunwale and stared into a wall of silent rain. He'd never been in such strange weather before. All around him was white fog, but it wasn't just fog, it was a thick blanket of rain that soaked stockings and jerkin and turned May into December. The only way he knew they were coming into a port was because anchored galleons emerged from nothingness like ghost-ships. A disembodied voice called out from a cargo tender or fishing boat, making him jump like the English priest. He gripped the wooden rail with a mixture of fear and excited anticipation. His whole body was at odds with the static nature of his surroundings: his heart was beating as if there were a high wind and he was running a race. They were here! Somewhere on the land they had yet to see, his father was sitting or sleeping or eating or fighting. Marcos felt the boy in him wanting to jump up and down with excitement. But it was all so quiet. Where were the warships? Why hadn't they heard any gunfire?

He had mixed in with the mariners during the crossing and picked up as much as they could tell about the never-ending Flanders war. Spain was trying to break the Dutch defences. In their ranks were ragged Portuguese, Catholic Flemish—'careful with the Flems, boy, they speak every damned language there is and tell lies in the lot of them'—Irish mercenaries—'never trust an Irishman: he'll stand you a drink and cut your throat for your purse as you drink it'—and Holy Roman Germans —'bloated, sausage eating bastards, but handy in a fight'.

Thousands of men were dying every week, the sailors said, some in military skirmishes, the rest victims of the climate and hunger. Mercenaries were angry as hell because they hadn't received a pay packet in months, years in some cases. English pirates were raiding the Spanish galleons that brought over the soldiers' New World silver, and ships that did get through the English Channel were just as likely to be raided by corsairs. One of the sailors had said that the Turks—they called all North African pirates Turks—were sailing as far north as Iceland: they had taken a fancy to the blondes.

There was danger in one form or another on land and sea, and locating his father was not going to be easy. It would take time, determination. Perhaps it might be wiser to stay with the Italian, go on to Amsterdam, get used to the country and the people and *then* make his way to Flanders. He looked into the whiteness around him and decided on the devil he knew.

"Marcos!" Ludo's sudden voice intruded upon his thoughts, making him jump out of his skin.

"Yes!"

102

"Go and sit on my cargo. Make sure no one slips anything out without my permission. No one is to touch anything with my mark on it, understand? I assume you're staying with me."

"Well, yes. Actually, *patrón* I might just stay with you until...."

"Stay or go. I've told you, Marcos, I do not own you. You attached yourself to me, remember. Stay or go. Do as you wish." A broad hand gripped his shoulder. "But whatever you do, you mind your tongue. What *I do* is no concern of yours—or anyone else's. Do I make myself clear?"

The hand gripping the shoulder of his leather jerkin was a vice. Marcos tried to duck down to escape the pain, but the pressure just increased.

"I will provide bed and board, clothes as required, and in return you do as I say, you don't make comments, and you don't ask questions. Those are my terms. If you don't like them, you can 'get off' right here and now." Ludo lifted his hand.

Marcos nodded his head frantically, his mind racing with possibilities: the merchant was up to something! That secret business in the *cortijo*—whatever it was—there was something afoot. He knew it: men as big and tall and elegant and devious as this one did not make a living out of tea and spice. He could watch what happened, investigate the sales; perhaps start a small business himself. Men who bought tea and spices also bought wine; he knew lots of men in the Sanlucar wine trade. He'd return home a successful merchant wearing a rapier and a fine cape and.... Before all that, though, he needed to find out why the little onions in the little sea chest were so special.

As if the devil himself were reading his mind, a voice whispered in his ear: "Sometimes curiosity can be very dangerous, Marcos. I've a good many Dutch friends, Protestant to a man, and they're all partial to a spicy bit of Spanish sausage. They make it out of plump Catholic boys."

Marcos turned round, but his benefactor had vanished in the mist.

Chapter Thirteen
Amsterdam, early June 1635

Leaving a glorious day of bright summer sunshine, Marcos followed Ludo through a door into a netherworld of peat-filled grates and dark afternoons. It wasn't the typical atmosphere of Dutch taverns he had already come to know—that particular hush broken by hearty guffaws and back-slapping camaraderie —this place was a composite of scents and sounds he could not name. There was one odour in particular, a pleasant aroma, but not the usual malty smell of warm beer, nor of the clear liquid that they served in thumb-sized tumblers that smelled like a woman's perfume. He stopped and inhaled.

"Coffee," said Ludo. "Like it?"

"It's wonderful."

"Doesn't taste as good as it smells, but you can add it to your list of new experiences and accomplishments."

Marcos gulped. The bastard knew about his journal. He knew everything—all the time! But the Italian wasn't interested in him. His eyes were scanning the darkness: an eagle-owl detecting its prey in the half-light.

Groups of men smoking curled-stem pipes were gathered around circular tables. Above, on a balcony, six or seven burghers huddled in negotiation. One smaller table was occupied by a single client. Ludo put a hand on Marcos' shoulder and steered him towards a corner. A stub of candle stuck in a wine bottle flickered as they disturbed the heavy air.

"Why's it so dark?" Marcos asked.

"So people can't see each other, I expect."

Ludo removed his wide-brimmed hat and placed it conspicuously on top of his miniature sea chest in the centre of their table.

The black leather brim was now bent so low at the front it nearly touched Ludo's thick beard when he wore it. Marcos had cheekily remarked that it wouldn't work as a disguise if he didn't remove the feathers. Anyway, he'd said, he couldn't see the point of Ludo trying to disguise himself with the hat when he was so tall that it bobbed above any crowd of heads like a drowned man in the sea.

Ludo had whipped round, grasped Marcos' shoulder and dug his thumb under his collar bone, saying, "Never, ever say that again, boy."

Marcos now surreptitiously touched the bruises. He wasn't altogether sure if Ludo had been referring to his hat or the drowned man; he suspected the latter. Ludo was usually jovial, but Marcos had discovered to his cost he had a temper as black as his hat, and when a dour mood was on him he looked like Death himself.

Nevertheless, Marcos felt he was right: the hat did make Ludo more conspicuous—and that must have been his intention, for Ludo never did anything without a purpose.

Ludo now settled himself into a chair and, leaning back in his customary manner, gazed around. "Dark is what they are used to," he said. "Light is a special commodity in the Low Countries, and your average Dutchman is too tight-fisted to waste money on candles. Candles offer no material return by definition."

"You don't like the Dutch, do you?"

"On the contrary, I enjoy them greatly: trying to out-manoeuvre them is one of my favourite pastimes. Successful strategy is the finer point of profit, Marcos. If you don't like—" He was interrupted by the serving girl.

Marcos observed the way the plump wench looked at Ludo. What did women see in him? He wasn't good-looking. Could they smell his money?

"I've ordered coffee for you to try, but not at this table. You're my servant, remember; you should be over there." Ludo nodded in the direction of the kitchen area. "But stay close and keep an eye out for onlookers. I'm expecting company and I want to know who sees us talking. If you notice anyone taking a special interest, follow him. Find out who he is and where he lives, if you can. I'll see you back at the lodging tonight if we are separated."

"Yes, sir." Marcos got up, doffed his soft cloth cap and bowed. It wasn't a fatuous move, Ludo's tone was too serious for that.

"Chat up the waitress," added his master. "See if that man up there by himself is a regular or if he just came in today."

"How shall I do that? I don't speak Dutch—or French—and she won't have any Latin."

"You'll manage. Languages are only an obstacle to people with no imagination. Do you have an imagination, Marcos?"

Marcos looked across the dark room and focused on an empty table; in one chair he saw himself decked out in velvet and frills like a Spanish grandee; leaning across the table, gazing into his eyes, was Alina. She was wearing a satin dress, its bodice cut so low he could see the rise and fall of her sun-touched breasts. He grinned.

"Of course you have," said Ludo, laughing. "I remember a splendid family pennant. Plenty of imagination." He waved a hand of dismissal.

The man sitting on his own above them took it as a signal. Ludo watched him get to his feet, then snapped his fingers, once, twice, to call Marcos back. Strong, swarthy fingers beckoned the boy close.

"If you're thinking of getting into petticoats, look after yourself. These girls look clean and healthy with their rosy cheeks, but they're as dirty as any tavern tart inside. Understand?"

"Yes, sir."

"Good, and find out about *him*." Ludo inclined his head in the direction of the approaching Dutchman. "Go on!"

The man waited until Marcos had made his way through the tables to the kitchen area, then moved into the chair the boy had vacated.

"Signor Ludovico?" he said.

"Master Simonis?" replied Ludo. He raised an interrogative eyebrow, lifted the hat and tapped his small sea chest with a forefinger. "You are a treasure seeker, I hear."

Marcos leaned against the high trestle table that acted as a bar at the back of the tavern. The waitress placed a small white china cup beside him and smiled. He winked and lifted the cup. Keeping his eyes on the girl's blue gaze he gulped the hot brown liquid. The wench smiled as his eyes opened in shock and surprise. He would have spat out the foul tasting stuff immediately, but she was in his direct line of fire: she'd put herself there on purpose. He moved the scalding, bitter liquid around in his mouth and forced himself to swallow. The cheeky wench laughed, said something incomprehensible, and raised a hand holding a bowl of brown granules. With her free hand she spooned some into his cup and stirred. Marcos stared at the brown poison. He was going to have to drink it. The girl mimicked his wink and waited until he had the cup to his lips again before skipping off to serve new customers.

Marcos took a very small sip. It tasted better. In fact it was quite nice. Crossing one leg in front of the other and leaning sideways with an elbow on the high bench behind him, in what he considered the appropriate stance for a coffee habitué, he took in his murky surroundings. The door to the street opened, and in that instant of light something on the balcony caught his eye. Something had glinted. That something was a pair of round spectacles on the round face of a gnome-like creature from a children's fairy tale: a shoemaker or a tailor. Whoever and whatever he was, he was bending down, observing Ludo through the balcony railings with far too much interest. Marcos looked for the girl; now he needed to find out about two men. But exactly how he was going to learn anything at all was quite beyond his imagination.

Ludo's visitor, Peter Simonis, tried not to stare at the sea chest on the table. He spoke good Spanish, but he was as nervous and as excited as a schoolboy. His words came out in a squeaky rush. "Forgive me, my name is Peter Simonis. I am an accountant from Haarlem."

Ludo waited for the man to say more; when he didn't, he replied, "Relax, Mr Simonis, we have plenty of time. Or do you have another engagement?"

"No."

"You are interested in my tea, spices, silks? Which?"

Peter Simonis went white. "They told me you had... they said...."

Ludo put his large hands on the table and bent forward to whisper, "*They* said? Who said?"

"I...." Holding the sides of his chair, Peter Simonis gathered his strength and started again, "I come from Haarlem. I represent a consortium. We are tulip growers, connoisseurs. We were advised about you."

"You heard I had bulbs to sell."

"Yes."

"And decided to contact me."

"Yes."

"Good. Now, what are you looking for, new colours?"

"We are looking for a Viceroy."

"A Viceroy—purple flames—very striking."

Ludo waited, marking a slow march with his right thumb, letting the silence drag on until Mr Simonis had beads of sweat on his brow. Then Ludo sighed and gave his one-dimpled grin, saying, "Well, today you are in luck, sir."

"I am? You have one?" Peter Simonis could barely speak. "Is it very expensive?"

"Very."

Ludo watched the man's hands creep onto the edge of the table to steady himself. The nails were clean and well-manicured. Mr Simonis was a professional gentleman, a friend of doctors and lawyers. His syndicate would be a group of rising men: the educated middle-class, the new bourgeoisie itching to demonstrate their hard-earned wealth and consolidate their status in any one of the United Provinces' smaller towns. Here was the very challenge he had spoken so lightly of to the boy. Professional Dutchmen like these could drive a bargain like a Levantine prostitute with a brood of multi-coloured bastards to feed.

"What can you offer?" he asked. It was barely a whisper.

"For one?" Mr Simonis' eyes were glued to the small sea chest. "You have got only one Viceroy? Nobody else will be able to acquire another from you?"

"Not one, no, *various*."

"Various?"

"You may have one, or you may have all of them. But if I let you take them all, then I...." Ludo paused, as if in a moral dilemma. "I'm not sure I should let you have them all, Mr Simonis. A monopoly...."

The tulip-grower licked his lips and with sudden confidence said, "I will purchase all the bulbs you have. You may draw on my bank for cash, or I will pay you myself in coin in two days' time. But I would like at least one Viceroy for myself. Perhaps we can come to an agreement."

Ludo registered the change of tone. "The lust for private acquisition, I see. Well, we could consider separating the sale into two lots, one for your syndicate and one—as a special sale—for your personal pleasure."

"May I see them?"

"Here?"

"Ah, yes, how foolish of me, I should have arranged a private room. As you see, I am not accustomed to these transactions."

"Don't worry, we are out of the way here. I don't think we can be observed."

Ludo made a show of scanning the area around his table. Looking up, he too noticed the gnome-like creature in spectacles. One of Mr Simonis' colleagues keeping watch? Or perhaps a rival grower or a florist wanting to know what he was up to?

Whichever, it served to spread the word that he was in business. Swallowing a smile, he removed his hat from the small sea chest, unclipped a gold chain from his doublet and with an elaborate dumb show of secrecy opened the lock. Holding the lid upright with one hand, he separated the straw nests in the compartments of the top layer.

Peter Simonis put forward a trembling hand and poked at the straw, revealing the top of a glass vase. He tapped the crystal with a fingernail. "What is this?"

"A 'nightingale's eye' vase. It is how the Turks grow their finest bulbs. The bottom is a globe for the bulb and, as you can see, the stem of the vase is just tall enough to support the growing stem of the flower. In this way a Turkish pasha can plant his seed and watch his priceless tulips from conception."

"Ingenious!"

"The passion of sultans, my friend. You are getting much more than a flower when you buy from me, Mr Simonis, you are purchasing part of the exotic East." Ludo studied the man's face; his whole countenance was transfused with pleasure. "And this as you know is named Viceroy, but it is not a *vice-roy*, it is the very king of *violetten,* of all known tulips.

I also," he added quietly, "have others hitherto unknown in the West." He closed the lid.

"Here?"

"Here. One of them is named *Nur-i-Adin*—The Light of Paradise. Had I known I was to meet with a true connoisseur I would have acquired one for you; unfortunately, it is already promised."

Peter Simonis let out a small cry. "If I had known!"

"Never mind, for now I am willing to sell you three Viceroys."

"And the new breeds? Can I not have just one of those?"

"I could let you have one, perhaps. You could also commission me to get authentic bulbs from Constantinople. I shall be returning to collect new bulbs after the winter. They flower earlier there. Indeed, you may be able to persuade them to flower earlier here if you know your horticulture. Imagine looking into the snow one cold morning and seeing beautiful indigo, rose and purple patterned blooms glittering like jewels in the frost."

Marcos tried to calculate how much the man in spectacles could see from the balcony. Enough to know there was a transaction taking place, enough to see a buyer's offer rejected then another offer made, enough to see the buyer place a brown packet in the seller's hand and then, after a further exchange of words, call for a pen and ink. Words were written on a piece of paper pulled from an inner pocket. Then, after a few more minutes of negotiation, something else was taken from an inner pocket.

"It's a New World emerald, worth a fortune and genuine—I can guarantee."

Ludo sighed. "I'm sure it is, Mr Simonis. I'm sure it is, and very lovely too, but of absolutely no use to me; it's for a woman."

"Give it to your wife, then; a stone this big will make her rich when you die."

"If I ever have a wife, sir, she will be rich when I die with or without this bauble."

Nevertheless, Ludo held out his hand and the Dutch accountant placed the ring in his large palm. Holding the stone up to the candle, Ludo watched the flame turn green. He bit the gold, then tucked the jewel onto his little finger.

"Very well, the ring for an offset of *Nur-i-Adin*." He snapped his fingers above his head and the plump girl appeared in an instant. "Brandy wine for two," he said.

The girl simpered and departed.

Ludo looked at the glowing cheeks of the man in front of him and smiled. "Happy? Good. Do you have a container, or are you going to stuff your pockets with treasure?"

The moment he and his buyer got up to leave, the little man with the spectacles who had been watching them from the balcony area above trotted down the staircase. Marcos dropped a coin on the counter and nipped out of the tavern door behind him. Ludo registered them go.

On his way back to their lodging, Ludo bought some gingerbread at a stall and, keeping a careful grip on the miniature sea chest, sauntered along the busy canal as if he had no particular place to go. At another stall he bought a painted monkey on a stick and spent a few moments playing with it, chatting to the Moorish vendor about this and that before moving on again.

At the door to their lodging house, he pushed the toy into the front of his doublet, then extracted a small, double-edged dagger from an inner pocket. Slowly, he pushed at the main door with an elbow. When the door was wide open he waited a good minute before stepping over the threshold, then he took the narrow staircase up to the second floor as fast as he could. He repeated the same procedure at the door to the rented rooms. But no one was in lying in wait, and no one appeared to have followed him.

Once inside his apartment he sighed, popped the dagger back into his doublet, and put the chest on a low sideboard, setting his black hat on top of it. He unbuttoned his figured-silk doublet, removing the syndicate's promissory note and Mr Simonis' paper bill for funds to be drawn from an Amsterdam bank. This system of exchange that Sir Geoffrey Fulford had found so amusing was ideal for these transactions. Tomorrow he would transfer it to his personal account, and paper would convert into gold.

It was the perfect arrangement for merchants who spent their lives travelling from one place to another: safe, reliable, effective and convenient. It made no sense to undermine it. The Habsburg emperor and the Spanish king were confusing religion with pragmatism. The future was in the north, and they should be wooing the busy, business-minded Protestant to their benefit, not trying to ruin his business.

However, much as he had tried to belittle the plot in Spain, it was, as he had hoped it would be, already proving lucrative and amusing. There was something tremendously ironic in watching predestined Calvinists gamble. For that is what Mr Simonis' syndicate was involved in, a particularly risky form of gambling. They had very probably just spent a lifetime's savings on a parcel of bulbs that might or might not be what he said they were. The bulbs themselves might die in the first hard frost, be eaten by mice or trampled by a clumsy boot. Mr Simonis' group had no guarantee that their flowers would see the next spring or that the colours they hungered for would bloom as described. And this was a group of sensible, educated, professional men. They could claim to be connoisseurs— interested only in the horticultural aspects of the plants—but it was much more than bright colours in dull back yards they wanted to see. A root with offsets would produce two plants, possibly three within two years. In those two years prices might rise sufficiently to make two, three hundred percent profit on *each* offset—perhaps more. If they were careful and tended the plants well, they could become enormously rich. Nonetheless, as a diffident Englishman had once said, it was a foolish occupation for a man.

And not just men. Pulling the emerald ring off his little finger, Ludo thought about his rendezvous with the widow vander Woude. A message had been sent; she was expecting him to call this very evening. He examined the bright stone again and smiled, then popped it into a pocket. He wouldn't need it for Elsa vander Woude—it was for *her* to pay *him* now.

Ludo went into his bedroom, unbuttoned his shirt and pulled off his buckled shoes. Padding across the wooden floorboards in his stockinged feet, he went back into the main living room, poured himself some wine and sat down at the table to enjoy it. As he lifted the glass he noticed something strange in front of him. It was a beautiful little ship, finely shaped out of folded vellum. He put down the wine and picked it up. On the stern a place name was printed in ink—Lisbon. On its prow was an exquisite depiction of a bird of prey—*un azor,* a goshawk—and a Spanish grandee.

He turned the vellum barque around and bounced it up and down as if on a rough sea. They had agreed to his demand. The conspiracy was launched. Despite all he had said the conspirators were still convinced. So now he could really inflate prices, and by making an astounding profit for himself he would earn a ship.

He wanted to chuckle, to rub his hands and enjoy the prospect of wealth, but he didn't; he couldn't, precisely because this little barque had been left on his table, in his privately rented apartment, meaning *they* knew exactly where he was and what he was doing, and this made him very uneasy. It was one thing to walk through city streets carrying a large sum of money, then to come through your own front door dagger in hand in case someone was lying in wait to rob you. But knowing someone could get through locked doors into your lodging—this was another matter. This was a special game with hidden rules and very serious implications. He dropped the vellum ship on the table, then picked it up again, looking for clues.

It wasn't the hawk on the prow that made him nervous. In his experience, Spaniards rarely carried through an effective plan; the Spanish noblemen he knew couldn't even organize the papers on their desks. They weren't practical or forward-looking—the way they were exploiting the New World silver and making no attempt to invest it for the future was testament to that: spend, spend.... No, the risk and the consequences weren't in Madrid, they were in Rome. The English priest, John Hawthorne, had intimated the Vatican secret service was involved—and they were not to be trifled with. If he failed to do what the Vatican wanted, this folded white vellum would be replaced by a flat square of black silk. And if he succeeded it would also be replaced by a square of black silk. Either way, they would eliminate him to destroy links and evidence.

He dropped the little ship back on the table and slowly drank the rest of the wine. *Unless....* He leaned down and pushed the ship around the table like a child. Unless he did what they wanted, created an unholy financial scandal, left the speculators in an embarrassing mire of their own making, took possession of his little ship in Lisbon and sailed due south into a Moorish corsair port. Even the Black Order, the most secret and efficient of the various papal agents, would have trouble locating him on Ibiza or in Morocco. He could take a fine house overlooking the harbour of Salé, have his own harem of lovely foreign slaves... of lovely foreign slaves like Alina... like Alina herself.

Now *there* was a possibility. He could join the corsairs and have a little fun at sea like his own father, then sail up the Tamar and spirit Alina off as a slave. Alina, Alina, Alina—why was she still with him? He had no time for blushing maidens, not that she had behaved like a blushing maiden in his cabin that day; and if the fat old Cornishman had had his way she would be round with child by now—by him or his feeble son. The thought made him put a hand on his doublet; there was a dull, hollow pain just between his ribs.

"Boh!" he said in his mother tongue. "Nothing but trouble."

At that moment Marcos swung through the door. The boy's face was flushed from running and he collapsed in a chair.

"What's that?" he panted, pointing at the table.

"A threat, or a promise, I have to decide which." Ludo held the little ship up on the palm of his hand. Without taking his eyes off it, he said, "Who was he?"

"Umm...."

"You lost him."

"It's a ship?"

"It's a ship. You lost him."

"I lost him."

Chapter Fourteen

Elsa vander Woude patted her hair. It felt very strange. *She* felt strange, quite naked without her cap. No one had seen her hair like this for years, not even her husband. Everyone she knew would be outraged, a woman of her age standing without her cap. Shocked by her own temerity, she checked her little watch against the gilt clock standing on the mantel shelf. Cornelis had bought both of them from an Italian, not her Italian, though. She thought of Ludovico as *her* Italian. The large timepiece over the empty fireplace was a replica of a clock in Florence. Cornelis had been to Florence; she had never left Amsterdam. Italy for her consisted of the names of rival states: Venice and Genoa. Ludovico said he came from Genoa, which worried her at first because it was allied to Spain. Spain was the Duke of Alba and the worst threat for any Dutch child: 'Be good or the Duke of Alba will get you.' But Ludovico was not like the Spanish *dons*. Ludovico was not like any man she had ever met. She patted her hair again, tucking a pin in tighter, making it hurt as penance. Without a cap, her hair might come loose.... Elsa dared not finalize that thought, yet it was precisely for this that she had set her cap aside.

The clock made a lurching click as it told the hour. Now she checked the clock against her little silver watch. Such a pretty thing: its shell-shaped silver case as darling as any brooch, but it had to stay hidden. Such ostentation would draw attention; a widow was not expected to adorn herself like a girl. Elsa smoothed her thumb over the silver; a pretty thing, but a sad memento of her husband's dying, and her guilt. One interminable winter afternoon she had watched the minute hand until hypnotized; she had fallen asleep. When she awoke

Cornelis was gone, and she had neither said farewell nor called their daughter to his bedside: a burden to carry to the grave.

"I am destined to live time slowly," she said to no one, "but it is not in my nature."

Three sharp knocks on the front door roused her from self-pity and changed her concept of time for months to come.

Elsa opened the front door herself and led the man she called Ludovico up to the first floor of the narrow house and into her private sitting room. Josie and Greit, her two servants, had been given the night off and instructed to stay in the kitchen or their adjacent room when they returned. The order caused the girls hours of speculation, which would have appalled her had she known. Elsa hated gossip in any form.

The large Italian strode into the modest room and crossed the black-chequered floor directly to the window. Resting his miniature sea chest on the shallow sill, he stood at an angle and looked down at the canal below. Men were loading goods into a sling to be winched into a neighbour's attic storeroom. A scruffy lad was loitering near them, but he wasn't watching the workmen or the machinery.

Elsa went to her sideboard and began to pour red wine from a decanter. Cut glass chinked against fine crystal: her hands were shaking; she half-turned to see if her visitor had noticed.

"Sometimes," Ludovico said, watching the goods being manhandled into the sling, "one forgets how much hard labour is involved in trade transactions. A merchant travels all the way to the East, to India or beyond to make purchases, risking his life at sea and on land. He arranges for the goods there to be packed and transported; there's always trouble with the coolies stealing or failing to complete the job. Then he has to sail back through typhoons and stifling heat, and even when he returns with his goods there is a whole range of hazards and misadventures that can make his entire journey a perfect waste of time. If that sling breaks, now, and the tea or coffee, rice or sugar spills out, a whole year's work will sink in that filthy canal. Such a lot of trouble for nothing."

Elsa went across to the window. The boy she'd noticed hanging around earlier was wandering off toward the city centre. For some reason Ludovico grimaced and picked up the miniature sea chest. Tapping it, he continued, "This is much easier and far more interesting. Where shall I put it?"

Elsa indicated a low table set between two chairs. Then, picking up a glass of wine for him, she asked, "You had a safe voyage?"

"Actually, no, it was full of incident—shipwrecks, pirates, all the dangers of the high seas. Thank you."

She barely heard his words, just standing near to him made her heart quite literally flutter. A wife, a mother, a grandmother-to-be and a widow for two years now, but this man made her feel like a schoolgirl. An unwitting hand twisted a button on her black dress.

Ludovico noticed the hand and said, "Black pearls. Are those the ones I brought you?"

"Yes. I thought they would be more useful as buttons."

"Oh, Elsa, can you never have anything for the pleasure of it?"

"I have pleasure in my life. That is...." She stopped abruptly. What would he think? A statement like that! Her cheeks went pink and he burst out laughing.

"Relax, good lady. I shall spend my visit at your window so your neighbours can see you have nothing to hide. Isn't that why you people light lamps but never close curtains, so you can all see into each other's lives? Come, let us stand at this window and conduct our business here, then your good neighbours can comment on how long it took us to come to an agreement. Your reputation is safe with me."

His eyes, however, said otherwise. The significance of the absent cap was not lost on him.

Elsa, embarrassed beyond measure, returned to the cabinet for her wine. Suddenly what he had said regarding his voyage registered. "Pirates! A shipwreck? Heavens! Your cargo! Tell me about it at once." She sat down as a wave of genuine fear touched her cheeks.

"Only if you will stop calling me Ludovico—I'm known to all the world and his wife as Ludo. May I?" He indicated the vacant chair in front of her, the chair Cornelis had so rarely occupied.

"Of course, please sit down, how rude, forgive me." Elsa heard herself gushing and swallowed hard, straightened her spine against the wooden back of her chair and tried not to fidget.

Ludo lowered himself into the chair facing her and began to explain how his ship had nearly capsized in the Bay of Cadiz.

Elsa's face drained of colour. "You lost the bulbs?"

"No, no, all quite safe. I had a cargo of single shade *colouren* in a special perforated barrel, some silk, tea and so on in the hold, but it's all safe. I kept your special commission with me at all times. It's in this." He tapped the casket on the table between them. "Do you like it?"

Elsa traced a hand over the smooth leather and gilt hinges of the miniature sea chest. "How curious."

"Made to your specifications; bulbs need air, as you said. See, these perforations here. I've also got a little something extra that I think will surprise you." Ludo unclipped the key from his doublet and turned the small locks.

Elsa held the arms of her chair to contain her excitement. He had brought her special new bulbs all the way from Constantinople—special bulbs just for her. No one else would have them. She stared as he lifted out a handful of straw packing and revealed a glass vase.

"Whatever is it?" she gasped.

"The Turkish are master glass-makers; they call this filigree design 'nightingale's eye'. See how rods of colour cross in and out? It's supposed to be like the eye of the nightingale. Have you ever seen one?" He lifted the small vase and placed its special globed base on the wide, flat palm of his left hand. "This is how the Sultan displays his tulips. You, my dear, will be the only woman in Holland, perhaps in all Europe, to have such a treasure."

He put it down on the table between them and carefully lifted another glass container from the chest. In the globe at the base was a single, dull, tulip bulb. It could have been a wrinkled onion, except no one would keep a vegetable in such a beautiful container. The stem of the vase was tall and narrow for the growing stem of the tulip and decorated with an intricate filigree design. In the evening light the glass was shot with pink and mauve, a treasure in itself.

"Ah," sighed Elsa. "But what is the bulb? It must be very special."

"This is *Dur-i-Yekta*, which means Matchless Pearl." Ludo leaned across to touch her cheek and raise her chin, "You see, I shall always bring you pearls."

Elsa felt her face flush again, but a sharp little doubt made her catch her breath. "Forgive me Ludovico—Ludo—but how can I be sure the bulb is what you say? It is impossible to remove it from the vase."

Ludo leaned back in his chair, "Now what sort of question is that? Have I not risked life and limb to bring it to you? I could have sold it a dozen times, each at a higher price, but no, Elsa vander Woude commissioned me to bring something special from a foreign land, and here is the most special thing I could find. Do you have any idea how difficult it is to obtain these bulbs? They are cultivated by the Sultan himself. He keeps a whole retinue of gardeners who are trained in the fine arts of horticulture and prolonged torture, so they can punish would-be thieves in the most horrific manner imaginable. My dear, what I bring you is the exotic East in all its dubious splendour."

Elsa tentatively pushed her plump fingers into the straw in the chest, "What else do you have?"

"What else do you want?"

"I will take all you bring."

"And you can afford that?"

"I can afford what I have to have. Tell me your terms."

And so the haggling that she so enjoyed began. Her husband had been a careful lawyer and every guilder of his fees had been put to good use. But once those fees had furnished his home and his one child had been educated for her station in life, once he had paid to see her safely married into the burgher class and had no debts of any description, he had no alternative but to keep his money at home in a strongbox, the banking system being too new for a cautious man. In her youth, Elsa had been trained to keep accounts and to account for each guilder spent. They had never been short of money, for Elsa also had an instinct for thrift, and so between them they had earned and saved little short of a fortune. And then Cornelis had died, and his wife lost her sense of purpose.

One day in the market she bought some strange little bulbs to plant in pots in her house. They grew into tall flowers ablaze with the colours of summer. They brought life back into her dark, silent home. After they had bloomed, she stored them as she was told, and the next autumn she planted them in her vegetable garden, safely marked so the girls wouldn't pop them in a stew. One viciously cold April morning, she looked down from an empty room at the rear of the house and saw bright yellow and scarlet hats among sprouts and cabbages, bursts of colour amid the last slugs of grey snow. Here was something to look forward to during the tedious winter of her life.

That spring she purchased more bulbs, and while doing so met a man who told her about wonderful striped blooms, purple flashes on wax white petals, and she had to have them. Cabbages and carrots made room for a flower garden. She watched and waited through another dreary winter until one day, through sleeting drizzle, tall violet, mauve and rich royal purple blooms shone out with the reds and yellows above the winter's lingering snow. She stood at her back door and laughed with delight. Now, indulging the other side of the thrifty Dutch coin, Elsa started to gamble. She bought new varieties, propagated new colours and patterns, and sold just a very few of her fine collection to a group of tulip-growers who called themselves connoisseurs. One of these staid men, who had gambled and won on offsets from late-flowering hybrids, introduced her to Ludovico da Portovenere.

That day they had done business in full view of her fellow countrymen, but then he had come to her house at night to confirm their arrangement. He had stayed for two hours, sitting in Cornelis' visitor's chair in Cornelis' old office. Four months later he had returned with new bulbs. After she had paid him the price agreed upon, he had given her a soft leather bag containing eight black pearls. During his remaining days in Amsterdam he had visited her more often than was necessary for a purely commercial enterprise.

Elsa touched a black pearl now, as if for luck, and said, "I have arranged a light supper. Would you stay and share it with me?"

"Of course."

"First, I will pay you for these."

She collected the fee from the funds still kept in Cornelis' strongbox, then they supped on cold chicken and sherry syllabub and finished the decanter of French wine.

Elsa, tipsy on the excitement of her new acquisitions, relaxed in her chair and watched the dashing Italian eat the last of his dessert. Her thoughts became tangled; she had no words for what she wanted next. Leaning forward, she tried to focus on her long-handled silver spoon and finish her syllabub. Scooping the sweet mixture from its tall glass, the significance of the spoon handle made her smile. *When you sup with the devil, use a long spoon.* "Oh dear," she sighed, as her left hand opened two priceless pearl buttons.

Before he left, Ludo said, "I shouldn't want you to rely on me, Elsa. It wouldn't be wise to treat me as your only...."

The word 'supplier' sounded too crude, so he kissed her brow and tucked the sheet under her ample chin, then said, "There are considerable dangers in my trips to the Levant. If I do not return one spring, think of me kindly when you look at your precious flowers."

"Are you saying goodbye?"

"I hope not." He sat fully dressed now on the side of her bed. "But I have to be realistic—and honest, too."

Elsa stared with fear. "You *are* saying goodbye. Forever?"

"No! Not unless you want me to."

Taking her warm left hand in his, he continued.

"I'm also going to be a little unwise. I'm going to tell you something I should not say yet. At least, not until...." He kissed each soft-fleshed knuckle in turn and in a low voice said, "I want to make as much of my business in as short a time as possible now for two reasons. Before, I only had one, but you, my dear, have given me a very special motivation. First, though, let us consider your situation and mine regarding these tulips. I shall return to The Levant on the next ship and bring you more special bulbs to plant before October. But that will only be a business between us—and you are perhaps going to laugh at me, but after tonight it is going to be difficult to receive payment for the next transaction. Do you understand?"

Elsa squeezed his hand and moved her head from side to side so that her unpinned hair shifted on the starched pillowcase behind her like a cloud before a storm.

Ludo smiled at her. "Think, *carina*. What's the point of you keeping all these fabulous flowers to yourself? While I am away, you can sell your more humble bulbs, breed offsets from the better ones, make yourself a little richer, and in the process increase demand. Prices can only go up, Elsa. If you set a trend in motion for men and women such as yourself to breed and sell bulbs, when I return I can—how can I say this without being vulgar?"

The buxom widow now sat up straight. "What? What are you saying?"

"I'm saying that if you indulge in a little more trading yourself, which, let's admit it, you're very good at, you could become a very wealthy woman."

"I don't need to be a wealthy woman, I have all I need here, except...."

"Me?" Ludo kissed her mouth softly. "But I cannot always guarantee to be here, not in Holland. And even if I could, oh Elsa, this country would kill me. My home is Italy where there is sunshine all the year. Even when it rains there is sun in Genoa. If you could just...." He sighed dramatically and traced his thumb over the soft pad of her cheek. "Just a daydream—I saw you coming to my country."

"How could I... how could a widow make a journey to Italy? What would people think?"

"People wouldn't think anything if you were no longer a widow."

Elsa stared.

Ludo got to his feet, buttoned his jacket and smoothed out his fancy cuffs saying, "The trouble is, and this is what I was trying to explain about the buying and selling of the bulbs, I am not a wealthy man like your husband. I'm not in any position to.... Of course, if we could find a way to sell our bulbs at a significant profit, that would change things. We could then make a very fine home wherever we liked: we could live like a king and queen in a land where summer lasts more than two weeks a year. We could have a house overlooking the Middle Sea. You could have your own terraced garden and gardeners to help you, and...."

Elsa clenched the sheet covering her breasts, not knowing whether to laugh or cry.

Ludo bent down and touched her nose with his, then whispered, "Decide what you want to do, my dear. For now, a sweet goodnight."

He was nearly at the door before she spoke.

"I know someone who trades professionally."

"That would be an excellent start!"

"But how... I mean, how will this help you?"

Ludo returned to sit on the side of the bed.

"I supply a few fine bulbs now, and the promise of many more of what you call here 'superbly fine' ones, later. You could find one or two agents and negotiate terms with them so they get a generous percentage on each transaction. Or you could just stimulate sales yourself, increasing your profit percentage in each transaction. That will keep prices high, and rising higher. Knowing I shall return with *exceptional* bulbs, you also tell new connoisseurs and growers about me and what I can supply. You could, if you think it appropriate, take down-payments on a future price for your own special bulbs. But keep prices rising all the time. Show a few select people your garden and let them make offers for offsets, or if you can bear it, let them have complete bulbs, whole beds after flowering. Have you got any you want to part with now, while they are out of the ground?"

Elsa didn't know how to answer. Ludo knew she wouldn't want to sell even the most ordinary of her precious tulips, but he was offering her a chance of a life she could never have believed possible, an opportunity to live, really live before her hair finally turned grey. He waited a moment then muttered a name and some numbers. Elsa liked numbers.

"What?" she demanded. "How much?"

"Five hundred and fifty guilders."

"Say it again."

"I know—it's hard to believe. He bought a *bizarden*, purple with a white border, for forty-five guilders last year and sold it this March for five-hundred and fifty."

Elsa sat up straight. "Twelve-fold profit!"

"*Brava*! That was quick! Tomorrow I'll send you some plain bloom *couleren* as bait or ballast; use them as you will to get humbler people started. I'll let you have two *rosen* as well— ruby flames on white. They are very pretty. In fact, when I saw them I thought those pretty things might have a special meaning in my life. Start with these two with the connoisseurs; see how much they will fetch."

Ludo kissed the widow slowly then murmured, "A new life, ah, my love, my love." Then he got to his feet and crossed to the door. As his hand lifted the latch he whispered, "Shall we discuss details tomorrow?"

"Come in the afternoon."

"So your neighbours won't gossip?"

Elsa saw his exaggerated wink in the candlelight and stifled a very girlish giggle. She did not see the way he skipped down the stairs, or hear the way her front door was opened onto the Prinsengracht and closed loud enough to wake clacking tongues.

Elsa slept soundly for a few hours, then woke with a start, seeing her late husband's clerk, Paul Henning, look up from his desk. In her waking dream he was sitting at the desk he no longer occupied, because Cornelis vander Woude's practice no longer existed. Even if it had, Paul Henning would not have been there, because his wife was bedridden and his elderly mother was too ill to care for their young children. Henning had chosen to live on his meagre savings and care for his family rather than pay a few cents to a servant, whom he was sure would leave the girls to run barefoot in the street and forget to feed his infant son.

"Henning!" said Elsa out loud. Just the man: loyal, trustworthy, and in need.

She pulled on her nightgown, got out of bed and opened the windows wide to let in the early morning sun. For a moment she stared out at the new day, and then sat down at her writing desk to compose a carefully worded letter.

Dear Henning,

I send you this note by hand so you have time to consider its contents before my weekly visit at midday. As you may know, I have become increasingly interested in the cultivation of tulips, which, as you may also know, command high prices. The matter is this: I need someone trustworthy to act as a salesman for me, someone who will deal with all matters relating to commercial transactions on my behalf. Naturally I will pay for this service, a percentage of each sale would seem appropriate.

As you are not able to leave your family for a full working day, this would provide you with some income and be a means of paying for domestic help (your dear mother is growing too frail for household chores). Indeed, you might think about becoming a 'florist' in your own right. These men make a very good living as brokers.

Please think about my suggestion. I shall visit Marie later, as usual. Today I have some fresh cream for her and some pretty ribbons for the girls.

E. vander Woude

After she had sealed the letter, she went to the door to call one of the girls and stopped in her tracks. *My God, the bed!* She put a hand to her mouth to hide her smile and shame. "What has become of you Elsa vander Woude?" she said to herself. "You are a hussy!"

Ludo slept later than he should and woke with a headache and a bad temper. French wine. Why could the French not make decent wine like the Italians?

Marcos was blacking boots and shoes in the sitting room, whistling tunelessly. Ludo struggled out of his hard, narrow bed and snarled, "Stop that."

Marcos put down the fancy new shoe he had been polishing.

"Not that."

"What?"

"Stop the noise, not the polishing."

"Sorry."

"No, stop both and get me some seltzer and some oranges."

Marcos huffed, "Don't think we've got any oranges left, you had them yesterday."

"Sir."

"Yesterday, *patrón*, sir."

"Oh, never mind, I'll get something myself. Finish those shoes; I'll need them in an hour."

Marcos lifted a new, high-heeled, bright-buckled shoe and spat elaborately over its square toe. "Can you actually walk in these?"

"Better than wearing boots in this heat."

"It is hot, isn't it? Seems funny being hot in a place where they say it always rains."

Ludo pushed his feet into dainty Turkish slippers, pulled on a robe and went into the sitting room. "It won't last."

"D'you come here every year like this, then?"

"Like what, then?"

Marcos rubbed at the heel of the shoe and without looking up, said, "Is it this selling that's made you rich?"

"This selling? What selling? What are you saying boy?"

"It's that I don't exactly understand what you're doing, sir."

"And why do you need to understand? It's none of your damned business. You only latched onto me as a means of finding your long lost father, whom you seem to have forgotten in the most unfilial manner."

"That's not true!" Marcos replied, hurt by the Italian's tone. "It's just that I want to learn and go back home with more than I came with—if I can't find my father—and if what they say in the streets and taverns is true, that's probably what's going to happen. I want to go home rich." He paused, regretting his words. "Richer than when I came," he held up the shoe and turned it in the air for inspection, "so I was sort of wondering if perhaps you could let me have a loan, and I could buy some of what you have and sell it."

"At a profit?"

"Oh, yes, that's what I want to do—make a profit, like they talk about with these flowers. There's hundreds of profit, they say, buying and selling your flowers."

"Hundreds of profit! Interesting concept. Are you going to embalm that piece of footwear or help me get my breakfast?"

"Oh, yes, sorry. There's some bread from yesterday and some ham and some beer. Do you want some of that tea stuff?"

"That 'tea stuff' is very expensive merchandise. Show some respect."

"Sorry. Do you?"

"Tea? No!"

Marcos busied himself in the kitchen area and picked up on the conversation he wanted to continue. "So what I was thinking was...."

"You want me to give you some bulbs so you can sell them and make hundreds of profit. And what will you give me in return?"

Marcos put a plate and a tankard down in front of the merchant and looked him in the eye, confused. "I don't understand. What do I have to give you in return?"

Ludo sighed, looked at the warm, flat beer and settled back in his chair. "I think we had better begin with the basics of commerce. Cut me some of that bread and ham—but wash your hands first."

While the boy dipped his greasy black paws into a wash basin, then turned a white linen hand-towel grey, the merchant instructed him in the art of buying at one price and selling at another, how one had to cover costs and make enough money to invest in new stock, plus enough extra to provide for the best quality ham, decent beer and fancy buckled shoes. Marcos listened intently and asked a few intelligent questions, then sat and waited until his master was near to finishing his food and all the beer had been drunk.

"But what I don't see," he said at last, "is how and why these Dutchies are buying things they've never seen and don't need, with money they haven't got."

"Explain," said Ludo.

"Well, last night I was in the Red Cockerel and a lot of odd bods were sneaking into a room at the back, so I sneaked in too. They were having some sort of sale, but there were only a few of those plant things you've got in your case. Some of them were signing bits of paper for flowers that didn't exist. Least ways I didn't see them; I s'pose they might be in people's gardens."

Ludo raised an eyebrow. "Well done. And how exactly did you follow these transactions? You said you had no Dutch."

Marcos lifted one of his master's boots and started to shine it with the linen towel. "Numbers are numbers, not as difficult as words. These are the softest boots I've ever touched."

"And these men, who would you say they were?"

"Oh, that's easy: butchers and bakers. They still had their aprons on. Some gentlemen. I followed one in like I was his servant; he didn't notice. There were a couple of gents like the one you were with a few days ago. The man that owns the Cockerel was running the show. They have a special code for when they go into the room—they go 'cock-a-doodle-do'. Sounds really stupid. I bet if you want to do business in the Golden Lion you have to go 'grrrrr'."

Ludo sat and stared at the boy for a moment, then said, "The answer is 'yes'. I will let you have a loan and some goods at rock bottom prices—and you are going to make us hundreds of profit with a cock-a-doodle-do."

He got up and went into his room to wash, saying, "And in the meantime I'm going to make *thousands* of profit with numbers on bits of paper."

Sometime later, he called out, "Marcos, where's that parchment ship?"

"On the sideboard, sir."

"You're good at pennants and pretty insignia. Can you fashion a sort of flag for it? Like the ones they use on ships to send messages."

"Toothpick and paper, easy. What's the message?"

"Draw a tulip on one side and write the word *si* on the other."

"Just that? *Si?*"

"Yes. You know what tulips look like, I suppose."

"Yes, *patrón*. They put pictures of them on the tables in the taverns where they do business. Why they make all this fuss over a bunch of flowers beats me. Still if they're good for business...."

The small boy who had slept against Elsa vander Woude's front steps ambled up the street to beg some milk and bread at another doorstep. He was hoping he might find an open door and get into a warm kitchen. Kitchen slaveys usually took pity on him. He was chilled to the bone and tempted to go straight back to his grandma's hovel, but he had to report to the monk, so he couldn't go far. He had only got a few doors up the street when he became distracted by workmen arriving to start work on a new house. As they passed him he begged a bite to eat. Workmen always had food and drink with them. Then he noticed a servant girl nip down the steps of the vander Woude house.

Quick as a pickpocket, he was behind her at a safe distance and following her down alleys into a humbler part of the city. The girl arrived at a street of modest cottages, then stopped at a door and knocked. It was answered by a thin man with hair standing up in a tuft. She handed the man a letter then turned to go.

A street vendor passed with a barrow-load of fresh bread. The boy snatched a stick of bread without being seen, thinking it was his lucky day. He'd got some information for the monk and he'd got something to eat. Perhaps he could leave now and spend the afternoon with his mates. But no, he should hang around and see whether the man with the tufty hair did anything about the letter; the monk would pay more for that.

The boy nibbled at the doughy bread slowly. Another of his teeth had worked loose and chewing was difficult. Perhaps he'd call it a day after all and make up some tarradiddle to satisfy the monk. It was a risk, though—the monk might look like a frog-faced old fool, but something told him the monk would be canny enough at detecting fibs. Instead, he hunkered down where he was to finish the bread and watch the door across the street.

Nothing happened for what seemed hours; then, just as he was taking a leak against a wall, he saw the widow he'd been told to watch arrive with a heavy basket. The door opened and she went in. The door closed. He settled back to waiting until, nearly mad with thirst, he ran off in search of a horse trough. It didn't take long, and he was back in time to see the woman emerge with an obviously lighter basket. Then she spent what seemed an hour kissing small girls goodbye on the doorstep and chatting to an old crone who wasn't much bigger than the kids leaning on a stick behind them.

Now he had to follow the woman home. This, he decided, was the last time. The monk could threaten him with hell and damnation, but he was not going to spend his days and nights waiting around to see if someone came out of one house and went into another. He kicked at a stone in the street with annoyance and nearly gave himself away.

He was in the process of planning what to do with the rest of his day when a voice called out, "Hey, Pieter!" and a friend invited him to take a beer in a nearby tavern.

The two boys stayed in the grubby drinking parlour until they had downed all the dregs they could lay their hands on and been chased back into the street. Pieter made an excuse and wandered back in the direction of the street he was supposed to be watching just in time to see the man come out dressed smarter than he had been earlier, his tuft of hair tucked under a black hat.

"This *is* your lucky day, Pieter me lad," he said to himself, and followed the man all the way to the big catholic Church of All Souls, up the steps and into the nave. The neat little clerk genuflected before the altar, then walked round to the confession boxes.

Pieter slipped behind a pillar and studied how he might listen in on the confession, but it was impossible—and he was being watched by a couple of old biddies counting beads.

Feigning interest in the ornate screen and tall saints on high plinths, he gazed around, then looked up towards the high roof.

Set into an alcove above the altar a rosy-cheeked Madonna presented her well-fed babe to the congregation. She reminded him of his mum, except his mum had been much thinner, and none of his brothers or sisters had ever been as fat as that baby.

The choir took their places; a service was about to begin. He was tempted to stay because he liked singing, but he had to see the monk first. Once outside, he ambled down the church steps and then quickened his pace, running until he arrived at the tavern he had been told to visit when the city clock struck five.

The monk, his bald patch shiny as a fresh apple, was sitting with a very tall man. The tall man had a face like a sour turnip and long legs wrapped around each other like serpents.

Pieter waited until the monk beckoned him to the table, then he delivered his information. The monk turned to look at his miserable companion. Turnip Face sniffed and stared at nothing. *Ah well*, thought Pieter, *there you go—I told her you couldn't rely on churches or churchmen.* His Gran spent hours on her knees, and they never had enough in the cooking pot.

Resigned to leaving empty-handed, the monk surprised him with a whole guilder, patted his head and told him to take it straight back home.

Lucky, lucky day!

The monk, who was a Franciscan friar, waited until the boy had gone, then turned back to his ascetic companion, saying quietly in a different language, "The man he described could be her late husband's clerk. He's unemployed with a dependant family. His wife hasn't risen from her lying-in." The monk shook his head, bewildered how such a humble family could become involved in—in what? He didn't even know what was going on. "I wasn't aware vander Woude's widow...."

The tall man was on his feet. "Silence, you fool," he hissed, brushing down the folds of his black, knee-length gown to cover his anger. "No names, and not another word until we are outside."

As they walked out into the afternoon light, the long-limbed Vatican agent said, "Don't use him again, for anything. Lose him."

"Pieter? He's the only breadwinner in the family. His grandmother needs him."

"Lose him."

The friar raised his hood and lowered his head. Boys fell in canals, but he couldn't arrange that. The child would have to disappear into a monastery, a closed order; but then how would the grandmother manage?

As they walked, the tall man said, as if thinking aloud, "If this man is her late husband's clerk, and if, as you say, he is still unemployed and has a large family to feed...." He paused and wrinkled his long aquiline nose. "What is that smell?"

"Smell? Oh, that's the beer factory."

The Roman shuddered. "And they drink it?"

"Gallons, Father."

"Don't call me that."

"No, Fa—"

"As I was saying, he'll need a friend. Someone to turn to when he doubts: someone to support and encourage him."

"And what might he doubt—sir?" But the man from Rome wasn't listening.

Brother Caritas, who was being used as a go-between and translator, because he had been born in Spain but had spent so long in the Low Countries he could speak Dutch like a native, was confused and disturbed. What they were doing, what little Pieter had been paid to do, was like spying. Whatever were they looking for? Why should a good man and a devout Catholic like Paul Henning be under surveillance? Surely this wasn't linked with the Inquisition, not here in Amsterdam?

And the vander Woude family, also good, honourable people, what about them? He tried to follow a sequence of thought but lost each half-formed idea in a maze of doubt. "To be honest, I can't see how these people... I mean, the boy is just a lad."

"Brother Caritas, do not concern yourself."

"No, but—"

"Brother Caritas, do not concern yourself. That is an order."

The friar lowered his head and tucked his hands further into his wide sleeves. As soon as he was able, he would go to the boy's cottage and get him away from this. The monastery on the road to Hoorn had an excellent school. Pieter was a bright lad, he would benefit in all ways.

The friar didn't reach the boy's home until late that night. Pieter, exhausted after his night on a chilly doorstep, was half-asleep over a bowl of warm bread and milk. Brother Caritas tapped on the open door and ducked down into the dark living space. Pieter's eyes widened with apprehension, obviously fearing another night in the street.

His grandmother struggled to her feet and touched the friar's sleeve. "You are welcome, Father. Will you take some milk with us?"

"No, thank you, Mother, I've come for Pieter."

"What for now?" whined Pieter. "I'm not spending another night out there."

"No, no calm yourself. I'm going to take you to a school."

"School!" squealed the boy.

"He can't go to no school, Father," said the old woman. "How are we going to manage with him gone? Take one of the little ones. They're no use to us yet."

"If you call at the Church of All Souls tomorrow, you might find they need a cleaner." Brother Caritas smiled at the old woman.

By now Pieter was hiding behind the old lady's skirts, clutching at the thin fabric like a life line. "Don't let him take me away, Gran, don't let him take me away," he wailed.

Brother Caritas pulled a soft purse from his sleeve. "I've also brought you this."

"You're not buying me!" Pieter was round the back of the cramped room and out into the street now, crying, "No, I'm not going!"

He ran full pelt, desperate to get as far from the friar as possible—he ran full pelt under the metal shod wheels of a vast beer dray. The driver didn't even notice the slight bump as the child's spine was snapped under the weight of gallons and gallons of fine brewed ale.

The friar stood next to the grandmother as the slow dray pulled on down the lane. Tears started in the gentle man's eyes, but the old woman was stern. "He's better off out of it," she said.

"Out of what?"

"This. All this. Poverty's no place for a child. Here, take this." She passed the soft leather purse back to the priest.

"No! It's the least I can do." He waved his hand in embarrassment.

"Take the boy, Father. Will you do that for me? I can't bury him."

Brother Caritas lifted the broken child in his arms and carried him off down the filth-lined street.

"Where'll he be, Father?" called the old woman.

"Is he baptized?"

The woman pursed her lips. "What do you think?"

For a moment the friar hesitated. "What the Lord gives the Lord takes away. He'll be in the monastery cemetery on the road to Hoorn. We'll see he gets a proper burial. Don't forget about All Soul's tomorrow."

The old woman sniffed and waved a hand as her daughter's first illegitimate child was carried away.

Chapter Fifteen
Crimphele, June 1635

Sir Geoffrey finished his morning round, lamenting, as usual, the absence of a proper gardener. The grounds should have been at their best in June, but all they had were straggly shrubs and unweeded borders. Feeling particularly low, he went in for his breakfast. There was a nagging, dull pain under his left shoulder and he lacked his usual appetite, but this was the one time of the day he could sit and eat in peace, so he followed his usual morning routine and went into the family parlour.

His wife Marjorie was at the table.

"My dear, what a pleasant surprise," he said, trying to mask his disappointment. "What brings you down so early?"

"A daughter's wedding, husband, or had you forgotten?"

Her tone could have soused herrings.

Sir Geoffrey selected a boiled egg from the food on the sideboard and sat down. Lady Marjorie cut him a slice of bread and passed it to him without a word. Not even the aroma of freshly baked bread tempted him this morning. Out of sheer habit he pulled the butter towards him and plastered a yellow layer over the brown bread. Then he sat and stared at the plate, knowing his wife was watching his every move. He sighed deeply; there would be no moment of tranquillity this day.

"Is there more to be done?" he asked.

"Of course."

"I thought you women had everything arranged yesterday."

"The banquet, yes; now we have to prepare ourselves. You too, or do you want us to go into this new alliance looking like Tamstock peasants?"

"No, no. I'm sure you—we—will all look splendid. Does Alina have a new dress for the occasion? Kate's are too short to share."

Lady Marjorie ignored the question. "The Rundells will be here before noon and John Hawthorne said he would come early. The chapel was decorated yesterday. Ceremony at two, so don't go off up the fields this morning."

"I'll send McNab up to Home Farm. We need to sort this year's lambs for market tomorrow."

"No, I need him. I want him in the kitchen area; he's the only one who can control Agnes."

"She'll be in full spate today. That kitchen's a hellhole at the best of times," said Sir Geoffrey, absently mixing his metaphors.

He took a bite of bread and half-heartedly tapped the solid egg in front of him with a spoon. "You should do a bit of culling once this business is over; I heard the servants discussing Thomas and Alina again last night. It's not right."

Lady Marjorie sniffed meaningfully, looked him in the eye and raised her eyebrows.

"What? Am I supposed to know something I don't, or is this tittle-tattle?" he demanded.

His wife shovelled bacon and bread into her mouth.

"What? Tell me. I don't listen at keyholes, I don't spy on people, and I never listen to gossip if I can help it; just tell me."

Sir Geoffrey was more than a little cross. There was a campaign against poor Alina, which was evident from the way the servants behaved toward her. Initially, he had assumed—hoped—it was because she was new and foreign, that it would die down with all the fuss over Kate's wedding. Apparently not. A spasm of pain ran down his left arm and he opened and closed his hand to ease the discomfort. His wife was, as usual, making him angry. "Well?"

"They aren't blind, Geoffrey. Not like you." Lady Marjorie took a gulp of ale and looked at him over the rim of the mug. "You can't stop servants gossiping."

"They should show more respect."

"Respect? For that hussy!"

A damp globule of masticated bread and bacon, an accidental expression of her vehemence, landed on Sir Geoffrey's plate. He put down his spoon and pushed his uneaten egg away. "Marjorie, why do you hate her so? What has she done to you? She's as good as alone in a new country; she has no family, no one to—"

"Aye, and there's the rub, husband."

"I don't follow."

"Because you don't want to. We talked about finding someone for Thomas from a good family."

"How d'you know we haven't?"

"You can defend her as much as you like, but you're her victim."

"Victim? Of what, for God's sake? If you mean I'm smitten, if that is what you are insinuating, you can stop."

"That's not what I mean, although you are and you are a fool for it."

Sir Geoffrey pushed back his chair, "Woman, you are talking riddles, and in this case I am not the one being foolish, you are. You should take more care with her. When I'm gone you'll have to step aside, because she'll be the lady of the house. Do you want her to someday treat you badly?"

"That won't happen," said Lady Marjorie, picking a piece of bacon gristle from between her teeth and wiping it onto the edge of her plate. "She'll never be a lady. She's no lady because she's not a proper woman. That's what all the gossip is about. Don't you have eyes in your head? Don't you ever listen to what's being said?"

Sir Geoffrey had reached the door to leave, he turned, "No, I told you, I never pay heed to gossip."

"McNab doesn't gossip."

Sir Geoffrey closed the door again. That was true: McNab barely said a full sentence twice a day. On occasions he reported labourers' misdemeanours, the odd theft, the sleeping in on harvest mornings, but McNab never told tales unnecessarily.

"What does McNab say?" he asked.

"She sleeps with Kate, not Thomas."

"Well, that'll be the boy's fault. I'll speak to him."

"It's not like that. McNab says she goes to Kate—like a husband."

Sir Geoffrey frowned, "Like a husband?"

"Oh for God's sake, Geoffrey, don't be so innocent. She's got you completely fooled. I said she'd never be a lady, because she's not a proper woman! Look how tall she is!"

"But she's got a woman's hair...."

"So has your precious king, wavy locks down to his waist I heard."

Sir Geoffrey shook his head. "No, no, no. In this you are very mistaken. If Alina goes to Kate's room at night it is because Thomas is not... I know Alina—I mean... I mean, you say I am smitten by her, well, that is true."

Slowly, he went up to his wife and stood behind her chair, putting his hands on her shoulders he bent to her ear.

"Marjorie, I have been faithful to you for more than thirty years. Not since I was at court—but that was different—it was years ago. We were younger then." He lowered his voice to a whisper, "But I've never been attracted to boys. I've never been tempted in that respect. Believe me; Alina is in every way, every inch a woman. Even at my age I recognize that. And yes, under other circumstances, I would get her into my *cold* bed if I could."

Keeping her eyes on her plate, Lady Marjorie said, "Not all of that is true. More people know about your private life down here—not in London—than you think. Farm folk like to gossip— especially about farmers' wives." She smoothed her bodice over her ample waist, gathered her skirts, began to rise, then sat down again as if an awful thought had occurred to her.

Sir Geoffrey waited for her to speak. "Well?" he asked.

"I was just thinking, once our Kate has gone—tonight— where that girl's night wanderings will take her? How much do you want a grandson, Geoffrey? You've as good as admitted you'll get her into your bed if you can."

Her tone was spiteful but Sir Geoffrey could see a genuine concern. He gave a wry smile. "Perhaps you should remember, my dear, it was you who set this whole business in motion. You've been nagging that boy for years about getting a wife. However, much as I would like to flatter myself, I regret you have nothing to fear."

Sir Geoffrey crossed the courtyard and took the path between the stables and the dairy, towards the hill. The grey and white local geese had returned to using the old lily pond, and were now spread across what had once been his mother's well-tended lawns like a flock of feathered sheep. There was plenty of forage for them both around and in the pond, which badly needed cleaning. He bent down to pull at some water weeds and felt the pain across his chest again.

"Is this what they call heartache?" he whispered to the green water.

A little wren bouncing among the thick leaves of the hedge caught his eye. "Is this pain because my dear Kate is leaving us again?" he asked her.

No, he said to himself, getting to his feet, *this is because of Thomas. Marjorie has misjudged the issue, it is not that Alina isn't a proper woman; it is that my son is not a proper man.* He felt tears well in his eyes and wiped them away with a shaking hand.

With heavy steps, Sir Geoffrey, a hereditary baronet born in direct line from a brave man knighted on a Plantagenet battlefield, made his way to the top of a low knoll. From here he could see the house and outbuildings known as Crimphele. His father's father had turned it from a Celtic fortress on the Cornish march into a family home. The Fulfords had kept their estate safe from land-hungry Saxons and Romans as well as

141

marauding fellow Cornishmen. They had lived through times of pestilence and famine, and father to son they had been true to their inheritance. But after Thomas it would all go to his wife's nephew, Percy. There was no other boy in the Fulford line. He had no brothers, not even a sister with a healthy son. If Kate produced a boy, God-willing, that would solve the problem, but Kate was in her thirties; it was too much to hope. No, the estate would all go to Marjorie's odious nephew Percy. Then it would be neglected, abandoned.

Percy would use his Crimphele income to live the high life because the title would finally give him access to the mincing fops and jack-a-dandies he aped. Percy had no sense of obligation. He would ignore the tenants and sell off the livestock and fields for ready cash. The house, too far from London and too expensive to maintain as a country-seat, would be sold or left to run to ruin. What would happen then to the families that depended on Crimphele for a roof and a regular wage? Who would provide for them, see they had a full pot in lean times?

He did not have the heart to go on. Lowering himself onto a dew-dampened tussock he rested his arms on his bony knees. Somewhere in the woods down by the old river a wood pigeon cooed to its mate, a jay screeched, a fat young cuckoo called from its foster nest. Sir Geoffrey bent his head and let himself cry like a baby.

Kate wandered along the cinder path arm in arm with Alina. It was a beautiful morning, so she had offered to open the main gate for the wedding guests with Alina as a means of getting them out of the house, while her mother spat at the servants and Crook-back Aggie stirred merry hell in the kitchen. There was plenty of time before she needed to start dressing for the ceremony; besides, she had Alina to help her. They might not be able to chat but they understood each other perfectly.

Kate squeezed her sister-in-law's arm in a moment of affection. "I'm going to miss you," she said. But, and she was ashamed of the thought, she was glad to be leaving.

Her new husband's home was near Looe, well away from Crimphele, well away from McNab. Having Alina in her room each night was comforting, but it also served to remind her of that which she would rather forget. Once she was married and in a Rundell household she would be safe, she could start again. That was what she had decided to do: start a new life and make it as good as her new husband would permit. It meant leaving Alina on her own, which was sad, but Alina was young, strong and independent, she would soon learn to cope.

As they returned from opening the gate, Kate noticed McNab cross from the barn towards his rooms in the servants' quarters over the stable block. From his rooms he could look down on the hall court from one window and observe this cinder path from the other. From the passage windows he could see the dairy and up to Paddon Hill. He knew who came and went in three directions—and what was happening in the house at all times. At any time, day and night—as she now realized—McNab knew exactly where the family were and what the servants were doing, or not doing. She had often pictured him as a large black spider suspended in his web, waiting. Now she saw him as the king of the castle.

As they reached the main house beside the stables, Kate shuddered and Alina hugged her close. A freckle-faced maid hurrying out of the dairy with a basket of eggs stopped in her tracks, and her jaw fell open.

"What is it, Meg?" asked Kate.

The girl didn't speak, just bobbed a curtsey and hurried back to the kitchen as fast as she could. Kate watched her go. Was Crook-back Aggie stirring up trouble for Alina? If she were, as like as not her mother was turning a blind eye, or encouraging it.

Walking on, Kate said, "When the time comes, Alina, I would sort out the kitchen arrangements in this house. You might be better off without Aggie, she's… a little… strange. Can't be easy with a twisted spine of course, but she can be difficult. I'd get her out of the house if you can. Get her into the creamery. No!" she began to laugh, "She'll curdle the milk and turn the cream. Find her something that's out of the house, well outside the house."

Alina smiled. Kate knew her sister-in-law had picked up the cook's name and knew the words 'milk' and 'cream' and 'house', but Kate feared the rest of what she had said was meaningless. Alina's vocabulary consisted of names and objects. It was so frustrating! She had never had a proper friend before, and she desperately wanted to confide in her new sister-in-law, to ask her about her home in Spain and how she had met Thomas. John Hawthorne had been particularly vague about that.

Kate sighed. Today this odd friendship would be over. She was to be married in the Crimphele chapel like Alina and Thomas, and then she would be gone. Except this wedding was not like their marriage. This time there were flowers everywhere around the house and baskets of petals to throw after the service. She had a beautiful ivory silk gown. Four dowry chests, containing much of what her first husband had provided, were being loaded onto carts at that moment. The thought reminded her that Alina had arrived with nothing more than the wine red gown she was presently wearing. She patted Alina's hand. "After I have gone, do remember that my father will help you. If, that is, you need help."

Alina smiled, but she did not seem to have understood.

John Hawthorne was in good spirits and conducted the service and Mass with confidence. Later, they ate duck and stuffed capons off silver plates, there were pies and puddings, candied fruits and sugar dainties, French burgundy and sweet Spanish wine, and everyone had an excellent time. The bridegroom, a genial, dapper man, was delighted with his bride, and the Rundell menfolk told jokes and laughed, and set the old great hall ringing for the first time in many years.

Sir Geoffrey knew he should have been glad; even his wife looked half-pleasing in peacock blue brocade. She'd actually laughed out loud with some wives at the table. Yes, it had all gone very well, but now it was time for Kate to go. The bridegroom was on his feet; his friends had already sneaked off to tie spoons and boots to the cart, no doubt. He got up and looked around for his son and daughter-in-law. Thomas had absented himself, and Alina was probably helping Kate with the travelling dress. A dog snuggled its head under his hand. "You'll do; come along," he said, and they wandered out to see what was going on in the courtyard.

It was another hour before Kate finally left, and most of the guests followed. Lady Marjorie settled in the family parlour, chatting with her sister. Sir Geoffrey cast around for a quiet place, then decided on his own chamber. As he climbed the wide, shallow stairs from the great hall, he remembered that he needed seltzer to settle his stomach, but he couldn't face going into the kitchen to ask for it. The stairs seemed steeper than usual. He began untying his cravat and removing his velvet jacket before he reached his door. Once inside, he threw the jacket onto his bed and slumped into his high-backed chair by the empty fireplace. He put his head against the wing of the chair and, being utterly exhausted, fell asleep.

One final grasping, searing pain seized him.

He was gone before he could open his eyes or speak another word.

Chapter Sixteen
Crimphele, June 1635

Crook-back Aggie began her campaign in earnest two days after Sir Geoffrey died. Everything changed on the day they found him, after little Meg had gone up for the morning slops and found him still asleep but not asleep in his chair. There was such a to-ing and fro-ing, such a sending of messengers here and there, such a to-do with the new Mistress Rundell coming back home, and the wedding guests that had barely reached their gates turning round and returning with condolences. Such a lot to cook for, and no way to be sure who'd be eating, such an awful lot of this and that she hadn't had a moment to gather her thoughts. On the second night, McNab surprised her by coming in to the kitchen to offer her a snifter of his Scotch whisky and a friendly word. He had been more sociable of late, that was true, but he was not one to waste words, so he had come with a purpose.

While they were chatting over who had been at the wedding and if they'd be at the funeral, and whether it would be a funeral befitting a knight of the realm or tucked away in the family chapel, it dawned on Crook-back Aggie that McNab was as nervous about his situation in the house as she was about hers. With Sir Geoffrey gone, they'd have to keep Lady Marjorie sweet or they'd both be at risk. Aggie was very aware that it had been her own failure to detect the direction of the wind that had sent the foreign girl here in the first place.

"You'll have to learn her lingo now, Aggie," McNab was saying. "You'll be taking orders in Es-pan-ole from now on. There'll be strange food and a different wine with every plate. I saw that in London when I was a footman; my old master dined with the Ambassador from Madrid. You never saw such a commotion of food. Six courses every sitting, even weekdays, everything on a separate plate. You won't be serving meat and veg on the same platter anymore. There'll be more washing up. You'll have Meg and Molly and young Clarice under your feet all day—every day."

McNab went on talking, but Crook-back Aggie was only half listening. She'd be taking orders from that saucy madam. But what option did she have? She couldn't leave; where would she go? Her mother had been glad to see the back of her: her brothers and sisters were still squabbling for sleeping room in the two-up-two-down tin miner's cottage.

Could she still rely on Lady Marjorie? She had as good as promised to protect her if—when—anyone accused her. Lady Marjorie understood: a woman as deformed as Aggie was always at risk.

If she hadn't got a proper home, and she had to sleep in the woods and beg a bite of food, people would lay all the crimes they could name on her. And prove them, too. It'd take just one girl to see her picking berries or herbs, just one girl who'd lost her beau, or one woman who'd miscarried; one woman who'd be expecting and see Aggie's crooked back and know her own child would be deformed—which was what had happened to her own mother—she'd be tried for a witch and burnt on the same day. No, there was no question of leaving. So she would have to hasten up what Lady Marjorie had already hinted at... and make herself indispensable at the same time.

Crook-back Aggie was not a chef, not a creative cook as befitted a noble family, that was true. She was not one to consider the senses—to play with a smidgen of saffron, a twist of nutmeg. Few foreign imports found their way into her pantry. Occasionally a stalk of wild garlic or a bunch of dry thyme might get stuffed up a bird's yellow arse, but, apart from chopping mint for a leg of mutton, she kept her herbs for more serious uses. She cooked plain food as per Lady Marjorie's orders and kept the kitchen budget modest.

No, Crook-back Aggie was not a chef such as you'd find in one the greater houses, but she had her strengths. She could wield a meat axe like a master butcher, strip and salt a pig in half a day, and spend the afternoon shoving its pink guts into its par-boiled intestines for sausages.

Making sausages was Aggie's one culinary joy. She'd stand at her work table, unconsciously shifting from one foot to another to ease her misshapen spine, and man-handle mushed-up raw meat mixed with stale bread and odd bits of offal that weren't fit for a dog's dinner into a pig's innards. And once she'd created yards of slippery pink sausage, she'd start her next favourite bit: strangulating this half-living umbilicus at regular intervals with a length of cord, separating it into three dozen or more separate life forms with quick twists of a knot and a sharp flick of her special little knife—a special little, clever little, sharp, sharp knife that she kept on her at all times, because you never knew when you might need a sliver of yew, a cutting of hemlock. As her bony fingers curled and shaped newborn sausages, the cord would tighten, the knife would snick, and plop, a slimy little creature left its maker to drop into a bucket. Then she would fetch her little dog from its sleeping place by the chimney or under the work table, cradle it into her arms and feed it the tastiest leftovers with her fingers. Finally, like a shriven soul, she would sit by her fire with her one true companion in her lap and rock herself into a doze.

For no reason other than her particular sixth sense, the tying of sausages came to Aggie's mind as she sat half-listening to McNab's hissing Scots burr.

"Don't they eat sausage in Spain then?" she asked.

"They do, but it's bright red and as full of spice as you can't taste nor see what you're eating. You'll have to get some of that red stuff in, they put it in everything."

"What is it?"

"Sort of pepper."

"Pepper! Pepper costs a fortune. Got to come all the way from the land of black fellers, and you never know who's had their hands on it. Lady Marjorie won't stand for that."

"Lady Marjorie won't have any choice, Aggie; she's the dowager now. We've got a new Lady Fulford, remember."

Crook-back Aggie slugged back the last of her whisky and pushed her cup towards the bottle. Keeping her eyes on the table top, she said, "Not necessarily."

"Ah," whispered McNab in a hushed voice, "Agnes, my dear, that's what I was hoping to hear." He refilled her cup and raised his own; looking into the cook's hooded brown eyes he said, "You shall be our saviour, Agnes, and I shall be your slave."

Crook-back Aggie waited until McNab had left the kitchen, then she very quietly climbed the service stairs to the first floor. From a linen press she took two face towels, then crossed the landing and went into Sir Thomas' room. She searched among the personal possessions on his bedside chest, but there was nothing that belonged to the foreigner there. No hairbrush with long, loose strands, no hair pins, nothing to show the Spanish miss was ever in the room for a moment. She opened his closet: two dresses, but they had once belonged to Miss Kate and she didn't want anything accidental happening to lovely Miss Kate. Without a sound, she left the room and went into Kate's bedroom. In the closet she found Alina's wine red dress. With her sharp little knife she cut three pearls from the bodice, then severed a piece of cloth from the torn hem. Tucking them into her pocket, she replaced used towels with clean and slipped back down to the kitchen unseen.

Chapter Seventeen

Alina sat on the warm stone wall and watched the last set of people drive away from the house. Crimphele had been as crowded as the Plymouth inn for days, which had its advantages: it was easier to escape. Thomas had also made use of the unusual circumstances to disappear, keeping to his private study since they'd returned from the funeral. At least she assumed he was there; she hadn't seen him anywhere in the garden, and thanks to the beautiful weather she managed to remain outdoors most of the day.

Being on her own was so much pleasanter; she was tired of trying to follow the gist of what people were saying, never being sure she was making the appropriate noises when they expected a response. And it was good to be out of Lady Marjorie's black gaze, even if it meant confronting McNab alone, something she dreaded with all her heart. One day he would get his revenge.

She waited until the gate-boy had closed the gate and was on his way up the hill to his parents' cottage, then wandered through the trees onto the path that led down to the river. Mistress Hawkins, the ferryman's wife, was passing from her small stone cottage to their ramshackle boathouse and beckoned eagerly to Alina the minute she saw her.

Snuggled into a bed of straw in a disused rowing boat were five pink-nosed, pink-bellied puppies. Ignoring the state of the dusty floor, Alina knelt at the side of the boat and picked up two, cuddling them under her chin. They smelled of sweet straw and warmth, and were adorable.

Mistress Hawkins chattered on—about the pups Alina assumed—but it soon became too complicated for both of them, so she got to her feet and said goodbye as best she could, and continued on her way.

Alina strode on up the river path to the Tamstock entrance to the house, then, on a whim, walked on until she was right above Crimphele and out in the pastures. Big red cows, like the ones she'd seen on their way to milking the evening she had arrived at Crimphele, followed her with suspicious eyes as she crossed their field. A few late lambs skittered away when she jumped down from a stile.

Enjoying the wind in her hair and the sense of freedom, she climbed on up to the more rocky barren area they called Paddon Hill. A grass snake sidled away into a crevice between some boulders, escaping from her or the hawk she'd noticed overhead. From here, she cut across the brow of the hill, and in the middle of a wide space of rabbit-grazed grass she found a series of strange standing stones, not a row or a square or a circle, but clearly organized by man into a group. She ran a hand over one, wondering if it marked a grave. Something about the stones made her shiver, and she wandered on until she saw a wall and something else that said men, women and children had once lived here.

Standing a little below head height was a carved stone: a wide, wheel-like circle intercut with a thick, box-like cross. Someone had scored a pattern in the turf beneath it. Kneeling, she traced a circle with a finger: a dried twig was caught in the grass. For a while she sat by the cross, studying its strange carving. A robin hopped from nowhere onto the lichened stone and chattered a warning: this was his territory, she didn't belong. Sighing, Alina got to her feet, shook her skirt around her naked legs and set off back the way she had come.

After re-crossing the cow-pasture though, she delayed the inevitable a little longer, settling herself on a low stone wall to look at the view. She could see right down to the mouth of the estuary, to where the sea went all the way to Spain.

Alina turned back to look at the cows and bit her lips. What had she done? What did she think she was doing, playing the princess in a stranger's castle? Was she ever going to fit in and become part of the family? No. And not just because she was from a different country; she was different altogether. These people were so staid, so... she searched for a word to describe their quiet way of life, the way they each went about their business and made dull conversation during meals. There was no shouting or calling of names, no rushing about, no scraped knees and tears. She could not imagine Sir Geoffrey had ever slapped his knee and roared at a joke, and he had surely never needed to pull off his belt and thrash Thomas the way her father did with the boys.

The boys—her brothers—what were they doing now? Hiding from their tutor; balancing a bucket of water over their study door, torturing kittens? Or were they chasing hens to get feathers for arrows?

A movement below caught her eye. Lady Marjorie was walking between the dairy and the back entrance to the servants' quarters. Now she was stopping at the steps that led to McNab's quarters. She disappeared from view. Lady Marjorie, miserable woman. And what had she got to be so miserable about? A fine house, a nice husband—well, no, not anymore. Poor Sir Geoffrey, he had been a good person. She was going to miss him. If she stayed. Alina looked back at the distant sea. If she stayed.

Where was Ludo now? He'd said he'd come. Promised he'd come. Why didn't he suddenly arrive and rescue her the way he had in Santander? Lift her up in his arms and rush her down to a waiting ship.... She felt tears prick at her eyes. At this moment she'd even run off with Marcos. Then she remembered Marcos's voice: *Do you know what's going on?* Yes and no, she now admitted to herself; yes, and mostly no.

Perhaps she should just leave, go on her own. But if she had learned one sensible thing in the past few months, it was not to act on impulse. Leaving, unaccompanied, was not an option. A woman on her own with no money or luggage was asking for trouble on a Plymouth wharf. What might a skipper demand for a crossing to Santander in his fishing boat? That was easy to answer. No, she had to wait until someone could take her, or at least she had a proper servant and enough cash to give her credence.

Alina waited a little longer and then slowly wound her way down the path that led into the old knot garden. As she opened the gate into the grounds she stopped and looked at her hand. The skin was softer now, and a plain gold band said she was Sir Thomas Fulford's wife: *Lady* Alina. She gave a heavy sigh; perhaps she should stay and make the best of it. Perhaps if she tried to talk to Thomas, if she found a way to make him understand her, he might find a way to make life easier.

With renewed energy, Alina headed for the great hall door and ran up the stairs of the Tudor tower.

Thomas was sitting in his high-backed tapestry chair, his hands gripping the carved wood at his side; a small book had dropped to the floor. He neither moved nor spoke when she entered.

"Thomas?" Alina sat down in the chair on the other side of the hearth. "Are you well?"

He looked towards her, his eyes glistening. He was crying. Alina dropped to her knees beside his chair and stroked his arm. He lifted his arm and put it around her shoulders, pulling her closer to him. She adjusted her position to lean over the arm of the chair. Softly, he stroked her long, wavy hair. They stayed for some time like this until he said, "I'm sorry. I'm so sorry for what we did, Alina. It was wrong. But you see I wanted you so much and—and I wanted to please Father. Now you are here and I don't know how to talk to you, how to act, what to say. I'm sorry. I am a very bad husband," he paused and added, "and the worst sort of son."

Alina let him talk on. He stroked her hair, gradually pushing it away from the lace collar of her dress, then he leaned over and kissed the nape of her neck. She looked up and they kissed for the first time.

Thomas dropped onto the floor beside her and held her close to him, and they kissed with passion. His hand sought her breasts and she undid the laces on her bodice, and there on the red Turkish rug before an empty fireplace they made love for their first time—like uncertain, anxious lovers, and then as two people who belong to each other.

Much later, after they had taken a frugal supper in silence in Thomas' room and had climbed into his high bed for the night, they made love again as husband and wife.

As the full summer moon showed its jolly farmer face through the thick-leaded panes of an inland facing window, they laughed and cuddled and snuggled, and then Alina started to cry, because it was all such a relief; she was going to be all right. Sir Geoffrey had gone but he had left her a legacy.

Lady Marjorie noticed the difference immediately. Alina and Thomas grinned at each other across the breakfast table. Her lips set like the clasp of her purse.

"Well, Mother," Thomas said, catching her expression, "I suppose I had better make the arrangements for the day now. First, I shall send to Radcliffe regarding the reading of the will. Do you need me to do anything specific?"

Lady Marjorie straightened her back and folded her hands on the table in front of her as if in prayer. It had come sooner than expected, but she was ready.

"Thomas, I have been running this house for thirty years. I see no reason to change the arrangement. Your father followed his whim regarding the estate and Home Farm; if you have any doubts or requests in that respect speak to McNab. He is more than competent, and knows far more than you ever will about management and husbandry. McNab will make sure we always have enough to cover our obligations." She sniffed and forced a smile, "You two run off and enjoy the day together. I'll see to what is needed."

Thomas looked first at Alina, then at his mother. "But...."

"No buts, my dear, off you go and carry on with your studies, or whatever it is you get up to in that library of yours. Let's be frank, Alina is never going to be able to run this house, let alone talk to tradesmen. I'll just continue with the housekeeping, it's what I know all about. Off you go." She waved a hand of dismissal.

Alina looked up at her husband. Lady Marjorie tried to gauge how much the hussy had been able to follow. Not everything, but tone should have told her what was what. She waited, wondering if the girl dared to challenge her, make a stand.

"*Ella va a ganar,*" Alina muttered in Spanish.

Thomas nodded as if comprehending, then shrugged his narrow shoulders in defeat.

Lady Marjorie picked up her advantage. "Send to Radcliffe as you wish, or ride over yourself, if that's what you want. You don't need to worry about anything here. I can manage perfectly well."

"As you wish, Mother, but you don't have to, you know. We are going to have to start sooner or later."

"Later, Thomas. Right now we have to clear up after a wedding and a funeral. I need to see to the books and discuss what stock needs ordering with Agnes. Really, I am far too busy at the moment to even contemplate teaching Arleen anything." She got to her feet as if to go.

"Arleen?" Thomas repeated.

"Yes, I think it sounds more English, don't you? Like Eileen or Elaine. Perhaps you might think about having her re-baptised, if she ever was. Nothing wrong with Sarah or Jane: Josephine perhaps. She looks like a Josephine, or we can just call her Arleen, that's close enough."

"Mother, what are you talking about?" Thomas' voice rose with indignation.

"I'm talking about what I want here, now your father has gone."

"What's that got to do with Alina's name?"

"If she's going to stay, I think you should try and make her more normal. She looks too... scandalous. It has to be said,

Thomas. She does not look like a fit person to run a prestigious great house such as this."

"Prestigious! Great! Mother, this is a country estate three weeks distant from London. What on earth is great about Crimphele?"

"We are. We are great. And that wench has no place here. Look at her—all that hair!"

Thomas grabbed Alina's hand and pulled her to him.

"Alina is my wife, legally married to me in the chapel of this *great* house. If you want to wear yourself out playing the housekeeper so be it. But she is staying, and you had better start being nice to her. Alina is Lady Fulford now."

He stormed out of the parlour, pulling Alina in his wake.

"Over my dead body," retorted Lady Marjorie to the open door, "and not a day sooner."

She sat down to get her breath back then screamed, "Agnes!"

Little Meg, who had been hovering outside the door to remove the breakfast plates, scuttled off to get the cook.

Lady Marjorie unclipped the huge bunch of keys at her waist and put them on the table. While she waited for Crook-back Aggie she counted them: twenty-three. There would be more as soon as she annexed those her husband used to carry.

The cook put her low-browed forehead around the door. "You called me, your ladyship?"

"I did. Come in and close the door."

Chapter Eighteen
Crimphele, August 1635

Alina walked down what had become one of her favourite paths from Paddon Hill and entered Crimphele's grounds via the upper gardens. It was really hot now, and she was anxious to get back into the cool house. As she passed through the gate, though, the angry hissing and honking of geese made her pause and consider finding another way in. She caught a glimpse of russet as a fox shot through the open gate, almost brushing her skirts.

"You cheeky thing!" she said out loud and started to laugh, then stopped as the fox's stink reached her. She scrabbled in a pocket for a handkerchief. With the fine lawn square tucked up against her nose, and keeping her head down for fear of attack, she bravely hurried past the geese; but as she approached the dairy and creamery the smell of warm milk and cheese penetrated the handkerchief, making her want to gag again. Hastily, she retraced her steps and took the side path round the old tower to enter the house through the kitchen.

As she stepped into the dull light, Crook-back Aggie and Meg stopped in their respective tasks and stared at her. Suddenly, Aggie was all over her.

"My, you look done in, milady. Take a seat and a sip of barley water. It's too hot to be out today. T'aint normal, this weather, too hot for us folk. 'Spec it's all right for you, though, like your country. Hot all the time there, they tells me."

The grotesque little woman fussed around with a cup and a jug, chattering constantly. The cup was placed on the rough work table and Alina drank the refreshing liquid gratefully. As she did so the cook remained standing behind her.

"Everyone black as coal in Spain, they tell me. Our Robert went there once. All the girls got hair like crows, he said. 'Cept you haven't, have you, milady? Yours is like gold, not like an old crow's wing at all, I'd say."

Alina felt her skin crawl as the woman put her hand into her hair. She jerked her head away and caught Meg's grin. Leaning across the table, she refilled her cup, "Thank you, this is nice," she said carefully.

Crook-back Aggie didn't move. "What you gawpin' at, girl?" she said to Meg.

"Nothing, Aggie, nothing." Meg turned back to the dough she was kneading, keeping her eyes low.

In the ensuing silence Alina felt Crook-back Aggie watching her, as if waiting for something. She placed her empty cup on the table, but as she turned to leave she distinctly saw Aggie make a quick winding motion with her claw-like yellow forefingers. Alina shuddered, realising the cook had pulled hair from her scalp. Swallowing a shriek of horror, she left the kitchen and hastened up the back stairs as fast as she could.

Up in the room she now shared with Thomas, Alina began to undress, hot and sweaty from her walk and the unnatural encounter below. Her breasts were getting larger, even the two gowns that had been made for her had become too tight. Thomas hadn't noticed, or at least he hadn't said anything. She wanted to tell him, but suppose she were wrong? She had grown up in a household of men; she'd never had a woman to tell her about these things. Kate was the only person that might be able to advise her, reassure her that what was happening to her body was normal, but Kate was miles away.

Thomas had left one of his books on his chair. She picked it up and turned the stiff pages. It was in English, not Latin as many books in his collection were; it was something about a King Arthur. Here was another reason she didn't want to tell Thomas yet. He might use her pregnancy as an excuse to return to his old life. He would go back to spending hours in his library; perhaps he would send her back to Kate's chamber. Then she would be alone again—and vulnerable—as Kate had been.

Alina walked over to the window and looked out at the hillside. McNab was striding down in his characteristic disjointed manner, his greyhound at his heels as always. Her brothers would have made fun of him, but she saw nothing to laugh at. There was something of the scorpion about McNab— his angular limbs and unusual height, his drab brown and black clothes, his colourless eyes—something that said *Beware* that would have made her wary even had she not intercepted the dreadful incident with Kate.

As he opened the gate into the knot garden he looked up at the house: Alina automatically stepped back and put a hand protectively over her belly. Had McNab followed her up the hill and waited until she was back indoors to return?

"*Dios ayúdame*," she whispered out loud.

Suddenly she wanted to be free of the babe inside her, to run downstairs, out of the door and keep on running until she reached the river and a boat that would take her back home. With the child, she was trapped. There would be no escape after it was born. On the other hand—Alina paused and considered an alternative point of view—a healthy child would put her in a stronger position. At the very least, the servants would have to treat her with more respect. She shuddered at the thought of Crook-back Aggie's fingers in her hair.

Checking first to see McNab was out of sight, Alina sat down in her shift on the window seat and opened the small book she'd picked up. King Arthur had a queen called Guinevere. They lived in a castle named Camelot. Alina began to smile; she could understand most of the words on the first page.

For a while, Alina tried to read the little book, then she dozed and woke up feeling very thirsty. She pulled her dress back on and went down to the parlour. Thomas and his mother were facing each other across the table: their attitude told her it was another disagreement.

"Ah, just the person we were talking about," said Thomas. "Come and sit down." He got up and pulled out a chair so Alina could sit beside him. His face was very flushed. "Mother is going to Tavistock to visit her sister. Do you want to go?"

Alina thought she understood. "All right," she said.

Thomas raised his eyebrows in surprise. "You would rather go off to Tavistock in this heat than stay here with me?"

Alina looked between mother and son and frowned. "If you stay here, I stay with you."

"That's what I said." Thomas reached for her hand on the table.

Lady Marjorie sniffed loudly, "I'm not leaving her here without me. If I go, she comes too. Besides, my sister will be glad to have her; she can get to know Percy."

Still holding Alina's hand, Thomas gave an ironic laugh. "Get to know Percy! Who wants to know that creature?"

"Don't you dare be rude about my family!"

"Well, it doesn't matter. When are you going? Tomorrow?"

"*We* shall go the day after tomorrow; I have to make arrangements for my absence first."

"Why? Is there some great secret to housekeeping?"

Lady Marjorie went white, but Thomas didn't give her a chance to speak. "What is it you're afraid of, Mother? That Alina might take over as queen of the castle while you are away? That you might get back to find she's managed perfectly well?"

"Arleen—"

"Alina. Her name is Alina or Angelina, if you prefer."

"Angelina! That's a doll's name if ever I heard one. We'll call her Arleen—" But Lady Marjorie wasn't able to finish her sentence.

Alina pulled her hand away from her husband. "Maria de los Angeles. That is my name. Call me Maria de los Angeles."

She was angry. They were arguing about her, deciding her life for her and not consulting her. Treating her like a small child or a servant. They decided what she would do, what she should eat, what she would wear. She stood up so quickly her chair toppled backwards, hitting the sideboard behind her and knocking a decanter of wine on its side so its ruby contents spilled over the floor.

"See! See what a clumsy bitch she is!" Lady Marjorie screamed. "I'm not leaving her alone in this house for ten minutes. That was a wedding gift to me from my father!"

Alina turned to look at her mother-in-law. Without averting her eyes, she reached out behind her and with a long sweep of an outstretched arm swept the decanter and all the glasses off the sideboard onto the floor. Then she leaned over the table and said in Spanish, "I live here. I make decisions about my life, and if I want to break every piece of your precious crystal I can, because *I* am Lady Fulford now, not you!"

Thomas jumped to his feet. "Alina, stop," he said.

But it was a plea, not a command.

Two hours later, Meg was bouncing down the service stairs like a child on Christmas morning, "Aggie! Aggie!" she hissed before her feet touched the kitchen flagstones. "She's expectin'!"

Crook-back Aggie didn't pause. She rolled a thick wooden rolling pin once to the left over a circle of raw pastry; once to the right, then once to the left again before she looked up.

Meg had her pinafore bunched in her hands and her freckles were alive with the news. "The Spanish woman, she's expectin'!" she repeated.

"I heard you," said Aggie, never taking her hooded eyes from her pie crust.

Deflated, Meg dropped her pinafore and collected a soft broom from the scullery to sweep flour dust from around the kitchen table.

"I thought you'd be interested," she muttered, confused and disconcerted by the grim line of Aggie's thin lips.

After a few moments, the misshapen cook said, "I'll need more eggs. Get yourself off to the dairy. We'll need a quart of cream and some more butter as well."

"Yes, Aggie," replied Meg dully and left the kitchen.

"Meg! Come back, you've forgot the basket. Where's your head, girl? It's only a baby."

Meg collected the provision basket from the scullery and came back to the outside door, "But it'll change everything here, won't it?"

Aggie lifted her grey pastry over an oval dish. "Don't see why," she said, and began to slice excess dough from around the rim with her sharp little knife.

She waited a good minute to be sure the maid didn't return, then wiped the knife on her skirt and laid it on the work surface. From a pocket she retrieved a large wooden clothes peg wrapped in red fabric. Slowly, taking great care not to break the thread, she unwound a strand of golden hair from its neck. Once she had it free she laid it flat on her floured table and carefully pulled the cloth from the peg's forked legs. She placed that on the floured board beside the single strand of hair, then she dragged her forefinger through a pot of soft butter and rubbed it between the forked legs. After that she put down the peg and picked up a small lump of raw dough; she rolled it into a ball between her fingers and laid it on the red cloth. Finally, she lifted the peg, and with a sharp finger nail eased a fat pin from its body, then moulded the dough over the tiny pin hole, sculpting it into a protruding foetus. For a moment she stared at her creation, then placed it on the cloth. Using the pin, she created a red fabric skirt to cover the wooden legs.

Holding the pregnant peg-doll in her hands, she blew into its face, she blew into the pastry belly; she turned it over and blew life up into the skirt. Then she let out a deep sigh. "Don't let it be too late," she muttered, and carefully placed the pregnant effigy back in her pocket.

Meg was right, of course, it would change everything. Between finger and thumb she picked the strand of hair from the flour. It had been round the peg-woman's neck for some time, and it was a potent winding charm. Suddenly Aggie laughed. "She's got life in her, that one. She's as strong as she looks."

Then she stopped and felt a chill run through her. She had to reverse the charm immediately. But how? If she put it on the cooking fire and burnt it, it might work faster—cause a fever—with drastic results.

"What shall we do, Perkin?" she said to her little dog under the table.

Still holding the strand of hair between finger and thumb, she sat down in the kitchen rocker and beckoned the wire-haired mongrel onto her lap. Once he was curled into a fat ball in her pinafore, she went on, "We've got to think. We'll have to watch our step now. If it's a boy she'll be the boss within a year. Then where are we with her ladyship and McNab? We got to act clever. Keep 'em all sweet till we know what's what."

With her spare hand Aggie stroked the rough fur of the mongrel on her lap. Looking down, she watched her fingers push through the creature's hair up against its head and back down towards the stump of its tail.

"So that's it, then. That's what you think: put 'em back, eh? And how do I put three bits of hair back on someone's head, Perkin, tell me that."

Tipping the dog back onto the floor, Aggie got up and went into her large pantry. On a high shelf, just within reach, was an earthenware pickle jar. She lifted it down with two hands and set it on a marble slab between the butter dish and the half-made pie, then poked her fingers into the vinegar and fished about among bits of carrots and slippery silver onions until, one by one, she located the second and third strands of hair. The sharp smell made her catch her breath: this charm was to tighten the stomach and provoke sickness. A dreadful thought brought Crook-back Aggie to a halt. Suppose that stupid maid Meg had just seen the woman vomiting and come to a conclusion. The charm could be working!

"Meg!" she hollered, dashing out of the pantry, "Meg, get back here this minute!"

Aggie was greasing pie dishes when the girl, hot from the weather and flushed from a few kisses with Toby in the creamery, wandered back into the kitchen.

With a voice like winter wind, Crook-back Aggie said, "How d'you know?"

Meg looked confused. "What, about the Spanish woman?"

Aggie nodded.

"I heard her telling the master. They was cuddling like two love-pigeons and he was saying 'clever girl' over an' over."

"Clever girl? She'll have to be now."

"It's a pity Sir Geoffrey isn't here no more. What d'you think Lady Marjorie will say? D'you think she'll be pleased?"

"That's none of our business."

Young Meg hugged the heavy basket to her and said slowly, "Ah no? Well I reckon it is. When you think about what she's—"

"Put that basket down, beat me two of they there eggs in milk and stop your blatherin', child."

Crook-back Aggie spooned sharp apples and seedy black currants into the pie dishes, then criss-crossed them with lattices of dough, all in silence. Meg mixed the eggs and milk, handed the bowl to Aggie, then skipped back to the creamery before she could be given anything else to do. Aggie poured the egg mixture over the pies, set them in the bake oven, then went to stand by the kitchen door for some air.

A blackbird rattled off a chirp of song and drowsy sparrows hopped around tepid rainwater gathered in the long dead fountain. She looked out over the kitchen garden and down towards the river. In not so many years' time she'd be an old woman in poor health. Like as not they'd send her away when she wasn't any use to them, earlier if they turned against her. She'd have to take extra care now; Lady Marjorie wasn't going to last forever—and the girl was not going to leave.

"Ah," she sighed, looking down at her little dog, "I'm a foolish old crone. You can't go against a wind. You have to make the best of what it sends."

Perkin snuffled and waddled round her to cock his leg against the door jamb.

"Better hope we aren't too late, that's all, boy," she said as he rolled in the gravel at her feet, wiggling his paws in the air for her to rub his fat tum.

McNab filled his pipe and sat down by the open casement. Evening birdsong filled the air, but his mood was too dark to take pleasure in it. She was with child. She had been too 'quick' for him. He drew in the tobacco and exhaled. His plan would have to wait a year. He owed the old master that. Sir Geoffrey had taken him in, set him up and valued his skills when others had pursued him for what he believed was right. For what he *knew* was right—and the other things they said he'd done.

Well, there was truth in what they'd said, not that he had suffered any remorse. Women like that deserved what they got. They were dirty. They spread their evil and disease just as fast as they spread their legs. Women like that *had* to be stopped. His accusers should be thanking him, not trying to punish him.

He sucked on his pipe and gazed out at nothing in particular, determined he wasn't going to let that old business worry him down here in Cornwall. He'd outwitted everyone so far. Tucked away in this valley, no one knew anything about what was happening in London, or anywhere else for that matter. People of consequence—like Sir Geoffrey and Lady Marjorie—either hadn't heard or hadn't connected the Crimphele steward with the dreadful tales circulating up country. No, all things considered, he owed it to his late employer to let the bairn live. Sir Geoffrey had never treated him other than as a loyal servant and an efficient steward. He'd seen his true worth and kept him on in a permanent position despite having no references. *Crimphele will be your home for as long as you choose to stay, McNab,* that's what he'd said.

But if that foreign flibbertigibbet told on him about Miss Kate, even Lady Marjorie might turn him out. Kate wouldn't say anything herself, of course, she wouldn't want her new husband to know—he'd taken enough risks marrying a widow, a woman with sexual experience; if she mentioned a word about what had happened that night she'd be on the rubbish heap. An experienced woman who'd already been married was one thing; a lusty widow who pleasured men beneath her station was another. No, Kate's situation protected him there. But this one, this Spanish tart, wasn't scared. When he looked at her she looked straight back. She'd have to go.

But she was carrying Sir Thomas' child—or the master's—so he couldn't harm the babe. As soon as they found her a wet nurse though, she could disappear. As soon as she'd finished the lying-in she'd be back up her path to Paddon Hill and lose her footing....

He would act as soon as she was out of her chamber, because if the child was a boy she'd be queen, and she'd have him out with no reference—again. He couldn't risk that.

McNab tapped the bowl of his pipe on the stone sill, then closed the window against the evening chill and prying eyes, conscious of having come to a decision. Lady Marjorie was still in charge, but it wouldn't last. He had to assume the foreign woman was going to take over, and that had to be prevented.

It wouldn't be difficult to manage. People would think she'd run off home, or fallen in the river. Falling in the river could easily be arranged. It would upset Sir Thomas for a day or two maybe, but he'd have the child.

One year. In one year's time he'd be safe. No need to worry about finding a new employer, answering awkward questions, being recognized, remembered or discovered. He'd stay safe at Crimphele, safe from the outside world. He flexed his bony hands: a year to the day. Time enough to create a faultless plan. Stealth and a strategy based on close knowledge of the prey: that's what his father, the best gamekeeper in Scotland, had taught him.

Learn your catch, laddie, his father used to say. *Learn your catch.*

This was the best part, the stalking.

Chapter Nineteen
Amsterdam, September 1635

Brother Caritas put his hands on the uneven stone floor of the side chapel, tried to lift himself from his knees, caught a foot in the front of his robe and nearly fell flat.

"*Mierda*," he said.

For a moment he rested on all fours like a soulless beast and looked about for a witness to his indignity. Tall saints, stone-faced in their own agony and anguish, gazed down on him, but not with pity.

"Madonna," he sighed, stretching his jowled chin towards the high roof, "why so many trials? Truly, I am suffering in mind and body. This climate is terrible. Did you send me here for rheumatics and the ague? Am I being punished for the comforts of Seville?"

Slowly, he closed the gate to the chapel. "I'm too old for this," he muttered, "too old, and too infirm of purpose. Hear me, I admit it. Tell him to find a younger man."

He set off down the side aisle towards the main door, mumbling all the while. "A man alive with the fires of certainty, that's who You need.... From now on I'm going to pray like a Dutchman, on my feet... body *and* spirit too weak. In Your mercy release me from this business... let me stay in a quiet monastery. I could keep the slugs off the lettuces, plant trees. That's what I'd like to do. Somewhere with orange trees, somewhere sunny and warm."

Realizing he had raised his voice, Brother Caritas turned to see who might have heard. For a full minute he stood facing the empty church. "There you are, You see?" he muttered under his breath, "I've been trying to tell You, this is no place for us—not anymore. Money grubbers, the lot of them. Babylon dressed in drab...."

The aging friar continued his imprecations against the Dutch climate, frugality and hypocrisy, the Dutch diet, especially bland, soft cheese, as he wandered down the nave of the vast church. By the time he reached the main door he had run out of complaints. He turned back towards the altar and forced his aching knees to bend again. "Forgive me, Madonna," he whispered, then struggled out into sleeting autumnal rain.

A cart piled high with plague victims rumbled by. Brother Caritas made the sign of the Trinity, uttered a rapid prayer for lost souls, then, pushing his thick fingers into his sleeves set, off in the same direction as the cart. Not to offer the dead Last Rights but to meet a tall man from Rome, whom he had lately come to think of as *La Bicha*—the serpent.

As Brother Caritas made his way along the narrow streets below, Elsa vander Woude stood in the doorway of her salon, beaming with pleasure. The room was alive with chatter as animated figures shifted from one coterie to another. Heads bent briefly together in whispers, then separated in knowing nods. An argument broke out by the chimney piece: *guilders, offsets, two whole beds....* A third party intervened as arbiter; voices became hushed but remained insistent.

Tulips, tulips: tulips by the names of admirals and generals, gaudy coloured blooms named after sober towns, everyone was talking tulips. And in her salon! Elsa sighed with satisfaction: such changes, such fun.

Josie and Greit circulated with jugs of ale and sweet sack. It was becoming very stuffy; Elsa moved round the edge of the room to open the window, then stood for a moment with her hands on the low sill, looking out at the autumn night. Ludovico had stood just here a few short months ago and set her new life in motion. She raised a plump hand to her throat and rolled a black pearl button between finger and thumb. *A hand passed over her breast, lips kissed her neck....* She gave a shudder of delight and brought herself back to the present. It kept happening, this physical memory. No matter how busy she kept herself, how tired she was when she went to bed, the shameless act of love with the Italian haunted her.

But these same wicked thoughts served also as a spur. Memories of that night in spring, and the unspoken promises she believed, had urged her into buying and selling on a scale she could never have imagined. Just this week she had speculated on a whole bed of *bizarden* tulips owned by a Haarlem florist. And her enthusiasm, her physical drive, had impelled Paul Henning into the speculator's market, too. He was already trading on the bulbs just in the ground and not to be lifted until after they bloomed in March, April or May. It was gambling, of course, and that had held him back at first, but he was as much a part of the new tulip trade as she was now, and making an excellent living. Good Paul Henning with a proper bank account: a fine, safe account of new money in one of the new Amsterdam banks. His wife, Marie, was out of her sickbed, his children all had sturdy shoes, and they had even hired a girl to do the chores. Once the worst of the winter was over they would be looking for a new home, something larger, more appropriate to his rising status. And here he was mixing as an equal in his late employer's salon with his wife and other gentlemen and their wives, all enjoying fruit punch and sweet wine, and celebrating a good year's trading. Such changes! Such *good* changes, bringing benefit to all.

Elsa turned her back to the window and sought out her late husband's loyal clerk. Paul Henning was not mingling as she had imagined; he was standing at the far side of the room observing what was going on around him, a very serious look on his face. Stopping for a polite word here and there, Elsa crossed the room to stand beside him.

"Henning, my dear, why so glum?"

"Glum? No, not glum, *Me'vrouw.*"

"Then what are you thinking? Dark thoughts, I fear, but I cannot see why."

"Forgive me. I feel a little out of place here. I was not raised to mix with the rich."

"Neither you, nor many here. Look, there's Matthias Brants, he's a butcher. Martin Joos, a fishmonger last week, now he tells me he has bought his own boat, which changes his status for the good. Look over there. Those two lawyers and dear Doctor Kreft are talking with—well, I don't quite know who, but you can see from the way he holds himself he wasn't raised a gentleman, either." Elsa caught herself and gushed on to cover her foolish words. "That's Kreft's son come to join them. See, professional status is all one here. Tulips are a great leveller, Henning. Don't feel ill at ease."

"No, I am not... how shall I say, awed by the company; it is only that I have never had the opportunity to mix like this. I wasn't educated for salons and soirées."

"Then you had better get used to them. Your girls should marry well. Take the opportunity to make contacts. Good connections are always useful. Think of your little Pauli. He must have a university education and a professional career so one of these fine gentlemen here tonight can take him into their practice. Think of that. You can afford it after this year. You'll set them all up...." She turned to him, eager to see the pleasure in his face, but was disappointed. "You're going to be a rich man, Henning. It's so much easier now we don't actually have to have the bulbs in our hands to sell them. D'you know, last week I sold a whole bed of tulips—the ones I bought near Haarlem last spring for—well, for an awful lot more than I paid, and they were already in the ground. The whole transaction took two pieces of paper. It wouldn't surprise me if that same bed of flowers doesn't get passed on at a tremendous profit four, five times before spring!"

"That's what worries me, *Me'vrouw*. To be honest, it is exactly that which worries me. If you—we—are buying and selling without seeing the product—well, anyone can cheat us.

Tell us they've got a bed of purple on white and when they're lifted they're just plain red or yellow. And buying bulbs and off-sets according to goldsmiths' weights doesn't seem to make much sense either. Since when was a big winter potato any better quality than a small, floury summer root? Something here is not right, *Me'vrouw*."

"Oh, you Doubting Thomas! You Jonah!" Bending her head to the concerned man Elsa whispered, "Does it matter? I mean, we've got some lovely flowers already, we know they are safe and right; what harm can a little speculating do?"

Paul Henning did not reply. Then quietly he said, "*Me'vrouw*, I was raised to understand that the respectable working man worked hard to keep his place. What I fear is not that I will fail to get rich, but that I will lose what little I have. Security is all. If you will forgive me saying, it was your late husband's motto, was it not?"

Elsa did not reply; she was not listening. Paul Henning smiled cautiously and Elsa vander Woude went on spinning an elaborate future for his family.

Above the hum of voices and laughter there was the distant clanging of the plague bell and the terribly familiar call, "Bring out your dead."

"Death is also a great leveller," Paul Henning murmured, turning back to speak to the *Me'vrouw*, but her attention was entirely elsewhere. A well-known member of the Stock Exchange had just entered, followed by a blond youth wearing excessively frilly collar and cuffs.

Ignoring Henning, Elsa made her way back across the crowded room to greet the newcomers. Again, she was obliged to stop for a few words here and there, so by the time she reached the door the stockbroker and his young companion were already in separate conversations. Moving towards the young man to discover his identity, she intercepted a wink aimed at her serving girl, Greit. Who was this? And what was he doing in this company? He was nothing more than an over-dressed boy with a silky yellow moustache.

Brother Caritas concluded his brief meeting with the man from Rome and set out for Paul Henning's small home as instructed. It had stopped raining, but the weight of his soaked habit seemed to bend his back. The old lady came to the door, a child nearly as big as herself clutched to her like a sack of potatoes. She had obviously tried to open the door with one hand, for when Brother Caritas saw her the child was sliding down her slight frame and would have landed on the floor with a thud had he not caught him. They shouldn't have left her on her own; she wasn't safe with—how many children? He'd been told to call at this moment because Paul Henning had taken his wife to the vander Woude supper party. He hadn't liked the arrangement, or what he was obliged to do next.

Without a word he closed the door against the damp night and followed the elderly woman into the tiny living room. There was a surprisingly pretty and obviously expensive child's cot in the corner, its slats carefully rounded, the headboard painted like a Delft tile with a boy and girl in clogs holding a bunch of flowers between them, and so new he could smell the varnish. He lifted the heavy baby up over the side and sat him on the soft mattress. The child looked up in annoyance and started to howl.

The friar popped his grubby forefinger in its round mouth. "No, no, little man. You be quiet, I need to talk to your grandmother."

The baby grabbed the hand that was acting as a dam and pulled back, his mouth now forming a gummy grin. Brother Caritas was captive. He sighed: this was going to be harder than he had feared.

He was saved by a small girl, who came trotting through the back doorway with a rag doll and a stick of liquorice. She was followed by her two older sisters, each with a sticky black mouth.

"Just what we need," said the friar. "Will one of you charming girls share a little of your liquorice stick with...." He tried to remove his hand without success.

The eldest said, "He's got you trapped."

"Oh, yes."

"He's always doing that. Sometimes he hurts."

"Yes, indeed, a very strong boy."

"He didn't use to be," piped up the middle girl, "he was like a bag of sticks when he was born."

"And what has helped him grow so well?"

"Cream. He likes cream."

"Pauli can eat cakes now," the youngest girl informed him, passing her liquorice through the slats of the cot.

Pauli grabbed the sweet-tasting stick and pushed it straight into his mouth. Released, Brother Caritas stepped back and rubbed his hands up and down the small of his back.

The youngest girl watched him, a serious look on her face. "Who are you?" she demanded.

He was about to speak but the eldest said, "Don't be rude, Tessa, it's the priest come for Grandma."

"Yes, yes, I am Brother...." He turned to look for the grandmother in the dimly lit room; she was asleep in her chair by the fire.

"Would you like some hot coffee?" continued the eldest girl.

"Coffee! What a treat."

"Our girl made it this afternoon. I can heat it up on the fire."

"We've got a maid," Tessa informed him, moving a three-legged stool nearer to the chimney and sitting on it. "You can sit in Daddy's place," she said pointing to a wooden chair. "He's gone to the ball. Our maid has got a boyfriend."

Brother Caritas eased his body into the chair and beamed at the girls around him. The old lady wasn't going to be of any use, but he was going to find out what *La Bicha* wanted to know without her.

173

Chapter Twenty
Crimphele, March 1636

Thomas took another turn down the length of the great hall and paused once more at the high window to stare up at the black night. He could see nothing save a gathering border of white crystals as the wind blew snow into a small drift against the iron-barred window panes. Cold as it might be, he desperately wanted to be out there in the blizzard, away from the appalling screams. John Hawthorne sat at the table by the fire, telling his rosary. Now and again he would say, "Relax, Thomas, it is all quite natural," or "Relax, Thomas, it will be over soon." But neither man knew if what was happening above was normal or natural; they knew nothing whatsoever about childbirth.

Alina had heard her mother giving birth on four occasions. She had heard her mother scream, but what she remembered most clearly was the silence after the last baby was born. Alina was frightened, not of the birth itself, but what might happen afterwards.

Lady Marjorie was in the room, arms tucked under her massive bosom, her pudding face pulled into an expression of extreme disapproval at what she no doubt saw as Alina's lack of self-restraint. Meg was there too, looking more frightened than Alina as she hovered behind the elderly doctor, averting her eyes when he delved under the tented sheet and sweat-soaked mound of nightgown.

Crook-back Aggie was sitting at the kitchen table scraping red clots of mud off soggy roots with her precious little knife. She had been banned from Alina's presence for months: Lady Marjorie had told her to stay out of sight until the child was born. It had been the same with her younger brothers and sisters; she'd had to live in the outhouse during each of her mother's pregnancies. 'One crook-back in a family is enough— you stay out of the way, girl.' Her father had fed and watered her like a dog.

Despite Lady Marjorie's injunction, however, she had kept a careful watch on the master's wife throughout the pregnancy, via Meg. Keeping the service stairs door open she had heard all the fuss at first light when the labour pains started. She had spent a good part of the day in an agony of her own because McNab was sent for the doctor and she feared, wrongly as it happened, that McNab would use the heavy snow as an excuse to return without him.

As night closed in, the girl's wails died down, and for a while it was quiet. Then there was an awful, heart-wrenching, guttural yell, and nothing.

As Aggie listened to the prolonged silence she became more and more nervous. She snipped the scraggy top off another little root and dropped it, mud coat and all, into a pot, then got up and went into the larder with a candle. The small flame picked out the glaze on an earthenware crock of pickles and the pink skins of her sausages hanging from a hook. She looked at them and realized she had forgotten what she had come in for, so she went back to the kitchen table and sat down again.

Perkin, her scruffy little dog, wagged its stump of tail for attention and jumped onto her lap. Aggie ruffled the creature's short fur up around its neck and smoothed the soft hair under its bristly chin. She looked at her hand—white hairs had caught in her chapped fingers. There was still no sound from above. Then the dog was on the floor and she was up the back stairs with her clever little knife shining like a dagger before her.

Crook-back Aggie shoved the door open, shifted the old doctor out of the way with a sharp elbow, and plunged under the tent over Alina's legs shouting, "Stop! Stop, milady. For the love of God, stop!"

The room was ablaze with candles and the light from a huge fire. Sweat was pouring off Alina's brow, and she was not silent; she was gripping the sides of the great bed and groaning like an animal.

Aggie put the knife between her teeth and slipped her left hand under the baby's head, rough skin against satin, she gently felt around its neck. The cord was tight. Was the child already dead? Keeping her left hand under the head she took the knife from her mouth.

"Meg, hold the head."

"Agnes!" Lady Marjorie screeched, "What do you think you're doing?"

The doctor tried to push in beside her, causing the sheet to fall up over Alina's abdomen and revealing the tiny features of a baby with its umbilical cord tight around its neck.

"Get out the way, you," snapped Aggie. "D'you want 'em both dead? Now Meg, do as you're told, hold the cheel's head up for me."

Trembling, Meg held the baby's head while Crook-back Aggie eased a dirt-grained finger between the chord and neck, then slowly, skilfully, she slipped her little knife into the gap and cut through the cord. Dropping the blade on the sodden sheets she cleared the baby's mouth and pushed Meg out of the way. Now she had the tiny head in both hands saying, "All right milady, push him out. Push with all your might, girl."

"Agnes, I told you," spluttered Lady Marjorie, "get down to the kitchen this minute."

"Shut up, you old bag. Heave, go on, girl, heave, heave and let's be havin' him."

Lady Marjorie blenched, "Doctor can't you...."

But the old man was studiously washing his hands of the distasteful business. Carefully, he dried them on a linen towel, picked up his bag and made for the door.

"I'll still be sending my bill," he said, and left the room.

Chapter Twenty-one

The baby, healthy and perfectly formed, was baptized Geoffrey Thomas Percy in the stone font of the family chapel. Thomas held his son in his arms and didn't know whether to laugh or cry with happiness.

John Hawthorne trickled drops of water over the tiny head and let his own tears fall with them. He spoke the words of Joshua: *"Be strong and of good courage; be not afraid, neither be thou dismayed: for the Lord thy God is with thee."*

John looked up at his friend and smiled. "Between us, I should admit I have not always been of good courage myself; I have doubted when it was wrong to doubt. I have, indeed, been dismayed. But this one moment, Thomas, this makes everything—the summons in Rome, that dreadful shipwreck, escaping from the pirates, the doubts and fears—worth it all." Then, returning to the words of the baptismal service, he said, "The Lord thy God is with thee," for the father and son at the Crimphele font.

There was no celebration after the baptism. Lady Marjorie returned to her chamber and Thomas spent the rest of the day going between his study and his wife's room. No wet nurse had been contracted; Alina fed the child herself, sometimes with Thomas sitting at the bedside. Lady Marjorie would have been outraged had she known, but she uncharacteristically stayed out of their way.

The harsh weather kept everyone indoors. A blanket of snow covered the house and grounds, muffling the usual clatter and clang from the kitchen and the shouts and obscenities from milking shed or stable. The dogs slept in a jumble by the great hall fire undisturbed. Thomas knew some of the servants joined them at night as in the old days, but he turned a blind eye.

There was no question of John Hawthorne returning to his mother's farm with the snow so deep, so for the next few days he slept in Sir Geoffrey's old room, and when his friend Thomas was not available for conversation he made use of his late patron's extensive library. He was, he realized, happier than he had ever been in his life. Crimphele was a haven. His brothers, all grown men with families of their own, no longer taunted him, but he knew they saw him as an extra mouth to feed in a lean season and resented his idle presence on the farm. Being at Crimphele was not only more pleasant than being at home, it also made him feel safer. Should the cardinal's men be seeking him he was much more difficult to reach in this domestic fortress, and the house had repelled many would-be intruders over the centuries. As far as he was concerned, it could snow till June, especially with this new air of tranquillity. There was a calmness, a quietude, a sense of repose. He searched for appropriate phrasing but couldn't precisely name its nature. It was a sense of peace, and it was quite new.

Returning to his room after the baptism, John regretted not having his journal with him. The day was worthy of note. Perhaps on this auspicious day he should start a new one that contained no reference to Rome. It would be like starting the new life he had promised himself in the Spanish hostel, and there were so many positive things to comment upon.

Later that evening, as the two men dipped spoons into Crook-back Aggie's murky broth, John asked, "Thomas, how difficult is it to make a book?"

"You've got to write it first."

"No, I mean, to create a book with blank pages, a journal."

"Oh, that. Not difficult at all. There's paper and parchment and soft vellum in my study. I'll show you how to make a leather binding, then you fold it round the paper and cut the pages. It was one of the few useful things I learned at Oxford."

"But you enjoyed your student years: you told me you would have stayed to take a degree if they'd let you."

"We Catholics aren't admitted for degrees, and that's that. Anyway, I was summoned home when James was killed, and Mother never let me go back."

"Your mother? I thought it was your father that needed you here in James' place."

"Mm, my father said he needed me, but he was already training McNab as steward then, so...."

"Seems odd that a Scotsman should be all the way down here in Cornwall. Where was he before this?"

"Great mystery; Robert says he just wandered up the lane one day like a beggar. They all hate him, but you never hear a word against him. They're all too scared of him to risk his displeasure—or Mother's."

"There's something about that man that makes me uncomfortable. He's not... right. He is not... I see no virtue in him no sanctity, no—"

"Sanctity! You must be joking! He's downright evil. Meg, if you're listening, take this dishwater back to Aggie and fetch us some proper food."

Meg, who had been standing by the door waiting to collect their plates, appeared at Thomas's side, her face drained of colour, "Sir Thomas, I can't say that!"

"What, 'proper food'? Can't see why. Tell her we need feeding. It's been a hard few days."

"Even harder for your wife," added John as Meg made her way reluctantly towards the kitchen.

"Alina hates him too—McNab. I've seen her go out of her way to avoid him. Sometimes I think she's actually afraid of him, which is strange. Alina's not afraid of anything, not even Mother—more's the pity. We'd have a quieter life if she were."

John nodded his head, but refrained from saying anything out of loyalty. Lady Marjorie paid him a small allowance for conducting services in the Crimphele chapel.

"Alina truly loathes McNab," Thomas continued. "You can feel her hackles rise when he comes into the house. He is pretty venomous, though."

"Venom conjures serpents. Serpents conjure evil."

"As we were saying. Ah, good, what have you brought us this time, Meg?"

"Cold ham, sir."

"Cold ham! It's freezing outside, we need something hot. What's going on?"

"Well sir, beg pardon, but the house is all sixes and sevens. Lady Marjorie hasn't given us any orders and Agnes is... not quite as usual at the moment, sir."

"I'll speak to my wife about it."

"She'll be lying-in for a while, sir. You shouldn't—that is...."

"Yes, all right. Off you go."

John looked at his friend. "Perhaps now is the moment, Thomas."

The two fair-haired, slight-framed men exchanged glances.

"You mean usurp the old queen's power and take over as lord and master of all I purvey? Yes, you're probably right. I'd like to start by getting rid of that damned steward, but I can't see how we can manage without him. He's too useful, and he's got a special arrangement with Mother, that's quite clear."

"It would make life a lot easier for Alina if you let her take control of the household. From what she's told me about her father's house she's more than capable."

"I'd rather let them sort it out between them, you know—woman to woman. Shall I get some wine? We ought to be dining with wine tonight of all nights. Later on we'll start on your journal, if you like."

Thomas got up from his chair, anxious to change the subject, and came back carrying a dusty bottle, saying, "I've made a pretty good book for my butterfly and moth studies, I'll show you."

Later that evening, the two friends selected the materials for the journal, but the light was too poor to continue, so they said their goodnights and went their separate ways.

John Hawthorne had no means of committing his thoughts to paper, but he spent a contented hour sitting by a warm fire putting them in order, selecting the precise words and arranging them in the correct syntax. Then he fell to thinking about Thomas' studies. The intricacy and accuracy of Thomas's natural history drawings were impressive. Butterflies and moths were perhaps not a normal pursuit for the owner of a large manor and profitable estate, but his proficiency in dissecting small, delicate creatures and drawing what he saw was undeniable. Nevertheless, it was a strange occupation for a Fulford. Thomas's brothers had been hard-living, hunting, drinking men, which of course had been their destruction. The eldest, Geoffrey, had been killed in a quarrel over a brood mare; the second son, James, had died of a fever brought on by prolonged winter revels. It had to be said, a quiet life was a safe life, and it was evident that Thomas, like himself, valued a quiet life. He sighed and made ready for bed.

As John was pulling the cold white sheet under his chin, folding it neatly over the blankets, he came to a decision: he would stay here at Crimphele until actually asked to leave. Thomas needed a companion, he could continue with the English lessons he had been giving Alina, and, above all, he felt safe in this old fortress of a house. It was a long, long way from the cosmopolitan intrigue of Rome.

So when the letter from Lord Rundell was delivered a few days later, John Hawthorne saw it not as a splendid rallying call to good Catholics but as a tremendous disappointment. He had already risked his life for his religion and wanted no more of it.

"He's fallen asleep," whispered Thomas, moving his forefinger across the soft tuft of hair on his son's head to the silken skin of his wife's breast.

"*Venga gordi*," muttered Alina, lifting her son into her husband's arms.

"He'll be as big as me in a year if he keeps taking his food like this."

"I hope not, that will finish me."

181

"No, my sweet," said Thomas settling himself in the chair by Alina's bed with the child in his arms, "I shan't let that happen. You must not be 'finished', there'll be more babies to feed."

"Oh, no, don't speak of that. Put him in the crib. He should sleep some hours and let me sleep too."

Thomas very gently laid the baby in the crib by the tall fireplace and returned to his wife. "If I sleep here with you tonight I can wake when he cries. I can't hear him from my room."

"Sleep only."

"Of course."

Alina smiled and pulled a pillow from behind her.

Lying in the warm bed with his wife in his arms and his son at his feet, Thomas felt close to tears, almost silently he whispered words from a poem he had memorized:

"And now good morrow to our waking souls,
Which watch not one another out of fear;
For love, all love of other sights controls,
And makes one little room an everywhere."

He tipped Alina's chin towards him and by the light of the fire traced her features. "*'My face in thine eye, thine in mine appears'*... I have never known such contentment. My darling wife, '*If our two loves be one, or thou and I Love so alike, That none do slacken, none can die.*' I shall love you forever. Can you love me just a little?"

Alina did not understand the words, but she understood her husband loved her, and knew she had been won by this love. He was not the man she had dreamed of, not the man she saw in her waking dreams: he was not tall, did not swagger, had no trace of vanity or a quick wit; but he was good and kind, and they had a healthy son, and now she was in every way a proper lady—she would not die an old maid. She kissed Thomas' cheek and sighed as he pulled her tighter into his arms. And they both burst out laughing like children for the joy of it.

Chapter Twenty-two

A thaw set in the day after Alina's child was born, then another cold spell froze melted snow in cart-ruts and turned the paved surface of the inner courtyard into a skating rink. Meg and Crook-back Aggie had already made the kitchen their home that winter, sleeping in rugs and blankets by the fire at night. Meg was only too happy to avoid the long trudge to and from her mother's cottage, but for Aggie the freeze was a boon. She could not bear to be out of earshot of 'her' baby and kept a careful watch via Meg on what was going on in the foreign woman's room. Except she now thought of Alina as milady or the Lady Arleen, Sir Thomas' wife—and something close to a saint. For Alina had not swaddled her son: the swaddling clothes that had been prepared long before the child's birth still lay exactly where Meg had put them on the bedroom chest. The baby's limbs remained untrammelled. "Thank the Lord," she whispered each time Meg commented on it. *Thank the Lord, and let the child never be at risk again.*

During the cold nights, Aggie often sneaked up the back stairs to listen at Alina's door, then she would settle down in her rocking chair in the kitchen with her little dog on her lap and fall asleep. Her nights, though, were disturbed by memories of the strangling and suffocating charms she had employed over the years, and their results. For they had always achieved results: some more drastic, some less drastic, but all effective. And this one? What had happened to channel this one into the child? Could her attempts to stifle the Spanish girl, to make her feel so trapped in Crimphele she would run back where she came from, or, and this might have needed a little extra power, lead to her drowning in the river—suffocation by water—could this charm have been channelled into her son? And had she, by saving the boy, saved the Lady Arleen and turned the spell? Her head was a-buzz with doubts, fears and regret, a deep soul-awakening regret. She had done what the old lady had wanted: 'Make her go', she had been told. And to keep her place at Crimphele she'd done just that. But now, with the babe alive and kicking at his covers she saw how stupid and unthinking she had been, because an old lady should die before a young one.

"I said, didn't I, that I was a stupid, stupid woman," she muttered to her little dog Perkin. "Why didn't you tell me? Ah, but you did, didn't you, my clever boy."

A second thaw eventually set the blanket of tranquillity slipping from the new roofs and brought in a major change. One of Lord Rundell's most trusted servants arrived with a letter. Thomas received the sealed document and sent the man off to the kitchen for some hot broth before sitting down to open it at the great hall table. John Hawthorne, who was putting logs on the fire, turned just in time to see Thomas's face go white.

"Bad news? Has there been a bereavement—your sister?"

Thomas shook his head, not trusting himself to speak. Tears pricked at his eyes. He wiped them away with the back of his hand like a child. Without speaking, he handed the letter to his friend.

> *Your presence is needed, Cousin. There is a very positive move in our direction. It is imperative that all Loyal Catholic Nobles are ready and close. Make haste and come to London. I have mentioned your name and Her Majesty wishes to see you.*

John Hawthorne read the words aloud, then gave Thomas a questioning look. "Is he saying what I think—that the king is ready to declare himself a Roman Catholic at last? You will have to go."

"Oh, John, I do not want to leave Criphele—not now."

"That I can understand. But you must; it is a summons. Lord Rundell is not a man to be refused."

"I know, I know. But I have a newborn son and a wife lying-in and... a house to keep." Emotion strangled Thomas's words tight and dry.

"I can stay here. Not in your place, obviously, but I can stay here and look after Alina and.... Really, it is great news, Thomas, great, great news."

"If it's true."

"Tsss! That might be considered treason," John Hawthorne said quietly, nodding in the direction of the kitchens. "Take care this man doesn't report your reluctance. It never does to trifle with those in authority—in very great authority, if you catch my meaning?"

Thomas sighed, "I catch your meaning. I'd better go up to my study and write my reply. Stay here and talk to the servant, find out what he knows."

With heavy steps Thomas went up the short staircase to his study at the base of the tower and sat down to write his acknowledgement and intention to ride post-haste for London. But a dreadful foreboding stayed his hand: with all his heart he did not want to go. His world was here; their room was his 'everywhere'. He wanted no more from life.

He found his mother sitting close up to her chimney piece in her room, hands stretched out over dying embers.

"May I come in?"

"You are in." Her tone was accusatory. "You've taken your time."

Thomas' first impulse was to offer an apology, then he bit back his words and ignored his mother's insinuation. He was master of Crimphele now; he could come and go, visit or not visit his mother as he chose. "I have some news."

"Oh, and I am worthy to receive it?"

"Mother!"

"What?"

"I am to go to London."

She turned to look at him for the first time since he had entered the room.

"Why?"

"Queen Henrietta has established a sort of Roman Catholic court. I am summoned by Lord Rundell."

"Well now!" Lady Marjorie sat back and placed her hands on her knees, "I knew marrying Kate off in that direction would do us some good. When do you leave?"

"As soon as I am ready."

The old lady got stiffly to her feet and opened a window. Peering out, she said, "Snow's melting fast. Roads will be like a marsh for at least another week. You should wait for better weather." There was a pause, as if she were in doubt. "Are you taking her with you?"

"By *her* you mean Alina?"

Lady Marjorie stared out at the leaden sky. Ignoring the chill draught, she said, "Your father never took me to London. I became the wife of a baronet and was never presented at court." She shut the window with a sharp movement and closed the catch. "And now that Spanish woman's to have all I was denied. A lifetime I've given to this house and never once enjoyed the privilege that goes with it."

Having no idea how to react, Thomas said, "Alina cannot travel at this time, and I'm summoned post-haste."

"Then you'd better go. What do you want me to say?"

What he wanted her to say was 'God speed', not to worry about his home, wife and child; that she would be there to support Alina and act as loving grandmother to the newborn. "It was just to tell you...."

"Oh, don't fret, boy. I keep telling you I've run this house for over thirty years; a few more won't matter." Lady Marjorie was on her feet now, ready for action. "I better get downstairs and get started."

Thomas wanted to say, *No, don't. Let Alina do it*, but Alina was still lying-in. Damn and blast circumstance and coincidence. This was altogether the wrong time to leave.

"Tell your Arleen not to concern herself; I shall carry on as before."

"Yes, thank you, Mother," Thomas muttered, and left the room.

After he had spoken to his mother, Thomas told Alina about the letter and why he was obliged to go. Alina barely said a word, merely asked him when he was leaving. Her cold attitude toward him thereafter was a cause of sorrow. Was she pleased he was going to court? Was she angry that he was leaving? Her silence saddened him beyond measure.

It took nearly a week for him to make all the relevant arrangements for his departure and what he feared might be a prolonged absence. He delayed as long as he dared: until his trunk was packed and re-packed and labelled, ready to be sent on later; until he had written out a document for his lawyer giving his mother power of attorney; until he had had two long sessions with McNab regarding Home Farm and other farms belonging to the estate; until his saddle bags were stuffed with personal belongings and Mark, the boy he had selected to travel with him as a servant, was fully equipped and desperate to mount his new pony. Then, when he could delay no longer, he went to say goodbye to his wife.

Alina was gazing out of her window at the dreary day when he entered.

"You're dressed!" he said, noting her day clothes.

"Oh, Thomas, I do not like to be shut here all day. I am like a prisoner. I will come down to see you go and wave like a mariner's wife."

"You can't, it's too early. Not even a month."

Alina seemed not to hear him. "Look. The snow has fallen from the trees. I was never in snow. Let us go down into the garden together before you leave."

"No, you mustn't. I have come up here to say goodbye."

"Thomas, please, only to say goodbye." Alina moved to get her cloak from the wardrobe.

"No! You will catch cold and the baby...."

"Meg can sit with baby. I will call her."

"No, Alina. No! Not yet."

"Are you giving me orders, husband?" Alina laughed, pushing at Thomas' shoulder with a warm hand.

"Actually, yes I am."

The smile died on her face. "You can't."

"Well, I am. I forbid you to go outside until your lying-in is over and...."

Alina turned from him out of his reach. Thomas sighed.

"Alina, please, this is difficult enough, don't make it worse. Come and sit here with me for a moment."

He pulled the two chairs by the fire closer together. Alina sat down and he leaned forward to hold her hand saying, "I really don't want to go. I told you. But I have to. I'll return the very moment I can."

Thomas repeated why he had to go, how, if all landowning Catholics united and the king showed his favour, they could improve their situation. How the king himself might convert and return the whole country to the one true Church of Rome.

Alina listened to what he had to say. He suspected that as with the poetry, she understood many of the individual words but not their composite meaning.

"What you say is you are to be at a royal court, with ladies in fine dresses, and dancing, and every night a masque. Like my father. He went to Madrid, and my mother with a small baby, she is in the house always, and no money to pay servants. Then she died giving him *another* baby."

Thomas squeezed her hand, then leaned over to kiss her. He wanted her to fling her arms around him and beg him not to go.

He could have found an excuse: he could have found a way to stay. But Alina was angry and resorted to cold silence.

"Speak to me, Alina, please," he begged.

Eventually, Alina said quietly, "Once more I am to look after a big house and care for a boy and—"

"No. My mother will continue—"

"To make me feel like dirt!" Alina jumped to her feet. "I will not stay in this room and I will not let your mother 'continue'! This is my house now. I gave you a son for your title. We are square, as you say, fair and square. You go because you don't need me now you have a son!" Her face was flushed with anger.

"How dare you leave! How dare you go away just when you make me like and love you! How dare you don't take me!"

Alina had no more words in English for her sense of deception and fury, so she launched into a tirade of Spanish. Turning this way and that she located the crockery wash basin and flung it across the room, then came the towels and hairbrushes, then any little thing she could lay her hands on.

Thomas evaded each item and slipped out of her door just before a chair splintered against the lintel. Meg was standing on the landing outside, her eyes as big and round as the tray in her hands.

"I'd wait, Meg," Thomas said. "My wife is a little upset."

When Meg relayed these words in the kitchen, Crook-back Aggie's pinched little face lit up with glee.

"... and when I went in, the chair was broken. She must have tried to hit him with it and all the towels and baby things were on the floor and the boy squalling fit to break your 'eart."

Aggie had stopped listening. Milady was strong, she was full of life, and she was showing her true colours. Sweeping a whole set of crystal to the floor in front of Lady Marjorie had taken guts; she had wondered then if milady had less of the lady about her than she should, and now she knew.

"It's not our business, Meg. You mind what you say. Put that tray down and give the stew a turn."

189

Disappointed, Meg went back to her kitchen duties.

At midday, after all the fuss about Sir Thomas's departure had died down, Meg took a tray of the mutton stew and custard dessert up for milady.

The Lady Arleen was sitting on the window seat, staring at nothing. Meg put the tray on the table, bobbed a curtsey and left.

"Her room's a shambles," Meg reported when she came back down.

Crook-back Aggie made no comment and remained as silent as the young mother above while they ate their own meal and then started on their afternoon chores. It wasn't until she was ramming a poker into the kitchen range that she suddenly stopped and said, "Best we go and clear up afore anyone else gets wind of it. Go and get the biggest wash basket you can find, Meg."

The girl frowned. "Gets wind of what?"

Crook-back Aggie didn't answer. She had just found the perfect excuse to collect the swaddling clothes, only Meg didn't need to know that.

She planned to wait until the girl had gone home and the household was asleep, then burn every winding wrap she could lay her hands on.

After Meg had gone off to get a basket from the laundry, Aggie sat down and patted her lap for Perkin. The baby was safe and milady had turned the corner, but the master going off changed things. If he was going to be gone a good while, which seemed the case, and there were just the two women in the house, there'd be some sort of battle for control. This time she was backing the younger against the older.

First things first, though. The swaddling wraps had to disappear, because as soon as Lady Marjorie saw what was happening with the child she'd have him wound up tight as a knot.

When Meg returned with the basket, they went up the back stairs together. Aggie knocked on the Lady Arleen's door. There was no reply. Quietly she turned the handle and peered in. Sheets and blankets had been pulled from the bed, not one movable object was in its place except the child's crib, which was empty.

"Oh my God," squeaked Meg.

"Lord above, help us, she's gone!" Aggie rushed to the window crying, "Go tell anyone you can to find the girl. Tell them to get onto all the paths going down to the river. Run! We've got to get her quick."

"I'll tell McNab."

"No!" screamed Aggie. "No—I'll find him. You get on outside and find her; she'll catch her death in this weather."

"How d'you know she's outside? She might be down in the hall—"

"I know because I know, now go!"

Aggie knew because she had spent so much time watching where the Lady Arleen went, finding out what she liked doing and how she managed to stay outdoors for so long each day. She knew about the walks up Paddon Hill, about the visits to Crimphele quay and her chats with the boatman's wife; about the way she'd wander down the riverside as far as the path let her, then how she'd sit in among the bushes on the river path for hours on end. And she knew McNab knew all this, and probably more.

Alina was not in the garden, nor on her way down to the river. She was up on the roof. During the long winter days, when getting out to her usual haunts was impossible, she had explored the house from top to bottom. Climbing the narrow winding steps in the last days of her pregnancy had been difficult, but right up until the day before the baby was born she had managed to get out onto the flat roof of the square Tudor tower.

On a clear day she could see the sea. Sometimes, with a little imagination, she would pretend to locate her home and see her younger brothers clashing wooden swords or chasing chickens.

She'd remember the rough and tumble of fighting with them in the hay loft, her skirt caught up round her waist and full of spiky straw.

Sometimes she'd see a boat sailing up the river to fetch her, a big man with black hair and a soft black beard at the tiller and no crew, so when they sailed back down to the sea they would be alone. Today though, she had scrambled up the stairs to look out in the landward direction. It was far too late of course, Thomas was long gone, but she wanted to send a message in the wind to say she was sorry, to beg forgiveness for her angry words.

Crook-back Aggie found McNab in the estate office doing his accounts.

"You're needed," she said.

"Oh, aye, and who needs me?"

"Sir Thomas—and me."

"Oh, aye?"

"Lady Arleen's not in her room."

"And what's it to do with me?"

"We need to find her."

"We?"

"She's our future."

"Oh, aye, you've changed your tune. How d'you make that out?"

Aggie sighed. "Will you stop this 'Oh, aye' malarkey and get your coat? The old mistress won't last forever. We can talk about it later. For now we need to get the young one back into the house—safely and in one piece."

McNab stretched his long arms out in front of him and cracked his knuckles, then said, "And it's the steward's job to look for daft wimin now, is it?"

"Yes. Go and find her. When you get back I'll tell you what I'm thinking. If you can't see what's what, I'd better inform you. First, go and get her."

"Where from?"

"You know."

McNab sniffed and gave Aggie a long look. "All right. Pass me that coat over there."

Aggie handed him his jacket and left the office.

McNab waited until Aggie reached the end of the cold corridor, then he flexed his hands and set off to find the Lady Arleen. He knew exactly where to start looking.

She wasn't down on a garden path right now, but she soon would be. And not in one piece.

Chapter Twenty-three

After her son left, the dowager Lady Fulford walked down the long gravel drive to the main gate. An icy, easterly wind pushed at her back as if impelling her out of the gate as well. But that was not going to happen. She was not going to be forced out of her own home, not by that haughty miss her foolish husband had brought into the family, that foreigner. It was nearly a year now, and she was still angry about the manner in which her wishes had been disregarded.

Over the years she had suggested a number of suitable girls linked to her family for Thomas to marry. After all, his own father had married into yeoman stock to consolidate his estate, and he had never made any bones about it. True, her father had provided a very substantial dowry, far more than the average landowner of his class could offer; but she wasn't related to aristocracy, and Sir Geoffrey Fulford had known that when he made his offer.

After their marriage, her father had risen in status and acquired a great deal more land, and her younger sister had also married well. Marrying wisely was, and she had stressed this on many occasions, the only guaranteed way to maintain the old religion and the old ways. But no, Thomas, for all that he was so easily managed in other respects, had turned his nose up at marrying what he described as an 'illiterate country girl', saying that if he married he would prefer someone he could talk to.

About what? she'd demanded, *bugs?* What girl was interested in bugs? *Butterflies, actually, Mother,* he'd replied, *flora and fauna*—as if flora and fauna were some form of higher calling. Then he and his father both fall for some girl no one could talk to about anything at all, and certainly no one could vouch for. Being a Spanish Catholic was no recompense. That straight back and imperious manner didn't fool her. The girl was a fraud. All that nonsense about her father being a grandee—no girl from such a background would arrive without a stitch to her name, and she'd seen the state of her hands that first week. Grandee's daughters didn't clean grates and plant vegetables. She'd secured her place now, though, having a healthy son.

Lady Marjorie sighed, closed the gate and stayed clinging to the cold wood, staring up the lane that led to the Tavistock road, the route her son had taken. She'd begged him not to cross Dartmoor in winter, it was too dangerous. If he were to die his son would inherit the entire estate—and the Spanish girl would reign as queen regent. It was a fear she barely dared acknowledge; it contained the dilemma she'd been worrying over since the moment the child had drawn breath. If she acknowledged the girl she called Arleen and stepped aside in her dowager status, she'd lose all she had worked for over the past thirty years. There was no dower house on Crimphele; she'd be obliged to sit back and watch the stupid girl undo all her hard work. The only alternative would be to go to her sister's and eat humble pie for the rest of her days.

She turned and started walking back towards the house. *Her* house. It had been easy with her eldest son's widow. She had got shot of her a month after he died, sent her back where she came from, nicely of course, because Margaret came from a good family. She had done it once, she could do it again. The Spanish girl needn't think providing an heir for Crimphele made her the lady of the manor. But the child did create a problem.

Setting her shoulders to the wind, Lady Marjorie started back towards the house. Mooning about wouldn't get her anywhere. There was a lot to be done; she had let matters slip over the past week. Then she stopped. From this direction she could see some of the new building. The roof over the stable block was shiny slate, black in the damp air. Behind it she could just make out the ugly old Tudor tower. There was someone up there. Whoever would be up on the roof on a day like this, and why? Shading her eyes against the watery afternoon sun she tried to make out what had attracted her attention. But no, it was a trick of the light; it must have been birds.

After reaching the barn, she turned right to look at the new south range, the two storey block that faced out over the creek, admiring the new façade with its lovely big windows and arhed doorway. The terraced garden was in a bit of a state; she had better mention it to McNab, get a couple of lads to tidy it up.

Thank God for McNab, she sighed. Not that she would ever entirely trust him. Another example of her late husband's soft-hearted misjudgements. McNab obviously had a 'past'. He'd been hired without references, Geoffrey wasn't even told the name of his home town or village. This had worked to her advantage, of course. All she'd had to do was suggest she knew more than he'd want anyone else to know and he was hers. At the very least he owed her the roof over his head. She didn't trust McNab as a person, but if there were a battle for supremacy she could count on his loyalty as a servant. And Aggie—Aggie owed her a lot.

Continuing with her inspection of the property, Lady Marjorie checked on the cleanliness of the new windows and entered the old part of the house through the main kitchen. It was deserted. Clear evidence she had been slacking; Aggie and Meg should be there. Looking across the empty kitchen, she noticed the door to the back stairs was open. Perhaps Meg was up there in the old tower block tending the fires.

Moving into the great hall from the kitchen, she sat down at the long table and studied the stairs that led to Thomas's chamber and study, then through to Kate's room and on up to the chambers she and Geoffrey had occupied. Then she turned and looked down to the left, to the door that led to the ground floor offices in the new south range with the modern bedrooms above. Solution found. The foreign girl could have her part of the house, the old part, and she would have the new. She would move into one of the new south facing rooms that overlooked the garden. The baby could have the room next to her so she could oversee his education.

Half-turning on the long trestle bench, she examined the width of the steps leading into the old tower. A wall could be built there. They'd have to put in a door of course—with an elaborate lock—to avoid comment. She'd claim winter draughts if asked. If Arleen wanted to get outside she could use the service stairs and kitchen access. She would never prevent her getting *out* of the house....

Perfect. The girl had married Thomas for his old family name; she could have the old family fortress to go with it.

McNab lowered his head to look through the low arched doorway. She wasn't in her usual place, but she was up here, he knew that. He knew her smell, and the narrow stairwell was full of it. Silently, he moved onto the roof. She was looking out over the other side, towards the west. That meant she'd fall into the main courtyard. A nuisance, but if everyone was on the south slope there'd be no witness. And if there were, he'd say she'd jumped.

Now he had two choices: slip behind her and upend her legs, or slip behind her and make her suffer a while, pay her back for the way she'd made him suffer all these months. Watching her, he became hot; her cloak and that damned hair were lifting in the wind, that long, thick golden hair that wound into his dreams at night, that wound into his thoughts when he was miles from the house or calculating prices, doing any damned thing but thinking of a woman. She drove him mad the way she walked swinging her hips, the way she left her hair down like a common wench. It had been bad enough with Kate; then Kate had gone and the Lady Arleen had taken her place, forced him to want her. Ah, how she'd made him want her.

Before she met her unfortunate accident he'd have her. Here on the roof of his mistress's house. And his mistress hot for him since the day he arrived, the old bitch. He opened his clothing and looked at himself with satisfaction. The girl would have it better from him than that spineless husband, and when she begged for more he would take his revenge. He took a step towards where she was standing with her arms braced against the chest-high parapet; he'd take her from behind.

Gritting his teeth with determination, McNab slapped a hand over Alina's mouth to stop her squealing. It was so easy. One hand over her mouth, the other pulling up her skirts, his upper body pushing her into the stonework.

The woman, however, was strong despite her lying-in; she had the strength of a lad in her. She shifted round, ducked down and twisted out of his grasp. He got her again, this time with her back to the wall. He was up against her front, thrusting at her, her breath came at him sweet as milk. His knees were between hers, almost there. He bent his head to bite her breast. And stopped. A tiny white fist moved at her chest. Two lake-blue eyes glared up at him. She'd got the babe wrapped to her chest like a peasant woman.

McNab gulped. Aggie had said nought about the babe. Under the cloak, wrapped up like that, he'd had no idea. He stepped back, and as he did so she slipped round him into the centre of the roof, her left arm guarding the child, her right arm ready to defend herself. He scrambled to close his clothing. In the same moment, she was through the small door and gone.

McNab leaned back against the parapet and tried to catch his breath. She'd speak out this time. He'd have to leave. Unless he got to Lady Marjorie first.

Chapter Twenty-four

John Hawthorne uttered the last words of the morning service, waited until Lady Marjorie had added her own supplications, then followed her into the family parlour for breakfast. For a few minutes they ate in companionable silence, then Lady Marjorie said, "It is a comfort to have you here, John."

"Thank you, milady, it is a comfort to be here."

"Why is that, John? Surely you have more important issues to deal with after all those years in Spain and Rome. You have seen the Holy Father himself."

"Only from a distance, milady."

"But to be on St Peter's holy ground—oh, I wish I'd been born a boy and had your opportunities. I would have made a good priest."

"I think, milady, that you would have made a good bishop, even a cardinal."

Lady Marjorie looked at the young man her husband had been so keen to raise from his humble status to see if he were being sarcastic. He was not. His smile was quite genuine. She let herself laugh out loud. "I would, I would, you're right. I have always been fond of purple and red," she said, and they both laughed.

The laughter was disturbed by a tremendous rumble, as if a pile of stones had been tipped into the great hall beyond the door.

"Whatever was that?" asked John Hawthorne. "It sounded like a quarry."

"Stones. Bricks."

"In the hall! Are you going to divide it again, as you did to make this parlour?"

"No, I've asked the men to wall off the staircase to the old tower block."

John stopped smiling, his stomach muscles tightened. "Thomas said nothing about it. I didn't know."

"Thomas left me in charge here, as always."

"Yes, of course. Lady Alina...."

"We call her Arleen, John. It sounds more English. How often do I have to remind people?"

"Yes, I was going to say the Lady Arleen will soon be ready to assume her responsibilities."

Lady Marjorie stood up. "The wall will be built by then."

"You mean....?

"I mean that the *Lady* Arleen is not in her senses. She was going to throw the child off the roof—my grandson! She tried to kill my grandson!"

John gaped. "Off the roof?"

"McNab saw her. Called to her, ran up to the roof and stopped her. We are forever in his debt."

"But Alina—"

"Is mad. I knew she wasn't normal the moment she set foot in this house. All that hair, the way she stands and stares. It's not normal. I knew it. I said to Geoffrey—I told my husband, I...." Lady Marjorie began to undo the ribbons of the cap that covered the stubble on her head in agitation, then caught the priest's expression and stopped. "You don't believe me?" she demanded, straightening her shoulders and sitting taller in her chair.

"No, milady, it's not *you* I don't believe."

Lady Marjorie retied her ribbons, somewhat looser this time, and focused her attention on some detail in a tapestry above the priest's head. "You have always taken her side. That is your error. I cannot help your misplaced charity." She began to get to her feet.

"Apart from anything else, you have to remember that I have control of all housekeeping and power of attorney for my son, as his dear wife cannot read. I have taken charge of the child and given instruction she is not to be allowed near him. She will have her quarters—I *could* turn her out in the street, but no. So we need a wall. Two walls actually, but it's not a matter that need concern a priest."

"But it is, milady, indeed it is."

"It is not. This is a practical matter, not a spiritual matter, and I shall deal with it. I do not expect you to intervene in this affair in any way. Is that clear?"

"Yes, milady." John bowed his head and got to his feet, for his patroness was now standing.

Lady Marjorie pushed her chair back under the table, calmer, once again in complete control. "As I was saying, it is a comfort to have a priest to conduct services here again, but you know we have managed for a long time without one. In fact I don't believe they—we—have had our own full-time priest since dear Queen Mary, and that must be nearly a hundred years. So if you find that you are called away, or you're fortunate enough to be called back to Rome, or to Spain, please don't worry about us here. We are not, after all, family. We have no obligations to one another."

Lady Marjorie left the parlour to supervise her walls, and John Hawthorne sat down again. It was a dismissal. And another lie. He and Thomas were far too much alike—they were 'family'. His mother had never said... his father had been dead twenty years, but she had never openly said her husband was not his father, yet John knew he was nothing like his older brothers. And there was another piece of evidence: what landlord let a widow with under-age sons continue the tenancy of a large dairy farm without good reason?

Sitting down again as if winded, John considered what had just occurred, and came to a pleasing conclusion. Lady Marjorie had released him in more ways than one. If he had been dismissed, he was no longer required to obey her orders.

By-passing the rubble and workmen, he ascended the steps to the tower chambers. On the left lay Thomas's room, then his study, and the room that had been Kate's but was now used by Alina. He stopped at this door and knocked softly on the sturdy wood. There was no answer. For a terrible moment he envisaged her shut away in the ancient dungeon built into the hillside beneath the house, then there was another colossal rumble of stone on stone and he realized that Lady Marjorie wouldn't have needed to wall off the old tower if she'd taken such a drastic step. He knocked again, louder this time.

Alina heard the knocking on her door, but could not lift her head. She had screamed and screamed and ripped the sheets and covers of her bed to shreds, but no one had come. No one had answered her begging despair, "My baby! Don't take my baby!"

And now it was another day and someone had come, but it was the wrong sort of knock, a soft apologetic tapping. She ignored it. Meg wouldn't bother knocking if she had brought little Tomás back to her. She was too exhausted to fight anymore, too exhausted to even lift her head. Lying here on the cold stone floor she was going to fall into an icy sleep and die.

Chapter Twenty-five
Amsterdam, 20th April, 1636

The Journal of Marcos Alonso Almendro

He's back, I saw him on the quay. Spices from India, silk from Cathay, olive oil from Italy and wine from Spain. No sign of his precious little sea chest this time. He's either brought a barrel load of tulips from Turkey or none at all. Perhaps he's as sick of them as I am. Tulips, tulips, tulips, it's all anyone talks about here. Everyone wants to get in on it. Yesterday two weavers sold their looms to buy four bulbs. I didn't bother to round up the weight. Business is so good I can afford to let a goldsmith's ace-weight go here and there. Only the Dutch would think of weighing plant roots on goldsmiths' scales. Maybe it makes them look more precious.

I can tell him I'm a professional florist now. I trade flowers you can't see because they're in the ground in winter and on dark shelves in the summer, but I am a recognized florist! More and more people are using promissory notes the way he suggested, so he should be pleased. It's easy, but sometimes I get fed up. I suppose I should be thankful I don't have to risk my life with Turks, or risk losing my cargo at sea like him. Quick, easy and very, <u>very</u> profitable, which he said it would be. Ludovico da Portovenere knows everything!

I've ordered a burgundy velvet doublet made to measure by a proper tailor. Everyone here wears black, but not me. I wear something colourful and do more business in the taverns as a consequence, as they can see me through the smoke.

I've got 700 guilders in the bank. Henning said a family could live on that money for 2 or 3 years. He's a good man, but he's too cautious. I'm taking this money and whatever else I can make back to Spain with me so Mamá won't have to run the hostel and we can have a proper home of our own.

I shan't tell Ludo about the bank account, but I am going to tell him I'm not his servant anymore. I've saved 3 year's money in less than a year, and the way things are going prices can only go up. He can polish his own shoes from now on.

Elsa opened her front door exactly as she had done the year before. The difference was that this time she put her arms up for an embrace, and she was wearing dark blue, not black.

Ludo kissed her, but not as she had hoped or imagined.

Elsa leaned back and looked meaningfully into his eyes. "My servants have been given two days' holiday."

"Ah, well, that changes matters."

He winked and kissed her as expected, then let himself be led by the hand up to her sitting room, where she poured him a glass of French wine. Elsa did not see his grimace.

"Remind me to bring you some decent red wine. I've got plenty, and a few carafes of a special white wine from Liguria: it is refreshing if you keep it cool."

Elsa sat down in her usual chair, and he sat facing her across the small table.

"You haven't brought your sea chest!" she said. "Did something terrible happen?"

"Yes and no."

Elsa couldn't hide her disappointment. "Oh, Ludo, no pretty tulips and no pretty vases. Why?"

Ludo gave a rueful smile and began to tell his story. "The truth is, I haven't travelled to the Levant as we planned..."

Elsa gasped as Ludo went on to explain how he had been waylaid by corsairs.

"But how did you escape? They are cut-throats."

Ludo gave her a wry, half-dimpled grin. "Yes, but I have my contacts. I cannot say they are no danger to me; I'm as much at risk from the rabble of common pirates as any merchant..."

Instead of telling her about where he had really been— Genoa, Rome and Madrid—Ludo rambled on about winter storms, how people assume the Middle Sea is a great lake but its crosswinds and currents can be mortal; how storms blow up out of nowhere, and how this year he had been forced to insure his 'rich trade' goods at an exorbitant fee. As he chatted on out loud, he mused silently on how different it would all be when he had his own ship. He would make sure every pirate out of Morocco, Algiers or Portovenere itself respected that vessel. His ship. It was what he had always wanted. Odd, because it was a dream he could have realized much earlier. Except, of course, this ship came free. Well, more or less; Elsa and this vinegary wine were part of the price he had to pay.

Sailing back from Holland along the south coast of France into the Ligurian Sea that autumn, when he still intended to revisit Turkey for more bulbs, Ludo had experienced a sort of epiphany. He belonged at sea, could never commit himself to live inland. If he ever settled, it would be back in Portovenere surrounded by churning waves. A small island-like town full of colourful characters, fishermen and pirates, who never had a dull tale to tell.

In February he had actually set sail for the Levant, but on the stage between Genoa and Ostia he had picked up a piece of diplomatic gossip that had spiked his gut. He'd stopped off in Rome to verify the unpleasant news. What he had overheard proved to be true—or as true as anything related to Vatican politics was true. The Pope was actively opposing the Catholic Habsburg emperor because the Habsburgs controlled so much territory they could oppose his Holiness on any issue, and win. The Vatican *did not want* Spain to regain her lost Dutch provinces. Learning this meant he had to return to Spain. Not to tell anyone, naturally, but to find out their view on things. Instead of sailing east he had taken a passage to Cadiz, sailed up to Seville via Sanlucar, then travelled overland all the way to Madrid in a draughty stage coach. And having acquired the assurances and promises he needed, and taking possession of a hefty bag of Dutch money, he'd travelled all the way back again to Seville, taken a boat to Sanlucar, and hired a horse and trap to go to a Spanish nobleman's *cortijo*. Finally, on the return to Sanlucar with a box of special bulbs and a lot more Dutch guilders, he had made some difficult decisions. But Elsa most definitely did not need to know any of this.

"Yes," he said, "I have had some unpleasant adventures, but never fear, I have got you some very, very special bulbs, but not many, and— alas!—no pretty vases."

Elsa beamed. "Where are they?"

"I left them in my lodgings. You are disappointed."

"Oh!" Elsa went pink. "How can you think that? You know...."

"Does she want me or my flowers, hmmm?"

Ludo flirted for a moment or two, but his mind was elsewhere. He was back in Holland to raise Cain with this tulip nonsense, then take possession of his promised reward. There *would* be a ship for him as soon as Count Azor heard that the Dutch market had crashed. The king and his advisors in Madrid evidently had no inkling of the Pope's back-handed politics and still seemed to think tulip mania would, if not bring down the new Protestant economy, cause sufficient embarrassment to jeopardize faith in Amsterdam's banking system. Then suddenly he was listening to the woman in front of him.

"... and they have become so very expensive, you can't imagine what people are prepared to pay...."

"Prices are still going up?"

"Exactly as you said."

"And you have become a marvellous businesswoman; I can hear it in your voice. Excellent. Let us celebrate." He raised his glass. "To someone who knows more about superbly-fine tulips than anyone in Holland. To my Tulip Queen."

Elsa laughed. "Your Tulip Queen," she said, and clinked her glass with his, then laughed again at her own lack of modesty. "Listen to me, aren't you shocked?"

"Not yet. Perhaps we can arrange for you to shock me later."

Elsa blushed pinker still, "Oh, I...."

Ludo grinned and cocked his head on one side. "Not too much later. First, tell me about Haarlem. Everyone is talking about Haarlem."

"Oh, yes. That boy Marcos spends his life on the canal up to Haarlem. I think he's doing very well. He trades almost exclusively with lesser bulbs, of course, through promissory notes. Do you know he had the cheek to come to one of my salon evenings without being invited?"

"You knew who he was, then?"

"Not at first, then he tells me to my face he's your partner. I mean, really, I *know* he's your servant and here he is standing in my salon drinking my wine and—well, I suppose this is what's happening, all sorts of people are changing their status and their ideas about status." Elsa got up to refill their glasses.

"Money, as I said to Henning, is a great leveller. Except one can't buy class or good manners."

"Henning, is he doing well?"

"Oh dear, poor Henning, he's not as happy as he should be. And so many good things have come about! His wife is well, and they have moved into a house someone gave him for one single Admiral of Leiden bulb. Just one! And do you know, he was angry. I said to him, 'Look, if a professional man such as an attorney wants to exchange a house for a flower, let him! Let him! Think how it is raising the prestige of your business.' But he was still angry. You should speak to him, Ludo; try to make him see how much good he is doing for his family."

"I will. Arrange a meeting for me and send a note to my lodging."

Elsa began to say, "Ludo! That won't be necessary. I want you to stay with me here in this house—"

But Ludo silenced her. "*Carina, carina,* think—that is going too far. You have already scandalized your late husband's friends and acquaintances with your tulip transactions; I fear both they and their wives gossip about you enough already. If people see me enter, which they do, they should also be aware that I come only to visit."

"Are you hungry?" Elsa asked quickly, changing the subject to cover her disappointment. "I have prepared a cold supper. Could you bear to drink some cold sparkling French wine? It is very good, although I have to say it goes straight to my head."

"In that case, let's have supper with sparkling wine," replied Ludo. He was very pleased with what he had heard regarding Marcos and Henning, and the effect of sparkling French wine on Elsa would be enjoyable, as long as he were able to leave at a reasonable hour.

Elsa left the room to collect their supper from the kitchen. Ludo got to his feet and walked over to the window. A barge was inching its way down the canal below. A group of boys in a small rowing boat were stuck behind it. Poor lads, these dull waterways offered no opportunity for high spirits: little wonder grown Dutchmen couldn't resist a gamble. The King of Spain and his Conde-Duque de Olivares might be hopelessly overestimating the outcome of the tulip mania, but whoever had suggested it in the first place knew his terrain.

But who had suggested it? And why? That question bothered him. There was the distinct possibility that Olivares was playing some sort of bluff, or using the Dutch tulip plot as a smoke screen. He had the king focused on events in another country, thus diverting royal interest away from domestic issues, which from what he heard were not healthy. Olivares was surely too astute to believe this tulip scandal would divert funds from the Dutch war against Spain. Was Olivares also aware the Vatican was playing a double game? Was Olivares part of that game? The manner in which neither he, nor any minister he had spoken to in Madrid, was ready to even consider the possibility that Pope Urban was not wholly supportive of their king or their claim to the lost Dutch provinces was suspicious in itself.

Ludo folded his arms and sighed. Looking out of the window again he imagined a ship climbing a steep sea. Raise the odds as high as they would go and then, oh dear, no more credit—splash—the vessel descends on the high surf's downward slope—down, down, down—until it sinks out of sight. But *his* vessel would not succumb. He and his ship would stay afloat.

He turned back to the table and drank a little more of the rasping wine. *God help us both if the sparkling white is as bad as this,* he thought. Poor Elsa. Well, not poor Elsa, very wealthy Elsa. Pity she were not a bit younger and a bit more of a woman. Somewhere, there had to be one woman, one woman with enough character to cope with him and life in a pirate stronghold. Then he saw her, as vivid in his imagination as the ship on the high seas. Alina, the countess on the quayside—Alina....

Ah, well, at least she'd got what she wanted; respectable wife and mother by now, no doubt. What the English called the 'lady of the manor'. Alina had understood the deal with Sir Geoffrey from the beginning. A sharp mind and a pretty face. He smiled at the memory.

Elsa, coming into the room carrying a tray, saw his smile and smiled back, thinking it was for her.

Chapter Twenty-six
Crimphele, 2nd May 1636

Journal of Maria de los Angeles Catalina Fernanda
Santoña Gomez de los dos Castillas:

For my Husband Thomas,
Red Wine Red

The week my father said he would marry that woman, I tried on my mother's wedding dress. It is this colour, dark red with tiny pearls. That day when I put on the dress I knew I was not born to do servants' work and run after little boys like a nurse.

But now I have a boy of my own I want him with me, to wash him and look after him. Do you know I am only allowed to see him when Meg takes him to the kitchen patio? Now your mother is ill Meg brings him to my room, but I always have to let him go because he cries when he is hungry and I have nothing for him. Did you know this was going to happen? Is this why you never write me a letter? Did you know she was going to make walls so I can't go into the hall or the front of the house? There are doors in these new walls, but only she got the key. Why did you let this happen? You do not want me now that you have the son your father wanted. I knew that, but not that you are cruel.

I am embroidering the white curtains round the bed to stop me going mad. I did not like sewing when I was a girl, but here I have only your books. There is nothing for me to do. I can go outside through the kitchen but she keeps all the other doors locked.

I am a prisoner but she lets me go outside through the kitchen because she wants me to run away. I'm not going to. You want me to go away so you can have your quiet life back, don't you? You said I was everything to you. This is not true.

I am writing this in your butterfly journal so I can be sure you read it. It is my journal now. You can try to get rid of me and everything about me but I know you will never burn this with your butterfly pictures. One day you will see these words and know the pain you caused. You have got all your butterflies organized in colours so I write my thoughts in colours, the colours of the embroidery thread in your bed-hangings.

I came to England in red wine red. Sometimes I think Ludo did what he did because of that dress. If I live all my life and longer I will ask myself about that day and why I did not return home and why I let him make our marriage.

Did he get a good price for me? I know he sold me. Just like the girls the Turks take along the coast. He knows their language. He is like Bluebeard. But he is not cruel like you.

I stabbed my finger and there was blood this morning. The needle is very sharp. It is called a crewel needle in England. A cruel needle. My blood is the same colour as this embroidery wool. Thomas, you have my blood on your bed hangings to remind you I was here.

The Turks came to Tamstock last year. Mistress Hawkins told me. Her husband hides her and the boys in their loft and they have night torches to throw down if pirates come. He loves his wife and boys.

Be aware—if the Turks come again I will let them take me and our baby.

Be sure, I will leave and not come back. And you will never find us. Would you try to find us, Thomas?

I am sorry that I broke your equipment and some of the trays with your creatures but I am very angry with you. Why don't you write? I send you letters but you never answer.

"What's in this pot, then?"

"What's it to you? Poke your beak any further you'll lose it."

McNab straightened up. "Very thin broth."

"Lady Marjorie's having trouble with solids."

McNab lifted the lid of another pot, sniffed. "This for us?"

"Might be if someone gives me peace enough to finish it."

"So she's eating different to us?"

"Always has done. You don't suppose *they* live off turnips and pig liver, do you?"

Aggie watched the angular steward out of the corner of her eye. He'd never come poking round her kitchen like this before, leastways not when she was alone in it. He wanted something, or he wanted to know something.

"Her ladyship's still unwell," McNab said baldly.

"And don't we know it. Spends all day on the pot, won't let no one in her room 'cept Meg, and Meg's up two flights o' stairs every minute the day with trays of dainties and clean linen, no use to me as scullery maid no more. I need Clarice back in here to help me if you're to be fed like you're used to."

"Two flights of stairs?"

Aggie bit her lip and stirred the cauldron on the range. "The young 'un and Molly what's still feeding him morn and night has to be fed as well."

"I still say it looks thin," McNab had gone back to the small saucepan containing Lady Marjorie's soup.

"It's tasty enough. You want to try it?"

"If you'll join me?"

Aggie sighed and made a fuss of wiping two crockery bowls then ladling a small amount of the liquid into each. She plonked one down on the table in front of him.

"There, drink up. It won't kill you," she lied.

"So, Mr Henning, how are you getting on these days?"

Paul Henning looked at the Italian merchant and lifted his tankard of ale to avoid an immediate answer.

Ludo drank from his and said, "I hear you have moved into a new house." Then, looking not at the ex-clerk but at a table of noisy apprentices taking turns with a tobacco pipe, coughing and laughing, he added, "This is a jolly place. Do you come here often?"

"Only when I have to do business. The landlord uses a room in the back three nights a week for auctions."

"Auctions?"

"Oh yes, we have a proper auctioneer and a secretary who notes transactions in a ledger. Most transactions are tied up legally."

"Most?"

"There is an unfortunate custom of celebrating each sale with a pitcher of ale or wine. I'm afraid not all sales are notarized as they should be."

"But a buyer can be sure of obtaining what he has purchased?"

"Who can be certain of that? You can only take someone's word. A man says he's got a new variety of *violetten* or *bizarden* or *rosen* for sale. You go and see the row: it's labelled, but there's only one month a year when you can be sure what you're buying is what the florist is selling. It's gambling."

"You disapprove of gambling, Mr Henning."

"Yes, yes I do. Carpenters and shoemakers are selling their tools to buy tulips they can't see in the belief they can sell them on for a huge profit and never work again. I call that gambling. They are risking their livelihoods and putting their families at risk."

"Mmm, I hadn't considered this aspect." Ludo put on a grave face, pursed his lips and stared at nothing. It had the desired effect: Henning warmed to his theme.

"For the connoisseurs dealing in superbly-fine tulips, the ones named after generals or admirals, or a Semper Augustus, for example, well, that may be how people deal with legitimate objects of art. But for ordinary people, buying the less fine varieties, thinking they are going to be rich—what happens when there are so many of these ordinary tulips being traded they *all* lose their value?" Paul Henning tutted and took another sip of his watered ale.

"You think they will lose their value?"

"I'm not an economist sir; it's not for me to say."

"I suppose it depends whether you are talking in the long term or the short term."

Henning would not be drawn this time. He shook his head and focused on the content of his pewter mug.

"But people do make a profit, and a very handsome profit, I'm told, and you are doing very well in the process. Make hay while the sun shines." Ludo kept his attention elsewhere and watched the apprentices leave.

At the door to the street they stood back to allow two far more elegant gentlemen entry. Strangers. French, judging by their attire: wide lace collars and frills round the knees. Newcomers who didn't know they were supposed to surrender swords at tavern doors. Ludo turned to Paul Henning, who was also watching the new arrivals, and asked, "Do you know them?"

"No."

"French, would you say?"

"I really couldn't say."

"There are more French around nowadays, aren't there? I wonder why?"

Ludo didn't wonder, though; he knew. It was one of the things he had discovered in Rome. The French, supported by the Pope, had made a new treaty with the Dutch against Spain. According to his sources, the Vatican was in direct contact with Cardinal Richelieu, who ran France.

Ludo had spent a good while wondering how this affected him personally. If the conniving Florentine Pope was just playing games with the Spanish monarch and really backing the United Provinces through France, being too successful here could put him in real danger. No one in their right mind upset this pope. Among his secret agents were the assassins known as the Black Order. And now the French might be informing on him as well. Ludo shuddered and tried to bring himself back to his task.

His current plan was to send tulip prices sky high, as the Spanish wanted—and from what he had learned from Elsa, Henning and Marcos, that wasn't going to be difficult—then undermine the trust all these invisible sales were built on. He'd advise someone at a critical moment *not* to pay for a set of bulbs because the goods weren't worth the price. Word would go round; the market would teeter, then collapse. Then he'd collect his reward and disappear.

His attention was drawn back to the Frenchmen. Were they aware of what was going on here? And if so, would they try to stop it? Had the Pope informed Richelieu? More than likely. That way it would be the French who stopped the whole silly business, leaving the Vatican, untainted, to establish diplomatic relations with the rising and financially secure new Dutch nation.

But if he failed to create at least a scandal, the Spanish were going to be angry and there'd be no ship. It was all getting rather more complicated than he'd envisaged on that first ride back to Sanlucar with the irritating English priest. He gave an inward sigh and called for brandy.

The lad waiting at tables came up and asked, "What sort of brandy sir? We've got French brandy in now," then he lowered his voice, "or there's still some Spanish, if you prefer."

Ludo looked at the boy and said in a loud voice, "*Sono Genovese,*" then, looking around to see who was listening added, "*non m'importa,*" with an actor's flourish.

Paul Henning looked up, surprised by the histrionics.
Ludo smiled, shrugged his shoulders and said in a much quieter tone, "Tell me how you arrange promissory notes these days."

The ex-clerk took a scrap of paper from his pocket. "This is for a *violetten* worth six hundred guilders—an artisan's income for two years. You can take this note to the tavern of your choice and sell it on for seven hundred or eight hundred guilders. When you receive the money, you pay me the six hundred as agreed and keep the profit. Or you can gamble on the price of the bulb going up. If you wait and don't sell on for a week or two, you might make one hundred per cent profit, or more."

"And that worries you?"

"What worries me is that these common bulbs aren't like the special, superbly-fine ones traded between people who understand tulips and appreciate their beauty. I'm afraid there are now too many ordinary plants in circulation. Sooner or later they are all going to lose their value."

Ludo nodded sympathetically. "Don't think on it so deeply, Mr Henning. The plague could take you tomorrow. If you make a nice profit today, you are providing for your family tomorrow. Let your fellows enjoy their bit of excitement, and if they can put money in the bank, all the better. I suppose that is what they do, put their money in a nice safe bank account?"

"They may do. That is not the point. The point is, where will this lead? Where will it end?"

"You seem to know that, my friend. The question is not where will it lead, but *when* will it end? You—personally—just have to know when to stop. You are an astute man; you should be able to do that quite easily."

"Huh," said Paul Henning with more vigour than he was accustomed to use. "if it were my choice I'd get out right now. But my wife... she is buying new curtains, and we have fancy rugs in each chamber. She's probably buying the tea and silks you brought from Cathay this very moment."

"Well, I need customers." Ludo gave his lop-sided grin. "Trading with Asia and competing with your Dutch East India Company is always difficult. I don't return to Amsterdam each spring for the good of my health."

This time Paul Henning looked the big man straight in the eye. "Or Elsa vander Woude?"

Ludo cocked his head to one side. "Elsa vander Woude?"

"My late employer's wife believes you have returned to Holland for more than just the sake of your merchandise. I hope she is not to be deceived. Elsa vander Woude is a good, kind-hearted woman."

"She is," replied Ludo, genuinely humbled.

Greit showed Marie Henning into Elsa vander Woude's sitting room, bobbed a curtsey and left.

"Marie, how lovely to see you." Elsa was about to comment on how well Paul Henning's wife was looking but noted the manner in which the young woman's hands twisted her velvet reticule and refrained. "Is anything wrong? One of the children?"

"No, no, the children are all well."

"Your mother-in-law?"

"No, although I don't think the poor lady has much longer. She sleeps all the time, doesn't seem to know when it's night or day, but she's not a problem to us. We have a special girl come in to look after her. It's—oh, I am so ashamed I don't know where to start."

Elsa led Marie Henning gently to a chair saying, "Give me your cloak, dear. Greit should have taken it, I shall speak to her. She's not doing her job properly at all these days. She's developed an manner, I can't say what it is, but there's something different. I shall certainly speak to her about this. What a beautiful cloak, so light. If the weather stays this fine soon we shan't need them...."

Elsa chatted on, and gradually Marie Henning relaxed enough to speak.

"I have to talk to someone, you see," she said, "but I don't know who to turn to. If this should ever get out, my husband would die of shame."

"Then it's better if he doesn't know about it. All the best marriages contain secrets. What is it exactly that you don't want him to know?"

"Money." Marie Henning bit her lip. "Paul gives me housekeeping, but I seem to have got carried away with the new house. I've bought things—and now I can't find the money to pay what I owe."

"Well, that's easily solved. I can give you a loan and you can pay me back when you can."

Marie Henning sighed. "I hoped you'd say that, *Me'vrouw*, but I'm not sure that even you...."

"Have enough? Oh, yes, I have enough. And I don't think your simple needs will break my strongbox. How much are we talking about, ten guilders?"

"Two hundred." Marie Henning's voice was a whisper.

"Two hundred! That's more than I pay my two girls together in a year. Whatever have you bought for two hundred guilders? Can't you return something?"

"Then Paul will know, he'll see something missing and he'll guess. He's a very proud man; he'll be so angry."

"Oh dear," Elsa sighed, regretting her eagerness to help, not wanting to divert any of the money she had set aside for the new season's bulbs.

There was, however, the money Ludo had given her for purchasing: the money to help those who lacked the funds for cash-in-hand transactions. Attorneys, doctors, professors and other such men, he said, were often wealthy in terms of assets but lacking in cash. *Feel free to use this money for loans where you can be sure of repayment. Add the percentage you see fit,* he'd said. Well, in a way this was a tulip loan. If Henning had not accepted a whole house as a payment, Marie Henning wouldn't have needed extra housekeeping to furnish it.

"So it's for your new house?" Elsa said.

"Carpets—I couldn't resist them. We've never had carpets, and these are so beautiful, made of silk, from the East."

"Goodness, what a luxury."

Marie Henning hung her head in shame, "Yes, luxury."

For a moment the women sat in silence. Elsa examined how she was to arrange the loan and whether to charge interest, as Ludo had explained—as her husband had done when he had provided loans.

Marie Henning sat motionless, her head bowed, then quietly she said, "I have been tempted by beauty and comfort and succumbed. My parents raised me in the Catholic faith, but Paul insists we live like Calvinists. He says ostentation is sin, but... but the carpets are so beautiful. I couldn't resist."

Elsa nodded. She understood. After a few moments, she got up and called to Greit to bring them some refreshment; then, turning back to Marie Henning, she said, "My dear, you know I have always helped you...."

"Oh, don't think I don't know that, *Me'vrouw*. When I was so ill—we only survived because of you. I owe my life to you. The way you got Paul started again, and now we have a fine house and the girls go to school and...." She ran out of words.

Elsa ignored the content of this flow, trying to keep an objective perspective and look hard-headed, as she did when dealing with tulip connoisseurs, who always expected easier terms because she was a woman. "I will give you two hundred guilders, but I shall need something as security," she said plainly.

Marie looked at her without comprehension.

"I could spend two hundred guilders on bulbs and double it in a week or two weeks at the very most. If I give you the money it will not be working in my favour. You need to tell me what you can give me as security."

Marie's pale face showed her surprise. "Security? But you have known me since before I was married to Paul! Don't you trust me? I'm not going to run away, I promise." A thought struck her and she clapped her hands together as if in prayer. "The carpets! *Me'vrouw*, if I can't pay you back, I'll give you the carpets!"

221

Elsa looked at her, troubled by her lack of understanding, then she smiled. "Yes, all right then, the carpets. I will let you have the money until the tulips flower. In January they will start speculating on the lifting after flowering. Bulb traders are weighing individual bulbs and selling them according to weight now. A bulb in the ground naturally grows bigger, and if you're lucky it will grow offsets too, which you can then sell separately, and you've immediately doubled or even tripled your money. I'm sure your husband bores you with these details all the time; I know I would bore Cornelis if he were still with me. Anyway, don't worry about repaying the loan for now; your husband is going to very rich by next spring. Paul has told you about the rows of flowers we have bought near Haarlem?"

Marie nodded as if to say yes, then lowered her head again. "I know nothing of the enterprise, *Me'vrouw*. My husband never mentions anything related to business."

Fortunately for Elsa, who feared she had perhaps said too much, Greit came in at that precise moment with a jug on a silver tray. Elsa waited until the girl was out of the door and then waited a moment longer, looking pointedly at the door itself. Then she got up, opened it quietly, looked each way and closed it again silently.

"There was a time when one could trust one's servants." She waved a plump, jewelled hand as if to dismiss unpleasant thoughts. A large ruby and a row of sapphire glinted from separate fingers in the afternoon light.

Marie looked at her, fascinated by their sparkle, but said nothing.

"Lemon water?" asked Elsa.

"I've never tasted lemon, *Me'vrouw*."

"Exactly, and this is my point! You'll be able to buy lemons and *foie gras* and fill your rooms with silk carpets to your heart's delight by this time next year. Once we've lifted the bulbs after flowering we are going to be *so* rich—oh, you can't imagine! I myself sold three offsets last spring, reinvested the money in a new variety and used the leftover for—look!" she waved the ringed hand in the air.

Marie's eyes widened and she bit her lip. "You bought those? For yourself?"

"Wicked, isn't it!" Elsa chuckled like a naughty schoolgirl, "My daughter would be scandalized. I hide them when she comes to visit. But that's *my* secret; don't you tell."

The two women drank their sweetened lemon, Marie wrinkling her nose at the unaccustomed tartness.

"Now, back to our little matter," said Elsa. "All this security talk is really nonsense, but one should always, always keep money transactions on a business footing. So just between ourselves and for the sake of procedure, let's say that if you do not repay me by the last day of April, 1637, I will send for your beautiful carpets and sell them. How many are there, by the way?"

Marie Henning fairly danced back to her tall four storey house on the Keizersgracht. The new downstairs maid let her in and she went straight up to the second floor to check on her mother-in-law.

The old friar, Brother Caritas, was sitting beside the high bedstead, his head resting on the coverlet as if in prayer. He was asleep.

"Brother Caritas," Marie whispered.

He made no move.

"Brother Caritas," she said a little louder and coughed politely.

"Mmm? Mmm?"

Maria stayed by the door, unsure how to act. The friar had become a regular visitor at Paul's mother's apparent request. He seemed a good man, albeit a little slovenly. Not wishing to disturb him in prayer, she turned to leave, but just then he lifted his head.

"Ah," he said and cleared his throat, "*Me'vrouw* Henning."

"I didn't know you were here, Father, I am sorry to interrupt."

"This is your house, *Me'vrouw*."

"Yes, it is." Marie couldn't keep the pleasure from her face, but then she said, "I wonder, Father, when you have finished with my mother-in-law, could you speak with me for a moment, please?"

"A pleasure. Will this be in the nature of a confession, or do you simply need my advice as a cleric?"

"Both, I think. Oh, I have such conflicting thoughts. I am happy when I should be worried, I am pleased that we have money—we are going to be very rich—then I am ashamed for being greedy and wanting more. I do speak in confidence, don't I? I mean, you are a priest."

Brother Caritas levered himself from the low chair and smoothed down his grubby habit. Flakes of crusted porridge landed a little further down the rough cloth stretched across his belly.

"Dear lady," he said, "I am as silent as the wood in the confession box. Feel free to tell me all."

"Come down to my sitting room, Father. I'll call for some refreshment."

Marie aped Elsa vander Woude's expressions and deportment precisely. If she were to be a proper lady she must change her humble ways.

Chapter Twenty-nine

Ludo leaned back in his chair. "You'll make someone a good wife one day," he said, as Marcos removed his large empty plate and took it into the scullery. "Pity you can't manage more than these *gallette*. Still, one day bacon, one day cheese, I suppose we shan't get bored."

Marcos ignored the barbed comments and placed a small orange on the table.

"Dessert, sir?"

"Not another orange!"

"You brought them."

"Only as camouflage."

Marcos lifted another orange from the crate beneath their table with one hand and selected a wrinkled brown bulb from beneath it with the other. Balancing one on each hand, he held them to the light from the high window and said, "Oh, yes, excellent camouflage."

"Sit down and don't be so cheeky," said Ludo. "I need to talk business, so less of your flippancy. Here, take this." He removed a fat leather purse from inside his waistcoat and handed it to the boy.

"My wages?"

"You said you weren't going to work for me anymore, so you don't get wages."

"Present?"

"In a manner of speaking."

Marcos put the fruit and the bulb on the table and sat down, serious at last. He knew Ludo well enough now to know nothing came free. Lifting the purse from the table, he weighed it. It was heavy and still warm from being worn inside the Italian's clothes. It was a considerable amount. "What's it for, then?"

Ludo delayed a moment as he peeled his orange into one practised spiral; then, as if choosing his words and weighting them with importance, he said, "I don't want you to trade in anything except cash anymore. You can use that for loans."

Marcos looked at him enquiringly. "You want me to lend with this, so they can buy these?" He now held up the weighty purse in his right hand and the tiny tulip bulb in the left.

"Yes."

"I lend an amount of cash from this hand, and take it back for the purchase of one of these with the other, interest and profit all in one go?"

"Correct." Ludo popped a segment of fruit into his mouth and watched the youth beside him process the information.

Marcos repeated more or less what he had said before, adding, "That is, if someone hasn't got cash I don't accept goods in lieu; I offer to lend him the money? He takes a hundred guilders, for example, and promises to pay me back that money when he sells on."

"Divine in its simplicity."

"You old devil."

"Not so old."

Marcos got up, collected the orange peel and threw it into the empty fireplace.

Ludo spoke as the boy moved about the room, clearing away the debris of their meal. "You'll be known for carrying money, though, so watch your pockets. If you think you're being followed or feel you might be threatened in any way, get yourself into a public place and—"

"That reminds me," Marcos interrupted, "of something odd I was going to tell you, but it slipped my mind. I bumped someone outside the Black Cockerel the other day, a Spanish monk."

Ludo's head shot up. "Monk?"

"He spoke in Castilian Spanish." Marcos was now shifting oranges back over the few remaining bulbs in the box under the table.

"What did he say?"

"*Mierda.*"

"Marcos, stop that and look at me. What did he say?"

"*Mierda.*"

"Just that?"

"*Mierda*, then *disculpad*, I think."

"Proper monk, you'd say, tonsure and breviary? Or a friar?"

"What's the difference?"

"Monks live in monasteries; friars wander about all over the place."

"Must have been a friar then. Does it matter?"

"Yes and no. As I say, friars can be anywhere at any time. Oh, hell and damnation to the lot of them."

Ludo sighed and slumped down with his chin on his hands. how closely were they being watched? Knowing *he* was under scrutiny was understandable, but if Marcos was being followed too, was he also at risk? Should he alert the boy to what was still only a potential danger? A potential danger that involved a Dutch prison cell for the rest of his life, or no life at all because someone might eliminate *all* evidence of their involvement.

After a while he said, "Are you going off to search for your long lost father in Flanders this summer?"

"I could."

"You should. If you're going to travel overland in this damn country you should go now."

"The trouble is, how do I get through the blockade and not get shot?"

"Take a sea passage to Bruges and get in that way. Maybe wear a monk's habit?"

Marcos smiled. "Father Almond come to minister to the ailing and spiritually weak. Good job I learned my Latin lessons."

"There you are, then. Give me back the purse. There'll be time for this when you get back. *If* you decide to come back."

"Oh, but—"

"Don't fret, boy, you can have travelling expenses. Although monks sign a vow of poverty, remember. Marcos," Ludo's tone was different now, "if you don't come back to Amsterdam, if you find him and decide to stay and be a real man fighting side by side or want to get back to your mother, don't feel obliged to me here."

Marcos stopped what he was doing and said, "I've got to be back by September for the planting."

"What's so important about planting? Oh, you haven't, have you? You haven't bought bulbs yourself?"

Marcos sat down at the table again, his face eager with delight. "A whole row of *bizarden,* two *rhoot en gheel* offsets and a Generalissimo!"

"And what clever devil persuaded you into that?"

"*La señora* vander Woude."

Ludo looked Marcos in the eye with incredulity, then burst out laughing.

Chapter Thirty
Crimphele, 10th June, 1636

*J*ournal of Maria de los Ángeles Catalina Fernanda
Santoña Gómez de los dos Castillas

I am using pale blue wool to make white feathers. I start with pale blue, then stitch over and into that blue with white silk from Kate's old embroidery box. The feathers look quite real and the bird stands out from the background. I like stitching feathers. I do not like geese. We had a nasty old gander that lived for many years. He did not bother the boys but he ran at me every time I feed the hens. I hated those hens because of him. He ran at me with his wings open like two gates and hissed. The geese here are not so nasty, they don't attack me. They can't because I'm locked in this room. I heard the key turn this morning and pulled and pulled at the handle and shouted, then Aggie came and put a note under the door. I am sure it was Aggie, not Meg. The note says 'For safety's sake'. I don't understand what this means.

Geese are like guard dogs and Crimphele is a fortress. You said your great-great grandfather built it to keep people safe inside, is this what 'for safety's sake' means?

I want to be outside and not safe and I want my son with me. Robert's wife Molly is still feeding him with her baby.

Meg says your mother is very ill and does not get out of bed. But instead of leaving the doors unlocked so I can go to little Tomás they lock me in. I could have pushed Meg down, kicked her when she brought my food today. Why didn't I do this? Because I have lost my will to fight, because your servants are not servants, they are my guards. Sometimes I hear them listening at the door: up and down the stairs in their white aprons like guard dog geese, hiss, hiss, gossip, gossip.

They say the devil has cloven hooves, I say he has a long neck and wide wings, or your beige skin and your beige hair and your empty heart. I used to think the devil was something black and evil until I met him. That devil may wear black, look black, but his evil is rapid and fun. I wish I were unsafe with him.

Thomas, I am putting geese in your bed hangings for safety's sake. Each time you wake up and see these hangings you can think about how you kept me prisoner.

Alina sanded the page and went to stare out of the window for the tenth time that day. Behind her there was a scratching at the door and the lock clicked. She kept her eyes on the distance beyond the thick window pane; it would be Meg with another meal for her that she wasn't going to eat. Then there was a coo and a scratching sound, and the door swung open. Alina turned. It was indeed Meg, but with plump little Tomás squirming in her arms.

In two strides Alina crossed the room and clasped the babe to her, crying with relief and joy. Meg waited by the door, but Alina couldn't speak.

After a few moments Meg bobbed a curtsy and said, "Beg pardon, milady, but Agnes says to tell you the old... that lady Marjorie has passed away."

That evening after Tomás was laid to sleep in his crib in her room, Alina sat down to write to her husband again. This time it was a terse, urgent letter.

Crimphele, 12th day of June, 1636

Dear Husband,
I send this letter with Robert. Your mother has died.
He will tell you what has happened. Come quickly, you
are needed.
Your Wife,
Maria de los Ángeles Santoña de Fulford

Aggie had spent the day up and down the stairs preparing what she needed for the laying-out, then preparing the corpse with Mol Roberts' help, decking it in a suitable gown as befitted the old woman's rank. But her mind was on the young mistress at every turn.

None the less, it was a shock and surprise when Lady Arleen finally came down to the kitchen with her little boy resting on her hip. Aggie tried to still her hands, calm her breathing, fearing what the foreign woman might say—or do. Was she to be dismissed so soon? Lady Arleen's tone was gentle, though.

"Agnes, sit down please."

"Yes, milady."

"I want to ask you one question, then never speak of it again."

"Yes, milady."

"Why did you lock me in my room? It was you, wasn't it?"

"Yes, milady."

"Why?"

"So that you..." Aggie sought for words, diplomatic words that would convey what had happened since the new walls had been built, but would not convey all the truth of the matter.

She had locked the door and managed to keep the Lady Arleen shut in the tower block for the time it took the old woman to die. Everyone on the estate knew the young mistress had had no access to the old lady, not even on the day she died. Not even the worst of gossips could name her if suspicion fell; not that gossips cared anything for facts. Nevertheless, it was true to say the Lady Arleen had not seen her mother-in-law for weeks. She had been kept apart for safety's sake while tin mine powder, that some called arsenic—mixed with elder water and some arrowroot to slow its progress and alleviate the vomiting —did its work. As far as anyone need know, the old lady had died of an illness that was not uncommon in this area.

Crook-back Aggie, whose only memory of maternal love came from what little her old grandmother had been able to give, looked at Lady Arleen and smiled and shook her head. How could she say it was because the child needed a loving mother and Lady Marjorie was denying him that? She smiled a black-toothed smile and folded her hands over her flat chest as if to hold her contentment safe inside. There was nothing she would not do to protect the dear, innocent creature she had brought into the world. But she would tell the Lady Arleen none of this.

Chapter Thirty-one

John Hawthorne had just arrived back at his mother's farm after a visit to Truro when news came of Lady Marjorie's death. He set off immediately with the messenger, Toby, cutting across clay-baked summer fields to shorten the distance. Leaving the boy at the dairy to complete his day's chores, he walked round the stable block and entered the house through the door to the old great hall.

He expected the house to be in confusion: servants running hither and thither, Aggie all a-lather in the kitchen preparing funeral meats. He walked instead into a sinister silence and witnessed a scene he was to replay in his mind for many nights.

Alina had come into the hall through the now open tower door. She had taken a few steps across the uneven stone flags when the door from the new ground floor offices opened and McNab entered the vast room from the other end. They stood and stared at each other like two cats vying for territory: a honey-ginger she with young to protect, and a predatory, smoke-blackened alley tom.

Alina stood straight-backed, chin raised, but he could see she was ready to turn and flee. He felt, rather than saw, her choosing words—she was thinking in Spanish, preparing what she wanted to say to the Scotsman in her mother tongue. So when he spoke first, she was momentarily elsewhere and answered unprepared, stumbling over her words. It made her seem unsure of herself, and she was furious for that.

"Good day, milady. Are you wanting me for anything in particular?

"No, es que ...."

McNab carefully sidestepped into shadow. Alina now had to step forward to see him. He smiled and leaned into a tapestry of a battlefield.

Alina pushed her hands down the sides of her skirt, clenching her fists. "I was to call you later," she said. "Please, sit down." She indicated the long table.

McNab didn't move.

"I have to speak with you, sit down."

McNab still made no move.

"I said sit down," her tone was imperious. "Do as I tell you. I have charge here."

McNab sniffed and moved towards the table with insolent slowness.

Alina waited until he had settled his angular frame on the trestle bench, then moved slowly around the opposite side towards the empty fireplace. Standing with her back to the chimney, never once taking her eyes off her enemy, she said, "We need a box."

"A box? And what would that be for?"

Alina raised a hand and pointed upwards.

"Ah, the poor Lady Marjorie, God rest her soul. A *coffin*."

"Tell the man that does the wood things to make this."

"The carpenter? Yes, milady, right now. Will that be all?" McNab was on his feet, twisting to lift his legs over the trestle bench before she could reply.

"No. There is more. Sit. My husband is coming. When he is here he will decide what is to do. Until then I want you to continue with what is normal in your day. Make no changes until my husband does approve them. You understand?"

"Of course, milady. What changes are you thinking of?"

For a moment John wondered if she were getting ready to dismiss the creature herself, but she could not do that without Thomas's permission. He watched McNab trying to control his features. The man, odious in every way, had spent years keeping Crimphele solvent and running smoothly; he would, justifiably, be angry.

Alina was being unwise in this, John realized; she should wait. She was giving McNab motive and time to prepare a disaster: no ledger would balance. McNab could, and would, create such a monumental mess it would take Thomas years to rectify it. There were dozens of ways to set this estate in chaos.

But McNab said blandly, "I shall do my best to please, as always. Is there anything more, milady?" The last word was a sneer.

Alina, still clenching and unclenching her fists in her skirts said, "Not for now. Tell the carpenter what we need. And come back here this evening to speak about tomorrow."

"I always met Lady Marjorie in the estate office on Saturdays, ma'am."

"I will speak with you here. Come to this table, this evening."

That's better, thought John. *A public place and quick about it.*

McNab began to squirm. "Milady, we have the books and field plans in the office. It is where we arrange daily business."

"Not with me."

John had seen and heard enough. Alina didn't want to be alone in a confined space with McNab, in the same way Meg and the other girls would get out of the kitchen or the dairy the moment he entered.

"I think Lady Alina's instructions are clear, McNab," he said, stepping forward, pleased with himself for having the courage to speak.

McNab's head swivelled round on its long neck. "Very well," he said without expression, and got up to go.

They waited until the steward had left the hall, and then shared exaggerated shocked expressions like well-tuned friends or siblings.

"*Cuanto me alegro....*" began Alina, and burst into tears.

Crimphele, 7th day of August, 1636

Thomas,

Why do you not come? Is Robert with you? We are very worried. Molly, Robert's wife, is very sad and their baby is not well, he coughs and does not sleep. Our child is well. Do you not want to see him?

I understand now why I did not have word from you. Your letters were in her room. From these letters I can see that you are not happy, although your work in the library interests you. What is this work? Who is this queen that says a man may not go to his mother's funeral? Perhaps you have not had this news. It is strange you do not send word. Did Robert not reach London? He took ship from Plymouth. Or are you now so important in the court we are nothing to you? What is all this planning Kate tells me they are doing with the Queen? Kate says her husband is waiting to be called, but he does not go and she is happy for that. Your sister is well, she has a baby girl. She will come here soon. I am invited to her house with our son but I cannot leave Crimphele in McNab's hands. Agnes tells me the servants are angry because they do not get their money as they should. This is a matter for you. Come, please, before we lose our servants and workers. I cannot manage this house and estate on my own.

When you come I will tell you some true things McNab has done. Kate says I may, but this must be a safe secret.

I send this with John to be sure you receive it. <u>Please</u> return with him, we need you here.

Your wife,
Alina

Alina folded the letter, stamped the Fulford seal over the closure, and sat looking at it. Was there any point asking John Hawthorne to take it? She sighed. It was just like when she had managed her father's house, except Crimphele had a lot more land and a lot more people living on the estate. Her father expected his rents from his lands but he did not get involved in how they were run. He had never looked at an accounts ledger and he had certainly never shown her how to use one, or how to deal with tenants and their interminable complaints.

The Crimphele farmers wanted help with the harvest. What was that to Sir Thomas' wife? Aggie said Sir Geoffrey used to help them! A baronet cutting grass! It was hard to believe, but Sir Geoffrey had been a strange man. His wife had been strange *and* evil.

Colour rose in her cheeks as she remembered finding Thomas' letters in her mother-in-law's room. What kind of women were they—this queen and his dead mother—to prevent a man from being with his wife? The queen was French; why were Cornishmen going to her court? Kate knew but she wouldn't say. Was that because it was an important secret or because it was something dangerous?

Alina sighed again. She could not visualize Thomas being involved in a dangerous enterprise, nor could she imagine him stripped to the waist, scything hay like a peasant. Perhaps he had developed a liking for court life, as her father had. Perhaps he was involved in intrigues and dalliances and simply did not want her there.

She set the letter on her rack ready for John; he had promised to go to London. Soon they would find out what had happened to Robert and why Thomas did not return.

Chapter Thirty-two
Amsterdam, August 1636

Brother Caritas came down the stairs sideways, taking his weight on his right leg on each step, clump, clump, before attempting the next, clump, clump, right leg first. It was a slow process but his hip joints would permit no other, and this despite the fine summer weather. He was dreading another autumn. Each time he saw the tall masts of the Dutch East India fleet leaving the harbour he thought of running away like a naughty schoolboy; stowing away and not coming out of hiding until the ship had passed the Bay of Biscay.

But that was out of the question; he had to do what his abbot told him, and that was to do what the creature from Rome said he should. So here he was, up and down interminable stairs, two or three times a week, succouring the soul of a woman who didn't know he was in the room and asking impertinent questions of a goodwife who should know better than to answer.

Marie Henning was waiting for him, as usual, at the door to her first floor sitting room. He thought of this tall, narrow canal-side house as *Me'vrouw* Henning's property, having never seen her husband in it. The creature from Rome, however, did not need to know that.

The three little girls and the boy were elsewhere in the house; he could hear occasional high-pitched squeals, sometimes a shout of indignation or a howl of despair from the demanding Pauli.

"Brother Caritas, take a seat. Are you quite well?"

"As well as Our Lady permits, my dear, and how are you this summer morning?"

"Oh, as usual, although..."

"Yes?"

"Oh, just matters that occur outside my house and should not trouble me, but they do because they trouble my husband so."

"And he tells you about these troubles—and business concerns?"

"Oh yes, he does now. It was such good advice, Father. I encourage him to speak—as we discussed—and now he does. You were quite right. I think he is better for sharing his troubles."

"And now you can share them with me and troubles shared are troubles halved. It is an excellent system. My abbot advocates it."

She was pouring his drink, the tray being ready for his visit. Damned lemon juice: could it be this bitter mix that was provoking the pain in his hip? Very likely. He would have to buy at least two sugar buns as soon as he left to counteract the nasty sharp taste of the lemon.

Receiving his cup, Brother Caritas made a grin to hide his grimace and tried to swallow the first sip. "You still have lemons," he said. "I wonder they are not becoming scarce."

"I think they must be; their price goes up and up. All prices are going up and up." Marie Henning gave a resigned shrug.

"But it is not a problem for you? I mean, your husband's troubles are not financial? This house..." he indicated around him vaguely, making sure to spill some of the dreaded lemon carefully down his lap so as not to spoil the glorious carpet beneath his feet. "Oh dear..." He dabbed absently at his stained grey habit and waited for Marie Henning to pick up the lead he had offered.

"Rising prices? Oh, we are safe enough. The girls start at a new, fee-paying school next month. They will learn not just reading and arithmetic but writing, music and French as well."

"French now, is it? I suppose Latin is frowned upon these days. We do see many French in the streets nowadays, and I suppose it will be useful, if someone needs directions." Brother Caritas began to mumble. This task sometimes stretched his imagination beyond its limit.

"Mmm."

"Perhaps we should blame these French visitors for making prices rise. Do they buy your husband's tulips, do you know?" The woman shook her head. Mary Madonna, she was hard work today. "So, um..." He'd run out of ideas.

There was a silence and he was obliged to drink more of the lemon. Suddenly Marie Henning came to life.

"I think I understand now," she said. "I've been struggling for some days to comprehend, but I think I see it now."

Brother Caritas silently uttered a prayer for patience and inclined his head in encouragement. "Regarding?"

"There are new rules for buying the tulips. Now buyers do not have to pay for them in cash or kind unless the prices continue to go up. If they default—I am not sure what this 'default' means—then they only pay a small part or 'percent' of —oh, you know...."

"And this is what concerns your husband? What keeps his spirit low? I must urge you, *Me'vrouw,* to bring him to Mass and confession more often. It is what he needs."

Brother Caritas said what was expected of him and, task completed, was ready to be off. She did not understand what was going on; he did not understand either, but all he had to do was repeat this to *La Bicha* and he had completed his week's mission.

La Bicha would almost certainly know this 'default' and 'percent' business already, but that didn't matter; he was required to inform on what the ex-clerk Henning was doing and keep an eye on the Spanish boy that dressed like a heathen's parrot, not to obtain state secrets. Having acquired something to report, he was anxious to be off down to the nearest bakery, but Marie Henning was ready for conversation.

"That must be why so many more people, and quite humble people, not even skilled artisans, just ordinary labourers, can buy bulbs. How clever. They don't need to pay anything until they are paid. I think. Well, it seems a good system to me. I asked him to explain what is happening to me with these flowers, but Paul is such a pessimist, he sees the dark side of everything first. More lemon, Father?"

Chapter Thirty-three
Flanders, August 1636

Marcos waited until the small boat had pulled into the water, then lifted the soaking hem of his Franciscan greyfriar's habit over his arm like a toga and started to trudge up the beach. Sand sharp as grit pushed between the open spaces of his rough sandals and his feet sank down with each step. The dunes before him took on the dimensions of a mountain range. After a few more paces he stopped and looked about him: no one. Off came the hated undyed woollen habit and shoddy sandals. He turned and ran, light and lithe as a schoolboy, back into the sea. The cold water clutched at his genitals, taking his breath away. In a moment he was splashing back onto the beach, gasping, laughing with excitement and flapping his arms about him to warm his body.

Marcos turned back to face the water and caught the open-mouthed expression on the face of his ferryman still pulling back over the Scheldt. Raising an arm he waved and shouted, "Thank you, my son, and God be with you, ye sausage-sucking bastard! Shut your mouth, the tide's coming in!"

Laughing, he jigged on the spot, then sat down with a plop and burst into tears, because he had never been so frightened in his life.

"Never again," he said to himself as the sobs subsided, "never, never again. It's their war, not mine. I don't give a damn about kings, saints, soldiers or frigging tulips. I'm going home!"

But how? The boys in Flushing had robbed his money purse. They'd have done for him altogether if he hadn't been able to run faster than they did, even with the hated skirt dragging at his legs. The ferryman didn't deserve the coarse comments; he'd saved his life. If he hadn't shouted at the boys they would have pushed him over the sea wall and the filthy water would have sucked him down for ever. It started with a cutpurse and his mate, then, when he yelled at them without thinking in Spanish—a foolish action—the two cutpurses had become three, ten, a dozen louts chasing an innocent man of God. Well, that was the last of *Signor* Ludovico's great ideas—and the last he would see of the great Ludovico himself. He wasn't going back to Amsterdam, ever. He would find his father and return to his dear mother and serve at table for the rest of his days. A pity about the money in the Amsterdam bank, but if that was what he had to sacrifice for a decent, honest future, so be it.

Marcos sat hugging his knees, watching noisy gulls dive for fish, and realized he was starving hungry—and his breech clout was full of sand. In a moment he was back on his feet, stripping it off. For a satisfying few moments he scratched at his fair nether regions; then, gathering up the sodden robe, the cracked leather sandals and the gritty drawers, he began to make his way up the sand dune.

It took an age, sliding two steps back for every three steps forward. The fine sand shifted beneath his feet, and twice he slipped, so his robe and small clothes were covered with even more sand. Finally, puffing fit to burst, he breasted the dune and looked inland at Spanish Flanders for the first time. Nothing. Just more dunes topped with spiky grass.

"*Joder*," he sighed, and began to trudge down the shifting, sliding hill inland. But yes, there was something, someone: two people and a donkey. Two girls and a donkey with loaded panniers. Two pretty girls with huge eyes and their hands over their mouths. He waved. The girls looked at each other, squeaked something incomprehensible and started to run, tugging the reluctant donkey behind them.

"Hey!" called Marcos waving his free arm. Then he remembered he was stark naked.

Never mind, at least he had some idea which direction to take. Slowly, he pulled the gritty cotton drawers up over his legs and the fouled grey habit over his head, and all the time he was concocting a story: he had gone overboard—a ship full of missionaries to the New World—trying to save a child that couldn't swim. Despite massive waves he had rescued the child... but the weight of his habit had dragged him down, and the ship had given him up for lost, but he was an excellent swimmer so he'd disrobed in the water and swum to the shore and... That ought to get him a meal, if not a roof for the night.

Now, how had he come to be wearing a friar's outfit? For, you see, he was no friar, no he was the son of—even at that distance the girls had been pretty—he was the son of... not a Spanish nobleman, too risky... the son of a vastly rich Italian merchant who traded in precious jewels from Cathay.... Then he remembered the stupid bald patch shaved on his head and halted in his fabrications.

"*Joder,*" he said again.

Something caught his attention, not a noise or a movement, this time it was a smell. He sniffed. What was it? Horses? A farm? A farm would be good. He lifted his heavy woollen skirt and set off down the dune and up the next, then down and up, and slowly, panting with exertion, up the next. Soon he was sweating like a pig in a summer pen—and yes, that was what he could smell: hogs.

There were hogs, there were horses too, and at least a hundred men in a camp without sanitation that sprawled across the flat landscape like a giant cowpat. In the storm-brewing air the smell was indescribable.

Marcos searched the scene before him for banners, flags, anything to suggest whose army he was about to walk into.

"Oh dear God," Marcos groaned, "where the hell am I? Who are they?"

Stooping down, he selected a large handful of sharp flints. They could be deadly—as a last resort. He tipped them into his hood, tied the flax rope tighter around his slim waist and set off towards the camp. As he walked, the stones rattled together lightly in his hood like dry bones. Hmm, if he didn't need them as weapons he might pass them off as relics—some of the very stones thrown at Christ on the cross.

Chapter Thirty-four
London, October 1636

Thomas Fulford set down his quill and stretched his neck. Words swam before his eyes, the large illuminated text to his left blurred into wavy water-colours. He rubbed his eyes. They did not clear, so he leaned back against the prison bars of his tall chair and gazed at the huge, out of focus tome. The text went on forever. What had started as a joyful task had become a burden. He could not go home until it was finished, by a queen's command—a not so foolish or frivolous queen as many believed her to be. She said she wanted to give the translation to the King as a gift. A means, perhaps, of raising his interest in the old saints, for it was well known that this long-nosed, dark-skinned Henrietta of France, who spent her days at masques and balls and among the sycophants of her *petite* French court, was very active in persuading people back to the old faith. Her mother had been an Italian Medici, so her choice of the life of one of the more famous Italian saints had a certain logic.

It also carried a certain risk: this translation of *The Life of Saint Francis of Assisi* could very easily lead him to the tower. King Charles had been raised a Protestant. If his wife annoyed him, or if he found there were too many of *his* nobles in *her* court, he could cry treason and have each one hanged for threatening his title of Defender of the Faith.

Every single man dancing attendance on the French queen was at risk, because she was openly flouting the religious laws of England—Rundell was aware of that. The translation could, of course, just be a ruse to keep him in London, although he was doing nothing more than swelling the numbers of loyal

Catholic nobles at Henrietta's court. What Rundell really wanted him for was a mystery; they both knew he had no skill for politics or military campaigns.

Had it been any other translation task it would have been a burden of the very worst kind. But this—he smoothed a hand over the exquisite illumination in the original text—this was a precious manuscript from a monastery, saved from King Harry's hell-fires a century ago. It was an honour to translate it into English. A great honour.

Except he wanted not these honours, he wanted to be at home with his wife and child, not shut in this stuffy panelled room by day and trapped in treasonous talk by night. He stretched his arms out and waggled his bony wrists. What good would these be if it did come to civil war? They surely didn't expect him to fight; he couldn't lift a sword above waist height when he was a lad; he'd drop it for sure now.

How his brothers had teased him when he was young—*go on Tommy, we're the Saracens and you've got to stop us conquering the house....* Whatever the game, they handed him the longest, heaviest sword from the great hall armoury and laughed fit to burst when it dragged him to his knees. It was a bitter memory, sweetened only by the knowledge that it was he who now held Crimphele. In the end it had been the weakling who had inherited the estate and provided a healthy heir.

Closing his tired eyes, Thomas visualized white-blond wisps of hair resting on a soft pillow in a crib, then he saw the same precious head resting against the full bosom of his wife and felt tears wash his sore eyes. He had offered ten men and ten good horses, the content of his armoury if needed;, victuals for marching soldiers when they reached the Tamar Valley. What more could they want of him? His interest was the natural world, how humble bees, butterflies and moths stayed in the air, how mice and voles breathed underground, not the bellicose world of men.

From underneath his translation sheets, Thomas pulled a small square of thick paper and looked at the few words he had written earlier. An idea had been taking shape for some days now, and he wanted to share it with Alina. He also needed her to fulfil a request. If she chose not to respond to this letter—like all the others—that would say all he needed to know. She had never written a word to him about his son; her love had been a sham. Alina was nothing more than his mother had said—a fortune-seeker.

This project, however, was important and worthwhile. If nothing else it would divert him from his homesickness and persistent doubts. To make a start, though, he needed someone to send him his natural history journal. Perhaps he should ask his mother to do it, but even she had let their correspondence lapse. He breathed deeply to divert the effect of profound sadness and scanned the only three words he had written so far:

My Dearest Wife,

'My dearest wife' wouldn't do. Not even as a start. The letter had to be businesslike, to the point. He needed his butterfly journal and that was that.

While he completed the translation from Latin into English of the life of St Francis for the Queen, he was going to prepare his own book. It would be an illustrated text of English plants, animals, crawling and flying creatures set against quotations from the saint. The joy of the idea filled him with a sense of promise and raised his spirits. He saw himself sitting in his study drawing a butterfly onto one side of a page, then copying out a short Franciscan commentary on the next. His wife, looking over his shoulder, admiring his calligraphy and draughtsmanship, would place her hand on his neck, he would look up, they would kiss...

He dipped his quill into the ink and wrote:

Whatever reason you have to write me not a single word, I beg you, send my natural history journal, the one that is half-complete beside the specimen boxes and trays on my study table....

As he wrote he began to cough. His throat was sore, his head ached, his limbs felt like lead. But it wasn't a passing ague; the cough had dogged him since the day he arrived in London. He leaned back in his uncomfortable chair and tried to control his breathing—and the fear that he was never going to see Crimphele again.

Chapter Thirty-five
Amsterdam, November 1636

Ludo wove his way listlessly through the crowds, his lack of purpose at odds with the activity around him. Amsterdam teemed with people the way it teemed with rain: quiet, persistent, always there. Not like the tremendous skin-soaking downpours in Liguria that gave way to bright sunshine. The weather in Italy had a sense of drama.

Despite the new one-way system implemented by the practical Amsterdam city fathers, every turn he took was blocked by pedestrians or journeymen pushing handcarts. Once beyond the city wall it was no better; the alleys leading down to the quayside were choked with carts taking supplies to and from ships, or carrying wares to the new shops outside the city walls. Such industry; it wearied him.

When he finally reached the harbour itself, his way was blocked by a boy with an ill-balanced barrow of something agricultural, he sidestepped and dispatched a curt comment. He was out of sorts and bored, thrice bored. Dutch food was bland and boring. Dutch weather was depressing and boring. Elsa had become cloying and boring. The ease with which he could palm off paper sales of plants at absurd future prices had become predictable and boring.

It was time to get his teeth into something new until he could explode the bulb market and return to an unpredictable life. The trouble was, what? He had been politely but emphatically informed that a Genoese merchant was not welcome in the new Stock Exchange, which was a pity; he fancied himself in a short black cloak rushing around making a broker's fortune on commission. The 'rich trade' merchandise of silks and spices was increasingly falling into the hands of Jan Company—the ever-growing Dutch East India Company. Joining them was not an option: they kept the number of their directors to a minimum to maximize profits, and he wasn't going to work for anyone in an employee capacity. Rather than diversify, perhaps he should re-establish old contacts. Something would have to be done about his silk business if nothing else; he could not afford to upset the customers in Florence. The danger and the irony of his current situation was that he was becoming a victim of his own tulip trap. If he wasn't careful *he* wouldn't have anything to fall back on when the market collapsed.

Wandering along the water's edge, vaguely thinking about the next season's trade, Ludo decided to let the immediate future take care of itself. He might make contact with someone this very day, something might jump in his way—but not another damned barrow. This time it was a fat girl steering a mound of dirty linen, sheets and bedding from a returned vessel. *Madonna*, what a whiff! No wonder the girl had a turned up nose. Marcos had once asked him why the Dutch wore shoes to match their noses; he had slapped him for being a feeble joker, but the lad had a point.

And that was something else; he missed Marcos, and he was worried about him, too. Sending him off before the Vatican watchers could do him any harm had seemed wise enough at the time, but had he sent him into greater danger walking round battlefields looking for a father who like as not wouldn't recognize him if he saw him? Well, he'd be back; if just half of what he'd boasted was true, Marcos had a tidy sum in an Amsterdam bank and a considerable amount to come through real bulbs.

Checking behind him first, to make sure no ill-driven vehicle was going to propel him into the black waters of the Ijsselmeer, Ludo paused on the quayside and stared out at the scene before him. Flat-bottomed *fluyts* were receiving all manner of cargo from tenders: grain and cheeses, bricks and pipes. Smaller, lighter *jachts* bobbed unattended at their moorings. Beyond them, a vast East India Company *retourschepen* was being unloaded after a successful two year voyage, the source no doubt of the dirty linen. *Retourschepen* had berths for a dozen passengers, plus officers and company officials. A floating town. No wonder Jan Company was overtaking individual 'rich trade' vessels and putting brokers like him out of business. Still, one more winter and it would all be over: he would soon be sailing his own ship along the Middle Sea and... and February seemed a lifetime away.

His plan was to wait until January, then, taking advantage of the tension created by long, dark days and the anticipation of a springtime flowering, he'd hoist tulip prices as high as they'd go. Once people were ready to pay these prices, he'd introduce the doubts: 'You paid *that much* for something you haven't seen? How do you know you've bought *bizarden* tulips, they could be just plain colours? Prices are bound to drop next year, only Croesus could honour these credit notes....'

Undermining just one or two well-publicized deals might be enough. It would generate enough fears to create a general panic, and the market would crash of its own accord. In the meantime, he needed some diversion.

The chill drizzle became an icy shower. Ludo cursed, lowered his head so the rain dripped off the brim of his black leather hat, and walked back to the nearest decent tavern. Once inside, he waited for his eyes to adjust to the peat-smoke and tobacco pipe dimness, removed his cloak and hat, showed the doorman he carried no weapons, and edged his way between crowded tables until he found a seat. Leaning back in his habitual manner he took stock of who was there and what was going on. Then he paused and sat utterly still: there was de Kuyper from the Spanish *cortijo*, the ebony cane was across his knee. It *was* de Kuyper, and someone he didn't recognize: a well-dressed fellow in expensive but sober attire. Interesting. What might they be discussing?

Interrupting his thoughts, the serving wench plonked a tankard of ale in front of him.

"Not that," he said, "wine. No, brandy, Spanish brandy."

The girl looked at him with her mouth open. "Spanish brandy?" she mouthed.

He was about to insist, then decided he couldn't be bothered and said, "Oh, French, Danish, African—whatever you've got."

The girl looked at him as if he were mad, then turned without another word to fetch his drink.

Ludo folded his arms over his chest and smiled. The latest of the local followers paid to report on his whereabouts had come in looking like a drowned rat. Poor chap, he needed a decent meal. Ludo waved a hand at another serving girl.

"See that young man over there? Give him a dish of something hot and a tankard of ale—with my compliments."

Having dealt with his watcher, Ludo turned slightly in his seat and became a watcher himself. If de Kuyper was here it was because he had rarities to trade, and because he knew how high prices were going. Ludo thought of the *rosen* bulb Elsa boasted about: she'd sold it at sixty-five guilders in September and it had just changed hands again at six hundred and fifty. Everyone with any spare cash, and a lot without, were getting into the tulip market. If de Kuyper knew how serious the business was now, he might be trading his entire stock in the knowledge he would be very, very rich—for a time—on paper. Ludo gave a crooked grin to match a crooked thought: if anyone knew the dangers of future prices, de Kuyper did.

Maybe he'd just come to see his old mother and buy some rubbery cheese. Or perhaps he had come with the fancy Spaniard with the predatory name to see what was what.

His brandy, watered, was placed in front of him. Lifting the thick goblet, Ludo took another look at the tavern's clientele. No sign of Azor. Perhaps de Kuyper had been detailed to pick up information his own watchers couldn't provide. That being the case, he ought to look busy, show he was in control and still generating sales. There was a ship at stake.

Ludo sipped the thin brandy and began to formulate a plan. The place to be was Haarlem. The town was on the edge of the tulip fields, and the greatest amount of speculating among the widest range of people went on there. The Amsterdam tulip trade was dominated by professional men and the wealthier artisans. Elsa was doing a fine job here, the doyen of Amsterdam florists. She had become rather tedious in her attentions, but she was a splendid woman. Of course, she and all the other connoisseurs would suffer when the market collapsed, and if they were all made to pay up there would be a run on the new banks—which was what Azor and his schemers wanted—but Elsa had a money coffer in the house. She was surely wise enough to secure her reserves, keep an amount from her husband's business set aside for emergencies; she'd survive.

The greatest impact of the collapse was going to be felt in Haarlem—and Hoorn—he should go up to Hoorn, as well. Over the past few years, the people of Hoorn had lost nearly all their shipping business to Amsterdam; some men had fallen on hard times and were using the tulip trade like a lottery. It wasn't helping the town itself, but they were clearly hoping it would reverse their individual fortunes. In this respect, it might be a good idea to rattle Marcos's contacts bag—see what fell out. Ludo drummed his plump fingers on the table, in this he had been remiss; he had promised to oversee the boy's business and had done nothing.

Finishing his brandy in one gulp, Ludo got to his feet and dropped some coins on the table, paying for the weakened brandy and his follower's fare with an over-generous tip. He then made a business of moving his chair, putting on his hat and cape, getting to and opening the street door—giving de Kuyper plenty of time to recognize and acknowledge him if he so wished. There was no response; the crotchety old man didn't even look up. *No matter*, thought Ludo; he felt a lot better than when he'd come in, and with a lighter step he set off for his rented rooms to pack a travelling bag.

His immediate plan, however, had to be modified, for when he opened his door he found Count Azor and a long-legged man in clerical black waiting for him.

"There you are!" he said, and tried to look pleased.

Once more, he removed his hat and cloak, then hung them carefully to dry. Taking his time, he went to stand beside the blazing fire in the grate.

"As you see, gentlemen, from this splendid fire, I've found an efficient landlady."

Ludo rubbed his hands above the blaze, then turned abruptly and, switching to Italian so he could master any subtleties, said, "Now, what can I do for you?"

Count Azor looked at the thin man beside him and made no attempt to speak.

"I have some decent wine:. May I offer you a glass?" Ludo said amiably.

Father Rogelio spoke now. It was the studiously acquired voice of a cultured Roman. "No wine. We have come to enquire how your enterprise fares."

Ludo cocked his head on one side and gave him a half grin. "You know that already, *Padre*; you see everything I do through your watchers."

"Watchers have eyes, not brains. We want to know precisely what state you have arrived at in your negotiations and how much longer you intend to wait. I should tell you we are not pleased."

"Not pleased! I've raised the price of a single bulb to the cost of a new canal-side dwelling, plus coach house and horse and carriage. How not pleased?"

"You do not trade on the Stock Exchange."

So they were going to use his arguments against him. He'd warned them the Stock Exchange was almost certainly not going to be their venue. But who was he speaking to here, Spain or the Vatican? Whichever, it was Count Azor who had guaranteed his vessel, so it was Spain that needed to be coddled.

Keeping his voice low and pacing words against irritation he said, "No, the Dutch decided the Stock Exchange was not for gardeners and gamblers. Actually, I think this may have worked in our favour. They would have restricted trading by now and created all sorts of checks and balances."

"So you have failed in your task?" The Roman spoke to, but never once looked at, Ludo. The Spaniard watched him as behove his name, like a hawk. But the Spanish count was not the predator in this scenario.

Ludo was riled. He went to the sideboard and poured himself a large glass of red wine to cover his annoyance. A Genoese would not give a Roman the satisfaction of seeing him ill at ease. As he poured the wine he began to explain how he had established his tulip network and the results he had achieved thus far.

"I have three main brokers—"

"Only three?" the Roman curled his lip.

"Let me explain. Elsa vander Woude brokers deals among connoisseurs, they are only interested in 'superbly fine' tulips and have the money to pay for their transactions. These transactions become a matter of interest for lesser purchasers, who would like to belong to this elite, so they start trading at a similar level. Some do actually have special plants: they name them after admirals and generals and the towns they live in. I arranged for some of my supplies from Turkey to filter down in that direction—a golden bait.

"Then there is Henning. He arranges deals among artisans and professional men here in Amsterdam. I supply him with a wide variety of bulbs at a range of prices and he sells them on, taking a percentage. Lately he has been buying and selling on his own behalf, but that's his business and his risk. Young Marcos you know about, because you've kept a careful watch on him for a while, too."

The Roman ignored the comment, so Ludo continued.

"Marcos travels between the ale houses and taverns in Hoorn and Haarlem. He fixes deals among the unskilled and illiterate, who sell their wares, beg, borrow or steal to acquire bulbs, which they then trade on promissory notes. For them it's no more than gambling, but it serves to keep the prices of what they call *vodderij*—rag goods—which are sold by the pound in baskets, high. All this goes on in taverns. The beer and wine they consume blurs their logic nicely."

Ludo placed his wine glass on the chimney piece, bent to shift a log in the grate, then straightened up, saying, "Each of these three—and no one seems to mind that Elsa is a woman, except her neighbours, who need something to gossip about— each of these three has perhaps twenty-five to fifty direct and indirect contacts. Now, and this is why I think you are mistaken about the Stock Exchange, if just Henning's and Marcos's contacts sell through a tavern college auction three or four times a week, you can double or triple the number of sales generated. Let's just say you shouldn't underestimate the scale of business being done. Marcos tells me some of his contacts will buy and sell on up to five times in a day if bulbs are special, or someone *thinks* the bulbs are special—, or someone *says* the bulbs are special."

"You are suggesting some of these bulbs don't exist?" Count Azor asked.

Ludo inclined his head. "Who's to say? Half the year they're underground and the other half they're locked away in dark chambers."

"Haarlem, Hoorn and Amsterdam, you've hardly set the United Provinces by the ears." The tall Roman waved an effeminate hand in dismissal as he spoke.

"On the contrary, the rage has spread well beyond the borders of Holland to Utrecht and Groningen, and now they're buying like mad in northern France as well."

Ludo waited for a second to see if the reference to France would have any effect. He clenched a fist behind his back, thinking the whole scene was a staged play; they were just trying to wriggle out of rewarding him for his work. That made him very angry. It was one thing to be unscrupulous in a business deal, quite another to not honour a debt.

"In Haarlem alone," he said quietly, "not a big town, there are about four hundred florists. These are men who work solely buying plants from growers and selling them on to whoever can pay their prices. Prices are still rising. But soon—just wait until the next flowering—they will drop in a most dramatic manner. It will be as the Count and I discussed in Madrid. So I wouldn't say I have failed. Quite the reverse."

Count Azor gave a cynical moue and said, "You have looked to your own fortune?"

Ludo looked him in the eye, "I'm no gardener, Count. My interest lies only in a sea-worthy vessel. I thought I had made that plain."

He went back to the sideboard and took out the folded parchment galleon. Placing it on the palm of his left hand, he held it out to them. "A seaworthy vessel with a flag that has a tulip on it—like this."

Count Azor touched his moustache and turned slightly towards the Roman cleric.

Father Rogelio said, "Tell us how prices will fall and when this is going to happen. I fear it will be more difficult to engineer with all these... amateur arrangements. The Stock Exchange would have been easier to control."

"If you still believe the Stock Exchange is the answer to your political manoeuvring, perhaps you should assign someone with better connections here in Holland—a Dutchman, for example—to arrange it," said Ludo sharply.

Father Rogelio responded with quiet menace. "You challenge me, and all I represent? Is that wise?"

"I do not challenge you. As you said yourself, your watchers have eyes, not brains. I am giving you the information your informants haven't managed to grasp. I accepted a distasteful task for the promised reward of a seaworthy vessel." He looked directly at Count Azor.

The Spaniard avoided his eye.

Ludo placed the vellum ship on the mantelpiece. Keeping a large hand beside it, he turned to face his visitors once more. Trying to keep his voice even, he said, "I have stayed here in Holland for that promised reward and that reward alone. I have absolutely no interest in tulips or politics, or religion. Not that this charade has much to do with religion. What you two and whoever it is you represent are after is territory. For reasons I can't be bothered to fathom you're more interested in this strip of wetness so aptly named The Netherlands than the saving of souls. I don't know if you want the country back under Spanish control or whether you just want to prevent someone else acquiring it—frankly, I don't care. Perhaps you're thinking to harness the Dutchman's thrift and productive skills for your own benefit, or just want to punish his independence with your blessed Hail Marys. I repeat: I don't care."

Ludo paused, waiting for a response, but neither man spoke. He sipped his wine and waited; then, addressing Count Azor, he said, "When we renewed our agreement in Madrid I stated clearly I only cared about getting the ship."

Father Rogelio of the Roman curia exploded. "Ship! Ship! Who gives a damn about your blasted ship?" Getting to his feet he turned a look of hate on Ludo. "Men like you don't merit...." he began, then stopped. "Come," he said to the Spanish nobleman, who rose as he was bid.

As they went through the doorway, Ludo held up a hand and said quietly, "I would avoid conversing in Spanish, Italian or Latin in the street, gentlemen. Remember how your predecessors were chased off by rebels. Hollanders won't tolerate the Spanish—or high Roman priests. Remember what they did to your churches."

The two men stared at him for a moment, then as one turned and began to descend the staircase. It being too narrow for two abreast, the Spanish count, representing the King of Spain, was obliged to follow the base born cleric from Rome.

Ludo closed the door and poured himself another drink.

Holding an arm up against the light of crude tallow candles, the man who called himself Count Azor examined the Bruges lace of his cuff. He was in a foul mood. It had not been easy to arrange for a ship to be made available in Lisbon: months of paperwork, and now it looked like the Roman wanted to renege on the debt—or worse. The whole affair had got out of hand, and he was powerless to do anything about it.

What the Roman proposed to arrange after the market crashed might appear convenient to him, but it would not do. The Spanish government relied heavily on the Genoese for financial, military and mercantile support. If word got out that he, representing the Spanish government, had been responsible for Ludovico da Portovenere's disappearance, it might jeopardize the loans Madrid obtained from Genoa's bankers—and the private arrangements he made to finance his own lifestyle.

On the other hand.... He raised the other arm and bent to examine the fine lace against the candlelight; a globule of grease had embedded itself in a minute knot. On the other hand, it would silence any embarrassing revelations, and he need not be involved at all. Father Rogelio could make his own arrangement. He held his carefully manicured hands to the light and examined his nails. He liked to keep his hands clean.

The man from Rome, who was an ordained priest but whose agile mind and ruthless nature served the Vatican better in less pastoral issues, was also in a foul mood: the damned pirate had been far too successful. He poured himself a cup of sweetened wine and sat by the fire blazing in his own grate, thinking how ironic it was that most people's vision of hell involved leaping flames when it was flames that kept them warm on dark nights in inhospitable climates. Leaning forward, he poked at a damp log and remembered how the Genoese had done the same thing —to gain time and gather his thoughts. Clever. Ludovico da Portovenere might look a come-day go-day adventurer of the flashiest kind, but he was clever, so clever he needed to be stopped sooner rather than later.

As the wine and firelight began to take effect, the Roman put down his glass, slowly undid the buttons at his throat and eased his neck where the tight collar pinched. *A noose for the*

Genoese? he wondered. Not quite yet. Soon, yes, but he would see him humbled first. The others could be dealt with in a more accidental manner, and earlier, before they could point fingers and name names. They were only significant because they had dealt directly with this Ludovico de Portovenere.

Henning would be easy: a bump on the head and into a canal. The woman was large; she would have a sweet tooth. A box of tainted candied fruit would serve there. Tomorrow he would visit an apothecary; they always had such interesting concoctions to sell. Or perhaps marzipan mixed with vanilla: that masked most flavours, whichever the apothecary could provide.

Then there were the watchers. Caritas could be sent to a silent order. That would shut him up, mumbling, bumbling old fool—a mountain-top monastery somewhere chilly so his aching bones would be his mortification. The same for the feeble Englishman, but a different mountain top. He would probably like that.

That left the Spanish boy. Where *was* he?

"John!"

"Hello, Thomas. Am I disturbing you?"

"No, come in. Good Lord, you look frozen and worn out."

"It is cold."

"Sit down, here, come...."

Thomas raised an arm to indicate a fireside chair, but as he moved a paroxysm of coughing shook his body and left him speechless. John crossed the room to him but was waved away. Once he could speak, Thomas said, "Don't come too near. Just a second—let me get my breath."

John Hawthorne removed his coat without taking his eyes off his friend. Thomas had lost a lot of weight: his slight frame looked emaciated.

"Have you consulted a doctor?" John asked.

Thomas nodded. "Apothecary made up a draught for me—foul brown stuff—just makes it worse." He steadied himself and took another deep breath, trying to swallow the impulse to break into another fit coughing. "That's better.... Sorry to greet you... like this. Do, please, ... sit down." He got up and patted the back of his armchair. "I'll call... for a warm drink." His chest heaved between phrases and his face was suffused with colour. "We share my lad Mark... and a cook here. It's... like being a student in the old days. Mark... is in his element; I doubt he'll... return to our quiet Cornish... backwater."

"But you will?"

"Oh Lord above, yes," he said with a gasp. "But let's get you warm... before we think about that," he wheezed. "I'll get Mark to heat us some ale... with nutmeg and ginger, that'll bring the colour back to your cheeks, ... helps me, too."

"Ginger? Is that wise? Doesn't it make you cough more?"

"Perhaps. I thought that was what I was supposed to do, ... cough and expel the evil humour."

"It's not always best. A soothing draught with borage and honey would be more efficacious. Oil of chamomile will ease the hurt in your chest. How long have you been like this?"

"Months."

"Months! Then it is more than a winter ague."

"I fear so. It will improve... when the spring comes, when I get back to clean air... and good food... at Crimphele. But what about you? You look as if you've ridden... all the way from Tamstock."

"I have."

"All the way? Why didn't you come... by ship?"

"It would have been worse."

"Well, you're here now, and it is *so* good to see you. I haven't had word... from home for months. All I hear comes... via Rundell's family, but they haven't... been in Cornwall for over a year now either, ... all their news is second hand."

Thomas, his phrasing still punctuated by gasping breaths, went to the door and called for the boy Mark to bring them warmed ale. John sat by the low fire holding his thick riding coat and gloves on his lap.

"Let me have those," said Thomas. "Where's your bag? You're staying here with me, I hope."

The two friends sat together by the fire and chatted as if they had seen each other only yesterday. The warmth and cheer, and perhaps the ale, seemed to act as a restorative for Thomas, and his breathing eased.

John soon discovered Thomas knew nothing of his mother's death. So, choosing his words carefully as was his wont, and leaving out the weeks of wasting sickness, he gently informed his friend that his mother was no more. He didn't add that unpleasant deaths such as hers were not uncommon in the Tamstock area, although it was something that continued to bother him. Tin-mining folk died of sickness to the stomach, not gentry. But his friend could be spared these thoughts.

"And Alina?" Thomas asked quietly.

John handed him Alina's letter. "Read that first, and then I will answer your questions. It is all a sad business, and she has grown quite bitter. But read first."

Mark brought in their drinks and put them on the small round dining table, acknowledging John with a bow and a "How do, sir." Then he picked up the coat, hat and gloves and left the room as quietly as he had entered.

Thomas read Alina's letter twice, then sat in silence, a hand covering the pain in his chest. John tactfully left his side, went to the table and sat there nursing his warm tankard, waiting for his friend to speak.

Eventually, Thomas said, "I must go home."

"What is stopping you, Thomas?"

"The Queen and Rundell. They have got as many of us titled Catholics here as they dare. We, and a few academics, are involved in... how shall I put it? There are issues afoot."

"Issues? Do you mean schemes, plots, plans?" The priest's voice was a whisper.

"I do."

"Ah, then you *are* needed."

"As a foot soldier is needed in a battle, John. I'm here to swell numbers, nothing more." Thomas stirred fretfully, and a surge of coughs overcame him.

"But surely your promise is what counts. You can wait for the—event, occurrence, disturbance, or whatever is planned, just as well at Crimphele."

"Yes, but I have been set to translate a text for Her Majesty, and the book cannot be removed from here. You would enjoy the task. It's the life of St Francis; I'm making an English version from Latin. I don't know which monastery it came from, but it must have taken years to complete; there are three or four different sets of handwriting. The illustrations are exquisite. Someone has had it safely locked away out of sight for a hundred years, and now I am translating it. It's a fine privilege."

"Indeed," John smiled, "I would enjoy it." A thought came to him. "If I helped, we could finish the job in half the time and perhaps you could be released to go home. Or I could stay in your place and do it for you. Surely you should be released on health grounds; you are terribly thin. Let me take over."

"Would you? Would you really do that for me?"

John smiled. "Of course I would."

"I will have to talk to Her Majesty's secretary; it might take time. Perhaps I should go to Rundell first. It's not so simple: one cannot simply absent oneself from a queen."

"No, obviously. Oh, I nearly forgot, and this is of first importance. Alina told me she had mentioned it in her letter— what of poor Robert?"

"Robert?" Thomas began to cough again. A spasm shook his whole body. He dabbed a handkerchief to his mouth and bent over to ease the pain in his chest.

John leaned over to rub his friend's back, but again Thomas shifted out of reach. "No," he said shaking his head, "keep away." After a while he was able to breathe more normally and started again: "Our Robert from Tamstock?"

"Yes, he was sent to bring word of Lady Marjorie's demise."

"I haven't seen him. He never arrived."

The two men looked at each other.

"Robert is not the sort of man to leave his employment or his wife Molly and their baby son to go off adventuring."

"No," replied Thomas, "but if he was carrying a generous travelling allowance a cutpurse and his mate could have waylaid him in a Plymouth alley in broad daylight, or even on the road nearer to home. Was he to have come by boat?"

John nodded in reply. "It's easy enough to get a place on a barge working between London docks and the Barbican, but travelling by sea has its risks—I should know! Any sort of sea-going or water-side accident could have happened."

They were quiet for a minute, each considering the respective dangers of travelling to and from such a distant county as Cornwall. Then as one, they made the sign of the cross at similar thoughts.

Chapter Thirty-seven
Crimphele, Christmas 1636

McNab, his hands blue with cold, stamped mud off his boots and pushed open the new front door. His greyhound nosed ahead of him and pattered into the left-hand corridor that to the estate office, the sewing room, and what had once been the house-keeper's room.

Lady Marjorie had dismissed the housekeeper just weeks after the new south range was finished, and she had never been replaced. Aggie and McNab had taken on the two or three duties Lady Marjorie found unnecessary to do herself. The housekeeper had come to them from a much larger house in Devon and had referred to her past employers once too often. Lady Marjorie suspected, quite rightly, she was being compared and sent the woman packing.

Since that time, Aggie had told the mistress of the house what stores were needed for the kitchen, and McNab had kept her informed about the dairy, the creamery, and what produce was available from the estate. He also had regular access to the main house, because he kept the estate account books—accounts that since Sir Thomas' departure and Lady Marjorie's demise no one had troubled to oversee. Despite her earlier insistence, the Spanish woman never came near him.

But she was near him now, facing him in the narrow corridor. They would pass close enough for him to touch her, to reach out and grab that golden hair and twist it in his cold hands until she screamed, to pull her into his office.... She should cover her head like a modest woman, she dressed to tempt him....

Alina stopped in her tracks. "What are you doing here?" she demanded.

"Come to set the day's work down, ma'am. I always do, you know that."

"You are early."

"It's Christmas Eve, ma'am. We finish early this night, to prepare for the midnight service. The men go across to St Andrew's or up to the old chapel near Gurney; either way, it's a good walk from here."

"Very well." Alina turned and walked back to the sewing room.

McNab opened the door to the estate office and his greyhound went straight in and up to the cold grate. Plonking herself down with a sigh, she stared at the dead cinders.

McNab scowled. The skivvy Clarice hadn't even cleaned his grate that morning. It was part of the Spanish woman's campaign, of course, but she was a fool if she thought an unlit fire would send him on his way. How stupid she was to aggravate him. Revenge was so easy: altering two columns of figures was the least of it; winter planting could be delayed, sheep left out of the fold, wood not cut. There was a whole host of ways to get his own back. Except, ultimately, he was damaging his own reputation. The estate workers used to murmur against his obsessive timekeeping and attention to detail; now they queried his slackness. If he diverted too many funds, too quickly, it would come to light, and he was the only person to blame. And he wasn't planning to leave, not yet.

He had travelled far enough these past fifteen years. First from Scotland, then from the house near Birmingham, then the months in London—he'd been doing well there, but *she'd* got the better of him. Elspeth, they'd called her—Lady Elspeth. There was always one of them, taking advantage of her class to primp in front of him, to taunt him with her breasts or her hair, or the way she moved. Always one base, dirty woman who thought being gentry gave her the right to tease every male she set eyes on.

There was that other one in London—playing in front of the old lion at the zoological park. Poor mangy creature was locked behind iron bars and she was taunting it, laughing at it, thinking she was safe. She screamed blue murder when it growled. Well, *he* wasn't locked away, and he was never going to be. And it was up to him to teach women like that, show them they shouldn't taunt men.... They had to learn. But each time, someone found out and blamed him, not her!

He had to be careful now. Choose the moment. The Spanish bit would get what she deserved, then he'd go. He'd get right away, get to Plymouth and onto a ship for Virginia. Virginia. He gave a satisfied little snort. That's where he'd go. The name was right.

Pulling himself back to the present, McNab breathed on his ice-cold hands and began logging the estate-work completed that day. But his mind wouldn't focus on the task. A ship to a new land... start all over again... and this time as his own master. This time with all the funds needed to build his own house on his own land, and grow... tobacco. He reached inside his jacket for his tobacco pouch and sniffed. Tobacco. It could be done. And they wouldn't know until he was safely away down the Tamar and out, far out to sea.

Alina waited for what seemed an age, tidying threads in the spool-box, folding the linen they were hemming for sheets and towels; then, closing the door silently behind her, she trod softly down the corridor. She went straight to the kitchen to oversee preparations for the evening meal. All the household staff had been told they were to eat with her in the great hall to share the celebration of Christmas Eve. It was as close as she could come to making up for the one aspect of life in Spain she badly missed: long, communal meals with wine and joking, and very often song. They always sang Christmas songs on *Noche Buena*.

The spirit of peace and goodwill, however, was not apparent in the kitchen. Crook-back Aggie was rolling at her pastry in a fury, the wooden pin shooting up and down, up and down and across. Molly, who was married to Robert and was therefore known as Molly, Robert's wife—or just Molly Roberts—stood on the other side of the table. Hands on hips, she was giving Aggie a piece of her mind. Meg was tending a cooking pot with her back to them, evidently trying to stay out of the argument.

Alina started to say, 'What's wrong now?' then held her tongue. They would drag her into their perpetual arguing, and she was tired of it. Molly resented Aggie going up to the nursery; Aggie didn't want Molly preparing thickened soups and vegetable pap for the children in her kitchen. Instead of trying to arbitrate, Alina cut across them in the tone of voice she used when her brothers were at each other's throats.

"Enough! Stop! Tonight we have a special meal for Christmas. Tonight we are friends. Molly, if you want Aggie to make food for the children, ask her. Tell her what you need and when, then let her do it."

There was silence. The two women avoided her eye.

"Meg, while Agnes finishes the pies, you see to the children's food. Molly, who is with the children?"

"I only left them for a moment, milady. They're safe enough for a moment. They'll be up there on their own tonight."

"No, they will come down for the meal."

Molly stared at the Spanish woman. "But they're babies, milady. They should be asleep."

"They can sleep late tomorrow, we will all sleep late tomorrow."

"But, beg pardon, ma'am, they'll cry and disrupt your party."

"No, you and I will hold them and they will sit with us and play with spoons and share our food. They are our children and it is a special occasion."

Molly Roberts shook her head, then said, "If you say so, milady."

"I say so. Now go back quickly. McNab is in—go. Meg will bring you the children's soup and something for yourself if you are hungry."

Aggie's rolling pin had slowed down almost to a halt at the mention of McNab; she turned her head to catch a glimpse of the Lady Arleen's expression.

Molly, who did not like being in the wrong, cast a venomous look at Aggie and flounced towards the kitchen stairs to go up to the first floor children's nursery. Then she turned, placed her hands on her hips and said, "Lady Arleen, when you insisted I stay here to look after Sir Thomas's boy and said I could keep my Bobby with him for company, I was grateful. Most days I dreaded going back to our cottage with no husband there and his mother round every two minutes asking what had become of him and when was he coming home. She wanted to know what had happened between us to make him stay away—the old bi—biddy. Robert's the talk of Tamstock, now they've worn out the death of poor Lady Marjorie. But it's getting too much for me. You expect me up in that nursery with the fire blazing like a bread oven day and night. Sometimes I feel like I'm guarding the child, not nursing it. And it isn't *right*, any of it. I know it in my bones, it isn't *right*. What if Robert comes home and finds our cottage cold and empty and us not there? What will he think? He won't know I'm up here, which might seem very grand to some I could name but it's ever so lonely—and it means I have to deal with *her* all day, every day."

Molly pointed a finger at Crook-back Aggie. "It's more than I can stand, it is. They all know about Aggie in the village. Nobody likes her, not even her brothers and sisters. And now she's up in the nursery every day, gawping at baby Thomas fit to wear him out. Anyone'd think she'd given birth to him herself. It isn't *normal*. It isn't normal what she done when he was born, but she saved him, Meg said, so I shan't say more on that. But it wasn't *normal*, if you catch my drift, milady? Nor is the way she looks at him and ignores my little Bobby, who's much bonnier in every way, round and smiling, you'd never know he hadn't got a father anymore."

271

She waited for Alina to respond, but Alina only pursed her lips and stared back at her, daring her to say more.

Molly made one last attempt to win her to her side. "Lady Arleen, you want a party in the great hall like they used to have in the old days before Lady Marjorie, but it's not right. Not with the master away and Lady Marjorie gone."

Alina folded her arms across her chest and took a deep breath. She did not want to appear weak but she was close to tears. "Thank you, Molly, for your words. But *I* decide what is right and normal now. Please go back to the children; they have been on their own too long."

Molly clumped up the stairs. Alina left the kitchen and went into the great hall. Meg had arranged holly and winter twigs on the table, and places had been set using the family silver. She could almost hear Lady Marjorie's screech of horror: *Silver for servants!*

A place had been laid for her at the head of the table nearest the fire. Only half the long table was needed, because she had drawn the line at the estate labourers, fearing the event would get out of hand. She couldn't understand them when they spoke together. So there would only be Agnes, Meg, Molly Roberts, Henry the forester and his wife, Will from the stables, Toby from the dairy, Clarice the maid-of-all-work, and Susan from the creamery. McNab would have to be there, but she would pretend he wasn't. Perhaps he wouldn't come; Meg said he never socialized at fairs or the like. Meg hated him too, you could tell.

Alina took another look at the table setting. No place had been laid for Sir Thomas this year, but next year there would be. He and John Hawthorne would be home for Easter. She sighed and walked to the far end of the room. The floor had been swept and the suits of armour in the armoury corner had been polished. The swords on the wall glinted dully in the firelight. The daggers in a row below them actually sparkled. They must have been very dull and dirty, she'd barely noticed them before. There were eight short, sharp daggers.

And now there were seven. Alina removed the smallest and tucked it up her sleeve. Later, she would find a way to fit it into a pocket so she could keep it on her at all times, and never fear McNab crossing her path again. It was only a small weapon, but it would give her the upper hand. The upper-hand: a sword-play term. Her brothers had shown her its importance when they were teaching her what they had learned in their fencing lessons.

She opened the door to the tower to go up to her room and smiled at the sudden draught of cold air. Lady Marjorie had done them all a favour, the wall kept the great hall warmer than it ever used to be.

Chapter Thirty-eight
Amsterdam, January 1637

At the sound of feet on the stairs, Ludo opened the door to his apartment. Plump little Greit, cheeks pink from hurrying, was puffing up the steep staircase, her face a summer rose in mid-winter.

"Greit, how charming you look," he said in his accented Dutch.

Greit stifled a giggle with a hand over her mouth.

"Come in, child, you must be frozen."

"Oh, no, I mustn't! *Me'vrouw* vander Woude said I was only to give you a message."

He cocked his head on one side and smiled, holding out a hand. "So, Greit, you have a message for me."

"Oh, yes sir, here." She fumbled with her hand-knitted muff and withdrew a small letter. "*Me'vrouw* vander Woude said I was to be sure to put it in your hands and not lose it." Having done as bidden, Greit turned like a startled deer to make her escape.

"Careful, Greit, go carefully. It's very icy outside, don't run."

Ludo turned the letter over and sniffed it. Not a perfumed *billet doux*: what did Elsa need to tell him so urgently that it couldn't wait until supper?

Ludovico, come to my house quickly.

He sighed; Elsa was becoming very tiresome. For a moment he was tempted to throw the message in the fire. But he didn't; he finished dressing, put on his thick cloak and set off down the black-iced streets to the vander Woude mansion.

Greit opened the door. "Oh, it's you again!" she said in surprise, then opened the door wide enough to hide her face, saying, "Beg pardon, sir, I was forgetting my place. Don't tell *Me'vrouw* vander Woude, please, sir."

Ludo passed Greit his gloves and gave her a conspiratorial wink, making her bite her lip to keep from laughing.

Elsa was standing in her late husband's study holding a large sheet of paper with what appeared to be a list on it. She was wearing a vast, fur-lined, brown velvet housecoat. There was something about it—or perhaps it was the way she raised her arms when he was shown in—that reminded him of a captured she-bear he had once seen in Genoa.

"Look!" Elsa said, waving the sheet at him. "Look!"

It was a long list of names; admirals, generals and towns, classified under types: *bizarden* and *rosen* and *violetten*, then colours.

"Look," repeated Elsa tapping the paper, "*bruyn purper*! Brown and purple! And it's for sale. They're all for sale!"

Ludo looked not at the paper but at the woman; there was a distinct note of hysteria in her voice.

"Five Brabansons," she cried, "and an Admiral van Enkhuizen—to buy!"

Ludo was rather at a loss what to say. "An important sale, then?"

"Important! It's Wouter Winkel's *whole* collection!"

"And he's selling them all?" Now Ludo was concerned. Had someone instigated the end without him knowing?

"No, he's dead. They are selling his tulip collection to raise money for his children; they're orphans now—in Alkmaar."

"Where's that?"

"Up in the north. We'll have to go."

"Elsa, can we sit down and talk about this? Tell me what is happening and why it's so important, and please speak slowly so I can understand."

"Oh yes, oh, I'm sorry, yes, I'll call for some hot lemon."

"No! Not that concoction. Coffee, do you have any?"

Elsa nodded and looked at him. "Come, we'll go into my sitting room; it'll be warmer there." Despite everything, Elsa evidently still had qualms about talking with her Italian lover in her late husband's office.

Over the not unpleasant coffee, Ludo questioned Elsa about Wouter Winkel's tulip collection. He had, it appeared, been a connoisseur of humble origins who had actually grown his tulips from seed and propagated their offsets, so the collection was real, in as much as each name on the sheet Elsa now clutched to her bosom represented a real bulb. Over the years, Winkel had become famous for growing splendid, rare tulips, and the connoisseurs of Elsa's acquaintance had a very high opinion of the quality of his superbly-fine collection. Now it was up for sale by auction on the fifth day of February in Alkmaar.

While Elsa chatted on about different bulbs, colours and flames, stripes and frilled petals, Ludo considered how to turn the event to his advantage. He questioned her about prices. Winkel bulbs had been selling for vast sums for over two years. Sales at this auction would reach and go beyond anything paid yet. Good, but he needed to be sure of that, and he would raise them higher if need be.

"As a connoisseur yourself, Elsa," he said, "and someone who is very well respected, do you think you could arrange to make a few purchases privately, before the public auction?"

"To get the *violetten* they call Admiral van Enkhuizen, and the brown and purple?" Her eyes were huge. "Could we arrange that?"

"That's what I'm asking. Surely the auctioneers would be willing to sell to a lady such as you. We could persuade them." He raised an eyebrow. "All men can be persuaded by a beautiful face—and a few extra guilders for themselves."

Elsa giggled in a manner not dissimilar to her servant Greit, then her face fell. "But this will have to be for cash. All this will be for real money, no promissory notes—because of the orphans—the money will go to them."

"Ah, well, if you don't think you have enough cash—that's a pity. I've just purchased a share in Jan Company or I'd help you, as I used to do, but...." Ludo looked into the muddy waters at the bottom of his cup, "What a pity."

Elsa looked down at her cup too, her high excitement now deep disappointment. They finished their coffee in silence, then Ludo left her with just the briefest, sweetest peck of a kiss on her cheek.

Elsa waited until she heard the door to the street close behind him, then went back to her chair to stare at the fire and use its hot glow to warm her cold tears. How long she stayed there she wasn't sure, but she must have fallen asleep momentarily, for she woke with a disoriented start when Greit came in for the coffee cups. The girl bobbed a curtsy and went down to report to her friend that it looked like the Italian affair was over. The *Me'vrouw* had been crying.

Elsa looked at the little watch her husband had given her and checked it against the fancy clock on the chimney-piece. How much had this little watch and the clock cost? A lot of money. The watch had a silver casing. The clock had been made by a master craftsman—and the black pearls Ludo had given her that she had converted into buttons: how much had Ludo paid for them? And the jewellery she kept in her room and never wore; and the paintings Cornelis had acquired as payment in kind from different artists, and.... She got up and went down to her front door. Starting from there, she walked slowly around each room in her tall house, making a mental inventory of each valuable item that could be pawned to raise cash for the Alkmaar sale. When she got to her late husband's office she sat at his desk and wrote a list from memory. Then she took the key for his money chest from the ring at her waist. Over the past two years she had been using his savings; there wasn't much left. But she had her tulips as capital now, so she wasn't poor by any means. There was a fortune, the equivalent of a whole treasure trove, buried in her garden alone.

Cornelis would not have approved, but the vander Woude name still represented solid wealth. If she used the last of his funds to purchase the best of the Winkel collection, then in a month or two sold them on... why, she would make another fortune. This time, though, she silently promised her dead husband, she would only accept payment in hard cash, and that cash, in the form of tangible guilders, would come straight back into this very chest. Elsa laughed, problem solved.

She sat down at Cornelis' desk to write Ludo another little note.

Chapter Thirty-nine
Alkmaar, February 1637

Marcos had taken a long time to get to sleep; he hadn't been a in a proper bed with sheets and blankets for what seemed like years. On the *jacht* from Rotterdam he'd slept in his new cloak on a bed of grain sacks stuffed so full they felt like rocks. When he finally came to consciousness, it took a few moments to remember where he was, and then he sighed and curled back into the feather mattress to sleep some more.

He was half awake when Ludo came into the room and stood looking at his sleeping form for a moment. The girl that came in to do the housework and bring their meals had prepared a jug of warm ale and left some sweet-smelling, freshly-baked bread, but neither that nor the clatter she made cleaning the grate had roused him.

Ludo stooped to pick up a shirt dropped by the bedside and looked at the other clothes Marcos had arrived in. A good quality cotton shirt with plenty of frills, fine knee hose, an expensive leather belt, and a pair of fancy shoes wholly inappropriate for the snow and treacherous black ice on the streets outside.

Marcos opened a crusty eyelid and smiled. "Like them?"

"Good quality."

"French. They know how to dress, the French."

Ludo nodded. "You were in France?"

"I was everywhere."

"Hungry?"

Marcos sat up. "Starving."

"On the table by the fire. Don't bother to dress."

Marcos got out of bed, pulled a blanket round him and staggered into the sitting room.

Ludo watched Marcos drink some ale then said, "You couldn't find him?"

Marcos shook his head. "His name was on a list of men shipped back to Spain from Ostend. It might have been him. Alonso is a common name, could have been anyone."

"Then you went to France?"

"Mmm." Marcos watched Ludo raise an enquiring eyebrow and mumbled, "I sort of needed to get out of Flanders. Got a boat to Dunkirk."

Ludo got up. The topic was closed. Although Marcos knew he'd find out whatever he wanted to know sooner or later.

"Right, then," Ludo said. "Get yourself ready; you're making another little trip. Thick clothes, we're going in an open carriage."

"No. No, no, no," Marcos said firmly, shaking his head, "I'm staying here in the warmth and not moving for at least a week. Then I'm going to the bank to get my money and I'm going back to Spain."

"No, not yet, you aren't. We have got some very important business to oversee. You do need to get your money, though, in gold, from your bank; and call in all your debts. Apart from the planted bulbs you said you'd bought for yourself, have you got any others in your own name?"

Marcos shook his head again.

"Good. Don't buy anything at all from now on. We'll get this bit of the business over, then we'll get the first ship to Spain."

Marcos sighed. "What's 'this bit of the business'?"

"An auction in Alkmaar."

"Where's that?"

"No idea. But a lady is taking us in her private conveyance, so get your gear on sharpish. We're leaving in an hour."

At one point in the journey, Marcos decided he was still drunk in Ostend, or drunk in Breda, Antwerp, Bruges, or he was still in Dunkirk, still celebrating his escape from the ditches and bloody flux of Flanders. Freezing crystals of slushy snow shot up from the wheels into what little of his face he'd not been able to protect. He closed his eyes and tried to daydream the nightmare away.

When he opened them again, they were out in a desolate landscape with not a house in sight. He gazed about and eyed the big man sitting in front of him, whose usually benign expression had become a scowl.

Ludovico, as the lady called him, was tucked under a fur-lined wrap with the large *Me'vrouw,* and the *Me'vrouw* was leaning so close to her Ludovico that at each rut and rumble she tipped against him. Elsa, as he called her, was enjoying the journey, but her Ludovico most definitely was not, that much was obvious. Marcos focused on the flat lands beyond their shoulders and tried to ignore them, but the pained expression on the seafaring merchant's face made him want to laugh out loud. He winked at his *patrón*, a slow, wicked wink and the Italian responded with such a dramatic eye-rolling that he burst out laughing.

"What?" Elsa demanded.

"Er—that cart," said Marcos, pointing randomly in the direction of a capsized cart. He leaned out of the carriage to stifle his laughter and stared at the donkey cart. A greyfriar was tugging at the ass's head and trying to rearrange a cat's cradle of harness at the same time. It was the fat little chap he used to see before he'd gone away.

Eventually, Elsa's driver guided his two sturdy cobs into the narrow streets of Alkmaar. Ludo told him to take them into the town square and wait while he arranged accommodation. It wasn't a market day, but there were plenty of people out walking or standing around chatting despite the weather. Elsa rearranged the blanket around her, and Ludo dragged Marcos out of the carriage, marching him off down a cobbled side street.

The moment they were out of earshot, Ludo began issuing rapid instructions in Italian. "We might not get a chance to talk again. There's a lot more people here than I expected."

He was right; even in this narrow street there were half a dozen men, all dressed in black and wearing such serious expressions it looked like they were on their way to a funeral, not a highly publicized tulip auction.

"I want you to write everything down. I've got a journal for you in my bag. Every time you overhear someone talking prices, write it down. Tomorrow, at the auction, note down each sale, then write it up fully in the journal later."

"Why?"

"Ah, this place looks good enough. Do you think our Lady of the Tulips could lodge here?"

"Looks like beggars can't be choosers to me; all these people have got to sleep somewhere or they'll freeze to death."

"True. I'll get two rooms—you can have a truckle bed in mine."

"Very generous, *patrón*."

Marcos waited until Ludo had finished with the innkeeper and they were back in the street before repeating, "Why? Why've I got to write things down?"

"If prices go as high as this crowd suggests they might, we're going to publish a pamphlet. Next week there'll be such a buying and selling frenzy...." His words were drowned out by a clatter of hooves on cobbles; some dignitary had just arrived in town. "See what I mean?" he said.

There was no more time to talk, because they had to get Elsa into the inn, and she had to arrange for her cobs and the driver to be stabled. Marcos stood aside and let everyone fuss around him.

The ostler in the courtyard was grumbling, "Never had so many horses here at one time. They'll have to be double-stalled, too many in one space and not enough straw. We got servants sleeping in the loft...."

At this point, Marcos picked up Elsa's and Ludo's bags and started up the stairs to their rooms. He wasn't sleeping in any more lofts. He'd had enough of fleas and rats and straw in the past six months to last him a lifetime. Besides, he was *not* a servant.

Elsa had been allotted a partitioned area of a larger room. He and Ludo were going to have to share with two other men from Haarlem, who had already claimed the only bed. He bounced back down to the bar to give his *patrón* the bad news. But he was disappointed; Ludo was not as put out as he'd expected.

"Excellent! Perfect excuse to chat about the auction, discuss prices, question their validity." He gave Marcos a half grin. "You keep quiet, though. Let 'em think you're a proper servant, it'll lend credibility."

That evening Ludo and Marcos accompanied Elsa to the tavern once owned by the late Wouter Winkel. Ludo and Elsa were shown into the back room used for bulb sales. Marcos stayed in the main room itself to keep an eye on some of the rougher customers; Elsa had a great deal of money in her plain leather bag.

Quietly and privately, Elsa negotiated the purchase of the *violetten* bulbs and the Brabansons she so coveted with a very well-informed overseer from the town orphanage. A lawyer acting for the Winkel estate, who was also a close friend of one her connoisseur associates, wrote down every detail of the transaction. They agreed on 5,200 guilders for the *violetten* collection and 3,200 guilders for two lilac-flamed Brabansons. Then Elsa made offers for a few other individually named bulbs. In just over an hour she spent 12,404 guilders and settled up in hard cash.

The lawyer finalized the details of the transaction and they each signed their names on the sale document. *Me'vrouw* vander Woude was then given another sheet of paper stating where on Winkel's land the wonderful flowers would bloom. Naturally, she couldn't actually see what she had bought until the warmer weather set in and the tulips began to flower, but she could take possession of the bulbs when they were lifted in April or May.

On the way back to their inn, Elsa was as excited as a middle-aged woman of her upbringing could ever let herself be. "We'll all go to the public auction tomorrow morning. It will be thrilling to see what the sale achieves."

Ludo agreed because, as Marcos knew, that was his plan anyway, and Marcos nodded sagely.

The auction was to take place in the *Niewe Schutters-Doelen*—the headquarters of the Alkmaar civil guard, which struck Marcos as ironic in some way. He, Elsa and Ludo followed sturdy city fathers, a few of these accompanied by ample wives and eager sons, and the more humble members of the artisan class into the stuffy salesroom. Everyone crowded in until there was barely space to nod a head. Ludo led them around the edge of the room until they were standing to the right of the auctioneer's dais. From here he would have a reasonable view of who was bidding for what so he could, quite by chance, encounter them later.

Marcos waggled his elbows, thinking there wasn't room to put a dot on a domino let alone take notes, but it didn't matter because he had a good memory, and what he couldn't remember he'd invent. For now, he just had to listen.

While they had been waiting outside the guardhouse there had been a good deal of animated conversation as friends met friends and greeted acquaintances from previous sales. The air buzzed with speculation. Winkel's bulbs were justifiably famous; Winkel's bulbs *always* grew offsets; Winkel's bulbs *always* changed from plain to flamed in a season; Winkel's plants had magic properties.... Just saying your bulb had been in Winkel's ground would triple its price. Buy a bag of his least interesting *vodderij* 'rag goods' and next week you'd be a richer man.

Everyone was talking, except Ludo. He had made no attempt to talk to anyone, which in Marcos' experience was unusual and therefore suspect.

The hum of conversation gradually died to a reverent hush. There was a fair bit of jostling as men tried to get closer to the auctioneer's dais, but no one was rude and there was no pushing or shoving. Eventually they were jammed in so tight no movement was possible. Each person stood silent and alert, as if awaiting a great judge to deliver his verdict.

In the crush, Marcos studied Ludo at his side. He was holding his hat in front of his stomach like a shield and scanning the crowd. Marcos tried to follow Ludo's gaze. There were faces around them he vaguely recognized, but he wasn't tall enough to see much more, and it was so cheek by jowl he gave up.

"Who are you looking for?" he asked.

Ludo muttered something that sounded like "de Kuyper and the Roman." Then in a louder voice he said, "Farmers, most of them by the look of their faces. Peter Simonis is here, that's no surprise. And Henning."

"Hope he's buying for a client, or just come for the spectacle," Marcos replied. "Surely the man isn't foolish enough to—"

"Tch!" Ludo put a finger to his lips. "It's their problem, not ours."

As the town-hall clock struck ten, a tubby, baby-faced auctioneer entered the room from a side door and stepped onto the small dais. He lifted his wooden hammer to start. There was a collective intake of breath.

From the first moment, bidding was fast and determined. Henning was involved in the early bidding for single bulbs and acquired two at 200 and 400 guilders apiece. The next bulb was knocked down at 600 guilders and he stopped before that sale closed. Peter Simonis bid for a variety of lots, but he too backed down as the prices began to soar. Of the next hundred or so lots, four went for over 2,000 guilders. Bulbs were being sold for more than a hundred times their weight in gold. Sweaty hands rose above the sea of heads; taller men nodded; shorter men raised an entire arm.

There was no break in the pace or rhythm until the final four, three, two men pitched against each other for a famous *rosen*, Admiral Liefkins, which finally went for over a thousand guilders. After that, there were the last of the red-on-yellow 'crowns', then two good-sized Viceroys, which sold for 4,203, and 3,000 respectively. Then, finally, the mythical, dark purple tulip that some said could be bred to black.

Each lot had been knocked down at a record price, now everyone was craning their neck to see who was going to get the coveted black tulip. At last the gavel struck home. For a second there was absolute silence. Men turned to their neighbours, grinning and nodding knowingly, barely containing the urge to cheer. The self-restraint of their ample wives was sorely tested. The auction room hummed with excited approbation. That these people had not obtained the legendary bloom themselves mattered not; they had witnessed its purchase, and that in a land of traders was a very great deal in itself. They knew that this day's sale, and the astronomical price paid, would be a tale to tell over drinks for the rest of their lives.

Then suddenly they were off again for a whole bed of whites that had 'broken' last spring with hints of pink. The gavel hit home again and again, and men were still buying: they were into common pound goods and trade was still fast.

And then it was over, and everyone shuffled out of the stifling room into an ice cold North Sea wind. Cloaks were wrapped round warm bodies, hats pulled over flushed faces. It was freezing but nobody seemed to mind, and no one was in any hurry to leave the scene of the excitement. They hung around the main door of the guardhouse as if a particularly satisfying marriage had been celebrated. Record prices, they all agreed, record prices!

Each man wanted to relive the moment in which he had made his bids and failed to get, or had actually acquired his dream tulip; how he couldn't breathe for fear of losing it; how he'd have to be very careful over the next few years because he'd spent his entire savings; where he was going to plant the bulb; what he was going to sell to cover the cost.

Then someone came out of the auction room with an amazing piece of information. Men looked at the speaker open-mouthed, then turned to pass it on to those behind who hadn't heard properly.

"*Ninety thousand* guilders."

"How much?"

"*Ninety thousand* guilders!"

"Imagine!"

"All in cash! Real money."

The money raised for Wouter Winkel's seven children was *in excess of* ninety-thousand guilders. A fortune for each of them. No boy would ever need to work. The girls would have their pick of the most eligible suitors in Holland. Men slapped each other on the back as if they alone were responsible for the figure. The women smiled at each other, comfortably satisfied that they had done their Christian duty. Everyone was enormously pleased that they had not just saved seven orphans but made them immensely rich. Everyone was rich!

Whether they had managed to buy a bulb or just been part of the event, everyone went home happy. Not least Ludovico da Portovenere.

As soon as they had finished the midday meal, Ludo made his excuses and disappeared. Elsa stayed close to the dining room fire, chatting happily with people she would never meet on a normal basis and would probably never meet again. Marcos wandered outdoors on his own. He felt strangely downhearted, ill at ease. He wanted to be off, away from Alkmaar and all it represented, but Ludo planned to stay another night.

Marcos was in no mood for smoky taverns and slatternly serving girls. Unfortunately the air was so bitter, so biting cold, he had no choice but to get inside somewhere. He walked as far as the town square and went into what looked like a decent marketplace inn. Ludo was there, leaning against a barrel, holding court. Marcos sighed, went to a quiet corner out of earshot, and ordered a tankard of ale.

The crowd around Ludo swelled and changed. He was encouraging his earlier listeners to talk among the newcomers. The next time Marcos looked in their direction Ludo had gone. Without really wanting to, but driven by curiosity, he handed some coins to a wench with plaits round her head like a helmet and set off to see where his *patrón* had gone next.

Across the square there was another inn. Ludo was talking with another group of men. And then Marcos really did not want to know anymore. He turned and stepped back outside.

Keeping his head down on his chest and pulling his jacket collar up round his ears to avoid the worst of the North Sea blast, he nearly collided with a tiny donkey cart. The poor little beast was clip-clopping down the street, its long ears laid back to avoid the vicious wind. A greyfriar was holding its reins tucked up his wide woollen sleeves. Something about him reminded Marcos of the little old chap he used to see in Amsterdam and the friar he had seen by the upturned cart on their way to Alkmaar. Whoever it was, the hood hid his features, and it made no difference; apart from once wearing a similar habit, a monk of any description was nothing to him.

Over supper that evening Ludo asked Marcos about the notes for his journal. Marcos flushed; he'd forgotten all about it.

"Well, you'd better make a start now, it's important."

"What journal?" Elsa asked.

"I wanted Marcos to write down the prices reached in the auction."

"Why?"

Ludo gave a little half shrug. "Posterity. You might find it useful to know what was paid here—for famous bulbs."

Marcos looked at Ludo; he had never seen him this uncomfortable before. "It's too late now. I can't remember," he said.

"Elsa will help you. She has a great mind for numbers."

Chapter Forty
Amsterdam, February 1637

Two days later, back in Amsterdam, Ludo sat down and converted the list of sale prices Elsa and Marcos had made into a pamphlet describing the amazing auction in Alkmaar. Once finished, he stared at it for a while in silence, then handed it to Marcos.

"Here, find a reliable printer who'll check my Dutch and get this out as soon as possible. Best quality durable paper and clear print."

Marcos looked at the sheet of names and numbers. "What's it for?"

"Some people may see it for what is; a list of sales. Others might see it as a guide for future purchasing. The wise might take it as a warning."

Marcos shrugged. "Can't see the point, but it's your money."

Ludo waited for the boy to leave, then stretched his arms out in front of him, eased his neck, and pushed his thick black hair back from his forehead with both hands. "Nearly over," he sighed.

When Marcos returned from the errand, Ludo was laying his lightweight clothing in the bottom of a cabin trunk.

"What's all this? Where you off to now?"

Ludo gave the boy his half-grin and winked. "Time to find some sunshine."

"Home?"

"If that's what you want. You don't have to come with me. You could stay here."

"But you don't recommend it."

"No."

Marcos looked at the Italian and quite unconsciously adopted his stance: right leg slightly to the fore, arms across the chest, head held high. He sniffed and said, "So what's next?"

"You put your gear on top of this. I got it for you mainly; you've got too much for one carpet-bag. I made a fuss at the dock office about two berths for Genoa in our names; the purser has been paid to unload this at Sanlucar. You'll need to write the address of your mother's hostel on the lid."

"The ship's stopping at Sanlucar? Why don't I just keep it with me?"

"You can if you like. I thought it made a useful decoy, myself."

Marcos looked at him hard and wrinkled his brow. "Decoy?"

"Oh, Marcos, use your brain. Where's the first place they're going to look?"

"They? Who are 'they'? And how do 'they' know where I come from?"

"Depends which 'they' you're referring to."

"*Ai, por favor*, enough of the riddles! Explain."

Ludo ignored him and placed a pair of fancy-heeled shoes in the trunk. "I'm travelling in boots. You should do the same. Now, get down to your bank and withdraw *all* your funds, even if you're not coming with me. Call in all your loans and keep the cash on you. Don't leave a cent in any bank, understand? And don't accept any bank or credit notes."

"Why?"

"I think you're clever enough to work that out for yourself. Same as you can work out why this trunk is a handy decoy. If you can't see straight today, believe me, in a week's time you will."

Marcos looked at Ludo for a long moment. "You're going to undermine them, aren't you? Bring the prices down. Ruin the market. Henning, Elsa—ruin them all."

"I thought you knew that."

"I did. It didn't seem wrong then."

"So what's wrong about it now? If someone's been stupid enough to spend his life's savings on a brown onion, it's his look out. And actually I—we—haven't done anything wrong. We've barely done anything at all, if you consider the size of that crowd in Alkmaar. How many of them there did you even know: two, three, four? Did you force anyone to buy the stuff you started with? Did you have to persuade one person to buy from another and give you a commission for the privilege? No! They've all had the time of their lives, best fun any of them have ever known. Well, buyer beware, I say. All these sober-side Dutchmen with their Calvinist prudence and pruderies: hypocrites the lot of them. You saw them in Alkmaar, slavering, frothing at the mouth with greed and their 'covetousness'. They deserve what's going to happen."

Ludo stopped and held out his hands in a particularly Italian manner, "Maybe I'm wrong and prices will stay high."

"But you've already started the fall, haven't you? I saw you in Alkmaar after the auction. I heard you with those men from Haarlem in our room. *Best you sell on fast and best you sell for cash; don't accept a promissory note on these prices; make sure your next buyer's got enough capital....*"

Marcos sighed. "We'll be at risk, won't we? They'll blame us." He blew through his cheeks. "I thought I'd done with danger when I got to Dunkirk."

There was a silence, each waiting for the other to speak. Eventually, Ludo bent down to resume his packing, and Marcos said, "I'd better go and get my money, while I've still got two legs to walk on."

"They will want someone to blame, Marcos," said Ludo seriously, looking into the depths of the trunk, not at the boy. "It's human nature." Then he straightened up and with a rueful half-grin, went on, "The minute something that could have been avoided happens, people look for someone to blame. I've seen passengers on a ship blame the captain for a storm. If it makes you feel any better, I—we—have only participated in what was bound to happen anyway. Those prices in Alkmaar were absurd. We haven't *caused* anything. They were paying stupid prices for tulips long before we got here."

"But like you say, they'll be looking for someone to blame."

Marcos put his winter cloak back on. "I'll put my stuff in the trunk as soon as I get back, and pack a bag—for wherever we're going."

Ludo folded his arms and watched the boy go onto the landing and down the stairs, thinking how much he had changed, grown up. Those months in Flanders he refused to talk about had altered him. A likely lad had left on an adventure to find his father, and an apparently fatherless, serious-minded young man had returned.

Well, he wasn't responsible for Marcos. The boy had wanted to come to Holland; had stayed the first year out of choice and made a tidy sum out of commission and bulb sales of his own. Flanders must have been an unpleasant experience to make him so gloomy.

Ludo gave his head a shake; he had caught the boy's dark mood. He ran his fingers through his hair, pulled a black ribbon from a pocket and tied it back, then turned to finish the job in hand. Leaving out just sufficient to see him through the next few days, he finished his packing and set his travelling valise by the press in his chamber. Then he remembered something important. He went into the next room and took his parchment galleon from the sideboard. Holding it on the flat of his right hand, he bounced it up and down through imaginary waves, then folded it flat and tucked it into a pocket.

Marcos made his way along the crowded street towards the bank, all the time thinking about the trunk's destination. A woman blocked his way; she was bending down, wiping tears from a small boy's face with her handkerchief. It gave him a jolt.

If 'they' were looking for him, so that it was too dangerous to travel *with* the trunk... if 'they' knew their names were on a ship's manifest for Genoa, stopping in Sanlucar... if 'they' had his mother's address, was she in danger too? Would 'they' go that far to claim money or revenge? Were 'they' just angry florists and tradesmen who thought they were going to be extremely rich and were now extremely poor? No, because these men wouldn't have the means to follow him.

So it was something more serious. He stood stock still, considering the implication of Ludo's dark words and the immediate future.

Had his father reached home? And if so, was he maimed or whole enough to protect them? Was what they had told him in Flanders true? *Please God, let it be true*, he thought. *And let me get home safely as well.* He turned to see if he were being followed, stepped round the woman and child, and tried not to run.

Chapter Forty-one

"So who'll start? What am I bid for these Alkmaar *witte croonen*?"

There was a heavy silence. The auctioneer checked the price chalked on the florist's slate—1,250 guilders. He cut the price down to 1,100 guilders and started again. Not an eyelid flickered.

"At one thousand guilders, a pound of *witte croonen*...."

Someone gulped at a tankard of ale, the auctioneer swivelled to face him.

"No!" said the man shaking his head furiously.

The rest of the men hunched motionless around the tavern auction table. No one spoke.

The auctioneer pursed his lips and looked at each man accusingly, then he tapped his list dramatically and moved on to the next lot. It was the same. No one was buying. He drummed his fingers on the table and after what seemed an age said, "Well, gentlemen, if you don't need me, I have other things to do."

They waited like guilty schoolchildren until he had left the room, and then waited another minute to process what had happened. Then they were all on their feet, talking at once.

Within a week, news of this one small, failed auction had spread throughout the United Provinces. In tavern after tavern, town after town, in one way or another, the scene was repeated. Florists now held bulbs that a few weeks previously had been valued at five times an artisan's yearly wage and now couldn't be sold at a tenth of the price. Some shifted their better known bulbs on to connoisseurs at knock down prices, but the more ordinary flowers, the plain blooms and pound goods, the *vodderij* that labourers, grocers, and workshop apprentices had acquired, wouldn't sell at any price.

Back rooms once crowded with eager buyers who quacked or barked their silly codes to gain entry, now stayed empty. Desperate men, anxious to keep the collective panic at bay, tried to set up sales on street corners, at the doors to their houses. Florists who had made a fortune on paper were now in dire straits. Even if they could recoup the money owed in promissory notes, they no longer had a business. Many of them, who had been living well above their real income, were very heavily in debt. Some went from door to door, some set up mock auctions in tiny market towns far from Amsterdam. But the news had travelled far and fast and no one was buying. The tulip market was no more.

Everyone called in their debts. Anxious lenders insisted; tearful borrowers begged for time. *Wait for the flowering; wait for the tulips to be lifted, there'll be offsets, we can still be rich....* Professional men, city lawyers, doctors and merchants withdrew their savings from the new banks. Weavers sold their looms, carpenters their tools, butchers sold their knives: each man did what he could to pay off what he owed, knowing he would live in poverty for the rest of his life.

Henning went home to his wife and cried like a baby.

"But we have the house, Pauli," she said.

"It will have to be sold."

"We can live in a smaller house."

"A much smaller house, and what shall we live on?"

"But...." Marie Henning looked at the warm, richly patterned rug beneath their feet and bit her lip. She hadn't paid *Me'vrouw* vander Woude for the carpets. "We can sell the furniture. Someone will buy our lovely things."

"Everyone is selling 'lovely things'. Who's going to buy them?"

"*Me'vrouw* vander Woude will help us, won't she?" Then Marie gasped and put her hands to her mouth. The lady might have problems of her own. She might demand payment for the rugs. Nevertheless, she said, "*Me'vrouw* vander Woude will help us, I'm sure."

"Not this time. And I owe her a lot of money I cannot repay."

"*You* owe her money?"

"Her or that damned Italian. He's to blame, he got her started and she pushed me."

"Are we ruined, Pauli?"

"Yes, my dear, utterly."

Elsa sat in her chair facing a warm fire, but the fingers playing with her black pearl buttons were cold as ice. She stared at the bright flames in her hearth and saw only an empty money chest in a cold room. *I shall have to sell them all*, she thought. *All my beautiful tulips, I shall have to sell them all.* 'Who to?' said a silent voice. 'No one wants your tulips. They are worthless.'

"Good," she said aloud, "because I will never sell them. They may be worthless to you, to others like you, but they are everything to me."

I will send the girls away, she thought, *to save on their wages. I will live like a humble widow and bake my own bread and scrub my own floor, but I will never part with a single bulb.*

Elsa turned to look at her row of nightingale's eye vases in a dark recess of the room and tears started from her tired eyes. She had not slept since they had brought the dreadful news, and Ludovico had not come. The clock on the mantelpiece gave its lurching click as it told the hour. Automatically, she checked it against her little silver watch. Time had always been against her. Now with all the worry and the guilt and the crying she looked her years; he would never take her with him to Italy. She would be a humble, lonely widow for the rest of her days.

Chapter Forty-two
Amsterdam, late February 1637

The boy sneezed again and wiped his nose on his upper arm. The box he was holding wasn't heavy and wasn't large, but it was awkward and he couldn't manage it with one hand. Despite the dark, he had located the house easily because there was a lantern hanging above the door and the number was carved into the stone lintel. He'd been at school before the plague took his parents, so he could read numbers. But he couldn't use the shiny door knocker without putting the box down and standing on tiptoe. The wide step had been cleared of snow, but it was still very damp. Carefully, he balanced the box on what remained of his old leather boots, reached up for the knocker and gave a good strong rat-tat-tat.

Josie and Greit, huddled up against the kitchen fire to keep warm, exchanged a meaningful look. Talk of the devil.

"I'll go," said Josie.

"No, it's my job," said Greit, and scampered down the narrow hallway.

She paused at the door to compose herself: she would not smile and she would not offer a pleasant greeting. Slowly, in as dignified manner as she could muster, she opened the door. No one was there. She looked left, then right, then down, and saw a pinched little face and ten blue twig-fingers holding a fat box tied with ribbon.

"For the lady," said the messenger.

"From whom?" demanded Greit.

"The man."

"What man? What's his name?"

The boy shook his head, "Dunno."

"What's he like?" Greit hissed.

The urchin balanced the box in the crook of his left arm and raised his right arm to indicate height. "Tall," he said, "foreign."

"Hmm," huffed Greit, all womanly indignation. She took the box and shook it: bon-bons. "What sort of gift is that for a woman with a broken heart?" she said, looking accusingly at the child.

He didn't move, he was expecting a tip and dithering with cold. Another one caused to suffer by that—libertine. Greit wasn't too sure what a libertine was, but the word fitted nicely into her thoughts. "Libertine!" she said aloud.

The boy stared at her, then turned as if about to run for it when the plump serving girl put a warm hand on his bony shoulder and, bending down, whispered, "Would you like some hot soup?"

His face lit up. "Yes, please."

"Quick then," Greit pulled his ragged form into the hall and shut the door with a foot. "This way," and they nipped down the hall and into the back kitchen as quick as a pair of pickpockets.

"Here," said Greit, passing the square box to Josie, "you take them up. Tell her they're from *him*."

"Him?"

Greit raised an arm, mimicking the boy's action, then folded her arms across her chest and cocked her head on one side.

"Ah," said Josie, and went up the stairs.

She tapped on the sitting room door and entered unbidden, tutting because her employer hadn't moved. She'd been sitting like that when they brought up the tray with her midday meal and a basketful of logs. The food on the tray was untouched.

"A boy brought this for you, ma'am," Josie said quietly.

"What is it?" asked Elsa without looking up.

"A box of bon-bons, I think, ma'am."

"Who from?"

"From the Italian gentleman, ma'am."

Elsa sat up. "Is it Valentine's day? Give them to me." She tore at the ribbon, pulled the close fitting lid off the wooden base.

"A note, there has to be a note—something cheeky about sweets for his sweetheart—something." She poked among the sugar-coated fruits, the candied plums and cherries and sticky green marzipan pears; she lifted the box and shook it until each sweetmeat rolled out of place. There was no note.

"I don't want them. Take them downstairs, you girls have them. Eat them all. Burn the box; I never want to see it again."

Elsa threw the ribbon into the fire and watched it shrivel to nothing.

Josie waited to be dismissed and left the room as the *Me'vrouw* waved a hand. Back downstairs she put the bon-bons on the table. "They're for us," she said.

The skinny boy was sitting at the table, his hands cupped round a bowl of winter broth. When Josie lifted the lid off the box his eyes nearly popped out of his head.

"Sweetmeats," he said with awe.

"Here," said Josie, "you brought them, you get first pick."

He looked at her to see if she was joking. She wasn't, but he waited, he knew his manners. When she nodded, he plunged a dirty paw into the box and pulled out a sugared plum, gobbled it down, then slowly licked the sugar from his lips, "Mmmmm."

The girls' fingers hovered over the sweetmeats, then one after the other took their pick, holding their perfect little fruits to the light to examine their shape, their colour, to prolong exquisite expectation. As they bit into their candied fruits, delicately to savour the texture, sugary liquid dribbled down their chins.

"Mmmmm," they chorused, taking another and pushing the box towards the urchin again.

"Mine's got liquor in it," said Greit, removing a half-eaten red plum from her lips to look inside it. "But it tastes like vanilla."

"Uh-huh," mumbled Josie. "Clove, nutmeg and...." she popped a small, perfect cherry into her mouth and rolled it over her tongue, "sweet almond."

"Delicious," Greit sighed.

Within a few minutes the box was nearly empty. The boy rubbed at the growing, blackening lump on his neck under his untrimmed hair. "I haven't had nothing like this since the feast of Santa Claus. My ma baked cakes with me sisters. My pa gave me a pair of real ice-skates. Now there's just me." He pulled a white-dusted fig from the bottom of the box, popped it into his mouth, then sneezed long and loud. His mouth became covered in sugar and they all started to laugh.

Henning wasn't surprised by the note summoning him to the Prinsengracht, but it was snowing hard and everyone was indoors, windows shuttered against the cold. He knew his way, didn't need a light, but the silent white darkness was eerie and he felt himself hurrying, anxious to get out of the night, anxious to hear the worst.

They were on the bridge, as directed. Each grabbed an arm and heaved. The little fellah was so light he fair sailed over. They waited for the thud on the ice below, then legged it in opposite directions as instructed.

Henning opened his eyes just before dawn, but he couldn't move and he was so cold and so tired he drifted back to sleep again, forever.

Chapter Forty-three

Brother Caritas fumbled with the last of the buckles, hitching the dear little donkey he'd been allotted for the remaining winter months into the now familiar traces. Despite the finger-numbing cold the task had become easier, and this little beast was more amenable than the one they'd given him for Alkmaar. Working in freezing darkness, he had already humped three bales of straw into the cart to make it look full. It had been strenuous work and he was sweating. A guaranteed recipe for a chill.

"*Mierda*," he muttered, pushing back the rough-woven cowl from his head and wiping the back of his hand over his round forehead. His short arms and plump body weren't designed for physical labour such as this. Now, though, he was ready, ready to go—and never come back. Gritting his teeth against the pain in his right hip, he heaved himself into the cart, pulled his hood back over his bald head and turned to check the grey blanket from his cell pallet covering the straw. It would do; not even the officious Night Watch would poke around a plague cart.

Clicking his tongue, he twitched the reins and the donkey moved forward. Wooden cartwheels trundled quietly over snow-carpeted cobbles, and the little hooves barely made a sound. All the same, Brother Caritas held his breath; he hated telling lies and could explain this outing in no other way.

A sharp sense of wrong-doing was sending him back into the city this vicious night. He could not rectify the wrong, but he could do something to ease his conscience, and save his own skin. If they could remove human evidence as quickly and as easily as *La Bicha* had arranged that day... was he next? He was a witness *and* participant, although precisely to what was by no

302

means clear. The man from Rome, whose real name he did not know, had once flashed the Pope's seal past his eyes, meaning what he ordered could not be challenged. He could plead that, as a humble friar, he had been following the Church's instructions, except that wasn't going to get him out of this appalling business. None of it was remotely ecclesiastical: in fact it was downright evil. He had hated everything to do with the Inquisition in Spain, which was why he had gladly taken the road to France, then on to Flanders all those years ago.... Then this *bicha* arrives and tells him to report on the Henning family —good Catholic, Christian folk. What he had overheard this day, however, what *La Bicha* was arranging... he could not ignore. And it was his moral duty to warn those in peril.

The harbour was chock-a-block with vessels waiting for the worst of the weather to blow over. Once the blizzard ceased, it wouldn't be difficult to get a passage. He—they—just had to get away before *La Bicha* found them, and leave no clue as to their immediate destination. One day, of course, they would be found. For now, though, he'd think in the short term. He flicked the reins, clicked his tongue, and the donkey shifted into a reluctant trot.

When they finally reached the city, Brother Caritas left the cart a fair way from the foreigners' lodgings and tried not to hurry. The landlady let him into her house, terrified at the implications of a having a man of God arrive in the dead of night. They went up the stairs together and knocked on the Italian's door. No one answered. The old lady, fearing they were dead of the plague—and nearly a month's rent owing—opened it with her key. They weren't dead in their beds. They were gone.

Not long gone, however; there were red embers in the grate. The warm glow illuminated a pile of thick coins on the table. The woman started to count them.

"Every week to the end of the month," she grunted. "A real gentleman, that Italian, and no mistake."

"Where would you go if you were them?" Brother Caritas asked his little donkey, half an hour later. "Not the north, not in this weather. No southerner goes north if he can help it."

The cart turned out from the lee of the city wall and was met by a blast of white wind direct from Siberia.

"South, they'll go south, but not tonight, and not overland. So, assuming they know they need to get away, but they can't get a ship and they can't travel by road... hmm.... If you had to wait for one thing and keep out of the way of another, where would you go?"

The donkey didn't answer. It was too busy getting to a safe place of its own. As they neared the harbour, it broke into a sprightly trot and came to a dead halt at the main gate of a livery stable right on the wharf.

Brother Caritas looked around at the lights from the neighbouring taverns and stews and said, "Exactly, well done. Somewhere public, well-lit, and full of witnesses. And warm."

The donkey brushed up against the high, closed gate of the livery yard, rubbing crusted snow from an ear.

"The gates are closed, we can't get in there," said the friar, extracting an icicle from under his nose. "Or can we?" He had just spied a narrow door cut into the tall portals for the entry and exit of bipeds. "D'you think you could squeeze through there, naked?"

In a moment the cart was unhitched and he was stepping through the door. The donkey took no urging and hopped in after him. A beast of mythical proportions immediately lunged at them from nowhere. Chains rattled, fangs bared, a mouth frothed. The donkey skittered forward, nearly knocking the friar flat, and hurled itself against another closed doorway.

Brother Caritas lifted the latch on this wide door, sniffed the comforting scent of warm straw and sleeping equines, and gently pulled the bridle over his little friend's long ears. For a moment he leaned into the bristly fur of the donkey's neck, tracing an arthritic finger down its dorsal sign of the Holy Cross.

"You stay here now. You'll be safe here," he whispered. And for more than another moment he considered bedding down in the straw and staying there, too. It would have been so easy and not so surprising: a little fat friar asleep in the hay.

Ludo hurried Marcos down empty streets, through alleys and across private gardens until they reached the city wall and the snow-surfaced cobbles to the harbour. Despite the cumbersome bags and the slushy mush of garden mud, Ludo was surprisingly agile. More than once, it was he that offered his gloved hands as a stirrup to hoist the younger man over a wall. At the time Marcos was too scared to notice. When the Italian had said, "We've got to go *now*," he knew this was the end, that he would go too. He wasn't going to stay and 'risk it'. He didn't know what or who had finally set Ludo in motion, but it had to be someone powerful, because the Italian had really got the wind up.

On any other night the harbour scene would have been both beautiful and disquieting. As the snow ceased and the moon slipped out between laden clouds, Marcos could just make out ships lying spine to spine in the freezing Ijsselmeer. Stripped of sail they looked like butchered whales, carcasses white as snow, each corpse covered in a mantle of ice.

Ludo pushed him on, hissing, "What d'you think this is, a night time pleasure jaunt?" and propelled him towards a tavern. "Get in there."

Marcos opened the door into another world.

"It's full to bursting," he groaned, "someone's bound to know us."

"Get in! This lot wouldn't know the difference between a tulip and a toffee-apple."

Marcos was right in one respect, though; the tavern was full to bursting and noisy beyond belief. Raucous voices competed against a constant background din. Joking, cursing, and toasting the next round, a dozen Poles and Germans, who had timed it too late to get back into the Baltic, crashed their pewter tankards together. Danes and Icelanders, who sailed prepared for the worst of any weather but were glad of any excuse to stay in port, were enjoying a marginally more sedate drinking contest. A bevy of Frenchmen still wearing their frills and feathers were settled comfortably around a large table. Six or seven Italians had taken possession of a space close enough to the hearth to singe their breeches. In the corner farthest from the hearth, a huddle of Russians in bear skins crowded round a bottle of lethal clear liquor.

Ludo took stock.

'What? Marcos demanded.

Ludo frowned. "Various possibilities, various solutions, but not the one we're seeking. No doorman here to check for knives, which I don't like." For a moment he vacillated, then said, "*Boh*, it's noisy, public and warm; if we have to wait a day, two days, or a week, this should do."

He put his hand on the back of Marcos' neck and propelled him through the chaos, edging him into a space at the back of the room. There was nowhere to sit and nothing to sit on, so they stood—with their backs to the wall—not far from the scullery door.

When the friar came in Marcos nudged Ludo. "That's the old cove that's been following me."

Before he finished the sentence, Brother Caritas had located them and was pushing his way through the mêlée.

"You're being followed," he said in a dramatic Spanish whisper.

Ludo raised an eyebrow. "Not anymore."

"Not by me. Well, yes by me, but not anymore, if you see what I mean?"

Ludo and Marcos exchanged glances. Ludo leaned down, mimicking the friar's stage whisper said, "Friend or foe?"

"Friend, obviously! Aha!"

A drunk had toppled with a head-cracking smack onto a table. The front legs of his chair teetered forward just far enough to allow the friar to ease the back legs from under him.

"That's handy," he said, shoving the chair up against the wall. He was about to sit down when Ludo grabbed his shoulder.

"You've lost part of your skirt, dear. Been in a scrimmage?"

"*Jodido perro*," muttered the friar, trying to peer over his left shoulder. "Ah well, I've got another one." He pulled the rough greyfriar's habit up over his head and stood before them in the slightly more tailored black outfit of a Dominican monk.

Ludo bent now towards Marcos. "It has been my experience that humour often accompanies quite real danger. I'm reminded of our Mr Hawthorne in a splendid storm. Keep your eyes peeled."

"Have the chair," said the friar looking up at Ludo, "I can sit on this." He bundled his filthy old habit into a cushion and dropped it on the floor. "Have you ordered anything yet?" he asked hopefully.

Apart from wood, cloth and sacks of grain, the *fluyt* was already laden with untreated beaver pelts and pickled herrings; the smell was appalling. But after two days and two nights in the fug of tobacco and peat smoke they stank like kippers themselves. The Dutch captain, red-faced, beer-bellied, was taking a mixed cargo to Dublin by way of Southampton and Plymouth. He and Ludo had become the best of friends.

Word had gone round the tavern late that night: the wind had changed. A warmer south-easterly was blowing. Ice was cracking. Many crews left there and then. This skipper said they could wait until morning. One more night wouldn't matter; his *fluyt* was the fastest vessel on the Ijsselmeer.

"And you know why?" he'd asked in his cups. "You know why? Because I take out her guns! I say to myself, who wants to steal bricks and pots and sacks of smelly skins? We haven't met a pirate in thirty years. I have no guns and we're the fastest *fluyt* out of Amsterdam."

That morning there was a fairly dense white fog, although not nearly dense enough for Marcos: he became more and more nervous with each counting and recounting of sacks as the *fluyt* was loaded. He was just about to suggest they try for a passage elsewhere when Ludo led him over to the tender. For one happy moment he thought the greedy friar hadn't noticed and Ludo was planning to get away without him, but then the old boy came waddling up and took an age getting himself into the boat.

Delays had been making Marcos grind his teeth, but now, as they rowed out into the Ijsselmeer, he began to wonder if they weren't getting themselves into a trap. Why had the skipper, *Der harte Seevogel* they called him—same name as his ship, 'the tough old seabird'—why had he accepted Ludo's offer so fast? True, they'd watched him lose at cards for the best part of a night, so he needed a little extra from somewhere, but why all the waiting when other ships had set off at first light?

The tender pulled in against the pear-shaped hull of the *fluyt* and they climbed aboard. Then there was more standing around, with a whiff blowing up from the open hatches like the vapours from hell. Not that he cared about the smell or the cold, or having to sleep in the belly of a ship like a rat on a sack again; he just wanted to get away. Standing on deck here made them easy targets—even in the fog. If someone were waiting his chance—or two men—the friar said there were almost certainly two—now was their best opportunity.

Marcos stared around the way they taught him during that awful week in Flanders, when he was trapped behind enemy lines with no dry powder in his dead man's musket. The crew was busy checking cargo or ropes. No one seemed out of place—like a fat Dominican monk or a large Italian in a hat with the tail feather of an Indian cock pheasant.

"*Dios mío, vámonos,*" he groaned.

Unless the friar's 'two' were already on board, down there with the cargo, waiting. It made sense. Dispose of them at sea, no unexplained corpses. Marcos shuddered.

The skipper looked across at him and made some snide remark to the Italian. Ludo looked at him and winked.

Later, Ludo said, "Captain's expecting you to be sick as soon as they lift anchor. Oh, and I let him think you're my catamite. It'll help him keep his distance. Might even get us a proper berth."

"Wonderful. Is the priest coming along to marry us?"

"No, he won't be with us long enough to read the banns."

"Ah," replied Marcos, "that's comforting to hear."

"First port of call, there'll be a fast vessel bound direct for Cadiz."

"But not for us?"

"You can take the next."

Marcos was about to ask, *What about you?*, but noticed they were finally weighing anchor.

The fog lifted, and with the wind in their stern they were up through the Ijsselmeer and approaching Den Helder by afternoon. A persistent, unpleasant drizzle set in, but no snow or sleet or hail or hurricane. And no one rushing up on deck to chop them to pieces or push them overboard—yet.

The *fluyt* was faster and lighter in the water than he would have guessed from its pig-like design. Having grown up watching vessels loading and unloading in the Bay of Cadiz, Marcos thought he knew what a ship should look like, and this ugly tub was not it. But now, looking up at the square-rigged sails, he decided the *fluyt* had a certain style about it, functional if not elegant.

The Tough Old Seabird guided her through the sandbanks off Den Helder, then the small vessel reached out for the wind and they were into the North Sea at last. Away from Holland and the other petty-minded republican provinces; away from Flanders' dismal mud and the terrible, shaming memories of a week when he lost and found himself in the stews of Dunkirk. He was going home, back to southern Spain; sunshine and oranges, laughter and song, and a poorer but predictable, easier life.

Then everything went dark and there was no more sea. A huge galleon was tacking across their bows. Someone shouted.

Marcos gaped open-mouthed at portholes. Up to his left he could see the carving on the ship's prow and human figures on the deck. It was a magnificent three-decker, designed for crossing vast oceans—and firing broadsides at enemies.

Three guns boomed simultaneously. Noise crashed through the air, taking a topsail from a mast. Another gun boomed, but in that second the *fluyt* was turning to the north, and the ball overshot and landed in the sea. The *fluyt*—just twenty paces long—was fast and the skipper quick-witted; the crew was hauling on ropes and shifting sails, fastening down hatches, scurrying hither and thither, nimble as monkeys and as disciplined as naval mariners. The little ship leaned hard to starboard and pulled out from under the galleon's flank. With her stern once more south-easterly she was heading north out of the monster's sea road—directly for the Texel sandbanks.

The galleon fired again and overshot again. With an almighty creak and groan of timber it tacked to port, took position, and this time six guns fired.

Then Ludo was shouting in Dutch—bad Dutch, but they understood him.

"Get round the galleon's stern and across towards England! Don't risk the shoals!"

The captain nodded. "Hard to port!" he screamed.

The fat little *fluyt* heaved round again and slipped out behind the galleon, sailing due west for the Suffolk coast.

Marcos and the priest grabbed onto the gunwale as freezing water washed over the side. The priest shouted something obscene. Marcos threw up.

Ludo stayed with the captain. For once he was at a loss for words.

The Old Seabird slapped him on the back. "Close shave, as the English say."

Ludo blew through his cheeks.

The skipper laughed. "After a week on dry land we need a bit of fun."

It wasn't fun, though. They had escaped this time, but they were marked. Perhaps the galleon would follow them out into deeper waters to try again. Perhaps they should find a port, a safe haven, disembark and stay there for a while. They, no not *they*; three of them were too visible. Not that hiding in the long term was even a possibility. Sooner or later he would go home, and they knew exactly where to find him.

Hiding in the short term, however, would be convenient.

Alina pushed her way through the undergrowth, ducking under budding aspen and alder branches, ignoring the snagging at her skirt and the catkin dust on her shoulders. Up here, safely off the river path, was an ancient oak whose twisted roots formed a damp but comfortable seat. She lowered herself against the bole of the tree and stared at her boots, red with mud. Red mud; just like Cantabria. But not like Cantabria, because she used her hiding place there to escape her chores, and now she was avoiding those wanting to know what chores to do. She smiled; it wasn't very becoming: the wife of a baronet in muddy boots, tucked away in a thicket. But she couldn't stay indoors, not today with the scent of spring in the air. There were bright mauve and gold crocuses on the Crimphele lawn. Crocuses contained saffron; she would pick them later.

Coming down the river path, she'd glimpsed patches of silky bluebells in among the trees, and the copse below the house was full of violets and small yellow flowers she couldn't name. In Cantabria they had tall yellow daffodils and gentle narcissi in March. Easter wasn't until April this year, so there would be plenty of pretty blooms to pick to brighten the dark hall and lighten the gloom in the cold chapel. Thomas was coming home at Easter. She rested her head against the rough bark of the tree, listening to the different birds, watching through the branches and half-closed eyes the river below, waiting. Always waiting.

River birds that she could now name, thanks to Mistress Hawkins, paddled among the reeds. Coots with funny faces, grebes with spiky headdresses, humble moorhens, they might all have young in their nests by now. A frog lopped into the shallows; further out a swan opened its wings to the sunshine. It was a lovely, peaceful scene, a calming place to come when Aggie was in a sulk and Molly in a huff, and both children screaming for attention. Somewhere McNab could not find her, to ask in his most obsequious manner if there were any 'wee thing' he might do for milady.

The new McNab was more sickening than the cold-blooded lecher of before. The change was noticeable at the Christmas Eve supper. She had put him as far from her as she dared, although his rank as steward required him to be at the top of the table. He hadn't commented on his placement because, she realized when it was too late, the distance enabled him to watch her.

He watched her spooning gravy for little Tomás sitting on her lap, but she knew it wasn't the child that interested him. Later, when it was time for bed, she made sure Molly accompanied her up to her chamber, then she wedged a chair under the door latch in case he had a key.

McNab was different, not better. And she certainly didn't feel safe anywhere near him. She still carried the dagger in her skirt pocket, and kept it sharp. Alina shuddered and tried to eliminate McNab from her thoughts. It was too nice a day to spoil with unpleasant memories. McNab really didn't matter anymore, because she was going to the Lady Day hiring fair in Tavistock to find someone to replace him. Once Thomas was home, he could effect the dismissal.

Then it would be all over. With McNab gone and Thomas at home she could relax and enjoy her new life. What a relief it would be.

A pink-downed chaffinch hopped among the lower catkins, a thrush sang a few happy notes. Then there was silence, and she dozed.

A rowing boat broke the stillness, a lad rowing over from Tamstock. His oars dipped and splashed gently in the slow water. Alina opened her eyes and looked out across the river. Another boat came into view, an inland sailing barge bringing goods up from Plymouth for Crimphele and the village store. Someone was standing in the prow. A big man with a black beard and black hair pushed back off his face. He was standing perfectly still on deck, his arms folded across his chest. Ludo.

Alina caught her breath. Ludo.

Immediately, she was on her feet and pushing through the branches, snagging her skirt and getting her hair covered in pollen. She was on the path running down to the landing stage, she was almost at the landing stage, the sail was coming down and the barge was turning in—and she stopped. He must not see her like this: torn skirt, muddy boots. Changing direction, she hitched her skirt up over her knees and ran as fast as she could back up the path to the house.

By the time she got to the lower garden door, she was holding her stitch side and gasping for breath, but she pressed on, in through the nearest door, the kitchen, up the back stairs to her room.

What to wear, what could she wear? She hadn't got a decent dress, nothing suitable; nothing to show off in. She should have had the wine red dress mended. The dresses Kate had left in her press were too short, and Lady Marjorie's... she might be able to pull in the bodice of one of her velvets.

Alina dashed up the short staircase and into the old lady's musty wardrobe. Everything smelled of her: stale sweat and resentment.

Near to tears now, Alina cast about for something to wear—something—there had to be something. She opened a dust-covered press. Aha, black satin, muslin sachets of lavender, and dresses from the old woman's youth. She held the black satin against her. Having been folded for years it was far too creased to even consider. No, but what was that? A thick bundle rolled in linen, scented with lavender and sachets of lemon verbena: a gold brocade skirt with a separate, laced bodice; thick swirling discs and flurries woven into brocade the colour of old gold. It wasn't what she would choose, but it would do.

"Well," said Molly Roberts placing her hands on her hips in her usual indignant stance, "now what's she up to?"

"Nothing to do with you, I don't expect," replied Crook-back Aggie, handing her a plate of custard tarts.

"Some days you forget she's Sir Thomas's wife altogether. What would Lady Marjorie have said to this?"

"Lady Marjorie would have had a much happier life if she'd had half that girl's spark, instead of using up her life looking for faults. You taking this up, or they cheel going to die of hunger?"

"It ain't fitting, though, is it? Her going off with a bow 'n arrow hunting rabbits like...." Molly couldn't say what it was like so she settled for, "'tisn't 'propriate behaviour for someone of the Lady Arleen's class."

"She's filled your plate more than once this winter, so don't complain. I told you before, you got a roof over your head and a boy in the lap of luxury; best you stop moaning and criticizing."

"What's she up to, though?"

"It isn't for us to ask. She's not one of us; she can do what she likes when she likes and we're here to do her bidding. Just 'cause she's spent the last months shut in a winter house 'broidering them bed hangings, and sitting with us down here or up in the nursery and having no visitors doesn't mean we're her family."

Molly nodded her head in reluctant agreement. "You're prob'ly right. Having her round us all the time, coming and going through the kitchen bringing in pheasant and rabbits like a poacher, and feeding the boy herself the way she does.... No, you're right. I'd better take this up. I've left them long enough as it is."

Aggie took herself off to the pantry with her sharp little knife, cut a lump ham from the hanging rail, and returned to her work table. Peeling off the sticky muslin, she trimmed the discoloured fat from around the salted meat, then selected some slithers of lean and set them beneath the table for Perkin. For a moment she watched him devour the morsels, his stub of tail wiggling with pleasure. But even little Perkin couldn't distract her from Molly's words. Who was she to say what was fitting and what was not, she who'd been brought into service when she was ten and lucky for the place? She went to get the right sized kettle to soak the ham, still annoyed by Molly's criticism, and despite herself began wondering what it was that had set the Lady Arleen alight. It wasn't until the ham was in the kettle and she was pouring in the water that it dawned on her: the master. The Lady Arleen had said he was coming home for Easter. P'raps he'd come earlier.

Well, the ham would need some herbs, and if she called in at the creamery for butter and the dairy, where they kept the eggs cool....

"Meg," she called, "Meg, get a fresh pinny on, we got visitors."

Aggie wiped her little knife on her apron and slipped it into its little pocket, saying, "You stay there," to the wiry creature now chasing a pewter plate around the table legs.

Grabbing a basket from the pantry, Aggie bustled out into the kitchen garden, stooped to gather random bits of parsley and thyme, then skirted the scullery and nipped on round to the creamery. From there, she could return via the stable block and pass by the inner courtyard.

Alina fastened the skirt and pulled the brocade down over her hips. It was too short. Of course it was; they were all shorter than her, except for the men, and she stood shoulder to shoulder with Thomas. She tried to keep her breathing calm. The brocade was the most suitable garment; if she put another petticoat under it the flounces would show, but not her boots. There was no alternative to her sturdy boots. Damnation, they were still muddy.

A tall lad, his arms too long for his sleeves, led Ludo and Marcos up a steep path and into what seemed like a narrow alley, except it was bordered on one side with a high wall and on the other by tall trees. The air smelled of vegetation and eons of dampness. The footpath was slippery with leaves and slugs. Ludo pushed a low branch out of his face and touched the wall. It was alive, green and slimy with moss; Nature was reclaiming her own. Sooner or later, her trees and bushes, leaves and moist earth would consume everything short-lived man had constructed. He felt a tightening in his chest; the canopy of thick branches shut him from the sky.

The boy lead them to a door in the wall and stood back to let them by. He waited to see them into the Crimphele garden, then fled back down to the landing stage and boathouse.

The travellers walked into what at first seemed a beautiful terraced garden. Tall shrubs, verdant and lush, bordered the wall behind them. On the terraces however, were rows and rows of unkempt spiky rose bushes set around a dried up fountain. Having no interest in gardens, Ludo looked out at the view. From here one could see across the wide tidal river to a village. Turning his head he could see the Tamar estuary and the sea. He folded his arms and examined the prospect in detail, then turned again and examined the house: two storeys, and above them a slate roof and dormer windows. In the centre was a stone-arched doorway, and nearer the wall whence they'dd entered was what looked like a much older edifice with a square tower. It was at once elegant and rustic: what had evidently been a strategically placed fortress on the Cornish march was now a very fine dwelling. So this was Crimphele, this was what the old man had been so anxious to preserve.

Marcos was also taking in their surroundings. "Impressive," he said.

Hugging a full basket to her flat chest, Aggie peered around the end of the stable block into the inner courtyard. There was no one there and no sign of anyone having just arrived, so she returned to the creamery pretending she needed more butter, then loitered for as long as she dared, watching the drive from the main gate, but no one came. McNab passed her on his way to the estate office, carrying a bundle of labourers' tally sticks. No doubt he'd slip in a couple of extras and pay himself: she had a twisted spine but he was the crooked one at Crimphele. She ostentatiously ignored his questioning look, waited until he was out of sight, then made her way round to the front of the house.

They were standing on the terrace by the front door that no one except McNab ever used. Two men—no, a man and a boy. Later, she wondered why none of the dogs had come round barking and chastised herself for not keeping Perkin with her; he'd have told her friend or foe straight off.

The man was tall, well-built, dark as a Turk. He was wearing a cape and a wide-brimmed hat with a feather the like of which she'd never seen before. The boy was fair, not so tall, dressed in a fancy coat. There were wide white frills on his collar and cuffs. For a moment she assumed it was the Lady Arleen's father and brother, but there was something about the older man that said no. And that same something set her scuttling back to her domain, anxious to remain unseen.

A girl with too many freckles to be considered pretty, but comely nonetheless, opened the door and led them into a vast old hall. A high roof and tall windows gave it a sense of lightness. Arms and armour crowded one corner; in another was a door that probably led to the kitchens. There was no fire in the grate and no places laid at the long table. Ludo took stock: an aura of tradition and purpose pervaded the old great hall.

Marcos poked at the armoury. "Do you think they use any of this?" he asked, running a finger over a nailed leather shield. "It isn't very clean."

Ludo shrugged, "The English are a bellicose lot. Any excuse and they go to war."

Meg tapped at the Lady Arleen's door. "Milady, there's two gentlemen here to see you."

Alina tugged at the brocade bodice. It didn't quite reach her waist. Clenching and unclenching her fists in the stiff folds of the skirt, she said, "Thank you Meg, I'll be down in a minute. Show them into the hall."

"I already did, milady."

"Then say I'm on my way."

Alina waited until Meg had had time to go down the stairs. Taking a deep breath, she went out onto the landing, shutting her bedroom door carefully behind her. She crossed the stone flags and stood for a moment at the top of the wide staircase. The door in the wall below was open, and Ludo was there, looking up at her.

She, clenched her fists in her skirt and looked down at the man below.

"I can see your petticoat," Ludo said in Spanish.

"It is the fashion here. Where have you been, not to know that?"

He stood back as she came down the wide stone steps and through the door.

"My dear, you look—what can I say? Magnificent."

"Thank you."

Alina moved away from him to where Marcos was standing holding his hat. He made a bow, which made her want to laugh. She wanted to hug him like a brother and hear all his adventures right away, but it wouldn't do, so she bobbed a curtsy. They both started to smile, and the smiles turned into laughter.

Ludo, watching them, said, "You have changed, *carina*. The dress is ridiculous, of course, but you have the bearing to carry it off. As with Marcos, I see you have changed in more than just appearance."

Alina and Marcos stopped laughing and gaped at Ludo.

"Do you know," he added rapidly, covering an extremely rare moment of embarrassment, "I think it must have been this very week, two years ago, we first met."

"Oh, don't remind me!" replied Alina. "It was a lifetime ago, and maybe not *my* lifetime at all." There was a warning in her words. "As you were saying, I am not the girl you picked up on a quayside and threw into a boat to save her from a harem, which, by the way, will never be discussed here." They were speaking in Castilian Spanish, but in any language, as far as she was concerned, it was a forbidden topic. "Come," she said, gesturing with a hand, "we can talk in the family parlour, it's more comfortable than this great barn. Would you like some refreshments? Have you ridden from Plymouth? Are you hungry?"

Alina led them out of the hall into the room Sir Geoffrey had created, which was now hung with vibrant tapestries and warm the whole year round. Meg, who had been standing behind the half-open kitchen door, followed.

Alina turned to her as they entered. "Meg, bring us some small ale and some of Aggie's sweet tarts."

"Will that be for three or for two, milady?" asked Meg quietly, nodding her head in the direction of Marcos.

Alina stopped and considered the question. Marcos no longer seemed to be the Italian's servant. He had a certain swagger; his clothes spoke of money.

"Three, thank you, Meg. Also three for supper. Tell Agnes, please." She lowered her voice and added, "Get someone to help you make up Sir Geoffrey's old room and Sir Thomas's chamber, and light the fires as soon as you can."

Meg went off to the kitchen and the lady of the house returned to her guests.

She could feel Ludo trying hard not to stare at her. Her wealth of golden hair was the same and still uncovered, but her features, she knew, had lost their softness: her cheek bones were more pronounced, and she had lost weight. She caught his eye and he inclined his head, giving her his half-dimpled grin.

Then he slapped Marcos's back, who had no qualms about staring at her.

"So you would like to stay here?" Alina said, trying not to show her pleasure at their attention. "Should I divine your purpose, or do you want to go into lengthy fabrications about how and why you are here?"

"We came up river on a barge, a very slow barge. Our travelling bags are on the landing stage. A kind lady there said she would keep an eye on them."

"Mistress Hawkins, the ferryman's wife."

"A very well-dressed ferryman's wife."

"Is she? Yes, I suppose she is. She has a very fine green wool skirt and a blue cloak I like.... Does this matter? Her husband runs a ferry that goes across to Tamstock. If you came up the river you'll know we're in a sort of creek. You can get round to the village on foot, but it's quicker to go by boat. There is no inn in Tamstock, though. You could get a room in Carlington, or you could go into Tavistock; it's only half a day's ride. If you want to stay here, of course, we have enough rooms." Alina gestured above her with a hand and added equivocally, "You are very welcome."

Ludo inclined his head and said in English, "Milady is most kind."

She ignored the irony in his tone and said, "There are just the two of you? No servants?"

Marcos answered. "We had a friar with us as far as Plymouth. Ludo found him a boat to Cadiz. He wanted to get back to Spain as fast as possible."

"And you didn't?" Alina looked at Marcos enquiringly.

"Perhaps I should explain," Ludo said.

"Perhaps you should. I would certainly like to know why you are here. I cannot believe you were simply passing by."

"No, not exactly."

Alina inclined her head, copying the Genoese merchant's gesture and raised an eyebrow.

"We have been busy—in the Netherlands—buying and

selling."

"Ah, so you did go to Amsterdam."

"Naturally. I said I was going to Amsterdam."

"And you always do what you say." Alina caught Marcos's eye and tried not to burst out laughing. "Tell me during the meal. Then I shall verify it with Marcos."

Aggie was mashing stewed apples with the back of a spoon. "Well?" she said as Meg returned from the parlour with an empty tray.

"Don't know, but he's smitten with milady and no mistake."

"And her?"

"Likewise, and the boy's got a grin like a love-sick calf. They're speaking Spanish so I can't tell what's going on. I wish the master were here."

"Might be what the Lady Arleen needs, a bit of company."

Meg clutched the tray to her stomach. "That's some company," she sighed. "He's—ooh, I don't know how to say it. Different, special."

"Which one?"

Meg stared at the greying widow's peak showing above Aggie's wrinkled forehead, confused for a moment, then said, "The boy's nice as well."

Chapter Forty-five

After a supper of pigeon pie, which was rather more feather than fowl, Ludo waited until Alina and Marcos had gone to their rooms, then poured himself more of the late Sir Geoffrey's excellent Spanish brandy. The fire in the parlour hearth was nearly out. It was time for bed; his eyes were sore with fatigue. He picked up a candleholder, left the parlour and slowly ascended the short tower staircase. Alina had put him in the dead patriarch's chamber. He wondered if the old man had died there; she hadn't said. Reaching the first floor landing, he noticed a light coming from somewhere to his right. There was a corridor; they hadn't been shown this part of the house. He passed through a doorway and walked stealthily towards the candle glow.

Alina was holding a child in her arms, its head tucked into the crook of her left arm, legs tucked under her right, and she was crooning a lullaby. The Englishman's son and heir. He watched for a moment, until something he dared not name made him turn and quickly retrace his steps to the old tower.

There was a good-sized fire in his grate, and the bed covers had been turned back. It was all very welcoming. He put his candle on a table and crossed to the window, he could never sleep in a closed room, even in the worst of weather. Opening a narrow, diamond-paned casement, he breathed deeply. The night air was sharp and invigorating. He put his head out into the night and heard a fox bark. An owl screeched,; another answered. Leaving the window wide open, he sat down to remove his boots. His mind was racing, and his body would not relax enough for sleep despite his tiredness. He pulled the boot back on, picked up his cloak, blew out the candle and, after waiting for his eyes to adjust, left the room and went back down the steps to the first floor.

Moonlight was projecting shafts of colour through the stained-glass windows of the half-way landing. Alina was standing exactly where he had first seen her that afternoon. This time, however, she had her back to him. Holding a candle in one hand, she was opening the door to her room.

Alina froze. "Who is it?" she demanded.

"Ludo." He saw her shoulders soften, but she did not turn to him. "Do you have many ghosts here?" he asked.

"It's not a ghost that frightens me. I wish it were." Now she looked at him and gestured towards the nursery. "My son," she said.

"I saw." They were facing each other. "You are a tender mother," Ludo said, and bent to kiss her cheek, but she moved and their lips touched. He stroked her hair as if calming a nervous animal, then put a hand on her shoulder and bent to kiss her again.

"I am not as I was," Alina said.

"No, I can see. Get your cloak. There is a full moon; show me your garden."

Alina opened her door.

Molly Roberts watched until the Lady Arleen stepped into her chamber, then silently closed the tower door and returned to the nursery.

McNab put a hand over his greyhound's muzzle as the couple moved across the great hall to the courtyard door. It was as he expected. Keeping his hand on the bitch's collar, he got up to follow them outdoors. The Italian had taken her hand; they had reached the stable block archway and were turning to go left onto the front terraces or down to the river. He grimaced and followed. Loosing the greyhound's collar, she trotted ahead of him and turned right, then waited at the door to the staff quarters.

"Very well," McNab said, and slowly followed his beautiful hound up the wooden stairs to a bare, unheated room.

After he closed his door he said, "You're right, we don't need to follow them, as we know what's afoot. Aye," he sighed, "it makes me sad and it makes me angry."

The greyhound ignored him and began turning round and round on a thin length of blanket, making her bed for the night.

"She's failed me!" McNab stared at the dark beyond the thick panes of his window and gnawed at the side of his mouth.

The gentle greyhound lay down, rested her head on her paws and watched her master balefully as he began his customary nightly pacing.

"I'll not have her cheat me again. Oh, no. Enough is enough. I gave her the benefit of the doubt. I thought the bairn had brought her round, but no, motherhood doesn't cure a creature like that. There's no Madonna in her. And you know why? Because she wasn't churched! She hasn't been cleansed of her sin," he hissed, "fornication."

Cold fingers pulling at the buttons on his doublet, speaking ever more rapidly, he went on, "She hasn't been churched, you see. A woman has to be churched after a bairn. She has to be cleansed. That stupid priest with his soft ways and foreign ideas, he should have cleansed her of sin. A good woman can't go about with the sin of fornication in her, it's not right. They tempt men that way—the way she tempts me. God help me!" he cried.

He dropped to his knees on the bare floorboards, hands clasped in penitence before him. "Dear Lord, I beseech thee, save me from her. Make her leave us or make her die. Help me to make her die."

Alina and Ludo walked hand in hand like old lovers along the front of the house, through the black and silver rosebushes of the upper terrace and across to the garden door that opened onto the river path. Alina talked and Ludo listened: Sir Geoffrey and Lady Marjorie, Crook-back Aggie, Meg with freckles and a kind heart, the birth, Aggie saving the baby, the walls being built. She talked of all that had happened to her, but mentioned her husband only three times, and only in connection with his leaving.

They walked down to the river and looked across the still water. Ludo put an arm round her shoulders and pulled her into his cape. He looked down at her hair, that wonderful wild hair, spun silver now in the moonlight. She smelled vaguely of lemons; he wanted to bury his head between her breasts and stroke the smooth skin of her thighs. But he did no more than kiss the top of her head, then they set off back up the hill to the house.

Alina took him in through the kitchen door.

"Do you want anything?" she asked, still speaking in Spanish, as they had been all evening. "Some wine?"

"Only you—and a cup of water."

Alina shook her head and filled a cup from a jug. As she handed it to him she let his fingers touch hers, then pulled away and opened the door to the back stairs.

"You can get to your room this way," she said and stood back.

Ludo accepted what she was telling him and felt his way up the unlit staircase.

Alina waited until he had had time to reach his chamber, then twirled round and round until the heavy brocade swirled out. Lifting her arms above her head she twisted her wrists, snapped her fingers and danced across the kitchen floor. Then she stopped, tugged the uncomfortable bodice back into place, brushed her hair back with her hands and went up the stairs alone.

Aggie did not move for some minutes after the Lady Arleen had left the kitchen. Except for her hands, which brushed up and down, up and down the wiry hair of Perkin's back.

"There's a good boy," she whispered, "I said don't move and you didn't. What a good boy, not a woof, and them near enough to touch us. But they didn't see us in this ol' rocker, did they? Too busy looking at each other."

Aggie drew in a deep breath and pushed Perkin down to the floor. She leaned from the chair and picked up a short, dead candle warming by the fire. Its wax was soft now. She squeezed and rolled it, softening it to putty in her right hand; then, using both hands, she shaped a head and body, traced a cloak. In the pale light of the dying embers she examined its likeness, then leaned into the grate and rolled it in soot until it was completely black. When she was satisfied there was not a speck of white, she put the black wax figure to stand at the edge of the dying fire and blew on him, a soft blowing to start with, then a harsh puff that sent the black cloaked image backwards into the cinders.

Counting slowly all the time, Aggie waited until the wax began to melt and lose its shape—eight and nine and ten—ten. Ten days until he was gone—or was no more. Ten days was a long time under the circumstances. A long time. Maybe the master would come back before and put a stop to it.

"Aye, milady," Aggie sighed, "you're still a girl at heart, and girls were ever fools for a pair of sparkling eyes. But I'll protect you. I can't let you leave us, you see, not with that cheel in the nursery."

Crook-back Aggie wiped the soot from her fingers, then carefully unravelled the last golden hair from around a pin under her apron. She stretched it to its full length and began to wind it with whispers around her index finger like a ring. Winding charms, as she well knew—that poor, dear baby— could be unreliable, but this one was in her very own hand. She was winding milady to her and would not let this one fail.

The next morning at breakfast, Alina inquired, "Have you ever tried shooting March hares?"

The two men turned to look at her, surprised by the question.

"Mad as a March hare," replied Ludo in English, then switched back to Spanish, "that's what they say here, isn't it?"

"Yes, hares jump about on the spot at this time of year and do odd things. It makes them easier to catch, though."

"How?" asked Marcos.

"Bow and arrow, how d'you think?" mumbled Alina around a mouthful of buttered bread. "A gun would blow them to pieces. Anyway, by the time you loaded the powder the creature would be in another county."

"Isn't it easier just to trap them?" asked Marcos.

"That's cruel."

Marcos looked at Ludo and raised his eyebrows. Ludo shrugged.

Alina spread fresh dairy butter onto another piece of bread and said, "I used to go hunting with my brothers. I'm a good shot. Do you want to come with me? It's a good day for it, fine and dry."

Marcos said, "All right."

Ludo shook his head. "Field and forest are not for me; I get land-sick. I'll find a boat and explore the river."

"Be careful they don't take you for a Turk and shoot you."

Ludo looked at Alina. "Have they been up this far?"

"Your pirate friends? Certainly have, villagers talk about it all the time. They call any pirate a Turk here. They come up the Tamar all the way from wherever they come from, to steal the pretty girls." Alina lifted her mug of small ale and met Ludo's glance over the rim, her eyes shining with mischief. "There's an armoury at the end of the hall, if you don't have anything with you."

"That might be useful—purely for self-defence." Ludo gave her a slow wink, then added in a more serious manner, "I never carry a weapon; perhaps I should start."

Marcos picked up the change in the Italian's tone and wondered if what the friar had told them could still be a real threat. They had got rid of him in Southampton, but it wouldn't be impossible for him to trace them to Plymouth, or tell someone where they were going. He drank some ale and tried to set the doubts aside; glancing up he intercepted a look across the table.

Alina noticed him avert his gaze and said, "The ground will be muddy. I'll get you some over-boots."

Marcos missed every time, but Alina bagged two plump rabbits, and they returned for the midday meal in high spirits. Ludo did not appear until evening and did not say where he had been. He had a familiar, smug look about him, so Marcos assumed he'd been up to some sort of no good.

The evening meal, Aggie's boiled ham followed by a half-curdled custard, was a cheerful affair. Alina took Ludo into Sir Geoffrey's cellar under the tower stairs and let him select the wines.

"Do you know," she said, "I think this cellar must be magic, it seems to restock itself. Not that I come in very often."

Ludo tried to read chalked place names on the wooden racks.

"Mostly French," he said. "But the brandy's Spanish. Who delivers it?"

"That's what I mean, I've never noticed." Alina laughed and led him back under the low door to the family parlour.

She had gone back to wearing her own clothes and was more relaxed in every way, but she did not want to risk being in an enclosed space with him for too long, not with Marcos watching their every move.

That afternoon she had taken little Tomás out into the garden to play ball, and Marcos had joined them. The child was still too uncoordinated to kick and kept falling over, so Marcos held him under the arms and swung him until his little feet connected with the stitched leather and the ball went rolling down the garden terrace. Tomás had squealed with glee as Alina had made a fuss of trying to reach it before the dogs that were intent on playing too. Now the child was asleep, she was sitting with friends speaking her own language, and she couldn't remember a happier day.

Marcos couldn't stay awake. "I'm exhausted," he said. "All that fresh air, not to say what happened—was it only last week? —have done for me." Leaving his half-finished brandy on the table, he muttered, "Goodnight," and staggered up to bed.

Alina looked at Ludo. "What happened 'only last week' besides buying and selling tiulips? What have you been up to? Where have you been?"

"Everywhere, except the New World, and I haven't been very far down the African coast, yet. I plan to do both in the near future."

Alina soon realized he wasn't going to tell her what he'd been up to, either last week or this very day, so she said, "What would you do in the New World?"

"I'm a merchant. I would trade."

"And what would you trade?"

"Whatever they were willing to pay most for."

"They already have silver and emeralds."

"Perhaps they need flour. I'll take them flour and bring back emeralds—for pretty girls."

"What girl would accept an emerald from you?"

"One who likes me well enough to warrant something valuable."

They bandied questions and answers, the verbal sparring becoming more intense, and they both knew they were flirting. Eventually, Ludo reached a hand across the table and said, "You are a cheeky young madam. Come round here."

Alina left her chair and walked carefully around the table: she had drunk two large goblets of wine, then brandy, and was none too steady on her feet. She sat on his lap.

Ludo kissed her and she returned the kiss.

His kiss was very different: she couldn't help but compare. His mouth was a different shape, his movements less predictable. He kissed her under an ear and pushed her bodice off a shoulder to kiss the hollow of her neck. His hands were slow and deliberate, strong and warm. Quite different. A hand cupped a breast inside her shift and she knew this was not going to stop and did not want it to. She unlaced her top and slid down to the floor.

He removed his jacket, knelt down beside her and placed his forehead between her breasts. Alina placed her hands over his head and held him there. For a minute or two they stayed like that, then Ludo rolled away to open his clothing and Alina shifted further under the great oak table.

They made love there on an old rug set over granite slabs as if they were on the softest, down-filled bed. There was no hurry, no tearing or wrenching or pushing.

It wasn't until it was over and Ludo was lying on an elbow playing with a strand of her hair that Alina noticed the smell: the rancid smell of dog's breath. She turned her head trying to locate its source.

Two dim yellow orbs just above floor level met her gaze. The creature panted, came closer and licked her face.

"Ugh, no, go away, Perkin," she said. The dog wagged its stump of tail. "Shoo, go back to the kitchen."

Pausing to sniff at the Italian's boots, then snuffling up some fallen crumbs, Perkin slowly pattered off through the open door.

"What was that?" asked Ludo, pulling his clothes back together.

"Just one of the dogs."

Ludo laughed, but Alina didn't find it funny.

"Don't come to my room," she said, "not yet."

Chapter Forty-six
Crimphele, April 1637

Ludo was still asleep, arms and head pushed up against the overstuffed bolster. He was snoring, not loudly but perceptibly. Alina lifted the sheet from his broad shoulders and traced a line down his spine. For a man who appeared to do little exercise he had a well-muscled body—and scars. She placed a finger over what must have been a wide gash under his left arm: somebody had aimed for his heart and he'd moved just in time, or parried. He said he never carried a sword. Her father wouldn't have left their house without his sword. The gems in its hilt would have kept them fed and paid a household of servants for more than a year. She lay back on her pillow and sighed. Mixed memories: sometimes they made her sad, sometimes angry, but not until the last few days had she wanted to go back. Now, speaking Spanish again, making jokes with Marcos, alive with Ludo like never before, she was beginning to revise her ideas.

She levered herself up onto her elbows and looked out at the morning sun creeping in between the bed hangings; it was late. For a moment she contemplated getting up, then changed her mind and snuggled back against Ludo's sleeping form.

Almost immediately she was disturbed by a banging on the door. Reaching for her nightgown she got out of bed, then, closing the hangings tightly behind her, she called out, "Just a minute—who is it?" and went to the door.

It was Meg, her freckled face flushed from rushing up stairs and carrying important news.

"Mistress Hawkins sent her boy up, milady. He says there's a man on the early barge. Looks like it could be the master."

Alina gripped the door jamb, "Thank you, Meg. I'll come straight down."

She closed the door and stared at the bed. "Ah, well," she said to herself and went to the wash bowl, stripped off and washed herself thoroughly in cold water.

When she was fully dressed, with her hair in some sort of order, she went to the bed and touched Ludo on the shoulder. He was awake, had obviously been awake for some time.

"And now?" he said.

"Go back to your room, then go to breakfast as normal. My husband has come home."

It wasn't Sir Thomas after all. Mistress Hawkins could see that now: he was thin, a little stooped, but otherwise quite different. Whoever it was, he looked like he'd been in the wars: his shirt and what remained of his hose were torn, and he was that skinny his jacket hung like it was on a peg.

The stranger took his time, staggering across the landing stage like a man still drunk, or like her Jim after a long night on the water. Then as he came up to her and spoke she realized it wasn't a stranger after all. Her hands flew to her throat with the shock of it.

"Morning Lucy, it's good to see you."

"Robert? Whatever happened to you? We thought…."

"Aye, I don't wonder at that."

"Come in and have a cup of something, you look famished."

Robert looked at her and tried to speak. He had tears in his eyes, and suddenly he was sobbing.

"Come in, come in, my dear. Oh, you poor soul, whatever has happened?"

Mistress Hawkins led him into the ferryman's cottage and sat him by the kitchen grate. Then she sent her son Jimmy back up to the big house with a new message.

Alina waited until husband and wife were able to separate from each other, until Robert was holding his son, and with what little strength he still had was bouncing him in his arms.

She put a hand on Molly's shoulder and said in a quiet voice, "Molly, stay here tonight. We'll make up a room for you next to the nursery. Your cottage will be damp, wait until it's aired and clean."

"No, milady, thank you. I never gave up hope, you see. I went every week to sweep the floor and open the shutters. It's clean and aired. We'll just need some food, if that's all right? I didn't leave any because of the mice. But thank you."

"Of course, take what you need from the kitchen."

Alina smiled, adjusted Tomás in her arms and walked back into the house, knowing they were waiting for her to go. She had no place out here with the servants. Biting her lip, trying to control the urge to weep, she felt ashamed and guilty. Had *she* given up hope, or had Ludo's presence simply made her forget? Had Molly's words been aimed to hurt? If so, she had succeeded.

Tomás wriggled to be put down, "Not yet, *cariño*," she said, and went into the family parlour. Ludo and Marcos were still eating breakfast.

Ludo raised an enquiring eyebrow. She avoided his look.

"You're white as a sheet," said Marcos. "Seen a ghost?"

"Yes, actually."

"Your husband?" asked Ludo without expression.

"No. It's Robert, Molly's husband; he's come back. He was taken for a sailor in Plymouth. We—I—thought he was dead."

Alina sat down and settled Tomás on her lap. Marcos gave the boy a crust. He grasped it in his plump hands and began to suck on it. Alina kissed the top of his head, still fighting back tears.

"How did he get back?" asked Marcos. "Getting away from the English Navy can't have been easy. We saw them recruiting when we were in Southampton. Brutal lot."

"I don't know. I'm sorry—um—I have to take Tomás now."

Alina turned the child round and got to her feet. Tomás waved his crust over her shoulder as she carried him from the room and gave Marcos a gummy grin. Marcos waved back. Ludo did not look up.

Mistress Hawkins was full of news, so Ludo let her gabble on unhindered.

"... Robert was drugged or knocked on the head and taken onto a Navy ship. You know we hear about such things, but I never did rightly credit it till now.... They was in the Middle Sea, alongside merchantmen, cargo ships, you know, to keep them from the African pirates. Oh, my, what a danger. A Falmouth ship carrying tin was taken right in front of his eyes! Imagine! And they on board, the captain and like, couldn't do nothing, and him thinking they was going to be taken as well and he'd never see his son or Molly again...." Her voice rose an octave with each aspect of the drama. "Course pirates don't dare go for Navy ships, leastways that's what they say, so he was safe, but he wasn't to know that, was he? And they might have dragged him off like they do, to Africa and... it doesn't bear thinking about, does it? Like I said to her ladyship, if my Jim gets taken, what's to become of us? I tell you, sir, as I told her, and I'll tell the vicar himself if he asks. I've changed my prayers, that I have...."

Ludo could stand no more. He slipped the good Mistress Hawkins an English coin and made towards the rowing gig her husband was letting him use. She was still talking when he pulled out into the river.

Ludo rowed out into the current, then shipped the oars to see where it would take him. Not far and not fast. How could people live on rivers? It wasn't surprising Jim Hawkins had branched out from his ferry business into smuggling, or the 'free trade' as he'd called it. This part of the river was tidal, being so close to the estuary, and to be sure, Crimphele was ideally tucked away behind trees on the creek—perfectly situated for storing goods to be transported inland, but after getting the contraband up here from France or the Spanish coast there wasn't much adventure left. Was untaxed brandy really worth the effort?

The whole concept of the house and its estate, each worker in his place, each season demanding the same cyclical work, defeated him. How could Alina stand it?

Alina. If it weren't for her, this would have been the most tedious experience of his life. But sharing a bed with Alina....

For a few minutes he considered the possibility of taking her with him. Would she give up her child for him? No, never. And no, no, no, this was ridiculous! How would he manage with a woman in tow? Supposing there was trouble getting his ship in Lisbon. It was one thing for him to slip away on his own and hole up in a brothel or tavern to avoid pursuers, but he could hardly drag a fine-looking woman like Alina around without being detected. No, it wouldn't do: time to make a break.

He picked up the oars and rowed purposefully into the strengthening current, working physical activity against emotion. After a while, he sighted a quay on the Devonshire bank of the river and started to aim for it, but no matter how hard he pulled on the oars, how much energy he put into *not* thinking of the woman, Alina would not go away. The trouble was he wanted to be with her all the time. How much nicer, more interesting this day would be if she were in the boat. He had suggested it that very morning, after the nonsense about the husband arriving, and she had said no—because she had the child to attend to. She always had the child to attend to. In that respect she was just like Maria Grazia and Teresa, not that he'd ever contemplated bringing either of them into his life.

"Enough," he said to himself. "You're getting into what you vowed to avoid."

As if on cue, his thoughts were stopped by a pair of otters. Gambolling over each other, they rolled down the river bank and fell as a bundle into the water. He started to laugh, then halted as they surprised him again, emerging a few feet from the boat with green weed caught about their ears like pixie hoods. They looked at him, and he looked at them, and for a single moment none of them moved, then as one the otters dipped down under the dark water and disappeared.

Ludo manoeuvred his small craft toward a man-made quay and with a practised hand pulled himself alongside. Perhaps if there was enough interest he could bring surplus 'rich trade', silk and spices up here as 'free trade' goods himself—and maintain a clandestine relationship with the lady of Crimphele. It was worth exploring the possibility. Now that he knew what Tamstock and a few of the other riverside villages imported on moonlit high tides he could arrange something with them. Bring a boat up from the coast and stay a night or two. It might be amusing. He'd have to work out how to receive his revenue. If he had someone like Marcos here....

Of course, it all depended on the ship in Lisbon. If it was a decent sea-going galleon he wasn't going to bother bringing piddling cargoes of pepper to Cornish goodwives. Alina had joked about New World silver and emeralds. Not such a joke.

He climbed out of the boat and surveyed the hovels along the quay. Further up the hill was the usual square-towered church. There'd be a house for its vicar and a house for the local squire; and a solid mansion for the magistrate, no doubt. No doubt—all too predictable. He got back into the boat and pushed himself into the river, rowing upstream towards Crimphele. Time to pack.

Alina heard the door open because she had stayed awake, listening for that very sound.

Ludo slipped into her bed and pulled her into his arms.

"*Cara, cara, carina,*" he whispered, but said not a word about leaving.

Later though, as if hearing his thoughts, Alina said, "Take me with you when you go."

Ludo kissed her brow, lifted her chin to kiss her lips. "You are my love," he said, "my perfect woman, how could I live without you now?"

The next morning Alina awoke in a cocoon of love and reached across the bed. Ludo was not there. Tucked into the depression in his pillow was a perfect almond-shaped emerald set in heavy gold. She sat up to examine it. Very pretty, and worth a fortune. She let it drop from her fingers. It slid off the counterpane and rolled out of sight under the blanket chest.

When neither Ludo nor Alina appeared at breakfast, Marcos immediately smelled a rat. He went up the stairs and knocked on Ludo's door, then registered the empty chamber to convince himself the Italian wasn't merely off on one of his jaunts.

Marcos avoided Alina until the midday meal. When she came in to eat he searched her face for clues. Her expression told him nothing, and she didn't volunteer any information. Once Meg had left them, he said, "I should go."

"Why?"

"My mother. My father may be home now as well."

"Couldn't you wait, give your parents time together? What will you do if you go back? What are your prospects?"

Marcos avoided Alina's gaze and said, "I don't think I have any prospects. No trade, no inheritance. I am, as you have said more than once, a nobody."

"I've never said that. I said you were a boy. But that is no longer the case."

Marcos's head shot up. Was this a morsel of hope she was offering him across her table?

"Would you like to have a trade, a skill you could make use of in the future?"

He wanted to say, *Oh, I've got skills, useful, lucrative skills. I am a very successful tulip dealer. I could be a stockbroker, a financier, a wine merchant—actually, I'm already a rich man by ordinary standards.* Instead he said, "Do you have any suggestions?"

"Yes, I need a steward to run the estate, someone who can explain things to me in Spanish. I need someone I can trust."

"Isn't that for your husband to arrange?"

"Yes, when he is here I will ask him to arrange it. If you think you could live here, that is."

"You don't think your husband is coming back, do you?"

"Not really, not any more. He said he would be home for Holy Week, but he didn't come. I used to dream about Thomas coming home and imagine what our life could be like."

"Until we arrived?"

"Marcos, does... did Ludo ever *talk* to you?"

"About what?"

Alina gave a slight shrug, "Just tell you things."

"Oh yes, he used to tell me what to do, what not to do, where to go. To be honest, I can only be grateful. I wanted adventure, and my God he made sure I got it. But if you mean did he talk to me man to man, *confide* in me," Marcos paused and lifted his wine. "No. I don't think he ever *talks* to anyone, certainly not to betray his feelings. You may not have noticed, but he actually spends a lot of time saying nothing at all. About you personally—he's said nothing to me. If that's what you're trying to find out?"

Alina looked at Marcos, cocked her head on one side and gave a lopsided grin. It was such a perfect imitation Marcos burst out laughing.

"Are you angry?" he asked, wanting to say but not daring to say *Has he hurt your feelings the way you hurt mine?*

She ran a finger around the rim of her glass and pinged it with a nail, saying, "My dear mother-in-law had a whole set of these."

"And you broke them."

"How do you know?"

"A guess made on acquired knowledge. That was something he taught me."

"Well, it would seem I have learned nothing, and in this case I am the nobody. Can we change the subject?"

"Yes. Tell me what you need me to do," said Marcos, silently planning to stay forever—or at least until the husband came home.

Chapter Forty-seven
Lisbon, May 1637

Out on the broad, blue Tejo estuary, sunlight glinted off gentle waves. Ludo shaded his eyes; it was unseasonably warm and very bright for so early in the day. He drew the mule to a halt, pulled on the cart's brake and lifted the magnifying implement to his left eye. Keeping the instrument focused low to avoid the resplendence, he panned the scene. There were at least twenty vessels lying at anchor.

The new instrument was worth every guilder. He could see galleons and fishing boats, old galleys, their oars finally shipped after so much suffering; there were three-masted galleasses bearing gaudy pennants and other vessels he didn't recognize. Two of them were crossing the bar, moving out into the Atlantic Sea. Not Dutch *Retourschepen*, of course, not in a Spanish-held port.

Which of these wonderful barques, with their carved prows of splendidly over-endowed women and sterns gilded with curlicues, was his? Somewhere there should be a pennant with a tulip, or perhaps a hovering bird of prey. Or was he being naïve? It might only be a silly game to lure him back into Spanish territory then drop him into an expanse of water, alive or dead. Either way, the prize was worth the game.

He brought the telescope down a little further to examine the craft moored along the quaysides; but it was a jungle of masts, so he closed the instrument, tucked it back into his rough labourer's smock and released the brake on the cart. As the mule began its careful descent toward the city, Ludo scratched his beard and began to sing a bawdy song.

Once inside the old city, he let the mule pick its way down the shelved cobbled streets until he found a livery stable. There he negotiated a price for leaving the beast for a few hours, removed the rough-hewn barrow from the back of the cart and set off down to the harbour on foot, pausing to buy a stick of bread and some spicy sausage on the way. Within a few minutes he had selected a vantage point, the steps of a white church. It seemed appropriate, and it was on a main thoroughfare.

He upended the barrow and sat on a low step to eat. Immediately he was surrounded by a flock of stick-boned brats begging for bread, gaping open-mouthed at the meat. He threw them the remainder of his breakfast then, using a colourful mixture of ship-board Spanish and Genoese Italian, threatened to reclaim it in the most gruesome manner he could invent if they continued to pester him. They disappeared. He leaned his head back against an upper step, stretched out his dirty, sandalled feet and tipped his straw hat over the day's new growth of beard.

After an hour or so watching locals turn off to his left between tenements that could only lead down to fishermen's hovels and the harbour, he roused himself and directed his barrow to follow a little eel of a man and a bigger, hair-faced girl carrying an empty wicker creel.

It was a labyrinth. Narrow tenement balconies met one storey above streets that reeked of fish gut and ordure. Eventually the man and the girl with the creel stepped out onto the wharf. Thick-scummed wavelets lapped at slimy stones: a sea breeze brought not a whiff of open water but the rankness of rotting entrails and yellowed sea weed. The location had no charm, but he was getting his bearings. Behind him and to his left was the fishing quarter, to his right, tenders for freight vessels were being loaded ready for the next high tide. He set off towards them, stopping to peek into a dark quayside tavern on the way.

Weaving his handcart among the business of the quay, he did his best to look as if he were on an errand and avoid the other barrow boys who, not knowing him, would see him as a threat. Their sort would blow up a fuss for the pleasure of it if he weren't sharp, and under no circumstances did he want to attract attention. He searched and searched but saw no vessel large or small that might be his, so he turned back towards the taverns on the cobbled wharf. And then he saw what he didn't want to see. They were impossible to miss. A tall priest in black robes accompanied by a well-fed friar whose rolling gait gave the impression he was running on mismatched wheels.

Ludo crouched over the barrow as if fixing a stave and stayed bent double until they had passed. So he hadn't been over-cautious or naive; they were here waiting for him.

He gazed after the two men of God and wondered yet again why they hadn't tried harder to eliminate him earlier: set fire to his lodgings, a knife in a narrow street brawl. The friar could have dropped poison in his beer ten times during their stay in the tavern. Even the Den Helder broadside had been half-hearted; the captain could have blown them out of the water if he'd really tried. The only explanation as to why they had let him reach Lisbon was that the Spanish were expecting the Vatican agents to do the dirty work and the Vatican had, for reasons of their own, decided to make a show of doing the job but kept him alive.

Seeing the two men reach the more savoury end of the harbour, Ludo wandered back the way he had come until he found the dark tavern he'd noted earlier. Abandoning the barrow to its fate, he lowered his head and stepped inside.

The wine could have been used to scour decks, but he didn't say that. He said he was Captain Azor of Cadiz;, that he was dressed like this because he was doing some of his own maintenance. He'd got a new ship and was on the lookout for experienced seamen and some willing young lads to make up a new crew. Then he spent the rest of the day fending off tarts by staying anchored to his chair and chatting to old-timers about crossing the Lisbon bar, the geography of the West African coast, and the current situation with Berber corsairs. Later, he joined another table for a long round of dominoes, giving every appearance of slowly getting very drunk. Some time before leaving, he ate a huge plate of eggs and more sausage, then paid the landlord, tipped a coin down a cleavage and told them all to put the word round: seasoned mariners and young lads looking for a bit of adventure to be here same day next week.

When he finally got back onto the quay, boats were riding high on the full tide and lanterns were being lit. Crews were changing watch, while passengers were returning to their berths after testing their land legs. And there she was: a tulip on her pennant and close in to the quayside. An old-fashioned carrack that, perhaps in her distant past, had once been a useful round ship; not exactly a hulk, but most definitely not the clever, windward sailing caravel he'd dreamed of. The fact that she was floating at anchor did not even mean she was seaworthy.

Not knowing whether to laugh or rage, Ludo wiped his nose on his sleeve and turned round to collect the farmer's wheelbarrow. Someone had pinched it, of course, so he wandered on and turned about in the reeking labyrinth until he was walking back up into the city to locate the loyal mule he had acquired in Vigo. Tonight he would sleep at the farm again, and in the morning he'd decide what to do next.

Both he and the mule were half asleep when they came to a halt in the unkempt farmyard. The dogs set to barking, then recognized the mule and the smell of the cart and went back to their den in the open barn. Ludo struggled with the traces, left the mule in a corral and walked towards the house. Something large and soft appeared out of the gloom. A blanket, a sack, it was over his head, rolling over his shoulders, wrapped all around him. He was trapped, couldn't breathe, there was fabric in his mouth, in his nostrils, he was suffocating....

Flailing both arms, he push away his oppressor, then dropped to his knees and tried to fall out and away from under this woven sepulchre. He rolled, twisted and, heart beating fit to burst, struggled to his feet, tearing the fabric off his head. Then he was back in the black night and there was silence.

Would the next move be a dagger in his ribs, a noose around his neck? Would they try again with the sack? He couldn't hear a thing for the sound of fear in his ears.

For a moment he stood perfectly still, each sense trained on his surroundings. Gradually he identified noises. A dog whimpered in its sleep, a hen cluck-clucked. The mule snorted. Then silence again. He waited a little longer. But there was nothing, so he found his way into the house, climbed the ladder above the winter cow byre and fell into the straw-filled pallet he'd been given for a bed. For a while he fought sleep, trying to stay alert, but the sour wine and day's exertion overcame him.

He slept badly and woke early, opened the shutters of the glassless window and looked out across tranquil green hills. In the yard below, washing flapped in the morning breeze. A vast white nightgown lay sprawled in trodden mud.

Had that been his assailant? Had he walked into a harmless nightgown or had someone used it to smother him? He searched the scene and decided, with mixed feelings, on the former. Something about the voluminous garment tugged at a memory, but the foolishness of his fear and a sense of embarrassment set it aside. Later, however, while he was splashing water over his tired eyes, he remembered a painted petticoat rolled around a pole and set among dusty oleander bushes. Marcos! The boy was a genius.

Within an hour he was on his way back into the city. This time the farmer was driving the mule. A deal had been struck: if Ludo didn't return, the mule and cart were his to keep, on condition he never mentioned providing lodging for a foreigner or losing his precious handcart. There was no way Ludo could guarantee the man's silence, but it didn't really matter; he would be leaving Portugal just as soon as he could. Tucked under his legs was his travelling valise. It contained some of his Dutch gold, his plumed leather hat, the telescope, the folded vellum ship and a vast white nightgown.

Three hours later, Ludo had a new suit of serviceable clothes on his back and had been measured for another far more elegant outfit. He acquired a room with clean glass windows overlooking the harbour, then set out to obtain quality parchment, some writing paper, writing implements, sealing wax and a seal, and some paint for the pennant: blue on white for his personal arms, to be quartered with green for hope and a nod at Islam. Perhaps he would also purchase some lengths of green cloth to raise as a Moorish standard should the need arise.

He revisited the tavern and introduced himself. The tavern keeper indicated two men sitting quietly by themselves.

"Over there," the tavern keeper said, handing him a thick ceramic cup of what looked like urine.

Ludo sat down, and after a few minutes one of the quiet men came to join him.

"You're looking for hands," he said. The man, whose wrinkled face indicated he was somewhere between forty and a hundred, sat down and added, "Lorenzo de la Cruz, they call me Tosho."

"You haven't got a ship?"

"We used to crew on crossings to the Americas, made some money, bought a fishing boat, thought we'd settle down. Got caught on rocks a month ago, lost everything, need to start again."

"With your friend?"

"Brother-in-law, Javi."

"You need work then; what can you do?"

Tosho explained, in as few words as possible, that he'd been first mate on transatlantic galleons and skippered various different smaller craft. He'd been at sea since he could walk. They were from Galicia but knew enough locals to whistle up a crew, depending on where they were bound.

Ludo put some coins on the table, got to his feet and led Tosho out onto the quay. The brother-in-law, a brown-bearded, bear-like man, followed them out and came to stand within touching distance of Tosho. He nodded at Ludo but said nothing.

Ludo strolled over towards the water, the men following, and once they were on their own said, "For now, this is between us, and for now I only need a basic sailing crew."

"Where we bound?" Tosho insisted.

"Canaries for sugar."

"With a skeleton crew? We don't sail mystery ships."

Ludo studied something in the distance, weighing up how much to tell them and how much of the truth to weave into those words. Eventually he said, "We don't want people knowing our business. Sailors get drunk and blab."

"We don't."

"No, I can believe that. If you want work, find me a basic crew and tell them we're for the Canaries."

"If this is exploration we're not interested. Africa's for Africans." Tosho spat just beyond the Italian's new shoes and made to walk off.

"Not exploration, but not without a certain degree of— adventure," Ludo's long arm reached out, his hand closed over a bony shoulder. "There will be *excellent* rewards, and not just your pay. All I ask is that you say little and trust me until we are a mile out to sea."

The wiry mariner looked up at the Italian's face. Staring him in the eye, he said, "Booty?"

"Booty."

"You should've said before."

Tosho and his brother-in-law were waiting with ten others on the quay later the next morning. Ludo pointed at the tub with the tulip pennant. Tosho made the sign of the cross and muttered "*Dios mio, ayúdanos*" under his breath.

"I know," Ludo nodded. "We need to see what she'll do. Keep the tender close and have a spare boat ready at all times, just in case."

Javi tapped his brother-in-law on the shoulder and whispered in his ear. Tosho spoke, "He asks what state's the canvas in?"

"That's what we need to check. We'll put her over the bar tomorrow morning. If she sails, and if we're successful in the Canaries, you and Javi get to keep her at the end of the voyage."

Tosho and Javi exchanged expressionless glances. Javi bent once more to whisper in his brother-in-law's ear. Ludo thought he heard the word *niños*.

Tosho just turned to him and said, "All right."

"Why not go out to her now? See what needs doing before tomorrow."

Canvas slapped out into the early morning sun and *The Tulip* lifted her prow, an old hound roused by a familiar scent. For a moment she shifted unsteadily, then manoeuvred herself out towards the bar, where, catching her first whiff of open water in a very long time, she gathered all her old energy into one great leap and, head down, began to race out into the ocean.

The cannon boomed across the bay, reverberating off hill and house tops, sending every bird for miles into the air. Well-aimed, the ball crashed down onto *The Tulip*'s stern, down through the captain's cabin, down through the top deck onto the old tiller, severing it in two and shattering the helmsman's skull into splinters.

Ludo lowered the eye-glass and noticed the lace on his cuffs was shaking.

"*Va bene,*" he muttered, and lay back on the grassy hillside.

A lark returning to its territory nearby sang out. Two others dipped and rose above him, their undulating flight like a ship at sea. Ludo shaded his eyes and watched them skim, blithe and free, up and over the bright grass.

"*Va bene,*" he said again, then sat up and reluctantly lifted the spyglass. Two small boats were rowing in to shore. He started to count heads but had to stop to rub his eyes.

Two days later, a well-built, very elegant foreigner wearing a hat adorned by an Indian cock pheasant's tail feather entered the Lisbon harbour offices. He was carrying two rolled, sealed documents under his left arm and asked to see the Captain of the Port. A young ensign showed him up a shabby staircase and opened a door.

"Who shall I say it is, sir?" he asked.

"Never mind, I'll do that bit," said the elegant visitor.

"Captain, a visitor for you." The ensign stood his ground, curious to see what was going on.

The foreigner stepped forward and presented himself: "Don Mendo Fadrique Fabrizio de las Esquinas de las Casas y Rio Arriba at your service, Admiral."

The rotund Portuguese captain bowed in automatic response, then put a hand on his desk for support as his eyes took in the details of just what sort of man was interrupting his morning beverage. A half-eaten breakfast bun was sitting on a pile of unread documents: he flicked it onto his chair.

The visitor, Don Mendo, appeared not to notice. He was wafting a violet-scented glove at the ensign standing at the open door and saying something the captain couldn't quite catch.

Assuming it was another piece of introduction, the tubby Portuguese captain came to attention and said, "Harbour Captain at your service, my lord."

Don Mendo acknowledged the salute with another waft of violet scent, then stepped around the table until he was as close to the Harbour Captain as a fastidious man might get. In something of a stage whisper he said, "With respect, sir, I think you should dismiss your ensign. I come from—shall we say, I am on a very special mission... from Madrid."

The captain, who lived a quiet life and liked routine, was confused. He had never been good with foreign languages and this Spaniard—if he was Spanish, it was hard to tell by the name —was thoroughly upsetting his morning programme. Nevertheless, he signalled the ensign to go. It was all most irregular. He tried to stand taller, assume his dignity.

"As I said, this is a de-li-cate matter." Don Mendo's fancy coloured feather nodded on each syllable. He paused, scrutinized the Harbour Captain as if trying to judge his qualities, then touched at the curlicues of his very elaborate, very black moustache. "It is a matter of the very greatest secrecy. My orders, you see, come from *above*." A recently manicured forefinger pointed aloft.

The Harbour Captain opened and closed his mouth, but could think of nothing to say.

Apparently satisfied the implications had registered as he intended, Don Mendo continued, "Between you and me, sir, it has more to do with our Genoese bankers than our monarch, but I do not wish to be hanged for a traitor, so please forget I said that."

There was another pause. The Harbour Captain was lost. Except no, the don was waving a rolled parchment in the air; now he was catching on. Mouth agape, he stared at the document's ribbon and red seal.

The document flashed across his desk and Don Mendo let forth a sally of rapid Spanish that left the Harbour Captain struggling to keep up.

"You only need to see this, and then we can proceed as directed on this very tide. Timing is crucial, absolutely of the essence. I'm sure you can appreciate that, you being an admiral, which clearly I am not, but like poor old Medina Sidonia all those years ago—poor chap, he'd never been to sea in his life and there he was at war with the English, not an enviable position, no wonder we lost that one. Where was I? Oh yes— that we both have to follow orders—from *above*." Don Mendo tapped the document, as if sharing a mutually recognized confidence.

The Harbour Captain reached for the rolled vellum, but the foreigner was already breaking the seal for him. It was unrolled, but then, before he could read a single word, the other document was pushed under his nose.

"This comes from the *Conde-Duque* himself." The title was spoken with hushed reverence. "They are my personal orders.

Perhaps you should see this first. It contains all the relevant details for what must be expedited today."

The captain reached out a hand to locate his Venetian spectacles on his untidy desk. He hooked the wires over his ears and bent over the document. It was immediately raised above eye-level.

"Appalling handwriting, but as I say, and naturally, under the circumstances the Conde-Duque has had to do this himself —hardly something that could be trusted to one of even his private secretaries—he's famous for his illegibility in Madrid. You know that, of course...."

This Don Mendo rattled on at such a pace the Portuguese captain couldn't focus on the words. Then the two documents were whipped away and he found himself being propelled out of his office and down the staircase to the reception hall. A dark-skinned page carrying a heavy valise and rolled pennants was waiting there; a dishevelled Dominican monk carrying a cord-wrapped grey bundle stood next to him. Without a word of explanation they followed Don Mendo, who was directing the captain by a hand on his elbow, out onto the wharf.

And all the time, Don Mendo was gabbling something about Africa, gold, salt, sugar. He talked and talked until they were standing beside the tender for the *Maria de los Mares*, which had arrived the night before. It was the newest ship of the Spanish-Flanders fleet, returning home empty except for some woollen cloth and maimed soldiers. A rabble-looking crew appeared from nowhere and crowded on board and, before he could say his own name, the Portuguese Harbour Captain was watching the ship move out into the bay.

It was all so quick, the captain tried to explain later; and, as he was to stress many times to anyone who'd listen, there had been nothing on board as far as he knew to warrant such a theft. He never thought for a one minute the vessel was being stolen—commandeered, yes, but stolen. Who'd want a ship with empty holds and a consignment of one-armed, one-legged men?

Then he remembered the funny little vellum boat he had found on his desk when he got back to his office. He handed it to his next surprise visitor, a Count Azor, also from Madrid, who barged rudely into his office before the ensign could introduce him, inexplicably accompanied by a tall, thin priest.

When he saw the vellum ship, the priest, who he soon learned was Italian, flew into a rage the like of which the poor captain had never seen in his life. The count went the colour of the vellum he'd not had a chance to read, and the Italian priest shouted at him like he was a child for a good ten minutes.

The Harbour Captain waited until the two men had calmed down a little and made one last attempt to exonerate himself, saying, "But there was a Dominican priest to bless the voyage, leastways I think that's what he was."

The Italian actually started to splutter. In the end, as the Harbour Captain told his wife later that night, it was almost comical. Italians were too theatrical to be taken seriously.

Chapter Forty-eight
Crimphele, May 1637

Her husband arrived during a week of winter-chilled weather towards the middle of May. It was raining when he arrived, pouring down, so no one heard the trap clatter into the yard. The dogs, however, knew. Confined as they now were to the stables, they barked and jumped, yelped and howled until Alina herself opened the inner courtyard door to find out what was going on.

At first she didn't recognize him. All she saw was John Hawthorne with a piece of waxed cloth over his head to protect him from the downpour, and an old man next to him wrapped in shawls and a blanket. When she realized, her blood ran cold, then hot, and she didn't know what to do.

"Alina!" called John, dismounting from the trap and running to the great hall door. "Alina, my dear, here we are at last."

Alina dashed through puddles that soaked her woolen skirt, across to the trap. She dithered around the carter as he lifted Sir Thomas into his arms, ferried him across to the house and deposited the baronet in his ancestral seat like a sack of beans. She waited while John brought in the hand luggage and paid the carter before calling Meg.

"Get Toby to bring those boxes in out of the rain!"

Thomas rested his head against the back of his chair and struggled for breath.

Alina dashed to the kitchen door shouting, "Aggie! Aggie!"

First Perkin, then Crook-back Aggie jumped out of the fireside rocker. "Yes, milady? Is something wrong?"

"Come quickly. No, make a hot draught for a...." Alina had forgotten the word for *fiebre*, "hotness—fever!"

"The baby!"

"No, Sir Thomas is here, but *está malo*, he's bad."

Aggie rushed towards the pantry for honey and blackcurrant jelly. Alina returned to the great hall. Toby and Marcos were hovering next to Meg at the door.

"Carry him up to my chamber," Alina ordered. "Nowhere else is warm enough, except the nursery and he can't go in there. Meg, arrange a chamber for Mr Hawthorne."

In a very short space of time Thomas was tucked in Alina's bed, the fire in her chamber had been banked up, and Alina was pacing between the window and fireplace to calm her nerves. Meg brought the hot drink to the room and left as quietly as she had entered. Glad of something to do, Alina sat by her husband.

"Thomas, can you sit up? We have a hot drink for you. Here, let me help you." He weighed nothing; their son had more flesh on him. "What has happened to you?" she whispered.

Thomas opened his rheumy eyes and tried to smile. "I'm sorry."

Alina had to bend over him to hear what he said. He put out a bony hand and touched a strand of hair that had fallen onto her shoulder, "You've put your hair up."

He tried to say more but started to cough. She waited for the dreadful rasping to subside, then held the cup of blackcurrant and honey for him to sip.

He could barely swallow and waved it away, "Later," he whispered hoarsely.

Alina took a deep breath; her husband had come home to die.

She must have stayed by the bed watching Thomas struggle for breath in his half-waking sleep for some time, for when Meg knocked at her door again she was stiff and cold despite the blazing fire.

353

"Beg pardon, milady, but Mr Hawthorne says can he come in, and Master Tomás is crying for you and Agnes says would you mind if she took a look at the master to see what remedy might help him or should we call the doctor?"

Alina shook herself awake. "Send Agnes up, then tell Mr Hawthorne to come. I'll go to Tomás when there's someone here, you see to him for now. But don't bring the baby in here."

Crook-back Aggie was waiting outside the door. She hurried in, keeping her head low, and grasped Sir Thomas's hand.

"Permission, milady, I need to see how hot he is."

Aggie held her master's hand in hers, then stretched up over the edge of the high bed to gently put her fingers under his chin and slid them down to his chest over the thin linen of the nightshirt. "He's having trouble breathing," she said, "and he's much too hot, *much* too hot. His brow's dry and he's not sweating, which isn't right, milady." Delicately, as if Thomas were made of glass, she placed her other hand over the one on his chest then bent as if to listen.

"Can you help him, Agnes?" Alina asked quietly.

Aggie shook her head. "I'm not sure, he's bad and that's a fact. We need to clear his chest then make him sweat it away, milady."

"Can you do that?"

"My old grandma called this pleurisy, I think. Sir Thomas, can you open your mouth sir, so I can see your throat?"

Thomas opened his mouth; Aggie looked, then shook her head again.

"I know what to do, milady, and what'll help him, but I don't know what *he'll* do, if you know what I mean? I can bring him remedies, but...." she lowered her voice and whispered without drama, "it might be up to him—at this stage."

"He's very bad?"

Aggie nodded.

"But you can help him." It was a plea.

"Willow bark, and crushed willow leaves in fruit syrup for fever: purslane, mallow and quince in syrup of violet with

354

liquorice for the quinsy of the throat. I'll pick fresh lungwort and lovage and we'll boil 'em in beer. He should drink that as hot as he can and as much as he can, to expel the poison vapours, but...."

"But?"

"He's very weak, milady." Aggie tapped Sir Thomas' shoulder gently, as if reassuring a child, and started to walk to the door. As she held the door handle, she half turned and said, "Thank you, milady."

"Thank you? For what, Agnes?"

"For trusting me, ma'am. For your respect."

Marcos did not see Alina again for two days. After helping to carry her husband up to her chamber on that first afternoon he went out to the stables then wandered into the dairy looking for something to do.

His head was full of half-formed ideas and half-recognized emotions. Inexplicably, he felt a tremendous sense of disappointment, not that Sir Thomas had returned, but that what had returned was worth so little. The creature Alina had married had seemed a flea of a man at the first meeting; knowing he was now also an invalid disappointed him in a way he could not name. Ludo as a rival was understandable if not acceptable: he could see why Alina would prefer him; but this feeble shell in dull clothing—this was not right.

After making a lightning visit to his mother, John Hawthorne stayed at Crimphele while Alina tried to nurse her husband back to health. As Molly remained absent he was happy to entertain the boy Tomás, and as soon as the weather improved John pulled him around the gardens in a wooden trolley. Sometimes they went up to the pond to hunt frogs, then played peek-a-boo around the overgrown knot garden until John's back ached from so much bending. On rainy days they stayed indoors and played around the great hall table until Tomás got fractious and squealed for *mamá*, then he bumped him up and down and recited "Ride a Cock-horse" until his knees ached.

And he enjoyed every moment. He would rest his face in the child's sweet-smelling hair and wish this wonderful creature were his own, then become sad as he remembered he had made vows to forgo this almost indescribable sense of delight, felicity, blessedness. Each evening as he tried to write his thoughts in his journal he struggled to find the words to explain how he felt, and fell to wondering if it were a sin for a priest to want a son of his own.

Sometimes Marcos would come in and the child would stretch his arms up to be lifted in the air. Marcos jiggled him at shoulder level, then tossed him high, causing the child to scream with delight and sending his self-appointed caretaker into a panic. John could not get used to having Marcos in the house. In his eyes the boy, who admittedly was no longer a boy, didn't fit, didn't belong.

When the crisis was over and Thomas had come through the worst of his fever, Robert arrived at the house to pay his respects. John was delighted to see him and questioned him with appalled curiosity about being pressed into service, about what happened with the corsairs and how he had escaped being captured or killed.

Robert had returned, God be praised, but Thomas was cross with what John told him about Molly. She had developed a pert attitude and refused to come up to the house during this critical time to help Alina with the child.

Exactly two weeks after their arrival, John, now dressed in country worsted breeches and leather jerkin, took little Tomás on his shoulders and set off out of the Crimphele grounds to visit his aunt and beg a cream bun. He was in the act of showing Tomás a bird's nest in the hedgerow on the way, when two men riding well-fed, well-groomed horses appeared round a bend on the puddle-littered track. Their horses filled the lane, so John, taking care not to scratch his tender burden, stepped back against the hedge to let them pass.

"Excuse me, friend," said one in accented English. "We seek the house of Sir Thomas Fulford."

John went cold: these were no Cornishmen come to see their cousin or acquaintance. They weren't messengers from Lord Rundell either. Could they be from the queen? He searched their appearance for some clue to their identity. They were well-dressed, but not attired in the foppish feathers and lace he associated with Queen Henrietta's French court. Nor did they look like the plain folk now calling for stricter adherence to the Protestant faith and seeking out recusants. Could they be officials come to check on the head of a Catholic family who was breaking the law by holding religious ceremonies in a private chapel?

Or—he swung the child down to his feet to give himself time to think—perhaps were they not Protestants seeking Sir Thomas, but foreign Catholics seeking the priest known to lodge in his house.

"You're looking for Crimphele?" he asked. If they didn't know the house there was a good chance they didn't know Thomas. "Can I help you?"

He pulled the child back into his arms and kept his head behind the boy's robust frame, as the two men looked at each other.

The man who had addressed him spoke again. "We must speak with Sir Thomas."

Speak *with*, not speak *to*: he used English the way Alina often did, in direct translation.

"Well, speak freely," John said, trying to sound the very opposite of the quaking, timid being he felt.

"You are Sir Thomas?"

"And this is Master Thomas. Say good day, Tommy." John wiggled the boy's hand like a puppet in mock greeting.

The two men exchanged glances again. "It is private, sir. Not to speak on the street."

They're Spanish or Italian, thought John, *saying 'street' not lane.*

"Then let us walk back to Crimphele together," he said calmly, while his mind raced through alternatives. How could he prevent them getting into the house before he had spoken to Alina?

The two men rode beside him, checking their horses to match his walking pace. At no point did they exchange a word. *The second one has no English*, John surmised. They had come for him, not Thomas. He was being recalled to Rome—or sent elsewhere.

When they reached the inner courtyard, he just managed to say, "Wait here, I will send a groom for your horses," before the dogs hurtled from the stables, baying and yapping, then circling the visitors in silence like a pack of wolves. The bloodhound wouldn't hurt a chicken, the mastiff slept out with the ewes at lambing time; neither had ever attacked anything as far as he was aware, but they were large and threatening. The smaller lurchers and terriers entertained themselves by snapping at nervous fetlocks and kept the strangers in their saddles. John had never cared for dogs, but he was grateful to them now.

"I'll just deliver this young man to Lady Arleen or his nurse," he said and disappeared into the great hall.

He hared up the stone staircase to Thomas's chamber, bouncing the heavy child in his arms and making him laugh at the fun.

"Alina, oh God, Alina, listen, there's two men—I think they've come for me. Let them think I'm Thomas, I beg you. Don't let them take me, for love of the Virgin, don't let them take me!"

Alina lifted the child from his arms and stared at him. "What?"

Slowly he repeated what had happened and what he feared.

Alina looked at him hard. "Who has come for you?"

"The Cardinal's men, I'll explain later. Thomas knows. Come, quickly, please."

Alina looked inquiringly at her husband.

"I know about this," Thomas said. "Go with John."

Alina shrugged and walked to the door, "Come then, Sir Thomas my husband, it is rude to keep guests waiting."

They descended the tower stairs and went out to the courtyard. The dogs were still circling, yapping and snapping, and the strangers were still in their saddles.

"Dogs, heel," said John.

Alina turned her face into her son's fair hair to stop herself from laughing. None of the dogs obeyed, so she shouted, "*Perros, fuera! A la cuadra, ahora!*"

The Crimphele pack slunk back to the stables. Too late, she realised she'd spoken in Spanish and realised John was watching the strangers to see if they reacted, but they were so absorbed with the dogs they either hadn't heard her properly or they already knew Sir Thomas' wife was Spanish.

"I'll fetch Toby for the horses," she said loudly in English, and followed the dogs into the stables with little Tomás peering over her shoulder and her heart racing.

When she returned the two men were in the great hall and seated at the long table. Alina and John stationed themselves with their backs to the fireplace.

"So?" John began.

"We come," said the spokesman, "to call upon John Hawthorne that lives in this house."

"Mr Hawthorne? Here?"

"That is what we are told, Sir Thomas."

"He doesn't live here. Never has."

"Forgive me, his mother tells us he lives in this house."

"It is her way of speaking," said Alina. "When they were young boys he was always here. She says he *lives* here, meaning he is more time here than at her house. Like young boys together all the time, you know."

"But," said John trying to measure his words, "he went up to London."

"And became very ill," added Alina, quickly.

"We are told he is not in London. He is here, now. His own mother says this."

"Yes, well, that is because his mother is distraught, distressed, discomforted." Alina gave John a sharp kick in the shin. "And as Lady Arleen says, very angry. You see... he came back from London... and died here yesterday. His body is in a chamber above—not at her house—it's very painful for her, as it is for us." John rubbed a foot against his new bruise. "A delicate family matter."

The two men exchanged looks. "I am sorry to hear that," said the spokesman.

"Was it an urgent, important matter?" asked John. "Anything we can help with?"

Alina tried to extract her son's fingers from her hair and moved him from one arm to the other, staring all the time at the man who was doing the talking.

"Pardon, but we have to tell our master this news and—excuse us, but we need to be certain that this John Hawthorne is dead."

"Certain? God Almighty, have you no charity? The man's laid out in a chamber above." John sounded genuinely horrified.

Alina laid a calming hand his arm and addressed the two men, "Would you like to show your respects?" Out of the corner of her eye she saw John swallow hard. "Please wait, I will call my son's nurse, and then we will take you to see poor Mr Hawthorne's body. I cannot take a child to the room of a dead man."

Both men nodded.

Alina walked across the great hall and opened the door to the kitchens keeping her back as straight and stately as a queen. Once there, she plonked the large baby in Aggie's floury hands, saying, "Keep him here," then sprinted up the service stairs.

Thomas was half-awake; he smiled a greeting.

"Thomas," she hissed, "you are dead. Don't breathe. Two men will come to the chamber. Don't move."

Before he could reply, she had pulled the sheet up over his head, folded down the bed hangings, and was running back down the kitchen steps. She paused before opening the door, took a deep breath, clenching and unclenching her fists in her skirt, then sailed back into the great hall like a Spanish queen.

"Agnes has Baby, my dear," she said to John as she re-entered. "Have you warned them?"

"Should I warn them?"

"Well, it is you who tell me *la peste*...."

"Plague," corrected John.

"Is very contagious."

"Yes, indeed."

"*La peste*—plague!" said the one who spoke, and he looked at his companion.

"Come this way." Alina led them to the tower door. "This is why we have the body here and do not send it to his mother's house, to stop the spreading. We say nothing of this to his mother, to prevent her panic."

John nodded frantically.

"Here," said Alina as they reached the room. "You must cover your mouths. Don't breathe while you are in this room, and don't touch him."

Slowly, she opened the door to Thomas' chamber and stood aside for the two men to enter. They stayed where they were.

"Let me show you," she said.

Alina went across to the bed and pulled back the hangings, then pulled the sheet down over Thomas's pallid brow a few inches and stood back to let them view the corpse, making sure her own body masked the rise and fall of its laboured breathing.

"They were quite alike, don't you think," she whispered, "my husband and his late friend?"

Neither man made any attempt to enter the room.

"We shall miss him a great deal," Alina said, replacing the sheet and dropping the hanging back into place. "More than I can say in words."

The two men backed away then started down the stairs.

John followed them, making a show of offering hospitality, "A glass of beer before you ride back—where is it you have come from?"

They did not answer. Once in the hall, they replaced their riding gloves, moving towards the door.

"And you're not at liberty to give me this special message?" John persisted. "I'm sure I could help."

"Not now. It is not necessary now, thank you. Please say your dogs," he was losing his English in his anxiety to get away, "say them—go—keep off!"

Alina and John stood shoulder to shoulder once more and watched the men trot hastily out of the courtyard, then they turned into the great hall, shut the door behind them and fell into each other's arms in hysterical laughter.

"You are a very clever woman!" said John.

"And you are a very dead man, Mr Hawthorne."

Arm in arm they went up the tower stairs to tell Thomas all about it.

Marcos came into the courtyard just as the two men were leaving, and walked into the great hall just in time to see the once timid priest climbing the tower stairs like a helpless drunk arm in arm with the woman he loved, had loved since the day she knocked him flat on a Spanish galleon. Now that he had finally decided to stay for good, he must act.

Chapter Forty-nine

Molly Roberts walked into the main kitchen through the back door and found Aggie standing by the table helping Tomás spoon up jam from a half-made tart.

"What's he doing in here?" Molly demanded.

"Can't rightly say. The Lady Arleen needed someone to hold him and the woman as was supposed to be caring for him wasn't around—as usual."

"Give him to me. I'll deal with him now."

Molly put her hands under the child's armpits but he squealed and landed her a sharp slap on the nose with his wooden spoon.

"Ow! You little bastard!"

Aggie got to her feet, holding the child tight to her chest. "What did you say?"

"I said ow! That hurt."

"And then?"

"Well, he might be, for all we know. We've both seen the way she carries on."

Aggie shook her head in disbelief. "Have you gone mad, Mol Roberts? Raving mad? She's done more for you than anyone could, and that's how you repay her?"

"Oh Lord, here we go—Saint Arleen."

Aggie's small but hard, work-worn hand flew up and slapped Molly's face, "You evil, stupid woman."

"Evil? Me? I know who's the evil one in this house. And it isn't me!"

Fortunately, at that moment Meg arrived with a basket of clean laundry. She paused at the door, taking in the atmosphere and looking from one woman to the other.

"You two fighting again?" she said, shaking her head like a despairing mother. Dropping the basket of kitchen cloths on Aggie's rocking chair, she added, conversationally, "Don't see you up here much these days, Molly."

"That's what I was saying," put in Aggie, and she sat down to let the baby bang the table with his spoon.

Molly ignored the comment and said, "That's because it's all different now with Robert home."

"But he's working up here again. I just seen him," said Meg, smoothing out wiping cloths into neat squares. "You should bring your little Bobby up to play. This one here's all lonely now he hasn't got a friend." Meg pointed at the flour-covered babe in Aggie's lap.

"I've left our Bobby with my sister. It isn't right him playing with a lord. People should know their class and station and act according. He'll grow up too familiar if I let him play with him."

Meg shrugged. "Can't see it matters while they're this small."

"Well, it does," Molly huffed. "Now give him to me and I'll take him up to the nursery. Where's his mother?"

"Where she's been the last fortnight I expect, in with the master."

"Huh, that's something." Keeping out of spoon's reach, Molly picked up their future lord and master.

Meg waited until the woman was out of earshot and turned to Aggie, "What's got into her? She's getting worse, all these comments and hints—you'd think she knows some great secret."

"P'raps she does," said Aggie, gathering up bashed about pastry and clearing her board to start again. "P'raps she knows things that we don't know she knows."

"Oh Lor', don't you start," laughed Meg. "D'you need one of these cloths for that?"

That night, as Alina pulled off her clothes and put on her nightgown, her husband reached out an arm and said, "Sleep here tonight. I'm not really contagious."

Alina laughed at the reference. "But you need your rest."

"I shall sleep better with you beside me again."

Alina bit her lip and hesitated.

"Please," insisted Thomas, "just to sleep."

Remembering when Thomas had used almost exactly the same words, Alina climbed up onto the high bed, closed the hangings and slid under the warm blankets. He slipped his arm under her head and pulled her to him.

"This is where we left off, me holding my lovely wife after she'd just given me a perfect son."

"Yes," murmured Alina, "oh, Thomas, I wish you did not go then." She kissed the light stubble of his unshaven chin.

"We can start again, my dear. We can be as we were."

Alina looked at this husband who was but a cup of milk to Ludo's rich red wine, a summer breeze to Ludo's storm, a safe haven to Ludo's unchartered waters. She gave a deep sigh. Thomas was all that Ludo was not, and for that she should be grateful. *Start again, yes*, she thought, *but for all that I try, it cannot be as it was.*

"I am not as I was," she whispered.

But her husband was kissing her ear and didn't notice.

Chapter Fifty
The Isle of Ibiza, June 1637

Brother Caritas wandered out of the low white house and drank in the sweet, malty scent of dew-dampened summer grass. A red-gold sun was rising over the treetops, promising comfort for his old bones. Pagan man had worshiped the sun; the Teutons and the English had named a day of their week for the sun god that illuminated and protected, provided food and fuel.

The woman who had given him a room came out onto the rough-stone terrace and gabbled something at him. His native language was spoken strangely here but he understood: there was fresh orange juice, bread and goat's cheese for his morning meal.

His stomach rumbled but he didn't go back into her house immediately. He sat on the edge of the well and lifted his old grey habit above his swollen, arthritic knees. Asking forgiveness for a prayer made in such a posture, he thanked the Lord for deliverance. He was as close to home as he dared to get, and as the merchant had said when he'd brought him into the very middle of the island, even the archangel Gabriel would have a hard time locating him here.

It was not pure altruism, of course. The Italian had probably never done a purely altruistic thing in his life. He wanted him tucked out of the way here so he couldn't inform on his whereabouts, should, God forbid, the Vatican trace them to Ibiza. Which was not impossible; they had picked him up fast enough in England.

Some hours later, down in the crowded white town, Ludo was trying to pass the time in a game of dice. As his turn came, he made a fuss of wiping sweat from his brow, drying his hands on his thin cotton pantaloons, lifting the dice as if they would scorch his fingers then rolling them onto the dusty street. He leaned back to watch them fall. It was all a pantomime and his heart wasn't in it. The idle men around him guffawed, swore, spat and drank rough wine, content with the day they lived, but not him. He stifled a sigh, made a joke about *el Ludo* having no game left in him, which went right over their heads, then said he was off to find some food.

Instead of going down to the harbour, though, he walked up the steep terraced cobbles and round the back of the castle to settle himself on a wall and look down on the scene below. The galleon that he'd steered into one of Ibiza's narrowest, deepest coves and kept there for a full lunar month was now here in the main harbour. Stripped of sail and pennants, with a redesigned prow and newly painted stern, she was barely recognizable. They were taking longer than promised to do the job, but it would be worth the waiting. Soon he would have to make a decision about where he was going next, then raise a crew from among the dicing rabble that called themselves mariners or pirates, according to their histories.

Taking the galleon in Lisbon had given him immense pleasure, and while he was on this half-wild island he was safe from Vatican agents or anyone else contracted to kill him, safer even than in Portovenere. But, but, but—it wasn't enough. He didn't want to be here. He wanted to go back for Alina.

For the first week or so, he had been plagued day and night by her absence. He sought out other women to distract him, but Alina wouldn't leave him alone.

The past two years had been a disaster. He had lost his 'rich trade' during his second year in Holland, and failing to bring merchandise from Cathay for two consecutive years meant he had also lost his clients for silk in Florence and Seville. He had lost his reputation as a merchant, and now he'd lost the compensation, because the fine ship being re-fitted in the harbour was not, after all, the only thing he ever wanted.

Ludo folded his arms and observed the activity in the harbour below. A group of men were making an old-fashioned galley seaworthy. Turks, they called them in England, although there wasn't a Turk among them.

A flicker of an idea flitted by on the breeze. A half-memory of Alina saying the Turks came up the Tamar for booty and pretty girls.

Where was that galley bound?

He could take a galley that size up the Tamar—and when he —they—returned, his new galleon would be finished and waiting. Then they could sail for—where? Would she consider the idea of crossing the Atlantic and starting a new life in the New World? There was a lot of money in tobacco and sugar. No. Something held him back from the Americas, it was too crude, too rough-hewn and new; milady would want something more refined.

He would take her to Italy to live in a fine house on a Ligurian hillside. Or had he suggested that to someone else, before?

Chapter Fifty-one
Crimphele, July 1637

McNab watched Sir Thomas and Marcos coming back down the side of the lower field. They had been walking the Home Farm boundaries without him, checking his gates, stiles, hedges, and the quality of pasture. The master was planning to replace him with the boy, he was sure. He was showing the boy what was to be done, except there wasn't anything to be done, because despite slacking off he still had the estate in hand. No one could ever accuse McNab of shirking his duty.

He clutched the sturdy walking staff he had recently acquired, smoothing his thumb over the heavy knot of wood in his hand. If he didn't find an opportunity to use it soon he was going to be out of job.

The irony and injustice of it gnawed at him like oak-canker. It had taken all his inner-strength to resist punishing her ladyship, all his self-restraint not to tell Sir Thomas what a slut he'd married. And what was his reward? Replacement! By a foreigner whose face had never felt a razor. Ach, he'd like a cut-throat blade in his hand now!

"Come," he growled needlessly at his dog.

Pretending he had not seen the master, McNab cut off down behind the house, back to his office. There was plenty of work he could be getting on with there. Plenty he could leave the boy to sort out. If that was what the master wanted, that was what he would have, because McNab never shirked a job.

Thomas and Marcos walked along, side by side, chatting about this and that: Thomas curious to know about Marcos' home and Spanish ways, Marcos responding and reconciling himself to the fact that he could not help liking this very English man.

Lately, Marcos's attitude to a number of things had changed. His new life in Cornwall kept him so busy he had little time to fabricate silly plans or dream up grandiose versions of himself. He was surprisingly content. Although he did need to resolve his status in the house: he was an employee in as much as he rendered a service, for which Sir Thomas ought really to pay him a stipend, but he was living like a guest in what had once been Sir Geoffrey's chamber.

He now knew why Alina had been so keen for him to stay on after Ludo's departure; she had told him all the dreadful things perpetrated by the odious McNab. Now, however, with her husband in much better health, there was really no need for him to be at Crimphele, unless, as Alina wanted, Thomas was planning to dismiss McNab. As far as he knew, though, Alina still hadn't said anything to Thomas about this, so McNab was still in his post, and it wasn't a foreigner's place to decry a trusted steward without evidence.

Resolving this issue would also resolve his relationship with Alina. While he was being treated as a guest, and therefore a gentleman, he was still in a position to hope Alina might turn to him. As a gentleman he could risk declaring himself. On the other hand, if Alina only wanted him as a replacement for McNab he was effectively a servant, in which case he had no possibilities with milady, so.... So obviously he must find the right moment to speak to Alina *before* McNab was dismissed.

It was true that he had given up fantastical schemes for his future, but he could not relinquish his dreams for Alina. That is why he had stayed after Ludo deserted them, why he had applied himself to the tasks she had set him, to gain her respect. That he had found a way of life that suited him in the process was ironic, but not disagreeable.

Not that he needed to remain at Crimphele to be close to Alina. He could use his ill-gained Dutch money to buy a respectable house nearby and set himself up as a neighbour: that was very tempting. Then, when the ailing Thomas had a relapse, and he was bound to die sooner rather than later, he would be at hand to comfort the widow and persuade her to his way of thinking.

Marcos was on the point of asking Sir Thomas if he knew of a good house nearby, when he was forestalled by Alina herself coming down from Paddon Hill with a dirty-faced toddler clinging round her neck.

Alina kissed her husband's cheek and shifted her burden on to him. "He's getting too heavy for me; you hold him for a while."

Thomas took the child and lowered him to the ground, saying, "I think this young man is old enough to walk with us now. Come along, son of mine, let's see your marching legs."

Tomás looked up at his father and opened his mouth to howl, then caught sight of his good friend Marcos and raised his arms to be lifted again. They all burst out laughing.

"He knows who is the soft touch here," said Thomas. "Go on, give him a piggy-back if you want to."

Marcos lifted the child onto his back and set off at a bouncy canter towards the upper garden gate. Thomas took Alina's hand and they followed more sedately behind. When they got into the garden Marcos was poking sticks into the pond to rouse the frogs, the child clapping his hands with delight as each one plopped off a lily into the thick green water.

"We should have this drained and cleaned," Thomas said. "Can you see about it tomorrow, Marcos?"

"Yes, of course." Marcos knew this was the moment to ask: employee or useful guest. But he said nothing.

They wandered on round the old knot garden, Thomas prodding the overgrown herbs and straggly box hedges with the toe of his boot. "All this needs doing, as well."

"You better ask Agnes, first," said Alina, stooping to pick the drying heads of sharp-smelling rosemary for her chamber, "she's the one that uses the herbs; she'll know what needs pulling up or replanting."

"Perhaps we should pull the whole thing up and redesign the entire area." Thomas surveyed the low-lying jungle more critically. "Look what we've got: it's not worth having, not even pretty. Unclipped hedges that have lost all their shape; laurel bushes growing branches too close to the ground; self-seeded wallflowers and Lord knows what these weeds are. It's an abandoned mess. It does not fit with my ideas for a modern Crimphele at all."

"Clear the lot and start again," Marcos suggested. "We could plant tulips and hyacinth. They would do well here, protected from the winds."

"Tulips cost a fortune."

"Not as much as they used to."

"Even so, it's an unnecessary luxury for a country garden like this."

"Perhaps. When I have my house I shall grow them."

Alina and Thomas exchanged glances. Alina said, "When will you have your house, Marcos? Where?"

Marcos got to his feet and gave the frog-poking stick to little Tomás, who instantly threw it in the water. "Can we talk about this later?" he said.

"At supper," replied Thomas. "We'll have some of the special wine my father imported and discuss your future. But we don't want you to go, do we, Alina?"

"No," she said and then added in Spanish, looking directly into Marcos' eyes, "We don't want you to go."

It was the repeated use of 'we' that helped Marcos make his final decision. All that remained was to decide where to go.

They moved on. Geese were pecking at the balding grass of the lawns; they didn't raise their heads, but Alina picked up her son and held him protectively against her nonetheless.

"Put him down," said Thomas. "You don't need to protect him from these geese."

"A goose opening its wings and hissing is very frightening for a child. I did the same for my brothers when they were little. We had a big gander with a vicious beak."

Marcos looked at Alina. He had never heard her speak of her brothers before.

Sensing his scrutiny, Alina clutched her son closer. "This dirty boy needs a bath," she said, and set off towards the house.

A few minutes later, Marcos excused himself and followed her in. He needed to be in his room on his own for a while. His mind was a turmoil of possibilities and indecision.

Thomas returned to the pond, then began to stroll down past the creamery and round the front of the house to examine the state of the terraced rose garden on the south range.

The chairs they used during his convalescence were still in the sunny spot by the front door. Thomas sat down; he was more tired than he had realized. Within seconds his eyelids closed and he was soon sound asleep.

He woke up to find Molly Roberts cutting roses.

"Molly," he said, "how nice to see you."

"Beg pardon, Sir Thomas, I didn't want to disturb you, but milady sent me down to pick some roses and Aggie wants hips for syrup."

"No, no, that's fine, you are not disturbing me in the least. Carry on. No, on second thought come and sit here a moment and tell me how you people in the house use the garden. Agnes uses rose hips for syrup, you say."

Molly put her basket down on the ground, smoothed her skirt demurely and sat on the edge of the vacant chair.

"Well sir, it's not me as uses the garden as a rule. I'm in the house more."

"But if you had a say, you'd keep all these roses, you wouldn't plant something else as well or instead?"

Molly wet her lips and folded her hands in her lap.

"Like I say sir, Aggie's the one that uses the herbs—and other plants we don't know about. She's got *special knowledge*, if you know what I mean? You've seen her pantry, no doubt; it's like an apothecary's."

Thomas nodded, he had never actually been in Aggie's kitchen, but he would go now, out of curiosity. He had an inkling what Molly might be hinting at, but his mother had trusted Aggie, had used her skills for winter preserves and obtaining free physic from the hedgerows and meadows to treat ailments. Alina also, and justifiably, respected her skills. Regretting his openness with a servant, he braced himself for what Molly might reveal. Not that it would make any difference; Agnes had saved his son's life and very probably his own. He would not be prejudiced against her.

Molly was warming to her theme. "Course she doesn't just use what grows here in the gardens. She gets what she needs, powders and special potions, elsewhere—having this *special knowledge*. And her having this special relationship with milady means…. There was one particular concoction when your lady mother was still alive, sir, Lady Arleen made use of it while you was in London, sir, though they says as no she didn't, but *I* have to say—" Molly suddenly stopped talking and gasped. Then she let out a high-pitched screech and jumped to her feet, pointing wildly down at the river. "Turks! Turks! The Turks are coming!"

Chapter Fifty-two

Thomas could see the galley. It was a high-decked vessel with an elongated triangle attached to the prow as a battering ram. The sail was down so they were evidently aiming for the Crimphele landing stage or for Tamstock, but there was only one man on deck, as far as he could make out.

He turned to Molly and said, "Run up to your mistress, tell her to take the child and go up the hill as fast as she can. Call out to anyone you see to go with her. Don't leave anyone here in the house. They will attack it for sure; we haven't got enough men to fend them off."

Molly rushed off into the house through the main kitchen door, shouting at Aggie and Meg to go up the hill, the Turks were coming.

Thomas followed her in. "Drop everything you are doing and get up the hill," he ordered. Meg immediately flew into a panic and dropped a pan of hot milk.

Crook-back Aggie quietly wiped the long knife she was using on her apron and tucked it into her pocket with her other little knife; then, calling Perkin to follow her, she ignored Thomas and headed up the back stairs to the first floor nursery after Molly. Once more Thomas followed. By the time they arrived, Alina was standing at the nursery window with the baby in her arms and Molly was fussing with blankets from the child's cot.

Thomas said, "Get up the hill as fast as you can, all of you." Alina turned to look at him. "Go, please, for the love of God, go as fast as you can. I'll sort things out here and join you." Then he raced back down the main stairs and out to the stable, yelling for Toby or whoever was there to hitch a cart as fast as he could.

Alina opened the casement window and stared down at the river. It *was* a pirate galley, but there was only one man on deck, a big man with black hair blowing around his face. Had he come just for her? Or were there others? Obviously there were others; the sail was down so they had rowed all the way up the estuary. Would he let these men do damage? If she went down to the landing stage on her own and got on his boat, would they go back where they came from and leave everyone in peace? Memories of the corsairs in Santander sent a cold chill down her spine. How many did he have with him? Would he control them now as he did then?

"Molly," she said calmly, "I want you to take Tomás and do as my husband says. Where's your boy?"

"Up at my sister's, milady. They're up by the church; they should be safe."

Meg appeared at the door, her face strawberry pink as she skipped up and down with fear and excitement.

"Meg, go with Molly and tell anyone in the creamery, dairy and stables to go with you. Get as far up Paddon Hill as possible, and stay up there until someone comes to fetch you. Aggie, you know where the keys are; get them and go round the house locking all the doors, then go up the hill as well."

Alina lifted Tomás into a tight embrace and placed her lips on his fair hair. Then she pulled herself away and whispered something in his ear. She made a move as if to pass her child to Molly, then paused and gave him another kiss. Tears were running down her face and glistening on the boy's fine hair. Pushing little Tomás into Molly's arms, she said, "Go, quickly— and God be with you."

Alina followed the women back down to the kitchen. As soon as she had seen Meg and Molly off around the back of the house she turned on her heel, hitched her skirt into its waistband and raced back up the stairs to Marcos's room.

The controlled English diction was gone; now she was screaming in Spanish, "Marcos! Marcos, get weapons and come with me!"

They charged down to the great hall armoury. Marcos pulled a musket from its wall bracket. "We need powder and a fuse."

"In the wine cellar, I think." Alina was pulling the swords and daggers out of their holders and piling them on the table.

"Alina, stop! This is stupid. We can't fight a ship full of pirates," shouted Marcos.

"It's not pirates. Well, it is, but they're with Ludo."

"Ludo!"

"Stop gaping, get weapons you can use and follow me."

"What are you going to do?"

"I don't know yet." Alina picked up her bow and slung the quiver of arrows she used for rabbit hunting over her left shoulder. "Get the powder, quickly."

Before Marcos could say another word, she was heading for the front door, but Aggie was already there, standing on tip toe, trying to reach the upper bolts. Instead of stopping to help her she turned again, racing back to leave the house through the kitchen.

Marcos ran into the parlour and pulled at the cellar door. It was locked, so he dashed back to the armoury, grabbed a sword, which he had no idea how to use, and pushed a dagger into the waist of his breeches. Thomas suddenly appeared in the hall. Marcos waved the musket at him, the words for powder, fuse and flint box all forgotten in the panic.

"In here," Thomas produced a key, and together they collected the necessary items from their place in the cellar. "Has Alina gone?" he demanded.

Marcos pointed towards the front door and the river, not daring to say what he thought she was about to do.

"What! The river! I told her to go up the hill."

But Marcos was gone, leaving Thomas with the worst decision of his life: who to follow and protect as best he might— wife or son?

After bolting the front door, Aggie collected the bunch of keys Lady Marjorie had always worn at her waist from the sewing room desk. Starting with the housekeeping room, she dashed from one door to the next, selecting keys and turning locks as fast as she could with fat little Perkin panting at her heels.

McNab stayed by the open window of the ground floor estate office. He had heard Molly scream, heard what was going on, and was still undecided. There was a box of copper and silver coins sitting in front of him on his table. He had been counting out the labourers' wages. All he had to do was pick it up, put it in a bag, collect the other smaller boxes secreted around the office and his rooms, and walk away. They'd assume he'd been taken prisoner. By the time they realized what had gone with him, he'd be on a ship to Virginia.... Except there still wasn't quite enough money to set himself up in business for the rest of his life. Another couple of months and he'd be his own man, but not just yet.

He briefly considered taking the money and following the women up the hill, to demonstrate his loyalty that way. Then he remembered the Lady Arleen, and he knew what he should do. Ten to one it wasn't pirates at all, it'd be that foreign devil come back for her. And she'd go, desperate for him she'd be, wet between the legs—leaving her duties and her child and them that had taken her in, like the lascivious tart she was. He'd like to see that, to know that Lady Marjorie had been right all along.

"You stay here, lassie," he said to his greyhound, and he went out to the front door. It was locked and bolted. He went to the side office entrance, it was locked; to the great hall door, that was locked and bolted from the inside as well.

"Nothing for me to do, then," he said to the greyhound as he came back to his table, "unless I climb out the window."

John Hawthorne was in the chapel. He was cleaning a chalice and so absorbed in his polishing he didn't notice Aggie until she and the little dog were right beside him.

"Oh, Agnes, you made me jump."

The small woman ignored him. Looking about her, she said hastily, "Perkin'll be safe in here once I've locked both doors. You keep Perkin with you; I've got a job to do for milady." She flicked keys round a large metal ring as she spoke.

"A chapel is no place for a soulless creature, Agnes. Dogs have no place in a sanctified, sacred building."

There was no reply, only the sound of a lock being turned.

"How odd," John said to the creature snuffling at his feet.

He had never noticed how the front teeth of its lower jaw jutted out before—rather like a gargoyle. Then he had a most dreadful thought: could Agnes be using her familiar for some appalling purpose? What terrible mischief was she preparing that required a live animal in a consecrated chapel?

Alina was hurrying, although not running, down the narrow, tree-lined alley that led from the river path, when Jim Hawkins appeared round the bend.

"Pirates! The Turks is here!" he gasped. "Best you get back to the house, ma'am. Lock yourselves inside. It's a fortress, you'll be safe there."

"Thank you, Jim, but it's not pirates."

"Beg pardon, ma'am, but they'm pirates! I should know."

"Not the usual sort of pirate."

Jim Hawkins gaped; the woman was walking past him, carrying on like it was a Sunday stroll. "Go back, ma'am, go back! They Turks was damn near tying up when I left."

"Your wife and boys are in their hiding place?"

Jim Hawkins nodded.

"Then go up to the house and tell anyone you can find what you've just told me. We've sent everyone up Paddon Hill—you'd better do the same. If they are pirates and they do get up this far, they'll be expecting us to be locked inside—let's disappoint them. They can take the tapestries and the silver, but they will never, ever take my son." Alina walked on.

"You're never thinking to go down there, milady?" Jim Hawkins called after her.

"Oh, yes. Do you want to come and be a hero with me?"

The ferryman was aghast; he shook his head in disbelief and ran on up the path only to collide with Marcos coming through the garden door. "You vurriners—you'm mazed in the 'ead if you think you can reason with pirates. You got no idea what happens when Turks arrived on a quayside," he screeched.

Alina continued on down the path, desperate to get to the galley before the pirates could get up to the house.

When she reached the river bank, Ludo was standing on the galley's middle deck arguing with some men. He looked up, saw her, and barked something at the men. Two of them went below as he must have ordered, the third, a bandy-legged, square-set man with a curved cutlass at his waist, folded his arms and stood back to observe what their captain was up to.

Slowly, deliberately, as if in no hurry at all, Alina walked the last few paces down to the landing stage; then, stopping a good ten paces from the galley itself and keeping her bow behind her back, she took up her position: back straight, chin in the air. For what seemed a full minute she just stood and looked at Ludo, and he, smiling, looked back.

Finally, he broke the silence. Speaking in his Italian-accented Spanish, Ludo declaimed theatrically, "Here I am! *Mostafa*, your Chosen One, *Al Wadud*, the Loving One—come to fetch my princess."

"Your princess! Are you mad?"

"Mad with love. Yes, I accept that."

"What do you want?"

"You, of course. Get in. No point dallying about here." Ludo stared at her then said, "Do you know, you are even lovelier than I remembered. Tresses of golden hair... except you've pinned them up. Some of them; they're mostly unpinned now. Come along, get in and you'll never have to use a hairpin again."

Alina stared, one hand gripping the bow behind her back, the other hand clenching and unclenching in the folds of her skirt. "What do you mean, 'get in'?"

"I mean *get in*! Come aboard. Embark! There's a triplet for your religious little friend. I can't make it any plainer. And I can't keep this band of cut-throats shut up much longer; they've been like caged animals since we left open water."

"But what do you want?" Alina insisted.

"I want to take you back to—anywhere you want to go."

"In a pirate ship? You *are* mad."

"I thought you wanted to come with me! Wanted a more exciting life, you said...."

"I did. I don't anymore."

Alina hadn't known she was going to say that. She looked round for her husband. He wasn't there, but Marcos had arrived. He was further up the path with his musket primed and the fuse lit; he nodded at her and kept the musket trained, not on Ludo but on the pirate that was standing behind him.

"Tell him I'll shoot if he doesn't untie the galley," said Marcos.

"Tell him," Alina pointed at the man behind Ludo, "to untie your boat and leave us in peace."

Ludo was flummoxed. "There are two dozen pirates below deck, panting for loot, entertainment and some comely white slaves for the Salé market. If you don't come aboard—" His words were interrupted by a crackling sound in the undergrowth behind Alina. McNab had cut through from the lower terraces.

Ludo laughed, "Oh, ho! We have a faithful servant come to protect you." He blew through his cheeks with impatience then said, "Get a move on, Alina—come aboard my ship of gold. You've got no choice, anyway; there are three of you against a ship full of professionals. Get in and stop wasting our time."

"Go to hell—and take those bastards with you. I will not be treated in this manner. I am Lady Fulford, not a harbour tart or some foolish juvenile."

Now Ludo really lost his patience and stepped onto the landing stage.

Alina raised her bow and held an arrow ready to let fly. "Stay there! I'm a good shot, remember."

"Don't be absurd!" Ludo started towards her.

Alina let fly and the arrow grazed the shoulder of his left arm.

"You stupid woman!" he shouted in anger, pulling the arrow from the threads of his shirt.

"Not stupid, not stupid at all. I have finally learned to be wise." Alina was preparing the next shot. "That was just a warning. I can hit your heart from here."

"Oh no, you can't!" Ludo bent double and raced at her, grabbing her round the waist and knocking the bow from her hands.

Then there were what seemed like a hundred men swarming out of the galley and up onto the river bank. Marcos fired, missed, then had no time to reload before two pirates were on him, snatching the musket from his hands and pulling him down towards the galley.

Ludo called out to halt them but it was too late.

"See what you've done," he growled at Alina, "now they'll be up at your precious house and doing their worst."

"It's all locked up."

"That won't stop them. Ever heard of axes? Anyway, they all carry tinder boxes. It'll go up in flames. Get in the boat and I'll do what I can to round them up."

"That's blackmail!"

"So?"

Alina took a deep breath and pretended to relax in his grip, "All right. But stop them!"

Ludo put two fingers to his lips to whistle but no noise came, for his mouth fell open in disbelief.

A noisy crowd of hysterical, honking females in grey was hurtling down the narrow river path towards them, cursing and shouting for all their might. Behind them, beating at them with wings spread wide and feathers splayed like the devil's fingers, came two huge ganders, honking in angry disapproval. Behind them, brandishing a long stick in each hand, came a beetle-like creature: Crook-back Aggie.

"*Maria Santissima,*" muttered Ludo.

Alina looked around and would have laughed had the sight not scared her as much as Ludo's cut-throats, who were now dashing back towards their galley like a bunch of naughty schoolboys caught scrumping apples.

Marcos, who was being man-handled onto the landing stage, took advantage of the chaos and jabbed back with his elbows. Twisting out of the pirates' hands, he grabbed Alina and pulled her towards the boathouse.

"Oh no, you don't!" cried Ludo and tried to grab her back, but she was too quick for him and he was left with a length of skirt in his hands. Marcos snatched a cutlass from a dithering pirate and waved it menacingly at Ludo.

"Don't be ridiculous, Marcos," Ludo said, and lurched again for Alina, getting an arm round her neck.

Alina remembered the small dagger in her pocket: suddenly its sharpened steel was in her right hand, and as Ludo tightened his other arm across her chest she leaned to her left and bit his hand, simultaneously thrusting the dagger backwards, catching him on his hip bone.

"Agh!" Ludo cried, "*mala femmina!*" and let go.

The geese were nearly on them now, and McNab was standing beside Marcos. Alina noted his presence but ignored him. Feet planted firmly on the landing stage, she faced Ludo, who was dabbing at the blood oozing into his soft pantaloons.

"Go!" she yelled in fury. "Tell them to go!"

Ludo shook his head and turned to his quartermaster. As he did so a few of the braver pirates stationed themselves around Marcos and Alina like a pack of wolves ready to attack. Then there was a shot: a pirate fell. Then another shot and another pirate fell. At least two people were firing from the boathouse.

The shots brought to a halt the chaos. For a moment or two no one moved, then, with reloaded musket and fuse at the ready, Thomas walked into full view. He turned to see if Jim Hawkins was following him. As he moved, a pirate took a swipe at him with his cutlass, and he crumpled to the ground.

The tableau on the landing stage surged back to life and mayhem. The enraged geese had reached the quay. Each one was beating its wings frantically, heads snaking forward, vicious beaks snapping left and right. Every pirate ran for the galley except the quartermaster, who launched himself at Alina. McNab kicked him out of the way and seized her himself.

With one hand clasped round her waist, the other at her throat, McNab began to apply pressure. His long fingers squeezed. She couldn't breathe; she was choking, suffocating, too weak to use her dagger, which dropped to the ground. Then she was free and McNab was falling, and Marcos was holding the curved weapon he had threatened Ludo with, but now it was covered in a Scotsman's blood. He dropped the cutlass and caught Alina before she, too, fell to the ground.

Ludo held out his arms, shouting, "*Basta! Basta!* Enough!" Rattling off something in a language only the pirates understood, he turned and got back into the galley. He stopped and looked across at Jim Hawkins, who had a musket pointed straight at him, then at the husband on the ground, and finally at Marcos holding Alina. "Keep her," he shouted to them, "I always said she was trouble."

With that he slashed through the mooring rope, and willing oarsmen pulled the galley back into the river.

"They'll go for Tamstock," gasped Alina, tears rolling down her face.

"No, not Tamstock, another village perhaps, if he can't hold them. He's not wicked enough to let them loose here," Marcos replied.

"What have I done?" Alina was sobbing and shaking. Safe now in Marcos' arms, she wanted to vanish, die, and never have to remember this day.

Marcos traced the marks on her throat with bloodied fingers. "That Scottish bastard nearly killed you. Let me get you back to the house."

"No, I'm all right. Help my husband first."

Thomas was sitting up, his right arm cradled against his body, rocking himself against the pain.

"*Dios mío*, Thomas!" Alina was out of Marcos's arms and on the ground next him, crying, "Aggie, come here, quickly."

Crook-back Aggie, who had managed to shoo all the geese into the water, scuttled over to her master. The cut in his lower right arm was so deep they could see bone.

"Bandage," snapped Aggie. "Hawkins, get over here and carry him up to the house."

Alina tugged at her torn skirt, pulling away a strip to bind the gash.

The ferryman hunkered down beside Sir Thomas, grinning. "Proper job," he was saying, "proper job—we see'd 'em orf an' no mistake!"

"Stop ya clacking, ya gorp, and get him up to the house," snapped Aggie, who tied the bandage, then followed the group up the river path.

When they got into the gardens, she dashed round them to retrieve the bunch of keys from the bottom of the dried up fountain. The pirates might have got her, but they wouldn't have got the keys to milady's home as well.

Big Jim Hawkins lowered Sir Thomas as gently as he could onto the great hall table. At some point on the way up the river path the master had fainted, and that, said Aggie, was a mercy.

Chapter Fifty-three

In his near-death dreams, Thomas relived the events of that summer afternoon over and over again. Mostly, he saw what had *not* happened: their beautiful, yellow-haired child screaming in the arms of a pirate; his wife pulled onto the galley. He called out in his powerlessness. Alina wiped his brow, smoothed his hair and kissed his dry lips, then tried to get some rest on the truckle bed in his chamber—as when she'd nursed him through his earlier illness. It was that illness which nearly claimed him now, because Thomas had no strength to rally from his wound.

Aggie applied yarrow and lemon balm to staunch the bleeding, wrapped the arm in a poultice of agrimony and comfrey that she called knit-bone, then insisted they call a barber-surgeon. Robert fetched a man from Carlington, who stitched the severed skin back into place and wrapped it in a rag bandage. By the fourth day the wound smelled so bad Aggie pulled it off, washed the stitches in rainwater, and said they should leave the arm open to God's fresh air, as a weak branch on a tree repairs itself after a gale.

Perhaps it was that which saved him. There was no more fever, and at the end of seven days Thomas was asking to be lifted into a sitting position. Alina gently arranged his arm in a sling, then set a huge bowl of steaming broth on his lap and waited until he could manage well enough with his left hand to eat it alone.

Molly Roberts came back to help, bringing her child Bobby to be the young master's playmate again. She employed a new tone of respect with milady now. The Lady Arleen was a heroine. All on her own she'd saved everyone at the house and all the village of Tamstock from a hundred evil-looking pirates, and each of 'em with two of they curved sword things. And that black-haired devil who'd been such a charmer had brought them—shown 'em where to come, the traitor. Mistress Hawkins had recognized him straight off. Who'd have thought it? You couldn't know who to trust these days.

But the Lady Arleen, what had been such a haughty madam as wouldn't give you time of day when she came, had saved them. Shot the bugger with her bow 'n arrow, then stabbed him near to death! Mistress Hawkins reckoned he'd come to get her, but she wasn't havin' any of it. Oh no, Sir Thomas' wife was too much of a lady to have anything to do with his type.

What had happened to McNab was barely mentioned. His body was brought up to the house and Mr Hawthorne shocked them all by refusing to do a funeral, so they took him all the way to Tamstock church. Aggie, Molly and Meg each said they were too busy to leave the house for his funeral. Sir Thomas' lady stood in the courtyard to see the coffin taken away, as was only right, but few wasted their breath discussing it.

Despite his earlier decision to maintain his status as a gentleman, Marcos quietly moved into McNab's role. He spent the first morning after the so-called raid investigating the estate office. His two-year apprenticeship in finance in Holland meant it didn't take him long to see what John Hawthorne had suspected about the account books. Some days later, he began to find stashes of silver coin. The only sad note was the poor greyhound, who grieved her master's passing until Toby noticed she was in heat. She was taken off to the stables and shut in a stable with a healthy young dog of no fixed breed.

Once he had regained enough strength to sit, then stand, Thomas became peevish, cross that once again he was reduced to invalid status. He became uncharacteristically demanding, wanting to see his son, to discuss the estate with Marcos, to know that Home Farm had made arrangements for summer-growth lambs, that someone had started to tidy up the terraced garden, and a dozen other trifles that annoyed Alina intensely.

Thomas was in the process of giving her a list of instructions one morning when he finally noticed his wife's fatigue. Her face was drawn and white; she was losing weight and not sleeping well. How could she on that awful little bed? And it was all his fault. He got up, went to her and laid his thin hand on her cheek.

"My dear, you look tired. I'm so sorry." Thomas lifted her hand to his lips and kissed her knuckles. "I am selfish, forgive me."

Alina looked into his eyes, saw tears there, and burst out crying herself. She cried and cried, then between sobs, in English, she said, "Will there never be any peace? Can I never live a quiet life?" But the translation was too much and she slipped into her native language. "All this wanting and waiting, and you moaning, moaning all the time. I can't believe I've exchanged a handsome, exciting man for a miserable weakling like you." The words brought her self-pity to a halt. "God forgive me, Thomas," she said, reverting to English, "I'm sorry, but it's what I feel."

Thomas wiped a tear with his fingers and kissed her wet cheek. Holding her with his good arm he kissed her with passion. "Alina, Alina, my love, my love," he whispered, "don't cry. We'll be happy again soon, I promise."

"Do you?" said Alina, reaching for a linen towel and blowing her nose on it like a child. "What is this 'happy again'? You think about that and tell me before you start giving me orders for the day."

Thomas hung his head. "I'm sorry, too."

"Good, you should be sorry." Alina pulled away from him, strode out of the room and slammed the door.

Thomas went to the door to follow, to call her back and tell her—what? That he had found his natural history journal full of her writing? That he had examined his bed hangings to see if there really was a speck of blood and red wine wool stitched into it? Thomas was on the verge of tears again himself, ashamed and distressed that he hadn't wanted to believe what his wife had written in his journal.

One day, one day when they were more settled and more certain of each other again, he would ask for her forgiveness—for so many things. Then perhaps he would broach the subject of the ring. Find out where an emerald the size and shape of an almond had come from, because he was very sure Alina hadn't had it when she first came to Crimphele, and it wasn't something his sister had left behind. But as he thought this he knew he would never mention it, because he didn't want to know.

Alina went for a long walk up Paddon Hill and came back ravenously hungry for the midday meal. Marcos was sitting in the parlour waiting to eat. A place was laid for Thomas, but he had asked for a tray in his room. Alina plonked herself in her chair and started on a chunk of bread.

Marcos said nothing until Meg had served their food and was back in the kitchen, or at least out of earshot. "So?" he said.

"So, I don't know what to think, what to do, or what I have done. I walk and I think and I walk more, and I cannot find an answer."

"To what?" Marcos felt a hint of hope curl warmly around him. "What questions must you answer?"

"Oh, whether to stay here as I am or go back to being... I can't explain. I don't understand, myself."

"You regret not going with him."

"No! How dare he come here expecting me to run off with him like I was—any girl with no class who'd fall gratefully into his arms."

"So where is your dilemma? You have chosen to stay at Crimphele with your husband."

"Who nearly dies and leaves me wondering."

"Wondering?"

Alina didn't reply. Marcos waited for a while until she appeared calmer, then he put down his knife and said quietly, "If anything happens to Thomas I am here."

Alina looked at him, completely surprised.

"I mean, I have to be honest, if anything happens to Thomas I would like you to turn to me—to marry me."

Alina's eyes opened wide. "You're not just offering to take me home again."

"I will if that is what you want. But I would prefer to marry you first."

Alina laughed out loud, "Oh, Marcos, don't be silly! You're a nobody. How could I ever marry you?"

Stung, Marcos hit back, "Actually a very wealthy nobody. I have a small fortune in a Dutch bank, contrary to your precious Ludo's instructions, and another small fortune here in my chamber. I have access to a very lucrative business, which I can take up again the day I leave here—with or without you."

"So I would be the wife of a rich man—but not a lady."

"Not a lady, nor a countess nor a baroness, nor anything else you think is more important than loving someone for themselves and being happy like a normal person."

Alina pursed her mouth. "It's not like that."

"No? Well, that's how it looks to me."

"I can't leave Crimphele, and I shall never leave Thomas."

"Why ever not?"

"Because," she sighed, "it is all I ever wanted: a fine house, an estate, a title—and, more important, although you won't understand—I won't ever go because Thomas is for me. He's good and kind, caring and faithful. He could be at the royal court, but prefers his country home. Could be in the company of men all day, but spends time with his wife and child. He wants to know how the house is run and everything about the estate. My father did none of these things and I think my mother must have been very unhappy. What happened to her—being left to manage on her own all the time because her husband wanted to be fashionable and show off, and strut around Madrid like he

was an important grandee with a fortune to fritter away—
Thomas won't do that to me. So I will never leave him. Besides,
I love him."

"Then what is your problem? You have just answered your
own question."

"Yes, I have, thank you, Marcos."

They sat in silence for a while, sipping their wine, not
wanting to break this moment of confidence.

Eventually though, Marcos had to speak. "I'll leave as soon
as you can find someone to help with the estate. Do you think
Robert could manage until you get another steward?"

Alina reached across the table and took his hand. "Go home
to your mother before you do anything else. She must miss you
terribly. I couldn't bear my son to go away for years and years
as you have."

"I could take a message to your father."

"Yes, do! I shall write and tell him where I am and who I am
now."

"That's all that really matters, isn't it?"

"Is it so bad that I wanted to be the wife of *un hidalgo*—to
marry the son of a somebody—and have something of my own?
Marcos, can you really see me as an old maid?"

Marcos burst out laughing. "No, never!"

"Then go."

"I shall. I shall also return. One day you may need me."

"What will you do? Come back here?"

"No! I have always had it in mind to start a business. I'll set
up in Plymouth."

"What sort of business?"

"Wine and spirits. I have a fancy to make that perfumed
drink the Dutch like so much. Gin."

Chapter Fifty-four
Goa, India, December 1637

"Captain... I'm sorry, I don't know your name."

Ludo scrambled to his feet and made a polite bow. "Ludovico da Portovenere, ma'am. I own a ship but I am not its captain."

"My name is Leonora Gasca Figaroa. May I sit and speak with you?"

Ludo smiled at the good-looking gentlewoman who was addressing him in Portuguese, and held a chair out for her. With the softest brush of fresh, light cotton and the scent of warm sandalwood she sat at his table. Her young Indian page positioned himself behind her, holding open a parasol. It was well past noon and the sun still punishing.

Leonora shaded her eyes and looked out into the bay. "I am told you have a galleon with red sails."

"All stowed below, now. They are a deep red, the colour of good red wine."

Leonora smiled. "How lovely, but why?"

"A fancy I had. May I use Spanish with you, or Italian? My Portuguese is limited."

"Spanish will be fine. I have some Italian as well."

"Excellent. Regarding my sails, as I say it was a fancy, but they have proved less easy to identify in the distance than white, and they have saved us from privateers and pirates more than once. When we come into port, those who know the ship recognize her immediately, and then we have dozens of coolie boats anxious to help us unload. A useful fancy."

"Yes, because that is how I come to be here."

"So this is business, not pleasure?"

Leonora coloured. "No, I would never approach a gentleman.... Really, this is quite difficult, but I am forced to make commercial arrangements myself nowadays. My father started our business and then my husband ran it. My husband passed away last year and I have not been able to find a manager, so I have to try to maintain our contracts as best I can. Now we need another ship to transport our spices."

"That can be arranged. Would you like some tea?"

"Yes, thank you."

Ludo called the waiter for tea and leaned back in his chair. If she offered a big enough contract he could drop the Cathay leg of his voyage, which was by far the most perilous, and focus on India. He waited for the lovely Leonora Gasca Figaroa to speak again—silence normally unsettled a woman into saying more than she should.

"I also have a tea plantation in Ceylon, and cinnamon trees."

"Tea and cinnamon from Ceylon, and spices from Goa—all for Portugal?"

"And cotton; we have a contract to send tea, pepper and cotton to Bristol in England as well."

Ludo nodded. "And how can I help?"

The waiter placed a tray on their table: delicate china cups and a tea pot in the shape of an elephant.

"How pretty," said Leonora, picking up a cup. "Perhaps we should include a few dozen of these in our next consignment. Shall I pour?"

"I wasn't aware tea was so popular in Portugal and England," Ludo said.

"Oh yes, and growing more popular by the week, it seems. Both nations have a taste for it now. We all like tea and sweet cakes."

"Ah, cinnamon buns, yes, I remember. A thriving business, then?"

"Thriving. Absolutely thriving."

"Do you by chance also export coriander and cassia bark? I have a young associate in England; he deals in exotic plants and flowers. He'd be interested in coriander and cassia for a fragrant liquor he's trying to make in Plymouth."

"Oh, yes, as I said, I can supply a number of exotic spices."

Leonora sipped her tea. Ludo studied her face: almond-shaped eyes so dark they were nearly black, and not a single blemish or wrinkle despite the sun, perhaps not even thirty—and a rich widow. *Perfetto.*

"Tell me more," he said.

The End

Historical Note

In 1636, tulip bulbs in Holland were weighed on goldsmiths' weights, but many were worth more than their weight in gold. One Dutch merchant paid 6,650 guilders for a dozen bulbs at a time when 300 guilders would have kept an entire family for a whole year. The merchant was not a rich man buying expensive bulbs to enjoy for their colour; he intended to sell on and make a profit, as his fellow Dutchmen had been doing for the past two years. Records document instances of farmers giving up their farms to acquire tulips; men exchanged their homes for just one rare bulb. A pamphleteer writing in December, 1636, created a list of goods with their prices to demonstrate how much could be acquired with the 3,000 guilders men were prepared to pay for just one bulb. Among the items were: eight fat pigs—240 guilders; twenty-four tons of wheat—448 guilders; a ship—500 guilders. It was a madness that came to be known as 'tulip mania'. The prices paid for tulips in this story are based on recorded sale prices. The term *florijn* was in still use in the United Provinces until 1680, but I have used the term *guilder* throughout the novel to simplify what in those days was a complicated coinage system.

At an international level, the first half of the seventeenth century was a period of intense political and religious intrigue. Spain had lost its Dutch provinces and was engaged in a protracted war in Flanders. Cardinal Richelieu in France signed a treaty with the Dutch, and French ships raided the Spanish fleet bringing supplies to its army. The Habsburg Emperor, Ferdinand, had vowed to impose Catholicism throughout his empire before his death and was harrying the Spanish monarch, Don Felipe, to regain the Netherlands.

Acknowledgements

This novel is a work of fiction based on recorded events. All the characters are fictitious with the exception of named heads of state, the Conde-Duque de Olivares and Wouter Winkel of Alkmaar. The financial scandal known as tulip mania or the tulip bubble is well-documented and there is a great deal of information available on the Internet; however, I found Mike Dash's very readable and informative book *Tulipomania* particularly useful.

Many of the details relating to the Vatican are what might have happened given the circumstances, although in this respect truth may be stranger than fiction. I recommend reading Eric Frattini's work on Vatican espionage *The Entity*, which is both enlightening and chilling. For details relating to marriage and domestic life in Cornwall, I mainly used *Tudor Cornwall* by John Chyrnoweth. *Lost Country Life* by Dorothy Hartley is a fascinating study of how country-folk lived and worked on estates such as Crimphele. Crimphele itself is very similar to the National Trust property Cotehele in Cornwall. References to pirate raids by Mediterranean corsairs, known in the West Country as 'the Turks', are based on fact. A horrifying account of how one Cornishman survived the white slave trade can be found in *White Gold* by Giles Milton.

Lastly, I would like to thank all the people who have taken the time to write up their research or specialist areas of knowledge for use as free information on the Internet; your websites are too numerous to mention but I am indebted.

J. G. Harlond, Málaga, Spain

The Author

J.G. Harlond

Jane G. Harlond grew up in Devon and studied in Bristol, Portsmouth and the USA before finishing her academic studies with an M.A. in Social and Political Thought at the University of Sussex. She has lived and worked in a variety of different countries and is married to a retired Spanish naval officer. Harlond has two sons and five step-children, all of whom now have their own careers in diverse parts of Europe.

If You Enjoyed This Book

Please write a review.
This is important to the author and helps to get the word out to others
Visit

PENMORE PRESS
www.penmorepress.com

All Penmore Press books are available directly through our website, amazon.com, Barnes and Noble and Nook,, Apple iTunes, Kobo books and via leading bookshops across the United States, Canada, the UK, Australia and Europe.

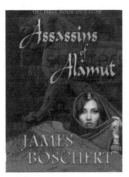

ASSASSINS OF ALAMUT
BY

JAMES BOSCHERT

An Epic Novel of Persia and Palestine in the Time of the Crusades

The *Assassins of Alamut* is a riveting tale, painted on the vast canvas of life in Palestine and Persia during the 12th century.

On one hand, it's a tale of the crusades—as told from the Islamic side—where Shi'a and Sunni are as intent on killing Ismaili Muslims as crusaders. In self-defense, the Ismailis develop an elite band of highly trained killers called Hashshashin whose missions are launched from their mountain fortress of Alamut.

But it's also the story of a French boy, Talon, captured and forced into the alien world of the assassins. Forbidden love for a princess is intertwined with sinister plots and self-sacrifice, as the hero and his two companions discover treachery and then attempt to evade the ruthless assassins of Alamut who are sent to hunt them down.

It's a sweeping saga that takes you over vast snow-covered mountains, through the frozen wastes of the winter plateau, and into the fabulous cites of Hamadan, Isfahan, and the Kingdom of Jerusalem.

"A brilliant first novel, worthy of Bernard Cornwell at his best."—Tom Grundner

PENMORE PRESS
www.penmorepress.com

Historical fiction and nonfiction
Paperback available for order on line
and as Ebook with all major distributers

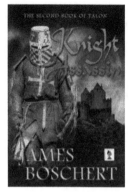

Knight Assassin

The second book of Talon

by

James Boschert

A joyous homecoming turns into a nightmare as Talon must do the one thing that he didn't want to - become an assassin again.

Talon, a young Frank, returns to France to be reunited with the family that lost him to the Assassins of Alamut when he was just a boy. But when he arrives, he finds a sinister threat hanging like a pall over the joyous reunion. A ruthless man is challenging his father's inheritance, aided by powerful churchmen who stand to profit by his father's fall. When Talon's young brother is taken hostage, Talon has no recourse but to take the fight to his enemies.

All is not warfare, however; Talon's uncle Philip, a Templar knight, brings him to the court of Carcassonne, where Queen Eleanor has introduced ideals of romance and chivalry. There Talon is pressed into the service of a lion-hearted prince of Britain named Richard.

Knight assassin is a story of treachery, greed, love and heroism set in the Middle Ages.

PENMORE PRESS
www.penmorepress.com

Historical fiction and nonfiction
Paperback available for order on line
and as Ebook with all major distributers

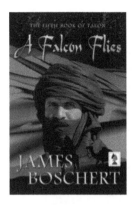

by

James Boschert

The fifth book of Talon

Talon returns to Acre, the Crusader port, a rich man after more than a year in Byzantium. But riches bring enemies, and Talon's past is about to catch up with him: accusations of witchcraft have followed him from Languedoc. Everything is changed, however, when Talon travels to a small fort with Sir Guy de Veres, his Templar mentor, and learns stunning news about Rav'an.

Before he can act, the kingdom of Baldwin IV is threatened by none other than the Sultan of Egypt, Salah Ed Din, who is bringing a vast army through Sinai to retake Jerusalem from the Christians. Talon must take part in the ferocious battle at Montgisard before he can set out to rejoin Rav'an and honor his promise made six years ago.

The 'Assassins of Rashid Ed Din, the Old Man of the Mountain, have targeted Talon for death for obstructing their plans once too often. To avoid them, Talon must take a circuitous route through the loneliest reaches of the southern deserts on his way to Persia, but even so he risks betrayal, imprisonment, and execution.

His sole objective is to find Rav'an, but she is not where he had expected her to be.

PENMORE PRESS
www.penmorepress.com

Historical fiction and nonfiction
Paperback available for order on line
and as Ebook with all major distributers

Penmore Press
Challenging, Intriguing, Adventurous, Historical and Imaginative

www.penmorepress.com

Lightning Source UK Ltd.
Milton Keynes UK
UKHW02f0804060918
328419UK00011B/683/P